LOST IN UTTAR PRADESH

EVAN S. CONNELL

LOST IN
UTTAR PRADESH

NEW AND SELECTED STORIES

COUNTERPOINT

BERKELEY

Library of Congress Cataloging-in-Publication Data
Connell, Evan S., 1924–
Lost in Uttar Pradesh : new and selected stories / by Evan S. Connell.
p. cm.
ISBN 978-1-59376-175-2
I. Title.
PS3553.O5L67 2008
813'.54—dc22   2007043829

Jacket by Gopa & Ted2
Interior by David Bullen Design

Printed in the United States of America

COUNTERPOINT
2117 Fourth Street
Suite D
Berkeley, CA 94710
www.counterpointpress.com

Distributed by Publishers Group West

10 9 8 7 6 5 4 3 2 1

CONTENTS

Preface   ix

Lion   3

Hooker   10

Nan Madol   30

Proctor Bemis   48

The Walls of Ávila   63

Arcturus   85

The Land Where Lemon Trees Bloom   119

Caribbean Provedor   131

Octopus, the Sausalito Quarterly of New
Writing, Art & Ideas   144

Election Eve   153

St. Augustine's Pigeon   169

Bowen   205

Assassin   217

Mrs. Proctor Bemis   222

Noah's Ark   239

Puig's Wife   261

Guadalcanal   290

Yellow Raft   294

The Cuban Missile Crisis   298

Ancient Musick   304

The Palace of the Moorish Kings   319

Lost in Uttar Pradesh   338

Publication Credits   361

PREFACE

Stories speak with a thousand voices. A woman in Colorado told me that she watched a lion follow a cow up the mountainside. She watched until they were out of sight, the cow slobbering and bawling. What surprised me was the intelligence of the lion. It recognized a need for privacy because humans are dangerous and it understood that it could make the cow walk to the breakfast table.

"Guadalcanal" originally was titled "The Marine." Nobody has paid much attention to this story, but I always thought it said something about the deterioration or degeneration of men at war. Years ago I reviewed a book by a philosophy professor who had been in the Army during World War II. His job was to interrogate Nazi functionaries picked up behind the Allied lines, and he kept a diary. Long afterward he read what he had written at the time and felt shocked by his behavior. The diary seemed to have been written by somebody else.

"Yellow Raft" is another WWII story. I was a Naval Aviation cadet and graduated from Pensacola on VE day—a meaningless coincidence. After being released from service I returned to college and roomed with a swarthy muscular friend known as "Blossom." We had gone through months of Naval Aviation training together, but at Pensacola we went different ways. He chose advanced training in multi-engine bombers. I chose fighters because I wanted to fly a Corsair, known to the Japanese as Whistling Death. My infatuation with that graceful killer had begun on a hot afternoon in Georgia while several hundred cadets marched back and forth on a dusty parade ground in obedience to the snarled commands of a Marine drill sergeant. All at once four midnight-blue Corsairs streamed out of the clouds, shot over our heads with a thunderous roar that made the ground tremble, spiraled upward almost vertically and disappeared in the clouds while we continued marching. We understood that once upon a time those Navy pilots had been cadets and had stopped by for a quick visit.

Blossom was ordered to the South Pacific as a patrol bomber pilot while I was still at Pensacola.

After the war, students again, both of us signed up for what is known rather stiffly in the academic world as Creative Writing. I do not remember anything he wrote except for a forty-page love story that included one paragraph about a raft he had seen floating on the Coral Sea. What this had to do with a love story I have forgotten, but the raft stayed where it was, a yellow flower on the Coral Sea. I told Blossom that if he couldn't sell his story within a year—maybe I said three years—I would steal his raft. He laughed and said all right.

Thomas Mann's resonant "Disorder and Early Sorrow" has been a lodestone, providing material for two novels and five long stories, three of which are in this book. Mann evidently did not think much of "Disorder" and wrote it only because a German literary magazine asked for something to commemorate his fiftieth birthday.

"Arcturus" was the first child of Mann's story and while writing it I kept his little masterpiece on the desk beside me. I wanted to recreate the stuffy German paterfamilias, Dr. Cornelius, a figure almost impossible to like or completely dislike. Several editors rejected it, among them George Plimpton at the *Paris Review*, who told me that at first he thought he was reading "Disorder and Early Sorrow." He did not mean that I had plagiarized Mann, only that I had duplicated the character. That is what I set out to do, so I felt oddly flattered. The story later was accepted by the *Western Review*, whose editor recognized the debt to Mann but thought "Arcturus" succeeded on its own.

Another child of Dr. Cornelius, "Saint Augustine's Pigeon," began to take shape when I was hit by a San Francisco pigeon while reading the *Confessions of St.Augustine*. I was outraged by such an insult, as anyone would be, and the longer I thought about this the more I became convinced it was no accident. I had been struck by a higher power. So what began with a capricious stroke resolved itself in the words of a medieval North African philosopher. This story, too, was at first rejected—mostly, I think, because of the pigeon. After all, one editor wrote with unmistakable distaste, we publish a family magazine.

No single character or image or disaster suggested "Puig's Wife." I remembered an absurd struggle on the sundeck of a dormitory, a

murderous assault late at night on a New Orleans street, the sexual
connivance of men and women, scraps from here and there. Collec-
tively these fragments had nothing in common. I could see no pattern, no structure. I wondered if Muhlbach, my stuffy replica of Dr.
Cornelius, might make sense of it. One critic remarked that the story
illuminates the mysterious dynamics of male friendship. That had not
occurred to me, but it doesn't matter. Wallace Stegner once asked a
class of students: If the nails a carpenter hammers form an interesting
pattern, is the carpenter responsible?

The Traveler, the Wanderer, that mythic lotus-eater, is frequently
useful and at times indispensable in storytelling. His ancestors go back
to our beginning when a member of the clan described what he had
seen beyond the mountain. "The Walls of Ávila" probably originated
when I thought about a carnival just outside that eleventh-century
town, shadows of boat-shaped swings racing up and down the walls. I
had seen Gaudi's peculiar cathedral in Barcelona, heard the butterpat
clap of gypsies dancing on a cobblestone street, listened to the shrill
passionate voice of a young woman singing while she approached a
foreigner in a café. I had watched a boy on a donkey delivering sticks
of bread the size of baseball bats. These and other Spanish moments
obviously belonged together.

Years afterward I thought there might be a sequel, when my lotus-
eater begins to feel that he will end up where he started, as though
human lives were elliptical. So he finds himself again in Spain listening to goat bells, following holy processions, feeling against his cheek
the sea breeze rising from Gibraltar, pausing to stare at a cataract of
lavender blossoms pouring over the ruined palace of Moorish kings
in Málaga, emblematic of his journey.

As for "Nan Madol," it sounds like a woman's name but is in fact a
sinister fortress of black basalt logs in a lagoon off the South Pacific
island of Ponape. I went there because I was not ordered to the South
Pacific during WWII, which left me indignant and baffled like a trained
rat without much to do. Someone pointed out that if the Navy had
dispatched me to a fighter squadron in those islands I might not
have come back. This was true. Still, I wanted to see that part of the
world. Long after the war I visited Ponape, Truk, a few others, gazed
at burned-out Japanese pillboxes, rusty landing barges, and thought
about what happened there sixty years ago. The visible reminders are

quickly dissolving. Nobody can be sure what Nan Madol looked like centuries ago but I doubt if it has changed much.

"Ancient Musick" is unlike the other stories and might not qualify as a story. It grew bristly as a starfish from Robert Burton's sui generis book *The Anatomy of Melancholy*, from Herodotus' account of Greco-Persian wars, fabulous monsters of the Middle Ages, alchemic mysteries, tales of phantom islands, the trial of Boethius, the arrogance of emperors, from this or that, a mosaic, a quilt of conflicting colors, perhaps a psychotic collation or recollection distorted by rage at the descent of the United States. It ends with a parable that may or may not seem relevant, depending on the reader.

I used to know Maria the hooker—Marla, Alexandra, Mikki, Gloria, according to her mood—elusive, dishonest, mystifying, one of those who have bedeviled mankind since the grandmother of Eve taunted some hairy ape. What became of her, I don't know.

"The Cuban Missile Crisis" grew out of hatred, fury, rage, whatever it should be called. During those terrible days we knew that millions of people could be annihilated by self-righteous officials in Moscow or Washington acting with the best of intentions. All of us were threatened, exposed, vulnerable.

"Election Eve" follows the trail of a sluggish Republican apostate, Proctor Bemis. He, too, is angry about the state of affairs: disorder, deceit, fascism masquerading as patriotism, betrayal, pretense. And he is annoyed with himself for eating too much. Well, what does a man do? At the very least a man can let the world know how he feels. And if the world is no larger than a cocktail party at the Wibbles, so be it.

"Proctor Bemis" tracks the fat ex-Republican ex-stockbroker to his country club, majestically motionless on a leather throne, complacent as Buddha, observing shadows creep toward the golf course while he nibbles Dutch cheese, munches cashews, waits for good old Bullock to bring the next Daiquiri. But he discovers that Pentagon generals have cooked up a scheme to drench Japan with poison gas. The earth wobbles. Insanity sprouts like mushrooms after the rain. Nobody cares.

And there is his conservative wife Marguerite, alarmed by everything. Security is what she values most. Telephone books contain devilish messages. Communist armies hide in Montana. Gang members paint frightening symbols on mailboxes, billboards, highway signs.

Criminals are pardoned by liberal governors and commit unspeakable crimes as soon as they are released. Nobody is safe. Danger lurks
behind every tree, every shrub, every shadow. Thieves, foreigners,
murderers. Mrs. Bemis has watched colored boys shuffle through the
Plaza. A man with dark skin brushed past her, nearly touched her. She
carries a whistle, just in case. The Plaza used to be so nice, one could
spend the afternoon shopping.

"Caribbean Provedor" is largely autobiographical, not entirely. I
think the surgeon from Ohio was, in fact, a New Jersey dentist, and
I seem to remember that I won more than seventeen games. And I
do not speak as much Portuguese as the story implies. The provedor,
though, was a brutal hulk. Unlikely possibilities became probabilities
whenever I thought about eight or ten dark nights on the Atlantic
between that steamy island and Lisboa. I did see the provedor go
ashore and saunter through customs with no trouble. The cheap watch
was not visible, so I might have been correct.

"The Land Where Lemon Trees Bloom" is not a wartime story,
despite the Nazi submarine. It developed awkwardly, unevenly, beginning with an outrageous, talkative merchant mariner whom I knew
fairly well. Under a different title the story bounced from magazine to
magazine. Editors liked one thing or another: Octave's butcher knife,
Hong Kong, the Peruvian whorehouse, a swimming pool packed with
sugar, this or that, but not enough to accept it. After quite a few rejec-
tions I changed the title, which suggested changes in the story. I cannot
explain why a haunting line from Goethe brought this about. Poets,
painters, sculptors, musicians, dancers, novelists, and other members
of that bedraggled fraternity live forever in a madhouse, one reason
being that their problems have no solution. Next time, they think,
next time I'll get it right.

"Bowen" was a member of that fraternity. I knew him well enough. I
watched him fall apart. He was a novelist and short story writer, at his
best quite good, and had spent some time at sea. He blamed himself
for surrendering to darkness, but he also blamed a neglectful public,
which seems reasonable to those who despise public taste. Near the
end we were driving across the Golden Gate bridge on a beautiful
afternoon. All at once he said: "My last book got six reviews. Three of
them were local." He was fifty years old.

"Octopus," a journal of the arts, was conceived, flourished, and expired in Sausalito, a village clinging to an unstable hillside just around the corner from the Golden Gate. Some of the houses are built with the garage on the roof. Tourists come to stare at this phenomenon and at a conglomeration of houseboats—expensive homes floating confidently on the bay, rickety scows stuck on the mud flats. A friend of mine lived in a collapsing bucket partly submerged during high tide. She didn't mind. Sausalito is that sort of place.

Bowen, the word man, and his partner Willie Stumpf, the money man who did not have much money, drunkenly resolved to create a publishing empire in Sausalito, natural headquarters for a journal of the arts, doomed to fail. They found a non-union printer who swore he could save them fifty percent. A good start. Along came Babydoe Slusher, Doc Arbuckle, a swindler who refused to say where he lived, Lucky Pizarro, Fingers, Spook the drug pusher.

Some years ago I floated down a stretch of the Colorado River to Lake Powell on a rubber raft alongside other rafts packed with vacationing college girls, airline stewardesses, a grocer from San Jose, and I do not remember who else. It took about ten days. Every afternoon we pulled ashore and set up camp. That much of "Assassin" is true. Otherwise, fact and fiction have become entangled. Ugly things happened in Vietnam, as everybody knows, enough to embarrass the nation beyond deliverance. Who can isolate the cause? Who imagined the sequel? Perhaps only an astrologer could explain how Vietnam and a raft trip and the buried lust of a bantamweight killer drifted into alignment.

Six nights a week Tessie listens to Reverend H. L. Hunnicutt broadcasting from Chattanooga. Gog and Magog prepare to wage battle against the kingdom of the Lord. O yea! O yea! Satan, loosed from imprisonment after one thousand years, readies his minions for combat. The hour is imminent! Are there not tidal waves, volcanic eruptions? Is not Heaven streaked with shooting stars? Are not four horsemen visible at dawn? How could Mrs. Stocking fail to understand? She teaches Religious Studies at the college yet ignores the mighty truth of Scripture. She smokes cigarettes and never stops reading books, some of them in foreign languages.

Tessie reflects on these matters while doing housework. Tweetwee the canary appears to understand: he sings to the sunshine, fluffs his feathers, creeps back and forth on his perch in the cage.

Reverend Hunnicutt has read out loud on the program a letter received from a gentleman in Dothan, Alabama, who saw for himself the Ark of Noah high up on Mount Ararat. With his own eyes this man saw cages for animals and birds, cages great and small. He saw hammers and ancient tools and pitch and ice on the mountain. Reverend Hunnicutt asks if listeners would pledge twenty percent of their income to feed and clothe the growing army of the Lord, which daily girds itself to battle Satan. Would not those who believe in Jesus express their love? For what is charity if not the Holy Spirit? Blessed are the generous! Alleluia!

Just like Uncle Gates, I got lost in Uttar Pradesh. And I have seen the Taj by moonlight and at noonday under a blistering Indian sun, have plodded up a dusty slope to the Ajanta caves, trusting Vishnu to guard my laundry bag and suitcase. I have walked across the bridge of lepers at Hyderabad, trying to conceal the pity and disgust I felt, lost my wits during a furious argument with a crazed rickshaw boy, quarreled stupidly about a chocolate fudge sundae in a hotel dining room, dodged rocks during a soccer riot, got myself poisoned by a doctor at the Calcutta public health service, shared a park bench with a foul-smelling Australian hooker in the muggy twilight.

Beyond doubt, India is a special place. Westerners who stay long enough begin to go mad and think the Western world insane. Late at night I saw a man with a blanket over his head sitting beside a little fire in a courtyard next to a pyramid of bones, an allegorical scene. And in a cluttered Delhi shop I uncovered a bunch of seventeenth-century Mughal drawings.

How stories originate may or not be apparent. A dream, a shock, memory, an insult, a startling perception—who knows what else? Many things contribute, at times rising from unsuspected depths. What moved Tolstoi to write about three hermits running on the surface of the water to catch up with the bishop?

Jung remarked that whoever speaks in primordial images speaks with a thousand voices; he lifts the idea he is seeking to express out of the occasional and transitory into the realm of the ever-enduring.

LOST IN
UTTAR PRADESH

LION

T HE BAWLING animal was part of a dream, but then Katia opened her eyes and heard it again. She lay in bed listening. Again she heard it. There were no cattle this high on the mountain. She threw the blankets aside and rushed to the window. At the edge of the clearing a pregnant cow was lurching up the slope, its eyes wild with terror. It stumbled against a log, fell to its knees, and got up clumsily. Strands of frothy saliva swung from the cow's muzzle. Katia watched it urinating and dropping pies while it attempted to run. The cow seemed to be trying to go downhill but for some reason it could not. The animal bawled and turned frantically toward the left and then toward the right, all the while staggering higher. She could not understand what was wrong with the cow, which plainly had lost its mind—rearing and flinging its head around as if that might solve the problem. Then she saw the lion. It was not a very big lion, not fully grown, but it was no bobcat. This was four times the size of a bobcat, with the heavy grace of a lion and the features of a lion, but the way it followed the cow was unnatural. It did not behave the way a lion should. Twenty yards behind the cow, which now and then jumped awkwardly, crept this adolescent lion, which did not appear to be excited or even very much interested, as though the two of them were circus animals trained to act out a scene. We do this every night, the lion seemed to say, what a bore. So he would lift one paw and set it down, then another, crawling forward without enthusiasm. Showing his broad lion face and stubby ears, his tail brushing the rocky ground like a rope, playing his part almost with embarrassment, he looked from side to side as though expecting the trainer's whip. His face gleamed with life and it was clear that he thought while he looked about. Oh yes, he said, we've done this many times. And a paw reached forward tentatively because the hard ground was littered with pine cones and he was a domestic lion unaccustomed to the wilderness. The morning is cold, he explained. The wind flows down from the peaks and I am hungry, but I will have breakfast pretty soon. Oh yes. All of this he seemed to be saying while he guided the hysterical cow up the mountain. Then out of the snowy pines flashed an irritated blue jay, but the lion paid no attention; troubled by something on the wind, disturbed, inquisitive, the lion swung his face toward the cabin and Katia knew beyond doubt that he was aware of her behind the glass. His focused glare was turgid with meaning—elemental, undisclosed, sealed within his nature. She wondered if the lion's expression might be different if her husband stood beside her at the window. And if at this instant the lion should speak, what would he say? Perhaps he would explain why he was guiding the cow up the slope. Well, don't you see? I was hungry and have found what I went looking for. I am within my rights. That is what the lion might point out. Then, having observed Katia, he slid forward like a snake because he did not want to step on a sharp rock or a pine cone. Oh, he was within his rights, yes, this almost affectionate lion who ignored the frantic creature just ahead. Katia saw that he had no intention of leaping on the cow, which seemed horrible—as though the lion had acquired a human brain. Each time the cow turned one way or the other so that she might go down the mountain, well, this patient young lion would lope the same direction far enough to prevent her from doing as she wished. And if she stopped for a moment because she was out of breath, well, he would pause, stroking the air with his tail. He was not in a hurry. Nevertheless, they ought to keep moving. Let us proceed, he suggested. Before long the journey will end. Oh yes, pretty soon. Five minutes. Ten minutes. Have you rested enough? Then suppose we climb a little higher. Come now. Katia realized that although she was in no danger she was shuddering with fright as well as from the cold. She thought about getting a sweater or jacket, but she could not leave the window. Now they were dancing—the immensely gravid cow lunging this way or that, her elegant partner following, the terrible dance whirling always a little higher. Oh, higher, if you please! Yes, that's right, that's where we shall go, whether you agree or not. And you will not see your friends or your home again because I am planning to eat you. You understand, don't you? Of course you do. You are not very smart, but you realize that you are going to be eaten. I can tell from the way you act that you know what I have in mind. Now let's be on our way. A little higher, not much. I could if I wished eat you right this moment, but I detect the presence of enemies so we must continue up the mountain until I decide we have reached a proper spot for breakfast. And you are the breakfast. Oh yes! Ho ho! Now let's be off. So they danced across the clearing. They had emerged from a grove of aspen behind the stream and Katia guessed that the cow had been driven from Gus and Betty Pruitt's ranch. Or maybe the cow unwisely decided to take a walk. Whatever happened, they must have been climbing quite a while because the Pruitt ranch was far below. From a granite outcrop beyond the shed it was possible to look down and make out black dots in the valley, which were cattle. She might have seen this particular cow although she hoped not. It shouldn't matter, but for some reason it did. Now they had stopped because the cow was blowing. The lion acted less considerate. Katia thought she heard him growl. Maybe the lion did growl because the cow bucked stupidly—a queer, futile bucking motion—and threw her muzzle at the sky before she resumed the climb. Katia wondered if the lion remembered the cabin, if it remembered seeing her inside. Perhaps it would bound across the clearing snarling and screeching to crash through the glass. It could do that. It might. She felt the solid thumps of her heart, she knew she was vulnerable and mortal. She watched the lion pick up one hind leg and daintily extend it a few inches while the half-developed body eased forward. The cow sensed this. She knows, Katia thought. What else does she know? Almost nothing. She can't be intelligent. And it seemed to Katia that the dance of death was not merely horrid but unjust—terrifying because the lion was going to eat both the cow and the unborn calf. She thought about running to the storage room for her husband's rifle and running outside to confront and kill the lion. She imagined doing this. Yet she disliked and mistrusted the rifle, which was a hateful object. Not once had she fired it. She had never touched it. Her husband would be able to kill the lion, she felt certain of this, but he was in Glenwood Springs for the twentieth reunion of his high school class and he would not come home until tomorrow. He would run outside and shoot the lion, but he was not here. I might be able to hit it, Katia thought. Suppose I shot the awful thing, then what? She looked through the glass with a troubled expression as though she were in a box at a theater and could do nothing except watch. She resented the fact that she was not a man. It occurred to her that she might open the window and shout at the lion and wave her arms. Or she could get a frying pan from the kitchen and beat on it with a spoon. Maybe the lion would run away. No, it would not. Whatever she did would be useless; she could not prevent the lion from doing what it had resolved to do. This seemed intolerable. She realized that she had covered her mouth with both hands to keep from screaming, and just then she noticed a quick movement outside. There on a tree stump sat a chipmunk. He sat upright, clasping a seed between his paws. He, too, was watching. He sat on the stump like a little person, fascinated by what was happening beyond the woodpile on the opposite side of the clearing. He sat erect, dumbfounded, one glossy eye appalled and shocked. Katia suddenly felt stronger because the chipmunk agreed with her. And leaning against the stump was an ax. The ax could be used as a weapon. But if she did not dare shoot the rifle, what good was the ax? With a furious squeak she hurried to the closet for a jacket, seized the camera, threw open the door and ran outside because at least she could take a picture. If there was a picture of the lion following the cow she could explain everything to her husband and he would believe her. He might become enraged. Maybe he would track the lion and catch up with it and kill it, so at least there would be some justice. He would skin the lion and they would use the skin as a rug in front of the fireplace. That would not make things right, but it would help. She had run almost as far as the woodpile when she smelled fried potatoes. She had been watching the ground for rocks because she had forgotten her moccasins and her last glimpse of the lion was his profile; now she was looking directly into the blunt triangular face. He crouched motionless as stone, yellowish and detached, like a carved marble lion in a museum. She tried to remember who had told her that you are much too close to a mountain lion if you smell fried potatoes when there aren't any. Sid might have told her. He had grown up on a ranch and knew about animals. He might have told her, but she did not think so. Somebody else had mentioned the peculiar smell. Maybe it was a joke because she had known absolutely nothing about wild animals when she moved to Colorado and married Sid. Or maybe she imagined the smell, but it was very strong. Now the lion was contemplating her with an acute dangerous gaze, with perfectly human lucidity. His mind had been aroused, he was thinking. If he decided to attack, she would not have time to get back to the cabin. He would move so fast that she might not even see him, she would be struck down almost where she stood. When Sid got back from Glenwood Springs he would find her body, or what was left of it, and the knowledge that her flesh might be eaten was an inconceivable idea. She watched the lion raise his head like a cat wishing to be stroked while he appraised her with luminous eyes and she fled to the cabin. After bolting the door she rushed to the window to take a picture but discovered that she did not have the camera. It lay on the ground near the woodpile. Both animals were higher on the slope. The chipmunk, too, had moved; he clung upside down to the side of the stump as though outraged or amazed. His tail arched over his back, one eye glowing like a gemstone. He was too alarmed to do anything. And at the base of the stump Katia noticed a miniature yellow flower with heart-shaped leaves. She was astonished because the flower had not been there yesterday. The tiny announcement struck her as a reproach, although she did not know why. She felt that in some mysterious way she had failed, as if by abandoning the cow she diminished herself. But this did not make sense. She glanced at the monstrous elk antlers Sid had picked up and wired to the top of the shed. The antlers were disembodied, oracular, beyond comprehension. She realized that she despised and feared this mountain where so much exceeded her ability to understand, where the boundaries established for civilization did not exist. She placed both hands on her belly. She, too, was pregnant. Winter had swept in arrogantly, fiercely; but now the valley stirred, triumphant with life. The tremendous promise of another season was imminent. The confident flower, the chipmunk clutching his precious seed, the grumpy blue jay—beyond doubt they were anticipating spring; but the desperate cow with a calf whose eyes had not yet opened—for these two the promise would end horribly among aspen shadows or beneath an enormous spruce or on some granite ledge and the murder would find an equal place in the cycle. I hate it, Katia thought. She felt sickened. What was about to happen could not be right. She watched grimly as the cow lurched and plunged, bawling, slobbering. Its expression seemed to have passed beyond fright; the cow appeared to be insane. And what of the lion? Did he appreciate his own

intelligence? They were traveling toward a place he knew, which
belonged to him, which he considered his inheritance, where the
dreadful play would end. Was he conscious of himself? For a while
he had been puzzled by what the wind reported so he had stopped,
doubtful, estimating the danger. But what came forth? Not much.
Oh, not very much. The lion's conceit infuriated her. Because he was
powerful, because he terrified everything on the mountain—except
perhaps the bears—because of this the lion went about his business
lazily. If I could kill you! she said aloud. Deliberately the lion had
frightened the cow away from the ranch, he had directed her to
climb the mountain, and a little above the clearing would be an
exciting place for breakfast. Oh yes! So he plodded back and forth,
this way or that, a shepherd minding his charge, exerting himself
only enough to let her know she could not go home again. Once he
lashed his tail to prove he was still on the job, a fact he wished to
emphasize. And like a good shepherd he kept his distance because if
she collapsed with fear and could not get up, well, he would have to
drag her to the table. That would be hard work. Even for a grown
lion that would be difficult. So he whipped his tail and grinned.
Almost shyly he crept closer, not too close, and she reared again and
tripped over a stone and let fall another pie; and when she tossed
her head to look for some escape he was vastly amused. He lifted his
grinning muzzle. He stared at her with friendly eyes. You won't
forget me, will you? I'm right here and you must do as I say. All right,
keep moving. Climb a little higher. When the time comes—if you
have been a good obedient cow—it will end quickly. I'm not quite
grown, you see, I'm not strong enough to drag your carcass up the
mountain and that is why I decided to let you do the work. Ho ho!
We must climb a little more, we two. Of course you're terribly
upset, but never mind, we're almost there. Before you realize it I
will be on your back. Yes indeed! Stop complaining. And don't think
you are clever enough or swift enough to escape. No no! But the
cow lifted its muzzle, lowing for help, and Katia who stood at the
window with both hands protecting her belly thought she could
guess what dull recognition stirred its brain: the cow feared not only
for its life but also, dimly, for another life. Then it stopped, exhausted,
drooling. The lion snarled. Katia was positive she heard this. However, the cow did not move. The lion waited. At last they resumed

their obscene journey, the cow staggering between two evergreens while the lion followed attentively, and then all at once they were gone. Katia looked for the chipmunk; he, too, had vanished. But after a moment he popped up on the stump and continued nibbling his seed, or another, while he kept watch, knowing quite well that the world is mutable and deadly and it is wise to avoid mistakes. Oh yes, he knew quite a lot about lions and humans and owls and nuts. He had observed the performance but he did not care any longer, he had important things to do. Katia looked at the evergreens that stood unperturbed, quiet, absorbed by their own reality. She felt an urgent desire to leave the mountain—this prehistoric ridge where nothing mattered except food. She hated the granite boulders and the violent rain, the medieval forest, the grotesque shapes emerging at dusk, the unexpected barbaric music, the hideous shrieks of creatures annihilated by passion or by the claws of predators during the merciless night. She hated this unfeeling, amoral existence. She wanted to return to the city where at suppertime she might arrange silver heirlooms on a linen tablecloth, where it was possible to discuss poetry or attend fashion shows and concerts of classical music, where the values of the mountain could be denied. Overhead two red-tailed hawks slanted with the current. Perhaps they could see the cow and the lion. If so, what did the spectacle mean to them? Or were they, like the chipmunk, indifferent? She could not understand why she felt as she did, why she felt some responsibility toward the pattern of life; surely this must be the utmost conceit, yet she could not feel otherwise. She stood uncertainly at the window, listening and watching. The chipmunk had disappeared. The hawks were gone. There was not a sound. She wanted to scream against the emptiness, the terrifying silence. She was afraid to look at the shed. If the antlers were gone she did not know what she might do.

HOOKER

KOERNER STOOD beside a eucalyptus tree with both hands stuffed into his jeans, listening to the distant foghorns and watching. Fog seeped over the ridge above Sausalito. Before long the Golden Gate Bridge would be engulfed, then San Francisco. Everything would be submerged. In a little while, he thought, we can walk on the bed of the ocean like Captain Nemo and Monsieur Aronnax. Tomorrow the city would reappear, perhaps by noon, or it might not. In late summer one never knew. A cool breeze was pushing ahead of the fog like a pilot fish ahead of a shark. Koerner buttoned his jacket.

Well, now the problem was where to eat. I should learn to cook, he said to himself. Going out every night is bad for the stomach. And he began to think about his usual restaurants, but rejected them all, one after another. Gilhooley's—they must have a blacksmith in the kitchen, you need a hammer to crack the bread and the meat is tough as a sponge. Angelo's—that waiter glides around like a reptile and the minestrone tastes like furniture polish. Wimbledon—they slice a bar of laundry soap and call it cheese. I'd rather eat at the city jail. Then he remembered the Flying Dutchman. He had not been there in months.

The Dutchman's lounge was empty except for a girl drinking wine in front of the stained glass window. She had made herself the center of an art nouveau composition and almost certainly she knew it. Koerner hesitated. She wore a Stanford sweatshirt and a knitted cap pulled down until it concealed half of her face, but there was no mistaking the unusually long nose and the crazed turquoise eyes.

She glanced up, apparently surprised, although the expression was not quite true. After gazing at him for a moment she said, "Je ne parle pas Anglais."

Koerner laughed and walked over to the table.

"Vaya!" she muttered, scowling. "No hablo Ingles."

The deep nasal voice was familiar. And those insane eyes—there could be no mistake.

"Aye vant," she said, enunciating each word, "tew bee alone."

He looked at her deliberately. "I met you in Taos several years ago."

"I used to be a circus contortionist," she said. "Maybe that's where you saw me."

"At the Taos Inn. We drank at least a gallon of Carta Blanca. We ate guacamole and enchiladas and then we drove out to the Rio Grande bridge and I played 'Sewanee River' on the harmonica because I couldn't think of a number about the Rio Grande. It was freezing. You howled at the moon. Your name is Maria Czermak."

"During a performance the elephant went into musth and grabbed the fat lady," she said in her almost masculine voice. "It was terrifying."

"I've lost my appetite," Koerner said. "Circus or no circus, we knew each other in Taos. You haven't forgotten. You remember that night as well as I do."

She lit a cigarette and murmured through the smoke. "My name is Gloria Wonderlips." Then she tamped out the cigarette. "Listen, I'm Marla Jarecki. I can't talk to you. I have an appointment. Don't ask me to explain."

"How about tomorrow?"

"That's impossible."

"I'll call you."

"Don't even try."

"How will I find you?"

"Give me your number."

He printed it on a cocktail napkin. "I'll be here tomorrow—just in case."

"I know you," she said and brushed his cheek with one finger. Then she was gone.

He could not get over a feeling of disbelief. He had never expected to see her again. He remembered that while they were splashing hot sauce on everything and laughing and feeding each other spoons of guacamole and talking about places they had been—in the midst of all the frivolity it had seemed that something important was happening.

He remembered thinking that his life was about to change because of this half-civilized creature with turquoise eyes.

She had been to Mexico. She had visited Campeche, where he lived for six months. She knew about the hawks sailing along the sea wall with their white legs pressed together and how the Gulf lay flat as a slice of blueberry pie. The Mexicans built that wall to keep out pirates and Englishmen, he had said, and she laughed. They talked about the smell of gasoline after a fishing boat chugged by, and the terrible restaurant on the beach with fans nailed to the pink plastered wall and a mosaic tile floor and the TV set perched on top of a broken refrigerator. She remembered palm trees struggling against the afternoon breeze, and truck fumes and yellow-and-blue stucco houses and idiotic crowing roosters and flowers and tin shacks and jars of Nescafé and painted wheelbarrows and a troop of Catholic schoolgirls with gold-capped teeth. She had seen the Mayan ruins at Palenque, so they talked about that—lime-streaked glyphs, the unexpected drip of water from stalactites in gloomy passageways, mosquitoes, warm rain showers, orange and black lichen scaling the mottled white temples. He felt astonished that they had gone to the same places and had experienced them in the same way, and it had seemed to him that night in Taos while they drank Mexican beer and talked about Campeche and mysterious temples in the jungle that their separate travels must have brought them together for a purpose.

So he remained for a long time in front of the stained glass window with his elbows on the table and his chin cupped in his hands.

Finally he got up and wandered out to the deck. An immense threatening shape obscured San Francisco. Lugubrious foghorns groaned through the darkness. The Oakland bridge was being swallowed. Without doubt the end of the world was near. However, the fog did not seem to be drifting north and dinner was being served outside. He chose a table overlooking the yacht harbor.

"Stay away from that bitch," said a voice.

Somebody in a straw hat was smiling disagreeably. The stranger wore a necklace of Italian glass beads and a polo shirt with an alligator on the pocket. He stood like a woman, swaying just a little, with one hand propped on his fleshy hip. He reeked of deodorant.

"She is not a nice person," the stranger continued, pushing the words out of his mouth. "Do you mind if I sit down? My ankle is killing me. Of course it's none of my business," he went on after seating himself, "but you obviously were entranced by that slut. And I refuse to apologize."

"Who are you?" Koerner demanded.

"Clem Figgie. Oh, you're such a grouch! I've noticed you around town. Was she pretending to be Alexandra Nowosielska?" His features oozed contempt. "Czermak? Maria Czermak? Or did she pose as Marla Jarecki? Isn't she the darling?"

"Jarecki," Koerner said, annoyed with himself for answering.

"She married Jarecki when she was a child, so I'm told. Listen, dear fellow, that sweet thing stole my mother's wedding ring and six hundred dollars. Oh, the money doesn't matter. Well, it does. I'm not that rich." He sighed. "You don't believe one word."

He owns a boat, Koerner thought, I can smell the bay underneath that putrid chemical. He's never had a job, it's inherited—bonds, coupons, stocks, maybe a patch of the hillside. I don't like anything about him. That Fourth of July hat, the sulky voice, the beads, the alligator. He's a mound of grease and pastry.

"Well, she did," Figgie continued, twisting his necklace. "I assure you she did."

I'm losing my appetite again, Koerner thought. That deodorant is suffocating. "What makes you so sure?" he asked. "Just how do you know?"

"Who else? Quite foolishly I invited her to brunch at my place on Saint Swithin's Day and that same evening I discovered the theft. I've no idea why I should unburden myself to you, I can tell you dislike me. Oh, never mind. I was presented to Miss Alexandra, diamonds and all, at a Pacific Heights supper. She can pass, you know. Or did you? Nob Hill. Tenderloin. North Beach. Whatever she chooses to be. Tonight she is the Stanford graduate. And I'm not Clem Figgie, no indeed, I'm the Crown Prince of Nepal." He fanned himself with the menu. His plump boneless face glistened. "Suppose we go for a sail some afternoon. Imagine what a spanking time we might have. Would you like that? Now what do you say?"

"I get seasick in a bathtub."

"Oh! Oh! How amusing!" Figgie cried. "Well, sweet thing, I must be off. My friends are waiting. Bye!" he exclaimed, flourishing one hand. "If I can just manage with this ankle . . ." He eased himself from the deck chair, gasped, and hobbled inside.

I should have let him talk, Koerner said to himself. That was stupid. I could have learned a few things. Alexandra. Marla. Maria. The elephant assaulted the fat lady. What next?

On the following night when he pushed through the frosted glass door of the Dutchman's lounge he told himself she would not be there, but he could not prevent himself from looking. At her table sat an inscrutable Japanese tourist slung with cameras. This is absurd, he thought. I haven't seen her for at least three years, I see her for three minutes, she gives me an alias, pats me like a dog, waltzes off to some appointment, and I lie awake half the night wondering when I'll see her again. Well, I'll have a drink before dinner and concentrate on other things. Baseball. Politics. Travel. Yes, that's an idea, I could plan another trip. Think about the Canary Islands or Tierra del Fuego.

The bartender arrived, wiping his hands on a towel. "Are you by any chance William Koerner?"

"I guess so," Koerner said.

"Marla called. She's going out of town for a while."

"Anything else?"

"She'll be in touch."

"Thank you. I'd like a double martini."

No sooner had the bartender turned away than a voice asked: "Is Marla a friend of yours?"

The voice belonged to an earnest young man with pimples and a cowlick. He wore a blue nylon windbreaker that might have come from a drugstore and clipped to the breast pocket stood a platoon of ballpoint pens.

"My name's Orin," he said timidly, extending his hand. "I didn't catch yours."

"Bill," Koerner said without enthusiasm and accepted the hand, which was moist and felt like a tongue.

Orin grinned, exhibiting ragged teeth. "Hello, Bill. It's a pleasure to make your acquaintance. Do you come here a lot?"

"Not very often."

"I come here all the time. It's expensive, but it's a wonderful place to make friends. I was pretty sure I hadn't seen you because I've got a good memory for faces. I hope I'm not intruding but I wanted to introduce myself because Marla used to be my girl."

Koerner looked at him again. Brown glass eyes, expressionless wooden features. Orin resembled Pinocchio.

"Can you guess where I work?" he asked. "Can you?"

There was a medicinal smell about him, but that proved nothing. After a drink Koerner said, "I give up."

"The animal shelter!"

"Well," Koerner said.

"Yep," said Orin. "This sounds funny, but I like animals better than people. Do you have a pet?"

"At the moment, no, but I may get a Chihuahua."

Orin grew tense. "You should buy two."

"Why should I buy two?"

"Because they don't eat much!" Orin cried and slapped Koerner on the back. Then he became serious. "Bill, I'm studying for my vet's license. In fact, I already thought up a name for my clinic. I'm going to call it Orin's Pet Hospital."

"That's a good name," Koerner said. "Tell me about you and Marla."

Orin frowned. "I don't know why she doesn't call anymore. I can't figure it out. Maybe she thinks I don't amount to much but she's going to change her mind when she sees my clinic." Carefully he wiped his nose on the back of his hand. "I'll tell you something else that puzzles me. We always went to the movies in Novato or someplace like that because she didn't want to go into the city. She knows a lot of those bohemians in North Beach and I thought it would be fun to meet them, but she didn't want to. She knows Christopher Lloyd. He's a poet. They went to Stanford together. His picture was in the *Examiner* a couple of months ago because he took a swing at a cop. Did you ever read his poems?"

"A few."

"I don't have time to read. Working at the shelter—wow! You can't believe how busy it gets. Last week it seemed like everybody lost a cat or found a cat. Things always come in bunches."

"How did you meet her?"

Orin's carved head swiveled toward the dartboard, an arm came up, and one finger pointed. No, he's not alive, Koerner thought, somebody pulled a string.

"Right there," Orin said happily. "She was watching me so I challenged her to a game."

"And you won?"

"Easy. I'm pretty good. I can beat everybody around here except Dave Aretino. You think you can beat me?"

"I'm out of practice."

"I'll give you a handicap and bet you a dollar."

"Not tonight. So you invited her to the movies?"

"Yep. She sells leather goods and she had an appointment, but she promised to call me. I was afraid she'd forgotten because she didn't call for a long time. She's really strange. Sometimes she dresses up like a gypsy with gold earrings and a bandanna." He stopped to squeeze a pimple. "She told me not to give her any presents, but I wanted to anyway."

My God, she devoured him, Koerner thought. He doesn't know what happened. He dreams about the two of them caring for sick puppies at Orin's Pet Hospital. She bled Figgie, too, but six hundred dollars is less than he spends on Halloween. I wonder if she did rob Captain Alligator.

Orin pulled out his wallet. "Bill, I'm going to show you something personal because I trust you, but you can't tell anybody."

The wallet was manufactured plastic that unfolded with a harsh ripping noise. Orin thrust two fingers into a pocket and triumphantly brought out a Polaroid snapshot, which he slapped on the bar face down.

"Go ahead. Turn it over."

Marla was lying comfortably naked on a couch, smiling for the camera. Koerner stared at it. What she had done was to arrange herself exactly like Goya's Duchess of Alba.

Orin chuckled. "Boy, was I surprised when she gave that to me! You could have knocked me down with a feather. She got some friend of hers to take it—some girlfriend." He slipped the picture back into his wallet. "She made me promise never to let anybody see it because her parents might find out. She lives in the city on Pacific Heights and her father is president of a bank. You know, Bill, this is going to sound funny, but after I get my clinic I'm going to ask her to marry me."

It was like something from an old fairy tale. The youth invited the lady to eat his heart, so she obliged. And how does our lady amuse herself this evening? Koerner wondered. Does she wear a short tight skirt as she prowls the Tenderloin? Does she play Alexandra with diamonds on Russian Hill?

Then it seemed to him that he had guessed where she was—in North Beach sipping cappuccino at a sidewalk café, or discussing poetry with Christopher Lloyd in the Literary Lights Bookshop. No doubt she had met Chris Lloyd. His cultural status would attract her. He was, after all, a celebrated North Beach poet.

He remembered seeing Lloyd at Raphael's Café surrounded by unpublished disciples—an arrogant little magistrate with tousled hair and the nose of an Aztec prince, full of himself to the lip, as though the universe spiraled about his pen. There, it was said, at that secluded table in the nook, half-hidden by potted ferns, he held court if the mood settled upon him. Oh yes, quite by accident she would have met Christopher Lloyd. And how did he respond?

She would be out of town—that was the message. Pinocchio waited for her to call, but why should I wait? Koerner asked himself. Tomorrow I might sidle around North Beach and see what develops.

When he drove across the Golden Gate Bridge on the following night he could see fog beginning to obscure the city, and by the time he got to North Beach everything was damp. Coffee at Raphael's seemed like a good idea. Lloyd might show up.

Wallace the giant bartender wore a prodigiously loose Russian peasant blouse and Koerner once again felt amazed that a man could be so wide and thick. When he was not mixing drinks or keeping the peace Wallace liked to draw imaginary creatures to which he gave imaginary names and homes. He drew brendels and absquiths and mergolyns and presips and cocoranths and a great many others. He drew them with exquisite delicacy on the best Japanese paper and everybody who had seen him do these things with a pen lightly between his fingertips was reduced to silence. Koerner remembered several years ago when there had been trouble outside—a junkie waving a meat hook, threatening customers at the sidewalk tables. He could remember Wallace rolling toward the junkie with the massive conviction of a truck rolling downhill. The junkie swung the hook and connected, which may have been the worst mistake of his life. Wallace chose not to kill him, but when a siren came screaming out of the Broadway tunnel a few minutes later the junkie still slept his dreadful sleep on the pavement.

"You haven't been around," Wallace said pleasantly.

"Not for a while," Koerner agreed. "How's Raphael?"

"Oh, you know," said Wallace, and swept imperceptible motes of dust from the lustrous wood. "What can I get you?"

"Nothing right now. Have you seen Chris Lloyd?"

"Half an hour ago he went by."

"Which direction?"

"Columbus."

"Thanks. Tell Raphael hello for me."

Wallace nodded.

Lloyd probably was heading for the Bagel Shop or maybe the Triumvirate. He would be someplace in that neighborhood.

At the corner of Broadway and Columbus stood Reece—a mahogany totem pole. He wore tattered sneakers and a greasy unbuttoned overcoat displaying four hundred soup stains and he smelled worse than a cage at the zoo. He had grown a wretched billy-goat beard, perhaps to compensate for several missing teeth. His mouth twitched. He won't notice me, Koerner thought. He fried his brain so long ago that nothing matters.

"Hey, man," Reece said in his very deep voice, "got a cigarette?"

"Gave it up," Koerner said. "What are you doing on this side of the street? You used to be on the other side."

"Corners," Reece muttered, studying the traffic light. His tickets to Paradise had been counterfeit and now he stood on corners watching the signals change. Green. Yellow. Red. Green. Yellow. Red.

"You know Chris Lloyd, don't you?"

"Uppity Jack."

"Come on, Reece. Do you know him?"

"I know him."

"Seen him tonight?"

After a while Reece lowered his gaze to the fireplug. That seemed to be the end of it. Either he did not want to talk about Lloyd or he had forgotten the question.

"Marla Jarecki. Do you know her?"

"Ted Bristol."

"Come on, how about it?" Koerner said, lifting his voice above the traffic. "Marla Jarecki."

"Ted Bristol."

"He knows her. Is that what you're saying?"

"Ted Bristol Bones."

"How would I find him? Where does he hang out?"

Reece vanished, speeding toward some nebulous galaxy accessible to no one else. At last he returned: "Lights."

This could mean the traffic signal, but probably it meant the bookshop. "What does he look like?"

"George Washington."

"All right, George Washington. Now what does Ted Bristol Bones look like?"

"I told you," Reece said, as though speaking to a child.

"Anything else? Could you describe him some other way?"

"Cops," Reece answered lazily, "bug him."

"Cops bug everybody. Come on, now."

"Watch cap. Pea jacket."

"Good. Will he talk about her?"

Reece considered the fireplug. "Cops bug him."

"I'm not a cop."

"I understand that," Reece said.

Well, I could go either direction, Koerner thought. I could walk up Grant and hunt for the bard of North Beach, or walk down Columbus to the bookshop.

The signals changed and it occurred to him that he had seen Ted Bristol somewhere—playing chess in the park, maybe. He did resemble George Washington. Pea jacket. Watch cap. And somebody had said that Bristol was an ex-Communist who worked on the waterfront and knew Harry Bridges. Yes, well, he might be worth a trip. The signals changed again.

"Hey, man," Reece said, "got a cigarette?"

Koerner wagged his head.

Reece began to giggle; he covered his rotting mouth with a pair of leathery hands and he stamped his feet with joy.

Meanwhile the traffic stopped and started like a mechanical caterpillar. Green. Yellow. Stop. Red. Green. Start. Well, Koerner thought, I don't want to stand here until midnight. I see why Reece likes it, but I'd better track down Mr. Bones.

Beneath the peppermint-stripe awning of Literary Lights a bin of used books leaned against the wall. Ten cents apiece. He paused to look at the titles. *Great Golf Courses. Beginning Jiu Jitsu. Prehistoric Astronomy in Cambodia. Sailing for the Novice. Fix It Yourself. How to Bowl 300! Zulu Odyssey*.

He opened the Zulu book. There, dressed for action in pith helmet and rumpled white suit, the corpulent author sat enthroned like a provincial governor—a swagger stick across his knees—facing the camera with dignified reserve after what must have been an adventurous trip through Zululand. His eyes bulged, his formidable mustache drooped.

Koerner looked at the copyright page. The book was privately printed in Philadelphia in 1912. The spine was cracked, the faded linen binding spotted by rain.

On the title page beneath his name, Charles Duckett Grubb, the author had written with a graceful hand:

Millie—Dear Love
Charles

After reading a few sentences Koerner dropped *Zulu Odyssey* in the bin and continued to the entrance. No doubt this African journey had been the most exciting experience of Mr. Grubb's life, but the wearisome prose and the mind responsible for it explained why the narrative was privately published.

Inside, as always, Huong sat like Buddha on a high stool beside the cash register.

"Huong," he said by way of greeting.

The shining slit eyes did not move, nor did Huong speak, nor did anything about that oracular brown face appear to change.

Koerner went down the narrow staircase to the basement and looked around. There—beneath a wildly painted social protest mural—sat George Washington in watch cap and rimless spectacles, his pea jacket folded on a chair. He sat behind a three-legged marble-topped table with a tiny cup of espresso and he was reading Plato. He glanced over the top of his glasses with a suspicious expression.

"Are you Ted Bristol?" Koerner asked.

"Bones, that's me."

"I wonder if I could talk to you."

"Show me your badge."

"I'm no cop."

"IRS?"

"Neither one."

"What's on your mind?"

"Marla."

Bones did not close the book. He did not look friendly. Then he said: "Who wants to know?"

Koerner introduced himself and explained that he had met her in Taos. Bones considered this information. He rubbed his jaw. He had not shaved for a couple of days.

"You're a cop."

"Maybe I look like one."

Bones shut the book, leaving a blunt finger inside to mark the page. He had not made up his mind.

"Why should I talk to you?"

"Can I sit down?"

"You might be straight," Bones said. "You might be anything. She's got trouble enough. I don't want something bad happening to her." He waved at a chair. "You god damn better be straight." Although he did not sound hostile, neither did he sound well disposed.

Koerner pointed to the espresso. "How about another?"

"No. First off, her name is Mikki Novak. I don't like people calling her Marla. Maria. None of that crap. Her name is Mikki."

"Why does she call herself Marla?"

Bones sucked his teeth. He peeled off his glasses and held them up to the light. Apparently they were clean enough. He hooked them back in place. At last he said, "I never knew one to be satisfied."

This could refer to women, but there were other possibilities. I don't want something bad happening to her, he had said, and the George Washington lips barely moved. If anything bad happens to her now, Koerner thought, a couple of waterfront goons will come looking for me. I don't know what she means to this character and I don't know why I'm trying to play detective. Maybe I should go home and wait for her to call.

"Mikki wasn't always wild," Bones said, reaching for the espresso. "Could have been her ma. She was nuts. Smart old broad, but crazy as a sow on ice."

And what about you? Koerner wondered. How do you fit into this?

Bones got to his feet with difficulty and limped around the corner to the toilet. When he came back he said, "Who told you where to find me?"

"Reece."

"That hophead."

"He can surface if he wants to."

"How do you know Reece?"

"I used to hang around North Beach. He was always in the Bagel Shop."

Bones looked attentively at nothing. Then he said, "Reece was a good sculptor. Why did he blow his head apart? What a waste."

"I never knew he was a sculptor."

"Years ago. All right, sport, listen. Bad things came down I won't talk about, but I'll tell you this much. Mikki was a nice kid. I hear things about her I know aren't true. Max and Hilda taught her right. Then she had to go and get married before she grew up. Stupid."

"Jarecki?"

"They lived together. She was sixteen. I told Max to kill Jarecki." His expression changed. Evidently he had decided to say nothing else.

"Was she ever in North Africa?"

"What's North Africa got to do with it?"

"Well," Koerner said, "I'm a little embarrassed about this. We got sort of drunk in Taos and started speaking French. She has an unusual accent."

"You may be straight," Bones said with a smile like a razor blade. "Until now I didn't think so. She learned French in Martinique. I don't know about North Africa." He took a sip of espresso and all at once he appeared older. "I don't see her much these days. Once in a while she comes around if she wants to talk. Usually it's some bastard making trouble."

"Can you tell me anything about her father?"

"Doing time. It was a bad rap. He worked with me at Eckholm's shipyard for thirty-six years. I know Max." Bones opened *The Republic*. His grizzled face tightened.

This seems to be it, Koerner thought, he doesn't want to say anything else. She tells Orin her father is a bank president and they live on Pacific Heights. Attended Stanford with Lloyd. She told Figgie her name was Alexandra something. In Taos she was Maria Czermak. I wonder if she lies to Uncle Bones.

He remembered meeting her at the Taos Inn on a frigid January night. He had been almost asleep beside the fireplace when she walked through the lobby dressed like a stylish Navajo in purple velveteen with a hammered silver concho belt and soft tawny deerskin boots. He remembered staring at her because of the insinuating walk and those oddly tilted, expressionless eyes. She was aware of him, he knew, and she had walked past him with the long full Navajo dress swirling around her boots. And when he followed that swirling Navajo dress into the bar he was surprised to find her alone.

They had talked about Campeche and Palenque, and Tulum above the emerald water, and Isla Mujeres, and the wonderful Mexican menus that tried to make things easy for American tourists by offering beal cutle and sirloing steack and hors d'aeuvre and red snaper. Had she been to Copán? Yes. Ceiba trees under a white-hot sky, tin-roofed shacks beating back the sun. And while she was there a boy with a flute walked out of the tropical green fields like some antique Mayan god and seated himself on the sloping wall of the prehistoric ball court.

Then he had mentioned Petra.

Where is that? she said.

Petra, the rose-red city half as old as time. It lies below Amman, below the Dead Sea, in south Jordan.

Have you been there? she asked.

Yes, he said. It's a city carved out of a cliff two thousand years ago by Nabataean Arabs. In Jerusalem I met three Australians who were backpacking around the world. We hired a taxi to Petra.

I want to go there, she had said. Take me there.

Koerner blinked and stood up. "All those questions—I don't blame you for being suspicious. Thanks for talking with me."

Bones peered over his glasses. "You're no cop."

"No? Why not?"

"I saw Huong in the can. I asked about you."

He's almost friendly, Koerner thought. I might as well try one more question. "What can you tell me about Chris Lloyd?"

Bones removed his spectacles. He examined them for dust. He considered. At last he said: "Lloyd couldn't write his way out of a paper bag. Stevens. Pound. Jeffers. Those are poets. I still think you're a cop."

"Huong tells me you're a narc."

Bones, after one long indecipherable look, returned to Plato.

A fanfare of trumpets welcomed Koerner to the street and a patrol car with flashing lights contributed to the argument at Broadway and Columbus. Reece had not moved from the fireplug, but his hands were in the pockets of his coat and he had turned up the collar. He appeared to be on another space trip, so Koerner walked by without speaking.

Christopher Lloyd was not at the Triumvirate nor at the Bagel Shop nor Beethoven's Goose nor anywhere in the neighborhood. Well, then, possibly at Raphael's.

And there the poet reigned, uncombed, lordly, all but enshrined. There the bard of North Beach presided over his discussion table in a fern-shrouded nook, properly attired in a turtleneck sweater. Koerner hesitated. No. No, it would be impossible to join that clique. Some other time, perhaps, when Mr. Lloyd was offstage. Then it occurred to him that Wallace might know her.

Wallace, not quite as big as a buffalo, was drying wine glasses.

"Cappuccino," Koerner said. While waiting for it he folded his arms and studied the bottles behind the bar. Cointreau with a red ribbon. The frosty green Courvoisier. Dark brown Tía Maria. Black Jack Daniel's almost hidden by Wallace's tip jar. Galliano. Chivas Regal. The opulent Chambord liqueur surmounted by a gold crown.

"I've been wondering," he said when the cappuccino arrived, "does Marla Jarecki come in here?"

Wallace replied with a massive shrug and began rinsing a carafe. It was obvious that he did not want to talk about her.

I think I've blundered into a spiderweb, Koerner said to himself. This is becoming a very strange night. I should go home before something awful happens. Or maybe I'm imagining. He looked across the bar at the great Scottish slab of a face and the tightly curled ringlets. Wallace had a large head, but it seemed uncommonly small above his shoulders. From the side he resembled a giant turtle.

"How's the menagerie?"

"Oh," Wallace answered in his pleasant voice, "various creatures come to mind."

Just then the door opened and a squad of tourists entered, unmistakable vacationers from the Midwest, dressed for August in Wichita on a chilly night in San Francisco. They were damp. Koerner glanced outside to see if the mist had turned to rain and found Christopher Lloyd glaring through the ferns. His orange hair flew in all directions and his reddish eyes burned. He looked like a crazed parrot.

Koerner swung around to the bar. There could be no doubt that Lloyd recognized him. But how? They had never met.

Somebody was approaching. The rapid click of heels sounded like a woman, but the poet wore elevated shoes.

"I saw you in Taos," Lloyd snapped. "Maria pointed you out." He had the fierce eyebrows of an old man. At the tip of his nose a crusty wart stood out like the stub of a broken horn.

My God, Koerner thought, I had a feeling she was there with somebody, but not this dervish. "How about a cappuccino?" he asked. And to his surprise Lloyd hopped up on the next stool.

Wallace floated toward them with the peculiar buoyancy of enormous men.

"Remy," Lloyd commanded, folding his arms. After the cognac had been delivered he tasted it and approved. Then he said, "She is a nymph. Furthermore, she is unstable. Did you know that? Until recently she was hospitalized at the Marquis Emerson clinic. They should not have released her. She is capable of destroying herself. I tell you for your own good because she is capable of destroying not only herself but anyone who fails to recognize her condition." He lifted the cognac smoothly with his palms as though elevating the Holy Grail. "You assume that you met a charming fauve, but she is distraught and dangerous. I might add that I saw you talking to that shipyard intellectual. Whatever Bristol told you should be disregarded." He paused, scowling. Then all at once he waved impatiently. "Suppose we get this over with. When Maria was a child she was used by her father. Not once, mind you, not twice, but indiscriminately. Her father is a degenerate who has been sentenced to a long prison term. There is no way of predicting what may happen if he gets out. Do you understand? Now I have one more thing to say, but first, let me thank you for the cognac. Three days ago Maria and I were married." He sprang off the stool, made some incomprehensible gesture with both hands, and stalked out the door.

The discussion table was empty. Their guru having flown, the disciples scattered. Or perhaps they were congregating at another café. Well, Koerner thought, I can't guess what this is all about but I know that maniac is lying. They aren't married.

Then he began to think about Taos. Most of what happened was easy to remember because one scene led to the next; but later, when they were alone on the snowy plateau with Taos a distant sprinkle of lights, fragments were missing. He remembered that while she stared into the canyon he had looked carefully all around because of something malignant in the night. He remembered that he took out the harmonica and began to play, and invented a clumsy little dance on the bridge—as though this might appease the gathering presence—although he could see nothing unexpected except the oval moon riding over Taos mountain. And during the night while they slept together it had seemed to him that a mystery was resolved; but when he awoke in the icy Taos dawn she had vanished. She might have been a violent dream except for a hairpin on the floor.

"Hello," said a voice that was almost masculine.

He looked in the mirror. "Je ne parle pas Anglais," he said to her reflection.

After a moment she smiled. "Did you get the message?"

He turned around, startled by how close she was. Tonight, as Figgie would say, she had decided to become the Montmartre Apache—black leather cap, black leather pants and jacket with chains and metal buttons, little black boots.

"If it isn't raining we might take a walk," he said. "I have so much to tell you."

After a questioning glance at Wallace she agreed.

"Where do you want to go?" she asked when they were outside.

"Where? Oh, anywhere. It doesn't matter in the least. Why don't we go to the circus? I'm worried about the fat lady. No, I have a better idea. Let's go to the bookshop. Did you know you lost a hairpin in Taos? I kept it for at least a year, maybe two years. What do you suppose that means?"

"Taos was a long time ago."

He laughed. "Yes. I've tried to forget. No, that's a lie." I'm not making sense, he thought. "Did you know Lloyd was at Raphael's just now?"

She smiled again. "I waited until he left. You're the one I wanted to be with."

"Let's go to Campeche. We could have lunch in that terrible restaurant—that old radio blaring and those tiny paper napkins. Arroz con mariscos and cheese pie and Nescafé. My God, it was awful! Those yellow plastic glasses and bent forks and a bottle of toothpicks—I never thought I'd want to have lunch there again, but now I do. I remember that card table with a splintered leg and the mangy little mutt that was always scratching and will you come with me to Campeche?"

"Before you start packing, one or two things will have to be straightened out."

"Yes," he said. "And we can spend a while in Villahermosa. It's lovely. There's a fancy painted bandstand in the park and flowers and flowers and flowers and have you been to Villahermosa?"

"Stop dreaming."

"Will you come with me to the hermosa villa?"

"I might."

"I want to hear you say yes."

"Maybe. It depends."

"Maybe. All right, maybe," Koerner said. "Will you come with me to visit the stone deities of Tula? They stand on a pyramid like Egyptian pharaohs supervising the town and there was a guard wearing baggy blue trousers sitting in the shade reading a newspaper and a pig tied to a tree and while I was eating a taco the church bells began to ring and there were orange peels and roosters and Mexico everywhere. Will you—ah! We're here. Charles Duckett Grubb. I want you to meet him. This is his book. This is what he bequeathed to posterity. This is the chronicle of Charles Duckett Grubb."

She was faintly amused. "Is he important?"

"Nobody could be less important. I'm not sure how to explain. Listen." After pretending to clear his throat he began: "Since early childhood in a leafy suburb of Allentown it had been my fondest wish . . ."

"You idiot," she said, with an arm around his waist. "You won't get through the first chapter."

"I don't plan to," Koerner said. "Read the inscription."

"Millie—Dear Love," she read aloud. For a moment she was silent. Then she looked up with a friendly expression. "You sentimental fool. Who believes in love anymore?"

"Close your eyes and pick out something. Anything. I'll buy it for you."

"Now I remember," she said. "The guy with the harmonica." Obediently she closed her eyes and reached for the books. "All right, sailor, what next?"

"Try again."

"Did I pick something awful?"

"*Lost Horizon*," he said, expecting her to laugh.

"How about it, sailor? Will you help me?"

Koerner felt his breath catch. He took her hand and guided it toward another book while she stood close beside him with her head tilted. A streetlight shone on her sleeping face under the black leather cap. The wide cheekbones, long nose, and protruding upper lip were deeply sensual, a Slavic sculptor's dream of Aphrodite. When he let go of her hand she picked up the book he had selected.

"What's my little gift?" she whispered, slowly lifting her blind face. "What will you buy Marla?" Then unexpectedly she opened her eyes. "Oh, how sweet! *A Scarlet Treasury of Confessions*." She began to read: "The Countess gleamed white and naked in my arms—well, now really!"

"Who is the Countess entertaining?"

"Nietzsche. Would you like more? It was in the greenhouse that the Countess first lured me to my fall, behind the back of her husband. Oh, my goodness! We ought to read this in private."

"Mikki," Koerner said, "you have no idea how often I've thought about you."

"And I've thought about you. But first, cowboy, let's get things straight."

"I don't understand," he said.

"Who told you my name was Mikki?"

"Bones."

"I thought so. He tells people he used to know my father."

"What are you talking about?" Koerner demanded. "Mikki, will you stop lying?"

"My name is Gloria Wonderlips," she continued in a musical voice. "That old man used to be in the merchant marine, but he was horribly injured during a collision. I can't imagine why he tells people he knew my father. You can't believe a word he says. My father died years ago. He was a wealthy land developer in Pasadena. I grew up in Pasadena. I'm rich. Have you heard of Encantada Estates? The homes are incredibly expensive. That was one of my father's projects. Did I tell you his name?"

"No," Koerner said. "What was his name?"

"Alexis Masaryk. His grandfather was related to the Czar of Russia. They were cousins."

"Your great-grandfather was the Czar's cousin?"

"Yes. My great-grandfather was a Romanov."

She went on talking and he understood that she was mad—or half-mad—and to enter that turbulent world would be another form of madness. She had moved closer. He felt her thighs press against him and he could smell the black leather.

"Let's take the ferry," she said with her arms around his neck. "I know we can agree on a price before we get to Sausalito."

Suddenly the weight of her arms became disagreeable. Koerner held his breath.

"If that's how you feel," she said. "I have an appointment." She let go of him and wandered away.

Nan Madol

UNCLE GATES and Aunt Ruth lived in Springfield and every so often they came visiting, but I do not remember having much of a conversation with Uncle Gates until I was about nine or ten years old. One evening he stared across the dining room table at me and asked what I intended to do with my life. I told him I wanted to become an archaeologist. If that is true, he said, you must pay attention in school. I didn't like Uncle Gates as well as my father's younger brother Rodney who could pull a silver dollar out of my nose and throw animal shadows on the wall by manipulating his fingers in the lamplight. Once when Uncle Rodney was visiting us he winked at me and turned a back flip. Uncle Gates, who resembled a parrot, did not care about magic tricks or back flips. He taught history and literature at Springfield College and I remember thinking that I would hate to be in his classes.

Almost every summer he took a trip, usually with Aunt Ruth, sometimes by himself. He had traveled around Canada and Mexico and the Caribbean and Europe and once I asked my father how Uncle Gates could afford so many vacations. He made a killing in the market, my father said. I had no idea what the market was, or how one could earn money by killing something in it, but the explanation sounded reasonable.

Now Uncle Gates was on his way home to Springfield after touring the South Seas and my father had written to let me know that he would be stopping overnight in San Francisco. I was expected to entertain him.

He was seated in the hotel lobby gazing straight ahead when I saw him for the first time in twenty years. He had retired from teaching and he appeared much older. Wattles hung from his jaw. The backs of his hands were spotted. For a moment he did not recognize me. Then he exclaimed, William! You gave me quite a start. You are beginning to look like Rodney.

It had occurred to me that we could drive across the Golden Gate Bridge and take the road up Mt. Tamalpais for a panoramic view of San Francisco Bay. Uncle Gates thought that sounded like an interesting excursion. First, though, he wanted to get a coat.

I am unaccustomed to your foggy climate, he said. Come along, I'll show you my room. This is a splendid hotel. I knew right away that I would like it.

He had trouble getting to his feet, which annoyed him. He frowned and steadied himself on the back of the chair.

Your parents may have told you about my accident, he said as we walked through the lobby. It happened a year ago last Christmas. I slipped on a patch of ice and went down like a ton of bricks. I was knocked unconscious. My balance hasn't been too good since then. I thought I would get over it, but I haven't. Now let's see, where's the elevator? Ah! No, isn't that the fire exit? I seem to be a little turned around.

An African couple entered the elevator ahead of us. The man wore a conservative English suit, but the woman was dressed in an elaborate flowing gown. Uncle Gates studied them while the door closed and we started up. I could not tell from his face what he was thinking. He cleared his throat.

The elevator stopped at the fifth floor. He looked puzzled. Then he remembered the Africans. He shuffled to one side and politely asked if this was where they wished to get off.

As we walked along the corridor to his room he seemed to mistrust the carpet, lifting each foot higher than necessary. Inside the room, after fumbling for the light switch, he went to the window and pulled the drapes apart. There lay the huge sparkling bay, the bridge to Oakland, Treasure Island, the Berkeley hills.

You have a distinctive city, he said. What a shame these young people in California fail to appreciate it.

How do you know they don't? I asked.

Just look at them, he said. Now don't chide me, William. I am aware that times change. However, we should not ignore fundamentals. Would you like a glass of water before we start? Or perhaps you would care to make use of the bathroom?

No, I said, I'm fine.

I envy you those kidneys, he said. Pardon me. He walked into the bathroom, shut the door, and turned on the shower before using the toilet. All right, young fellow, he announced when he came out, let's tackle that mountain.

While we stood waiting for the elevator I remarked that it was a handsome couple we had met on the way up.

He nodded. Yes. I wondered where they might be from. I know very little about the regional costumes of Africa, despite visiting several of those countries a few years ago. All kinds of people seem to stay at this hotel. It's practically a United Nations. I can't imagine a crowd like this in Springfield. He pressed the button again and shook his head.

The Africans were talking to a clerk at the desk when we came out of the elevator, but Uncle Gates after one glance paid no attention. I suspected he had filed them in his mind under the appropriate label and that was that. He walked unsteadily but with determination toward the revolving door which was moving slowly, like the paddle wheel of a steamboat. These damn things, he said, you never can tell what they're up to.

Outside the hotel I told him I would get the car and bring it around, but he insisted he didn't mind walking. I remembered a dozen motorcycles parked on Geary in front of a liquor store and I hoped that by now the bikers would be gone, but they were loitering on the sidewalk—black leather jackets with steel chains and painted insignia, boots, beards, mirrored sunglasses. Uncle Gates glared at them.

What the devil is the matter with those bums? he demanded. Why aren't they at work?

Come on, I said and took him by the arm to prevent him from stopping. A couple of the bikers had noticed us.

He had trouble getting into the car. I am sorry to inconvenience you, he said while backing toward the seat. I am not as limber as I was at your age. After sitting down he lifted one leg with both hands and pulled it inside, then the other. My God, he muttered, there used to be a time when I could walk all day.

As we drove toward the Golden Gate he sat with his arms folded, oblivious to everything. At the corner of Van Ness and Lombard we slowed down for some police cars and a crowd of people, but he looked straight ahead.

Who on earth buys those knickknacks in the gift shop? he asked suddenly. I should think a place like that would go broke. Doodads! Nothing but doodads! Well, it's none of my business. What's the name of this place we're going to? Mount something-or-other.

Tamalpais, I said. Tamal Indians used to live around there. Tamal country. Tamal pais.

I understand Spanish, he said.

This surprised me a little, although I did not know why. He had traveled in a number of Latin countries so I should have realized that he would understand Spanish. He may have guessed what I was thinking because he remarked that languages weren't difficult. We talked about this for a while. He had learned to read and speak several European languages, but did not consider himself a linguist. Also, he had begun to study Mandarin. I asked if Mandarin would be of much use in Springfield and he replied that it had not the slightest value.

However, he went on, the process of learning can be remunerative. What a shame that most people wish merely to be diverted. There is greater satisfaction in a single page of Tacitus than you are apt to find in twenty-four hours of ephemeral entertainment.

He sounded very much like a professor. I was afraid he might start questioning me about Tacitus so I asked if he wanted the window rolled up. Fog obscured the bridge towers and it was getting cool.

I am quite comfortable, he said. Do as you please.

His answer reminded me of the Midwest where polite indifference signified good manners. I thought about his courtesy to the Africans and about his courteous response when I had suggested we go for a drive. I wondered if he really did want to go driving or if he would rather have strolled around Fisherman's Wharf or listened to the bongo drummers in Aquatic Park. Maybe he would have liked to explore Mason Street and ogle the hookers. I wished for Uncle Rodney who probably would have said the hell with a scenic drive, let's see what's happening in the Tenderloin. I imagined Uncle Rodney walking into a strip joint and astonishing everybody with a back flip.

Ahead of us stood the lopsided cone of Mt. Tamalpais, regarded by some as California's attempt to copy Fujiyama. Uncle Gates, communing with himself, did not see it until I pointed. He emitted a volcanic rumbling that I took for approval and retreated to his meditations. I tried to think of him as a young man before the clay hardened. I had seen him any number of times when I was a child, but he had been my uncle, an adult, whose face and form I knew without knowing anything else. What was he like when he married Aunt Ruth? Well, I thought, why not ask?

Tell me something that happened many years ago, I said. Anything you remember.

He turned his head and considered me with a grave expression. What have you got up your sleeve? he asked. Why should you inquire about my youth?

Because I don't know you, I said. I was always your nephew.

A foolish escapade. Is that what you have in mind?

No, I said. Anything. Something you've never forgotten.

This may have amused him because I heard a noise similar to a little cough. Then he said, You must give me a moment to think. You've knocked me off balance. I don't believe I've been asked such a question before. All right, sir, now that you've jogged me, I do recall a curious incident—my encounter with the Hungarian princess. It occurred in New York when I was twenty-five or so. Yes, twenty-five ought to be about right. I was studying for my doctorate and for some reason found myself at a party in an enormous apartment overlooking Central Park.

He paused. What was I doing there? he wondered aloud. Who invited me? Lord, it's been so long. Well, it hardly matters. Now about the "princess." I doubt if she was a princess, William; I suspect she belonged to some lesser order of nobility, but that is how I choose to think of her. At all events, the woman had more money than you could shake a stick at. The size of that apartment! Great God! Room after room after room. She lived alone. There wasn't another soul in the place—except for servants. And you will not believe this, but the woman took a fancy to me. She persuaded me to stay after the other guests departed. She was attempting to seduce me! What do you make of that, eh? I don't mind telling you, William, I was shocked.

But you must have known, I said. Why else would she want you to stay?

Uncle Gates hesitated. Finally he said that at the time the idea was inconceivable. He could recall feeling puzzled by her interest because she was several years older, and he felt intimidated by so much wealth.

Now what was her name? he continued absently. Hanlika. Magyana. Something of the sort. In any case, there I was sipping cognac in the middle of the night while doing my best to make conversation. We were seated on opposite sides of the room. She was lounging on a sofa covered with the skin of a polar bear and I suppose she expected me to join her. I didn't know what to do. There happened to be a large gilt mirror on the wall behind me and I became aware that she was watching herself while we chatted. That struck me as odd. It made me a bit uneasy.

And did you join her?

Ha! cried Uncle Gates and clapped his hands. I knew you would ask. I was a lusty young buck so it is natural to assume that given the circumstances I would take advantage of such an opportunity. However, I must say that woman revolted me. She might have been ill—I don't quite know. She was listless and pallid. She may have suffered from anemia. Or I suppose she could have been tubercular. Whatever the reason, I stayed put. Another thing. She crossed her legs frequently while watching herself in the mirror. It was most unpleasant. I wanted to leave, but I was afraid of seeming rude. And now I recall something else. She rambled on about the Hohenzollerns and Hapsburgs as though they were family friends and whenever she mentioned one of those names she would throw back her head and laugh like a jackass. To this day I recall seeing the inside of that woman's mouth. I could see black fillings in her teeth and strands of saliva. Most unpleasant.

Was she an impostor?

I think not. She brought out an old photo album with pictures of her father and mother and grandparents and I don't know who else. There were carriages and family retainers and horses and what appeared to be the wall of a castle. The grandfather was a burly fellow wearing a fancy military uniform with a chest full of medals. He had a great curling mustache and she told me he never missed a social event at the court of Franz Josef. The woman's father, I believe, had become some sort of industrial magnate. Impostor? No, I think not. In any event, William, there's my story of the princess. Nothing much happened. It didn't amount to a hill of beans.

Have you wondered what might have happened? What if you had decided to join her on the sofa?

No. No, I have never considered that. I was out of my element. As the saying goes, I felt like a fish out of water. Thank goodness I had sense enough to realize it. I would only have made a fool of myself.

Where do you suppose she is now?

Oh, he said after a pause, I rather expect she's gone.

The Sausalito art festival had just opened and I thought he might enjoy it, so I asked if he would like to stop on the way back from Mt. Tamalpais.

Uncle Gates stared through the windshield without expression. He was slightly deaf so he might not have heard.

A few minutes later I remarked that on top of the ridge we would be able to see the bay on one side and the Pacific on the other, but there was no response.

Those motorcycle bums! he said abruptly. What do they do all day?

They scare the wits out of everybody, I said, that's what they do all day. They ride up and down the coast like a swarm of hornets. I wish Picasso had drawn them.

That fellow was a Communist, said Uncle Gates. That man was a Communist.

I had hoped Picasso would give us something else to talk about. I tried to think of another subject. We could discuss relatives, but I didn't want to. I remembered how my parents would talk for an hour about cousin somebody from Leawood who married the daughter of somebody whose brother-in-law had bought the Spruance house on Wornall Road across from the Presbyterian church, or the youngest son of the couple from Grandview whose Chevrolet caught fire on Ward Parkway the summer before last who was engaged to the niece of Lucille Nordgren whose first husband had been promoted to vice president of something. I remembered lying on the porch swing with a glass of lemonade and asking myself why adults did this.

William, Uncle Gates said. Those little fishing boats we saw while driving across the bridge and now these tile-roofed homes clinging to the hillside—I am reminded of southern France. However, I've seen no vineyards. Nor, might I add, a single weathercock.

Stay another night, I said. We can drive up to the Sonoma vineyards tomorrow afternoon.

He answered politely that he wished his visit were not so brief. Then, folding his arms, he remarked that he had been to Europe several times and always looked forward to France. Germany, though, was different. As soon as one crossed the Rhine one knew it was Germany. I expected him to go on, but he seemed lost in thought as we climbed out of the eucalyptus groves toward the ridge. Hawks were soaring above the steep flower-covered slope and the Pacific looked like a puddle of aluminum.

How was your South Seas trip? I asked.

Nan Madol, he said. Now that was an experience! Not altogether pleasant, mind you. The humidity of those tropical islands—Lord, I could have been mistaken for a wet sponge. Those islands are worse than Springfield in August. I spent a week on Ponape and let me tell you that jungle is a steamer. I do recall one amusing moment. Some fellow arrived a day or so after I did and when he first showed up on the lanai he was a regular fashion plate. He must have watched too many movies. From the way he was gussied up he must have been expecting to meet Hedy Lamarr or Dorothy Lamour or one of those other movie sirens. I don't mind telling you, it was all I could do to keep from laughing. Privately I called that fellow Sir Gerald Poobah.

And what about Nan Madol?

Ha! Getting there was quite an event. I had met a British couple who wanted to visit the place, so the three of us got together and arranged for a guide with a motorboat. Well, the lagoon wasn't rough, but the way that motorboat hit the waves was like sliding on your gazimpus down a washboard. I was afraid I had injured myself.

Nan Madol. Nan Madol, I thought. It could be something spoken in a dream.

I don't recall what the name signifies, Uncle Gates said. I inquired, but whatever I was told has slipped my mind. It is remarkable how age creeps up on a fellow, almost before you can say Jack Robinson. He sat erect and motionless, frowning at the road.

From Ponape you crossed a lagoon?

He blinked as though waking up. Yes. I apologize. I was woolgathering. Yes, we reached the place after quite a rough motorboat ride, as I believe I mentioned.

Then he told me about Nan Madol. Just when it was constructed and by whom is unknown, except that the builders could not have been Micronesian because skeletal remains are those of a long-limbed race physiologically different from present-day islanders. Nor is it known how many centuries ago the fortress was abandoned. What has been learned is that the immense basalt pillars forming the walls were quarried from the volcanic summit of Ponape, but how they were carried down the mountain and through the jungle to the islet remains a mystery.

My British friends suggested levitation, Uncle Gates said, which may be as plausible as anything else. My God, those basalt logs must have weighed a ton apiece and they were piled on top of one another to a height of twenty or thirty feet. And a sinister place it is, William! I shouldn't care to spend a night there. Indeed, I was told that early in this century some Dutch or Danish anthropologist did just that, despite being warned not to. He went to sleep in a stone cist that may have been used to hold prisoners. Well, shortly before dawn the natives on Ponape heard a roaring noise, as though an army of men were blowing conch shells, and when they paddled out to get the anthropologist they found him dead. Now I don't know how much of that yarn to believe. What's your opinion?

I'm a believer, I said. But why was the fortress built? Who were they afraid of?

Exactly! Whom did they fear? What did they fear? According to legend, three hundred and thirty warriors kept watch over the sea beyond the reef, so it is clear that they anticipated an attack. Now who might their enemy have been? It's mysterious. Quite mysterious. He chuckled and nodded. Oh, another thing. The walls of Nan Madol are alive with lizards. Our guide said they taste like chicken, but I suspect he was joshing. The crabs, though, should be palatable. We saw hundreds on the tidal flat scuttling here and there. At all events, I'm glad I had sense enough to wear a hat, otherwise that sun would have finished me.

He quit talking suddenly. He looked exhausted. We had come to a view point on the ridge and I was gazing across the Pacific when I heard him say something else.

The walls of Nan Madol are black, William. Black as the very devil. Then he continued in a different tone: I consider myself fortunate. I have seen more than most people. Tourmaline, amethyst, emerald.

I wondered what that last remark implied, but he did not explain.

Mt. Tamalpais was rising directly ahead of us. He clucked with approval.

Your Aunt Ruth would appreciate this. I wish she could be here. Your parents may have notified you that she has been experiencing difficulty with her gastrointestinal system. The doctors don't agree on just what is wrong. Her spirits are good and I do my best to pretend, but I must admit it is discouraging.

Where will you go next summer? I asked.

That depends. I should like to stroll among the ruins of Persepolis.

There was very little traffic on the mountain road and not many cars in the parking lot. I pointed out the trail and told him that if we walked several hundred yards we could see more of the bay.

I expect I can manage, he said. Now you might give me a hand getting out of the car.

I helped him to his feet, but he seemed reluctant to start walking. He frowned at the pavement.

All right, he said at last, more to himself than to me.

When we came to a bench on the trail he decided that was far enough, so we sat down. He grunted with satisfaction and laced his fingers across his belly.

A fellow could sit here till the cows come home, he remarked. Yes, sir, it's a sight. He removed his glasses and polished them with his handkerchief. There was a little indentation on the bridge of his nose where the glasses had worn away the bone. Without the glasses he looked much less formidable. Carefully he hooked them on, cleared his throat, and said: The Germans have a legend about Frederick Barbarossa.

Barbarossa meant Red Beard and I knew it had been the nickname of a German emperor. I thought Barbarossa had led one of the crusades, but I couldn't remember anything else.

In a pedantic voice Uncle Gates asked: Do the ravens yet fly over the mountains?

I understood that he was quoting and I tried to identify it. Nothing reasonable came to mind. I felt pretty sure he wasn't quoting the Bhagavad-Gita, but I had no idea what it might be.

Once upon a time, Uncle Gates continued, a lowly shepherd stumbled upon the entrance to a cave in the Kyffhäuserberg—which is a mountain in Thuringia, William, as you may know. At any event,

the shepherd followed this passage deep into the heart of the Kyffhäuserberg, where he found the Holy Roman Emperor and six of his
knights asleep at a stone table. The sound of the shepherd's footstep
awakened Frederick from his slumber. Lifting his head, he asked: 'Do
the ravens yet fly over the mountains?' And the shepherd responded:
'Sire, they do.' Then Frederick said: 'We must sleep another hundred
years.'

That's quite a story, I said.

I have not finished, said Uncle Gates. The conclusion might be
noted. When the emperor's beard has grown three times around the
table Frederick and his knights will emerge from the Kyffhäuserberg
to exalt Germany above every nation of Europe.

I waited for him to go on, but that seemed to be all. I said I didn't
care for the end.

Nor do I, he said. When Frederick awakens let us hope there will
be no Germany. We have met with more than enough knighthood, I
believe. Yes. More than enough.

We sat on the bench and watched the afternoon. I suspected he
might be thinking about Aunt Ruth.

Finally I said, I hope you don't mind, but I invited a friend to join
us for dinner.

I do not mind in the least, he said, provided you had the wisdom to
invite an attractive young lady.

I told him she was a dancer and her name was Rachel, but I wasn't
sure if he heard. He appeared to be watching a ship moving toward
the Golden Gate. One of his hands began to tremble; he covered it
with the other.

I doubt if your great-aunt Megan is more than a shadow, he said. She
passed away when you were quite small. A most intolerant creature
much addicted to Old Testament morality—an eye for an eye and so
forth. Yet she was honest enough according to her lights and the absolute soul of kindness. I find that the memory of her returns more often
as time goes by. Perhaps it is because she symbolized the dichotomy
of our estate. We humans seem to contradict ourselves, yet we do not
contradict the truth—as Demades so perspicaciously observed some
centuries past. Maybe that is it. Well! he exclaimed, slapping his knee.
Enough nonsense! If you would assist me to my feet, young man, we
might wend our way toward the city. I am a trifle chilled.

It had been windy where we were sitting and I asked if he felt all right. He assured me that he was fine.

Do the ravens yet fly over the mountains? I asked myself as we started back along the trail. It was a musical question. Uncle Gates, I said, do the ravens yet fly over the mountains?

Sire, they do, he replied. Ah, William, half a century has elapsed since I came upon those resonant lines.

Music of a different sort began to reach us en route to Sausalito, but Uncle Gates did not offer his opinion until we came within sight of the amplifiers.

I fail to understand, he said, enunciating each word, how a sensible person could tolerate such noise. I should think it would kill every cat in the neighborhood.

I had planned to look for a parking spot, but now it did not seem like such a good idea. Apart from the boiler factory music, I guessed that his taste for painting and sculpture did not extend much beyond the Old Masters.

Perhaps we should return to San Francisco, he said. At what time are we to meet your friend?

I told him she would meet us in the hotel cocktail lounge at six o'clock. He made a rumbling noise and consulted his watch. I asked what sort of food he would like. Chinese? Mexican? Fisherman's Wharf?

It makes no difference, he said. My appetite is robust, although I do not care much for gizzard and liver. The young lady may have some preference. You told me her name.

Rachel.

Ah! I was thinking 'Hazel.' As Caxton observed in the suffix to his first book: 'Age crepeth on me dayly and feebleth all the bodye.' So you must indulge me, William. This has been a pleasant afternoon. My one regret is that I will not be here long enough for an excursion to those vineyards you mentioned.

He turned to look at the fog spreading across the bay toward Oakland and I expected him to say it looked like a blanket, which was the usual tourist remark, but he said: Well, that Middle East business worries me. Those sheiks have us in their pocket. I don't know what's going to come of it. I doubt if anybody does—certainly not those nincompoops in Washington. We've got to have a decent supply of oil.

He appeared to be falling asleep as we drove across the bridge, but as we passed through the tollgate he lifted his head. Did I tell you about George Neidlinger? You didn't know Mr. Neidlinger, of course. He represented some oil exploration outfit, though I don't recall the name. We had lunch together once a month at the Oxbow Grill for years and years. He died last August. He was a gentleman through and through.

I had not told Rachel much about Uncle Gates, only that he was a retired professor on his way home after a trip to the South Pacific. I thought it might be an awkward evening because she was reticent with strangers while he was a thicket of stubborn convictions and meditative silences. What were we going to discuss? Picasso had been eliminated. Oil sheiks? Frederick Barbarossa? I found myself wishing for Uncle Rodney with his bag of tricks.

You must have known Agnes Barstow, he said as we approached Union Square. Agnes and Howard were friends of your parents. They divorced quite some time back. Well, she took Howard for every cent. The judge awarded that woman everything—left him a pauper. It isn't fair. Howard worked hard all his life, yet the court sided with her. Agnes is a bitch! I apologize, William, for such a pejorative, but it happens to be appropriate. Howard Barstow ended up without a dime!

He was enraged by something that had occurred years ago. When he looked at me his lips were set. I felt shocked by the angry brilliance of his gaze. His right eye burned more brightly than the left and I remembered having read that this also was true of Czar Nicholas—that his eyes burned unevenly and made him terrible to confront.

All at once he cackled and poked an elbow into my ribs. I suggest you drop me at the entrance before parking the car, young fellow. I would like to spruce up a tad before supper.

When we stopped in front of the hotel he said, I propose that we kick up our heels this evening. You and your lady friend shall be my guests at the restaurant or nightspot of your choice.

I argued that since he was the visitor he should be my guest, but he would not hear of such a thing.

A doorman helped him out. Uncle Gates stooped a little, peered over his glasses, and slapped the hood of the car. I am feeling a bit friskier, he said. Toodle-oo!

By the time I got back to the hotel it was after six o'clock and I felt guilty about having invited Rachel. I hoped Uncle Gates would not start telling her about his dying friends and my elderly relatives. It occurred to me that he might have decided to lie down in his room for a while, which would give me a chance to talk to her.

In the cocktail lounge five men sat at the bar like department store mannequins, not moving, not speaking, all five heads turned the same direction, which meant that Rachel must have arrived. Indeed she had. She was wearing an apricot jumpsuit. Furthermore, she was talking with Uncle Gates. Her features always reminded me of Nefertiti—sleek, balanced, imperious. And being a dancer she walked boldly, with her back arched. Strangers asked if she was in show business; if they were sufficiently ill-mannered they would ask if she was famous. She had danced supporting roles with several ballet companies and frequently appeared in local productions, but the wheel of fortune only hesitated before moving on. She did not quite illuminate the stage. So, when her bank account dipped toward the horizon she would go to work processing orders at a securities firm.

Where have you been keeping him? she demanded and I had never seen her more radiant, which puzzled me. One time at a party I saw an old psychoanalyst almost as ugly as Uncle Gates surrounded by attractive women. It was curious.

We have been discussing the intricate polyphony of creation, said my uncle.

Well, I said, don't let me interrupt.

You didn't tell me you were driving to Mt. Tam, said Rachel. You should have invited me.

For goodness sake, William, sit down, said Uncle Gates. Don't just stand there. He contemplated me for a few moments with the frank indifference of an owl and then winked at Rachel. Now be that as it may, he said to her, continuing whatever they had been talking about, the in-dwelling spirit—the animus—will not be denied. Which puts me in mind of a remark by Nietzsche to the effect that an evening of music would be followed next morning by a cascade of insight and inspiration. Nietzsche wrote: 'It is as if I had bathed in a natural element.' And this, my dear, reflects your comment on the ballet.

Rachel did not lift her eyes from him. Or if she did glance at me it was as though she felt obligated. Uncle Gates would not let up. He started telling her about a performance of Stravinsky's *Firebird* with Maria Tallchief that he had seen in Paris forty years ago. I thought about trying to climb into their conversation, which might have been no more difficult than swimming to Oakland. Clearly they did not want to be interrupted so I ordered a drink and listened. It occurred to me that his memory had improved quite a lot. When he was talking to me he apologized for getting old and fumbled around for details as though he had lost something in the attic, but now he seemed to have no such trouble. Rachel sat erect with clasped hands and it appeared to me that she was not breathing.

Wagner. Wagner and Liszt, he said. Ah! 'A storm of enthusiasm raged between us and we filled eight days with so powerful a content that I am now stunned by it.' Thus, Rachel, the intermingling of creative faculties may prove explosive. Nor is the Wagner-Liszt eruption unique. After a meeting with Schiller, Goethe wrote: 'You have renewed my youth and have made me a poet again, which I had all but ceased to be.' Yet you speak of feeling shattered by that encounter with the prima ballerina.

My God, Rachel said, what are you telling me? You ask me to doubt my own senses!

Let us transpose this to the realm of literature, Uncle Gates said as though lecturing a student. Consider Stendhal reading two pages of the *Code Civil* each day before resuming work on *La Chartreuse de Parme*. Or the effect of von Humboldt on Darwin's chef-d'oeuvre.

I began to think about going for a walk. Neither of them would have noticed. I also thought it might be a good idea if I listened to Rachel more attentively. Her classic profile and the elegance of her carriage had persuaded me that not much else mattered. However, the vigilance with which she followed the mind of my decrepit old uncle was disconcerting. I looked at his bent shoulders and sagging face, the forehead like an onion, the brittle jaw, the feathery hair and liver spots, the ears that had lengthened while the rest of him shriveled. I thought of how he had felt his way down the hotel corridor, tottering on his heels.

Rachel asked him about Europe. She wanted to spend some time there, maybe a long time. She might get an apartment in London or Paris and become a celebrated dancer. If dreams came true this might happen. However, that is not the fundamental nature of dreams and she was smart enough to know it. Her ambition and talent did not lack intelligent direction, so it was odd that her career advanced in a circle. From stage to stage, then a tour of duty at the securities firm. I suspected she might be a little too intelligent for the dream.

France is powdered with the dust of centuries, my uncle told her. At noon the caravans of clouds whipped by a sea wind, the pink tile roofs, the rust-colored little roses. And the wisteria spreading—ah! Rachel, you must see those vineyards blue with spray and poplars bordering the roads. One night at a festival not far from Aix when the streets were decorated with paper lanterns I danced with the prettiest girl in France. This is your moment, Rachel. Do not lose it.

I looked at the expression on her face and found myself wishing Uncle Gates would go home. He reminded me of the wicked old magician in fairy tales. His glasses had slipped down his nose and his bright eye burned furiously.

Let me ask you a riddle, he said. If many things seem beautiful to us, what is more beautiful than any of these?

Tell me, she said.

More beautiful than any of these, Rachel, is what we have learned. Yet what can be more beautiful than what we have learned?

Tell me, she said again.

That which we do not comprehend.

Rachel looked at him very seriously. I had no idea what their conversation meant, but I had a feeling she would never be quite the same.

I will tell you where to find the crowns of three Visigoth kings, he said.

Where? she asked.

In the Musée de Cluny. They are made of hammered gold, Rachel, and the embellishment does not look precious to us—agate, rose quartz, rock crystal, irregular pearls of weak luster, and a few unpolished emeralds. They were recovered from the Guarrazar fountain near Toledo.

Is this another riddle? she asked. What do the crowns represent?

I cannot begin to imagine, Uncle Gates replied while stroking the tip of his nose. As Montaigne informs us, ideas are wont to follow one another, yet they do so at times from a distance and gaze upon each other but with a sidelong glance.

It seemed to me that he was getting insufferably professorial and there might be no end to it. I pointed out that regardless of how they felt, I was hungry.

You have developed into a sensible young fellow, said Uncle Gates, contrary to what I anticipated. Where shall we dine?

I had a moment of inspiration. Sire, I announced and thumped the table with both fists. I am a great eater of beef!

He eyed me sharply. Unless I am mistaken you are drawing upon *Twelfth Night.*

I didn't know. I thought he might ask for the next line or tell me I was getting a C-minus in the course.

If you scholars would excuse me, Rachel said, and Uncle Gates at once began struggling to his feet. He remained standing until she had left the table.

After seating himself he continued briskly: William, if I were your age I would grab that girl quick as a wink. There is some unique felicity to marriage, as your Aunt Ruth and I have concluded from many years of attachment. Socrates, to be sure, when asked if it were wisdom or not to take a wife, responded that whichever a man does he will repent of it. Still, you are not Socrates. Take my advice and marry that woman, you young squirt.

Rachel had scraped enough barnacles off his hide to fill a basket and I would not have been surprised if he suggested we all go dancing till dawn. But then Uncle Gates sagged and looked vacantly into space. I thought he had forgotten me. One of his hands quivered. Something seemed to be flowing through his mind or spirit like an underground river. I wondered again if he might be concerned about Aunt Ruth, whose illness sounded threatening, or about the emptiness ahead. They did not have children.

The African couple entered the lounge. Their almost iridescent skin and distinctive bearing caused people to look, but my uncle did not notice. The years Rachel dispelled had returned swiftly and he began talking less to me than to himself: Ned Scowcroft was the fellow who called the ambulance after my accident. He's all right. His daughter works for the government, although I have forgotten just what she does. He and several other men carried me to a park bench. I failed to get their names or I would have thanked them. Ned Scowcroft is a gentleman, but I can't say as much for his brother. Charles Scowcroft isn't worth a hoot! Uncle Gates slapped the table for emphasis. Then, lifting his head, he peered across the room. William, he said after a long pause, my eyes are not what they used to be. Does this place serve niggers?

Rachel was approaching, so he began to get up.

Please, she said and touched his shoulder.

He would have none of this. With an effort he got to his feet and there he stood, one hand trembling.

PROCTOR BEMIS

PROCTOR CYRIL BEMIS, lately retired CEO of Bemis Securities, hobbled into the Wyandotte Country Club with a shiny and swollen big toe that felt like a radish, reminding him of those eighteenth-century gentlemen afflicted with gout who had been uncharitably depicted by the likes of Rowlandson and Hogarth.

I hope Bullock's tending bar, Mr. Bemis grumbled, and continued talking to himself. That new fellow hasn't the faintest idea how to mix a Daiquiri. Lord, what if Bullock retires? He must be almost my age.

The young woman behind the desk said good afternoon as he limped by. He tried to think of her name. Aurelia, Astrid, Ingrid, something of the sort. Her voice reminded him of Robin.

Ha! he said aloud when he caught sight of Bullock. And his favorite chair, a maroon leather throne overlooking the golf course, was unoccupied. After lowering himself into the chair he gently placed his bad leg on a stool and scowled at the toe, which had acquired a life of its own. He could not understand why it ached and throbbed, because he was not one of those decadent Englishmen who sat around the club all day sipping port and munching buttered scones. I ought to give Chambers a call, he thought, but he'd put me on some jackass diet of shredded wheat or cauliflower. Maybe the damn thing will get better.

For several minutes Mr. Bemis sat with his hands folded on his belly while he contemplated the golf course—a pleasantly undulating landscape, green as a billiard table. He wondered how many thousands of hours he had spent whacking a golf ball and following it around. What a senseless, gratifying way to squander time. He turned to look at the fireplace where a pyramid of logs awaited Jack Frost; the fireplace was enormous, big enough for the great hall of a Viking manor. He looked at the mahogany sideboard where an elegant silver tray offered a tempting assortment of mints, nuts, fruit, and cheese. He looked at a crystal vase bursting with roses atop the piano. He looked up at the fancy chandelier, down at the Turkish rug glowing in late October sunshine. He peered across the rims of his spectacles at a series of framed Currier & Ives prints on the wall, and it occurred to him that no matter which way he turned he could see something agreeable. He grunted with satisfaction.

Bullock had noticed him, of course. Nothing in the lounge escaped Bullock. Another minute or so and Bullock would come around, preceded by a discreet cough to announce himself. What a gem he was, good old Bullock. He must have been here thirty years, Mr. Bemis thought, and one of these days he'll throw in the towel. Strange, I know nothing about the man. He has a wedding ring, but he never mentions his wife. I wonder if they have children. Where do they live? What does he think about? Is he a Democrat? Does he go bowling on his day off? Nice fellow. Seems intelligent. I expect he's bored, serving drinks to chattering biddies and retired old cranks. Well, I'm ready for a libation.

And at that instant, like a genie from a bottle, Bullock appeared with a newspaper. Perhaps you would care to glance through the *Tribune*, he murmured, bowing just slightly.

I'll get around to it, Mr. Bemis said. Did you have a mob for lunch?

Quite a crowd, yes. We catered an engagement party. The daughter of Mr. and Mrs. Poteet.

Engaged? I assumed that girl was about fourteen. The years run away from us, Bullock.

Indeed they do, sir.

Who is the boy?

I don't know, sir. I'll ask Mrs. Tuckerly.

Skip it, Mr. Bemis said. However, I'll celebrate the joyous occasion. My usual. And one of those pears from the tray—get me a juicy one. And a wedge of Gouda. Umm, and a few nuts. I love cashews. Don't be stingy with the cashews.

Bullock, after a slight dip of the head, vanished into his bottle.

Mr. Bemis watched a foursome of golfers approach the clubhouse. Clearly they had enjoyed themselves. He thought about the game eighteen or twenty years ago when he scored a hole in one. The drive had made him famous for several months. Now, of course, nobody cared. Indeed, most of the people who knew about it were gone.

Bullock soon returned with a Daiquiri, crackers, solid Dutch cheese, an absolutely magnificent pear, and a silver goblet brimming with cashews.

I took the liberty of inquiring, he said. The young man is Raymond Epp.

Epp? Epp? said Mr. Bemis. Doesn't sound familiar. Are they members?

Not to my knowledge, sir.

Bullock, tell me, what's our world coming to? Young savages whooping out of the forest to abduct our daughters. Have you a daughter?

Bullock grinned, displaying ragged yellow teeth. Three daughters and one grandchild.

Congratulations. I had no idea.

Thank you, sir. If you would excuse me, Dr. and Mrs. Altschuler are waiting.

Of course. Of course, Mr. Bemis said. He waved to the Altschulers, who had settled near the fireplace. Obviously they did not intend to join him, which was a bit of luck. Late afternoon was a delphic hour—between the dark and the daylight, as Longfellow had written— and Gladys would spoil it by talking too much. Silently he measured the shadows, reflecting that late afternoon might be considered analogous to retirement. There were troubling implications to such a parallel; nevertheless, life thus far had been good, very good. Except for the damned toe, all was well. So, feeling rather satisfied, Mr. Bemis tasted his Daiquiri, nibbled a wedge of cheese, and gazed out the window. Bullock, poor devil, couldn't afford such luxury. Year after year fetching drinks, lighting cigarettes, listening courteously to opinionated old bores, forced to watch his behavior every moment or risk losing the job. And at his age what else would he do? I wonder if he hates us, Mr. Bemis thought. Most of the members are decent, but I'd be hard put taking guff from one or two.

Just then, hearing faraway violins, he glanced at his watch: five o'clock. Every afternoon precisely at five somebody in the depths of the club turned on the music. He closed his eyes, peeled off his glasses, and held them in one hand while he listened. Was it Haydn or Mozart? A life devoted to marketing stocks and bonds had not left much time for the study of classical music; but now, God willing, there should be time for many things, all sorts of neglected activities. Retirement was not bad, not bad. Now he could do as he liked—paint flaming orange sunsets, go fishing, raise petunias, learn to rumba, have Phillips drive him to the club. And if he had not grown fatter than Samuel Johnson he might loiter by the swimming pool and flirt with pretty girls. The devil take conferences, brainless subordinates, sales pitches, telephones, and a ticker tape spewing information that was obsolete before it hit the basket. Indeed, if he wished, he might sit like Buddha on this red leather throne and do nothing but look wise. That sounded just fine. At a quarter to six Phillips would arrive—very nearly as prompt as the music. He would be chauffeured home, agree with Marguerite's complaints about a disorderly world, and settle down to supper. Retirement came pretty close to being the cat's pajamas.

Not so bad, said Mr. Bemis.

He quartered the pear, took a bite, and unfolded the *Tribune*. Little enough on the front page. Auto workers threatening a strike. Politicians posturing. Surge in oil prices. Bank robber escaped. It could be yesterday or tomorrow.

He scanned the second page. Corporate merger. Albino gorilla. He paused briefly on the third page to read about a basketball player caught in flagrante delicto with the coach's wife. But on the next page, he stopped:

U.S. Planned Mass Gassing of Japan
A long-withheld military document shows the U.S. was willing to kill 5 million Japanese in a toxic-gas attack to end World War II.

The highly specific plan—which authorities tried to cover up after the war—was drafted before the atomic bomb attacks on Hiroshima and Nagasaki in August 1945 killed an estimated 120,000 people and ended the war without an invasion.

The plan designated "gas attack zones" on detailed maps of Tokyo and other major Japanese cities. Only five copies of the original, top-secret study were produced, making it one of the most closely held documents of the war.

The proposal for the attack is revealed in a 30-page document that was deliberately altered . . .

Mr. Bemis lowered the paper, conscious that the sun was going down behind a cluster of trees; and as he watched it disappear he remembered an afternoon in Germany, east of Stolberg, when he had been nineteen years old and watched the sun go down behind some trees on a ridge. German soldiers were in the neighborhood. If they saw his uniform they would kill him.

After a while he adjusted his glasses and continued reading:

> . . . deliberately altered after the war so that historians would never see that U.S. Army chemical warfare planners had recommended a preemptive poison-gas strike.
>
> We obtained the original document. It bears inked-in changes, made in 1947. The word *retaliatory* was frequently inserted to make it agree with announced U.S. wartime policy which, by U.S. presidential directive, prohibited first-strike use of poison gas.

Mr. Bemis looked for the names of the reporters. Thomas B. Allen and Norman Polmar. *New York Times* special feature. So this must be a reprint or excerpt.

> It was known that top military leaders had discussed massive gas attacks on Japan during planning sessions in summer 1945, but most of the details were locked away in archives.
>
> The poison-gas study was finally located, but its release by the Pentagon was held up by the U.S. Department of State because of "possible political implications."
>
> U.S. Army planners, shocked at the high casualty figures during the Pacific island campaigns, saw a pre-emptive gas attack as the best way to launch the American invasion of Japan, which was to begin Nov. 1, 1945.
>
> It recommended that the U.S. Joint Chiefs of Staff issue "a policy at once directing the use of toxic gas on both strategic and tactical targets . . ."

Amazing, he said aloud, and wagged his head. This is extraordinary. Why, this is unbelievable. Before the invasion this gas attack would "disrupt national life in Japan." Disrupt national life—a military euphemism for genocide. Twenty-five important cities "especially suitable for gas attacks" had been chosen, including Tokyo, Yokohama, Osaka, Kobe, Nagoya, and Kyoto.

Kyoto? he said. Kyoto was the cultural heart of Japan; it wasn't an industrial center. He had thought about visiting Japan and had discussed the idea with Marguerite, who seemed amenable. She, too, thought Kyoto should be interesting. It was full of ancient Buddhist temples, museums, the old imperial palace, famous gardens, and beautiful parks. Kyoto had been founded in the eighth century when the United States was wilderness.

Gas attacks of the recommended size and intensity might kill five million people and disable that many more. Ten million casualties. Ten million? Mr. Bemis whispered. Five million dead in a few hours? We said we'd never use gas unless the Japanese did, yet these birds claim Stilwell wrote to Marshall, "We are not bound in any way not to . . ." He glanced up and there stood Bullock with an expectant look.

Another, sir?

Yes, by all means, Mr. Bemis said. This *Tribune* article, this piece about using gas during World War II, have you seen it?

Bullock tipped his head and squinted at the paper. No, I'm afraid not, he said after a pause.

We were on the verge of gassing ten million Japanese.

I was unaware of that, Bullock said carefully. When Japan surrendered I was eight years old.

So you don't recall much.

Very little.

Ah. Well, this business was hushed up for half a century. It seems General Stilwell wrote to Marshall that we should consider the use of poison gas. Vinegar Joe Stilwell.

He served in the Pacific, did he not?

He commanded our forces in China, Burma, and India until he quarreled with Chiang.

Chiang Kai-shek?

Yes. Chiang Kai-shek.

Bullock gazed at the paper with a determined expression, as though he meant to read it. Will there be anything else? he asked.

Nein, Mr. Bemis said with a German accent. Bullock had been a schoolboy during the war; even so, it was odd that he could scarcely identify Chiang and Vinegar Joe.

When he returned with another Daiquiri Mr. Bemis looked up from the paper and said, That poison gas story reminded me of the Lusitania. Did you know the Lusitania was packed with munitions for the British?

Bullock hesitated before answering in the same careful voice, In fact, sir, I was not. I was under the impression it was a passenger vessel.

Tons of black powder, thousands of rounds of ammunition. That ship was a floating bomb.

There was considerable loss of life, was there not?

More than considerable. British, for the most part, although a hundred or so Americans were aboard, poor devils. I doubt if any of them knew the hold was crammed with explosives. Umm, I've lost my train of thought. Ah, here's the parallel, Bullock. Members of Congress smelled something fishy—suspected the Lusitania was more than a passenger ship—and asked the Treasury Department for a bill of lading. Well, Treasury replied that it had been delivered to the State Department. And what do you suppose happened when State was asked for the bill of lading? State wouldn't disclose the Lusitania's cargo on grounds it was diplomatic correspondence. What rot! Now here we have the same hanky-panky. Let's see. Yes, here we go. Poison-gas study located, release held up by U.S. Department of State because of—listen to this—"possible political implications."

Bullock nodded and cleared his throat. If you would excuse me, sir, Mr. and Mrs. Joplin are waiting.

What? Ah, of course. I didn't see them come in.

Almost at once Mr. Bemis felt a hand on his shoulder and heard Joplin's voice: How's that appendage?

Hurts, Mr. Bemis said. I'm going to chop it off first thing tomorrow. Will you and Elise join me for a drink?

We're meeting Bradley and Sue, but we'll take a rain check.

Mr. Bemis pointed at the newspaper. Have you seen that poison-gas article?

Joplin straightened up. The smile left his face. I read it at the office, he said. We should have gassed those slant-eyed bastards—all of them.

Mr. Bemis remembered that Joplin had been a marine in the South Pacific and was badly wounded on one of the islands.

We let those Japs off the hook. We should have fried those people—the whole stinking bunch. Hey, there's Brad. Take care of that toe, soldier.

Bullock came back a few minutes later to say Phillips had arrived.

Quarter to six, is it? All right. If you'd give me a hand—I'm stuck in this chair like a walrus.

May I assist you to the car? Bullock asked when Mr. Bemis was at last on his feet.

No, no, I'll manage. The trick is getting started. Not sure if the toe bone is attached to the foot bone and the foot bone to the ankle bone and right now I don't give a hoot. I'll skip right along. Bullock, those Daiquiris are marvelous.

Phillips opened the back door of the Chrysler while Mr. Bemis, grimacing because the toe had begun to throb, crawled in. Tell me, he said as they rolled away from the club, can you identify Vinegar Joe Stilwell?

Excuse me, Phillips said. Vinegar who?

I'll give you a hint, Mr. Bemis said. He was removed from command after a squabble with Chiang. Chiang Kai-shek.

Phillips shrugged.

Were you in military service?

Vietnam.

Ah, that explains it.

Explains what, sir?

I didn't realize you were so young.

Phillips laughed. My kids call me the relic.

Now that's astonishing, Mr. Bemis said. What did you do in Vietnam?

Air Cav.

Mr. Bemis thought about this. Air Cav. Air Cavalry. I've just about forgotten our lingo, he remarked. Nip. Kraut. Limey. WAC. Dogface. Repo Depo. And when we were discharged we got the Ruptured Duck.

World War Two?

Mr. Bemis sighed. Yes. I was too young for the First World War. In fact, I didn't exist.

Phillips answered slowly, as though trying to remember a high school history lesson. The siege of Stalingrad. Russia was on our side.

Thank God, yes, Mr. Bemis said.

But they were Commies. Isn't that true?

Very true.

We fought the Commies in Nam.

Don't ask me to explain it.

Nam, Phillips said in a hostile voice. Gooks in the fog. They blew away my best buddy. I remember the look on his face.

I lost a pal, Mr. Bemis said. Not much changes. The weapons, the landscape, the enemy's name. Otherwise it's mud, fog, rats, flies, explosions, and blood. Where do you suppose the birds go?

What do you mean, sir?

They vanish.

I never gave it much thought, Phillips said.

Perhaps they dislike our company. You know, Phillips, I came upon the most extraordinary news. We were planning to saturate Japan with poison gas. Kyoto. Osaka. Nagoya. Tokyo. Casualties would have been five million, maybe ten million.

The Japs attacked Pearl Harbor.

Mr. Bemis did not reply. What Phillips had said was true, of course. But was it quite so simple? British economic interests in the Far East were threatened by Japan, and the British hoped for American intervention. Roosevelt clamped down on American trade with Japan six months before Pearl Harbor. Three-fourths of Japan's imports had been cut off by the Allied blockade. Well, God knows, he thought. The tentacles reached everywhere.

Why didn't we drop the A-bomb in Nam? Phillips asked. My buddy would be alive.

It's very real to you, isn't it? After all these years.

Like yesterday. We could've nuked Hanoi. Took out those slopes.

Turn Hanoi into a parking lot?

That wouldn't have broke my heart.

Back to the Stone Age, Mr. Bemis thought. LeMay chomping a cigar. Napalm. Calley. What's happened to us? What have we become? Jefferson, Washington, Adams, Franklin—would they recognize their country?

He did not say anything else during the ride home. He felt old and tired and dissatisfied.

At supper he said to his wife, I had a remarkable conversation with Phillips. He knows next to nothing about the Second World War.

Mrs. Bemis tasted her soup, onion soup, before answering. For Heaven's sake, why should he?

Well, Mr. Bemis replied while buttering a slab of pecan bread, I thought the war was an unforgettable experience. And this comment struck him as being rather witty; he glanced across the table to see if she appreciated it, but she did not look up from her soup. Phillips is young, he added, nevertheless I was surprised.

Proctor, she said, you are growing absentminded. Phillips is not young. Phillips is middle-aged.

All right, Mr. Bemis said. He lifted his glass of wine, observed the color, and took a sip.

How is your toe?

Pinot Blanc has nothing to do with it, he said.

You really should call Dr. Chambers.

My toe feels better, he said. Besides, after ninety-five years at the office I'm entitled to enjoy myself.

Was anybody at the club?

The Altschulers and Joplins. It was a bit early for the evening crowd. I had the place pretty much to myself, just me and Bullock. Good old Bullock. Nice fellow. He has three daughters. He brought me the *Tribune* and I found out we were getting ready to soak Japan with poison gas.

Mrs. Bemis looked at her watch.

During the war, he said. The Pentagon intended to gas a few million Japanese before our troops landed.

Robin and the children are going to stop by. They ought to be here in a few minutes.

Ah, good, said Mr. Bemis.

Mark's teeth are killing him, poor child. He's so anxious to have those appliances removed.

Mr. Bemis chuckled. They used to be called braces. I wore them. I hated them.

Mrs. Bemis put down her spoon. What do you think of this?

Of what?

Does the soup taste salty?

It's delicious, he said. I love onion soup.

Bouillabaisse is your favorite.

I could eat a bucket. Lots of shrimp and lobster.

You were talking about Japan. I interrupted.

Never mind, he said. Nobody cares.

Please continue.

He took a deep breath and everything seemed unreal. He stared at the elderly woman across the table but had no idea who she was. He looked down at his hands and saw the puffy, discolored hand of an old man reach for the carving knife.

Proctor, she said, is anything wrong?

I don't know how to begin, he said. It's as if those journalists got hold of a Nazi document.

What on earth are you talking about? Don't you feel well?

I'm all right, he said. The prime rib looked succulent and juicy; he touched it with the point of the knife. Fifty years, he said to himself as he began carving. Our State Department hid that plan for fifty years. Then, when they were forced to reveal it, the wording had been changed so it would coincide with official United States policy. That is criminal. That is treachery. That is treachery at the highest echelon of government. I've always believed in this nation. We elect a lot of liars and nincompoops—everybody takes that for granted. But this? This is ethical decay. This is beyond belief.

How are the Altschulers? she asked.

I didn't talk to them, he said. I waved. They waved.

Gladys has been quite ill. I understand she may have diabetes. That certainly would be a blow. They were planning a cruise to Bermuda. It would be a shame if they had to cancel.

Mr. Bemis nodded. He poured a glass of claret for her and one for himself. Did you know Phillips served in Vietnam?

Is that so? she asked politely. Do you like the asparagus?

Indeed I do, he said. We should have asparagus more often.

I'll make a note of it.

Phillips wanted to turn Hanoi into a parking lot. Nuke the gooks.

Well, Mrs. Bemis said, I have absolutely no use for Communism. Just look what happened to Hillis Fowler. I feel so sorry for Ted and Kate. But why in the world do they insist on keeping him at home? It would be so much easier if they put him in a veterans' hospital. I simply can't endure his presence. He's disgusting. He can scarcely move and he can't speak—those horrid moans are unnerving. I do feel sorry for him, of course, but why must we be forced to look at him? It's as if they wanted to remind us.

He volunteered.

Don't you think he would have been drafted?

Possibly. Probably. How should I know?

You are drinking too much, Mrs. Bemis said. It isn't good for you.

You're right, said Mr. Bemis.

We did everything imaginable to prevent the spread of international Communism.

Almost. We forgot to nuke the gooks.

I think we should have dropped an atomic bomb. The war would have ended in a minute.

That's right, he said. How about a little more prime rib?

Not another bite.

Where did you get this? It's very rich.

Stroud's. I enjoy shopping there. The butcher is so nice.

All at once Mr. Bemis felt dizzy; he wondered if he was about to faint. His heart gave a powerful thump and it seemed to him that he was in Germany lying on some damp leaves, holding his breath as a German patrol went by. He could hear them talking and he could hear their boots on the road. One of them coughed, not far away. Suddenly they were gone and he realized that he was able to breathe. From a distance he heard his wife; she was talking about poison gas, explaining how it would have saved American lives.

Somebody knocked at the door.

That must be the children, she said, putting aside her napkin. You sit still.

The door opened and he heard the clamorous young voices of his grandchildren. He sat at the table with his hands laced across his belly, waiting, and presently they rushed upon him. He chatted with Melanie about school, asked Mark about his teeth, listened to Robin, and thought about what he had read. The government lied. Not only did the American government plan to kill millions of people with gas, it lied. I used to believe, he thought. I never once questioned our government. How foolish. Maybe I stopped believing when Ike lied to us about that U-2 plane. I trusted Ike. But then he told us an unarmed weather plane accidentally strayed across the Turkish border into Russia with the pilot unconscious at the controls because his oxygen equipment malfunctioned—some cock-and-bull story like that. What was the pilot's name? Purvis or Powers, I think. And the CIA gave him a suicide kit. He was supposed to kill himself if he was shot down. Ike knew the truth, of course. Nobody, not even those spooks at the CIA, would try such a stunt without the President's approval. I've never forgiven Ike. He stood up in front of the cameras and he looked at us without winking and he lied. Since then I've never believed. There's the heart of it. Still, somehow, I thought we were fairly decent. Not bad, as nations go. In spite of napalm and McNamara and Johnson and those Bundy brothers and the obscene body counts—I thought somehow, even while the evidence piled up—I told myself this isn't what we are.

Mr. Bemis discovered that his plate had been removed and dessert was being served. He looked unhappily at the slice of Sacher Torte his wife placed in front of him. Marguerite, he said, this isn't enough for a mouse. If I held this up to the light I could see through it.

It's more than you ought to have, she said.

You are hideously fat, said Robin.

I am not, said Mr. Bemis.

You are, too! Melanie cried. You're fatter than anybody!

Well, maybe I am, said Mr. Bemis, but this is a special occasion. I don't see why I can't have a little more.

Mother's right, said Robin. You should go on a diet.

Mr. Bemis grumbled and decided to begin eating his torte before one of them took it away from him. And while he nibbled at it he realized that there might be Sacher Torte at the club. That seemed quite possible. He thought he would ask Bullock. Marguerite would never know.

He listened to the children squabble over something and for a while he listened to the women talk about a sale at some department store and he felt altogether at ease. Life was a thing to savor like a bit of chocolate. He reflected that his life so far had not unrolled dramatically, he had not made much impact on the world, but he had done well and had played his part conscientiously. One could take pride in that. He began to wonder what he might have done. If, for example, instead of marketing securities he had entered politics—what might have happened? Would he have risen high enough to affect the course of events? If so, faced with terrible choices, what then? Two hundred years ago the nation's leaders had been men of unusual character and vision. They articulated a promise—a brilliant promise, an eloquent promise—that their descendants had failed to honor. Why wasn't the promise kept? Who, or what, was responsible for the treachery, the lies, the incomplete truths, the reduction of morality to mathematics? And therefore, what did the future hold?

Something's bothering you, Robin said. What's wrong?

I'm hungry, Mr. Bemis said. He could see his wife and daughter look at him, assessing the words, measuring his face. After a moment they decided he was not going to collapse over his dessert. They continued talking.

He glared at the shred of chocolate torte and thought about his conversation with Bullock. How could an intelligent, perceptive man only a little younger than himself fail to identify Vinegar Joe? And Phillips, who could discuss Ho Chi Minh or Westmoreland or Hamburger Hill—Phillips knew nothing of McAuliffe or Rundstedt or Malmédy. In a few more years those names would be forgotten. Mr. Bemis frowned into space.

Are you ill? his wife asked. You've scarcely touched your dessert.

Nothing's wrong, he said. Then all at once he heard himself talking about the horrifying plan that two journalists had forced the Pentagon to divulge, but when he looked at his wife and daughter he could see from their identical expressions that he had not explained it very well.

Fifty years ago? his daughter asked. The plan is fifty years old?

Yes, he said.

That's like the War of the Roses, she said.

Mr. Bemis considered this. She was right. And yet, he thought, it shouldn't be forgotten. Because if we forget what we might have done—if we were capable of that, who are we? Fifty years ago we destroyed Hiroshima and Nagasaki in order to stop what Churchill called the vast indefinite butchery, and the scheme worked. Still, something in this calculation offends me. St. Paul condemned those who argued that one may practice evil if good shall come of it.

Would you like more coffee? Mrs. Bemis asked.

Yes, he said.

You're brooding, Robin said. Poking through that ancient stuff.

Mr. Bemis nodded. All the same, he told himself, this is a moral issue so we've not come to the end of it. And while his wife poured coffee he finished the torte and wondered if he might ask for another slice.

THE WALLS OF ÁVILA

Thou shall make castels in Spayne,
And dreme of joye, al but in vayne.
Romaunt of the Rose

ÁVILA LIES only a few kilometers west and a little north of Madrid, and is surrounded by a grim stone wall that was old when Isabella was born. Life in this town has not changed very much from the days when the earth was flat; somehow it is as though news of the passing centuries has never arrived in Ávila. Up the cobbled street saunters a donkey with a wicker basket slung on each flank, and on the donkey's bony rump sits a boy nodding drowsily in the early morning sun. The boy's dark face looks medieval. He is delivering bread. At night the stars are metallic, with a bluish tint, and the Spaniards stroll gravely back and forth beside the high stone wall. There are not so many gypsies, or *gitanos*, in this town as there are in, say, Valencia or Seville. Ávila is northerly and was not impressed by these passionate Asiatic people, at least not the way Córdoba was, or Granada.

These were things we learned about Ávila when J.D. returned. He came home after living abroad for almost ten years. He was thinner and taller than any of us remembered, and his crew-cut hair had turned completely gray although he was just thirty-eight. It made him look very distinguished, even a little dramatic. His skin was now as brown as coffee, and there were wind wrinkles about his restless cerulean blue eyes, as though the light of strange beaches and exotic plazas had stamped him like a visa to prove he had been there. He smiled a good deal, perhaps because he did not feel at ease with his old friends any more. Ten years did not seem long to us, not really long,

and we were disconcerted by the great change in him. Only his voice
was familiar. At the bus station where three of us had gone to meet
him only Dave Zobrowski recognized him.

Apparently this town of Ávila meant a great deal to J.D., although
he could not get across to us its significance. He said that one night
he was surprised to hear music and laughter coming from outside the
walls, so he hurried through the nearest gate, which was set between
two gigantic watch towers, and followed the wall around until he came
to a carnival. There were concessions where you could fire corks at
cardboard boxes, each containing a chocolate bar, or dip for celluloid
fishes with numbered bellies, and naturally there was a carousel, the
same as in America. It rotated quite slowly, he said, with mirrors
flashing from its peak while enameled stallions gracefully rose and
descended on their gilded poles. But nothing was so well attended as
a curious swing in which two people stood, facing each other, grasping
a handle, and propelled themselves so high that at the summit they
were nearly upside down. The shadow of this swing raced up the wall
and down again. "Like this!" J.D. exclaimed, gesturing, and he stared
at each of us in turn to see if we understood. He said it was like the
shadow of some grotesque instrument from the days of the Inquisi-
tion, and he insisted that if you gazed up into the darkness long enough
you could make out, among the serrated ramparts of the ancient wall,
the forms of helmeted men leaning on pikes and gazing somberly
down while their black beards moved in the night wind.

He had tales of the Casbah in Tangiers and he had souvenirs from the
ruins of Carthage. On his keychain was a fragment of polished stone,
drilled through the center, that he had picked up from the hillside just
beyond Tunis. And he spoke familiarly of the beauty of Istanbul, and
of Giotto's tower, and the Seine, and the golden doors of Ghiberti.
He explained how the Portuguese are fuller through the cheeks than
are the Spaniards, their eyes more indolent and mischievous, and how
their songs—*fados*, he called them—were not more than lazy cousins
of the fierce flamenco one heard throughout Andalusia.

When Zobrowski asked in what year the walls of Ávila were built,
J.D. thought for quite a while, his lean face sober while he gently
rocked a tumbler of iced rum, but at last he said the fortifications
were probably begun seven or eight hundred years ago. They had been
repaired occasionally and were still impregnable to primitive force. It

was queer, he added, to come upon such a place, indestructible when assaulted on its own terms, yet obsolete.

He had postal cards of things that had interested him. He had not carried a camera because he thought it bad manners. We did not completely understand what he meant by this but we had no time to discuss it because he was running on, wanting to know if we were familiar with Giambologna, saying, as he displayed a card, "In a grotto of the Boboli Gardens not far from the Uffizi—" He stopped abruptly. It had occurred to him that we might be embarrassed. No one said anything. None of us had ever heard of the Boboli Gardens, or of the sculptor Giambologna, or of the Venus that J.D. had wanted to describe.

"Here's the Sistine Chapel, of course," he said, taking another card from his envelope. "That's the Libyan sybil."

"Yes," said Zobrowski. "I remember this. There was a print of it in one of our high school textbooks. Good God, how time does pass."

"Those damn textbooks," J.D. answered. "They ruin everything. They've ruined Shakespeare and the Acropolis and half the things on earth that are really worth seeing. Just like the Lord's Prayer—I can't hear it. I don't know what it says. Why wasn't I left to discover it for myself? Or the Venus de Milo. I sat in front of it for an hour, but I couldn't see it."

He brought out a postal card of a church tower. At the apex was a snail-like structure covered with what appeared to be huge tile baseballs.

"That's the *Sagrada Familia*," he explained. "It's not far from the bull ring in Barcelona."

The *Sagrada Familia* was unfinished; in fact it consisted of nothing but a façade with four tremendous towers rising far above the apartment buildings surrounding it. He said it was a landmark of Barcelona, that if you should get lost in the city you had only to get to a clearing and look around for this weird church. On the front of it was a cement Christmas tree, painted green and hung with cement ornaments, while the tiled spires were purple and yellow. And down each spire ran vertical lettering that could be read a kilometer away. Zobrowski asked what was written on the towers.

"There's one word on each tower," said J.D. "The only one I recall is 'Ecstasy.'"

Dave Zobrowski listened with a patient, critical air, as though wondering how a man could spend ten years in such idle traveling. Russ Lyman, who had once been J.D.'s closest friend, listened in silence with his head bowed. When we were children together it had been Russ who intended to go around the world some day, but he had not, for a number of reasons. He seemed to hold a monopoly on bad luck. The girl he loved married somebody else, then his business failed, and so on and on through the years. Now he worked as a drugstore clerk and invested his pitiful savings in gold mines or wildcat oil wells. He had been thirty-two when the girl he loved told him good-bye, tapping the ash from her cigarette onto his wrist to emphasize that she meant it; he promptly got drunk, because he could not imagine anything else to do, and a few days later he began going around with a stout, amiable girl named Eunice who had grown up on a nearby farm. One October day when the two of them were walking through an abandoned orchard they paused to rest in the shade of an old stone wall in which some ivy and small flowers were growing. Eunice was full of the delicate awkwardness of certain large girls, and while Russell was looking at her a leaf came fluttering down to rest on her shoulder. He became aware of the sound of honeybees flickering through the noonday sun, and of the uncommonly sweet odor of apples mouldering among the clover and he was seized with such passion that he immediately took the willing girl. She became pregnant, so they got married, although he did not want to, and before much longer he stopped talking about going around the world.

J.D., handing Russell a card of a little street in some North African town, remarked that on this particular street he had bought a tasseled red fez. And Russell nodded a bit sadly.

"Now, this is Lisbon," J.D. said. "Right over here on the far side of this rectangular plaza is where I lived. I used to walk down to the river that you see at the edge of the card, and on the way back I'd wander through some little shops where you can buy miniature galleons of filigreed gold."

"I suppose you bought one," said Zobrowski.

"I couldn't resist," said J.D. with a smile. "Here's a view of Barcelona at night, and right here by this statue of Columbus I liked to sit and watch the tide come sweeping in. An exact copy of the *Santa María* is tied up at the dock near the statue. And whenever the wind blew down from the hills I could hear the butter-pat clap of gypsies dancing on the Ramblas." He looked at us anxiously to see if we were interested. It was clear that he loved Spain. He wanted us to love it, too.

"One time in Galicia," he said, "at some little town where the train stopped I bought a drink of water from a wrinkled old woman who was holding up an earthen jug and calling, '*Agua! Agua fría!*'" He drew a picture of the jug—it was called a *porrón*—and he demonstrated how it was to be held above your head while you drank. Your lips were never supposed to touch the spout. The Spaniards could drink without swallowing, simply letting the stream of water pour down their throats, and after much dribbling and choking J.D. had learned the trick. But what he most wanted to describe was the old woman who sold him the water. She could have been sixty or ninety. She was toothless, barefoot, and with a rank odor, but somehow, in some way he could not get across to us, they had meant a great deal to each other. He tried to depict a quality of arrogance or ferocity about her, which, in the days when she was young, must have caused old men to murmur and young men to fall silent whenever she passed by. He could not forget an instant when he reached out the train window to give her back the clay jug and met her deep, unwavering eyes.

"The train was leaving," he said, leaning forward. "It was leaving forever. And I heard her scream at me. I didn't know what she said, but there was a Spaniard in the same compartment who told me that this old Galician woman had screamed at me, 'Get off the train! Stay in my land!'" He paused, apparently remembering, and slowly shook his head.

It was in Spain, too, in a cheap waterfront night club called *El Hidalgo*—and he answered Russell's question by saying that Don Quixote, for example, was an *hidalgo*—it was here that he fell in love for the only time in his life. The cabaret was in an alley of the Gothic quarter where tourists seldom ventured. J.D. often spent his evenings there, buying lottery tickets and brown paper cigarettes and drinking a yellowish wine called *manzanilla*. One night the flamenco dancers were in a furious mood—he said he could feel the tension gathering the way electricity will sometimes gather on a midwestern afternoon until it splits the air. An enormously fat gypsy woman was dancing by herself, dancing the symbols of fertility that have survived a thousand generations. She was dressed in what he likened to a bedspread covered with orange polka dots. Raising and lowering her vast arms, she snapped her fingers and angrily danced alone; then all at once a savage little man in high-heeled boots sprang out of the crowd and began leaping around her. The staccato of his boots made the floor tremble and caused the *manzanilla* to sway inside the bottles.

"Everybody was howling and clapping," said J.D., and he clapped once as the gypsies clap, not with the entire hand but with three fingers flat against the palm. It sounded like a pistol shot. "Somebody was looking at me," he went on. "I could feel someone's eyes on me. I looked into the shadows and saw her. She was about nineteen, very tall and imperial, with her hair in braids. She began walking toward me, and she was singing. She sang to me that her name was Paquita—"

"She was improvising a song," said Zobrowski.

J.D. nodded. "It had the sound of a lament. Those old tragedies you hear in Spain, they're paralyzing."

"Just what do you mean?" Zobrowski asked.

"I don't know," said J.D. "It's as if a dagger was still plunged to the hilt in her breast."

Zobrowski smiled. "Go on. No doubt this young woman was beautiful."

"Yes. And she never stopped looking at me. I don't remember, but she must have walked across the room because I realized I was standing up and she was standing directly in front of me, touching my lips with one finger."

"I have had similar dreams," said Zobrowski.

Russell was listening avidly. "I didn't think Spanish women could ever get away from their chaperons."

"*Dueña*, I believe, is the word," Zobrowski said.

"There was no *dueña* for that girl," answered J.D. He was silent for a little while and then concluded his story. "Later that night I saw her walking the streets."

"Well, that explains everything," Zobrowski smiled. "You simply mistook her professional interest in you for some sort of transcendental love."

J.D. looked at Dave Zobrowski for a long time and finally said, "I didn't think I could make you understand." To Russell he said, "I find myself repeating her name. In the night I see her everywhere. In Paris, or in Rome, or even in this town, I see a girl turning away and my heart jumps the way it did that night in Barcelona."

"You should have married her," said Russell.

"I think he has done enough foolish things as it is," Zobrowski replied, and that seemed to end the matter. At least J.D. never referred to Paquita again. He spoke of the Andalusian gypsies, saying that they are a mixture of Arab and Indian, while the Catalonians are almost pure Sudra Indian. He gave this information as though it were important; he seemed to value knowledge for itself alone. But, looking into our faces, he saw that we could not greatly care about Spanish gypsies one way or another.

He had a pale gray cardboard folder with a drawing of St. George on the cover. Inside was a map of the geographical limits of the Catalan language, and this inscription: "With the best wishes for all the friends of the Catalan-speaking countries once free in the past, they will be free and whole again thanks to the will and strength of the Catalan people."

This was a folder of the resistance movement; it had been given to him, at the risk of imprisonment and perhaps at the risk of life itself, by a charwoman of Valencia. Zobrowski inquired if these were the people who opposed Franco. J.D. said that was correct. In Algiers he had met a waiter who had fought against Franco and barely escaped the country; this waiter had been in Algiers since 1938 and had no hope of seeing his family again, though he believed, as the charwoman believed, that one day Spain would be free.

After inspecting the pathetic little folder Zobrowski suggested, "I can easily appreciate your concern for these people. However you might also spend some time considering your own situation. Frankly, time is getting on, while you elect to dawdle about the waterfronts of the world."

J.D. shrugged.

"I've been meaning to ask," said Zobrowski. "Did you ever receive the letter I addressed to you in Vienna?"

"I don't remember it," said J.D.

"It concerned an executive position with the Pratt Hanover Company. They manufacture farm implements. I spoke to Donald Pratt about you and he was very much interested."

"No, I never got the letter," said J.D. "I was traveling quite a bit and I guess a lot of letters never caught up with me."

"Would you have come back if you had received the offer from Pratt?"

"No, I guess not," said J.D.

"We've known each other a long time, haven't we?"

J.D. nodded. "Since we were kids, Dave."

"Exactly. I would like to know how you manage to live."

"Oh, I work here and there. I had a job at the American embassy in Switzerland for a while, and to be honest about it, I've done some black marketing. I've learned how to get along, how to pull the levers that operate the world."

Then he began to describe Lucerne. It seemed far distant, in every dimension, from the days when we were children and used to bicycle down the river road to the hickory woods and hunt for squirrels. Each of us had a .22 rifle, except J.D., who went hunting with a lemon-wood bow. He had made it himself, and he had braided and waxed the string, and sewn a quiver, and planed his arrows. He did not hit many squirrels with his equipment, and we would often taunt him about losing the arrows among the high weeds and underbrush, but he never seemed to mind; he would go home to his father's tool chest in the basement and calmly set about planing another batch of sticks. We would watch him clip turkey feathers into crisp rhomboids and carefully glue them into place, bracing each feather with matchsticks until the glue hardened. We would sit on the washtub, or on his father's workbench, and smoke pieces of grapevine while we studied the new arrows. When he fitted on the bronze tip and banded each arrow with hunter's green and white Russell would watch with an almost hypnotized expression. But Dave Zobrowski, even in those days, was puzzled and a trifle impatient with J.D.

Remembering such things as J.D.'s bow and arrow we could see that it was he, and not Russell, who was destined to go away. We thought he had left a good deal of value here in the midwest of America. Our town is not exotic, but it is comprehensible and it is clean. This is partly due to Dave Zobrowski, who has always been vehement about cleanliness. That he grew up to become a physician and a member of the sanitary commission surprised no one. He likes to tell of disgusting conditions he has seen in other cities. While he was in Chicago at a medical convention he investigated a hotel charging the same price as the Pioneer House here in town, and he reported, all too graphically, how the ceiling was stained from leakage, how there was pencil writing on the walls, together with the husks of smashed roaches, and how he found a red hair embedded in the soap. Even the towel was rancid. Looking out the smoky window he saw wine bottles and decaying fruit in the gutter.

Visitors to this town often wonder how it is possible to exist without ballet, opera, and so forth, but it usually turns out that they themselves attend only once or twice each season, if at all. Then, too, if you are not accustomed to a certain entertainment you do not miss it. Russell, for example, grew up in a home devoid of music but cheerful and harmonious all the same. To his parents music was pointless, unless at Christmas time, when the phonograph would be wound up, the needle replaced, and the carols dusted off; consequently Mozart means nothing to him.

A Brooklyn police captain named Lehmbruck drove out here to spend his vacation but went back east after a week, saying it was too quiet to sleep. However, he seemed to be interested in the sunset, remarking that he had never seen the sun go down anywhere except behind some buildings. And he had never eaten old ham—he studied the white specks very dubiously, and with some embarrassment asked it the ham was spoiled. The Chamber of Commerce later received a wistful little note from Captain Lehmbruck, hinting that he might have another try at the prairie next summer.

Christmas here is still made instead of bought, even if we think no more of Christ than anyone else. And during the summer months the sidewalks are overhung with white or lavender spirea, and we can watch the rain approaching, darkening the farmland. Life here is reasonable and tradition not discounted, as evidenced by the new public library which is a modified Parthenon of Tennessee marble. There was a long and bitter argument about the inscription for its façade. One group wanted the so-called living letter, while the majority sought reassurance in the Doric past. At last we chiseled it with "Pvblic," "Covnty," "Strvctvre," and so forth.

J.D. knew about all these things, but he must have wanted more, and as he talked to us about his travels we could read in his restless blue eyes that he was not through searching. We thought he would come home when his father died, at least for a little while. Of course he was six thousand miles away, but most men would have returned from any distance. We did not know what he thought of us, the friends who had been closest to him, and this was altogether strange because our opinions about him were no secret—the fact that Russell envied him and that Zobrowski thought his life was going to rot.

Russell, to be sure, envied everybody. For a time after the marriage we believed Russell would collect himself, whatever it was needed collecting, because he went around looking very pleased with himself, although Eunice seemed a bit confused. He began to go shooting in the hickory woods again, firing his old .22 more to exult in its noise than to kill a squirrel. Yet something within him had been destroyed. Whether it could have been an insufferable jealousy of J.D.—who was then in Finland—or love that was lost, or the hard core of another sickness unknown to anyone on earth, no one could say, but it was to be only a few years after J.D.'s visit that we would find Russell lying in the garage with his head almost torn off and a black .45 service automatic in his hand.

"Here is where Dante first met Beatrice," said J.D., adding with a smile that several locations in Florence claimed this distinction, even as half the apartments in Toledo insist El Greco painted there. And he had a picture of Cala Ratjada where he had lived with a Danish girl named Vivian. We had forgotten, if indeed we had ever realized it, that in other countries people are not required to be so furtive about their affairs. We learned that Cala Ratjada was a fishing village on the eastern end of Majorca. Majorca we had heard of because the vacation magazines were publicizing it.

"I understand there's a splendid cathedral in the capital," Zobrowski said. "Palma, isn't it?"

J.D. agreed rather vaguely. It was plain he did not care much for cathedrals, unless there was something queer about them as there was about the *Sagrada Familia*. He preferred to tell about the windmills on Majorca, and about his bus ride across the island with a crate of chickens on the seat behind him. We had not known there was a bus across the island; the travel magazines always advised tourists to hire a car with an English-speaking driver. So we listened, because there is a subtle yet basic difference between one who travels and one who does not.

He had lived with this Danish girl all of one summer in a boarding house—a *pensión* he called it—and every afternoon they walked through some scrubby little trees to a white sandy beach and went swimming nude. They took along a leather bag full of heavy amber wine and drank this and did some fancy diving off the rocks. He said the Mediterranean there at Cala Ratjada was more translucent even than the harbor of Monte Carlo. When their wine was finished and the sand had become cool and the shadows of the trees were touching the water they walked back to the village. For a while they stopped on the embarcadero to watch the Balearic fishermen spreading their nets to dry. Then J.D. and the Danish girl returned to the *pensión* for dinner. They ate such things as fried octopus or baby squid or a huge seafood casserole called *paella*.

"Where is she now?" Russell asked.

"Vivian?" said J.D. "Oh, I don't know. She sent me a card from Frederikshavn a year or so ago. She'd been wanting to go to India, so maybe that's where she is now."

"Didn't she expect you to marry her?"

J.D. looked at Russell and then laughed out loud; it was the first time he had laughed all evening.

"Neither of us wanted to get married," he said. "We had a good summer. Why should we ruin it?"

This was a kind of reasoning we were aware of, via novels more impressive for poundage than content; otherwise it bore no relation to us. What bound them together was as elementary as a hyphen, and we suspected they could meet each other years later without embarrassment. They had loved without aim or sense, as young poets do. We could imagine this, to be sure, but we could not imagine it actually happening. There were women in our town, matrons now, with whom we had been intimate to some degree a decade or so ago, but now when we met them or were entertained in their homes, we were restrained by the memory of the delicate past. Each of us must carry, as it were, a balloon inked with names and dates.

So far as we knew, J.D. looked up only one of the women he used to know here in town. He called on Helen Louise Sawyer who used to win the local beauty contests. When we were young most of us were afraid of her, because there is something annihilating about too much beauty; only J.D. was not intimidated. Perhaps he could see then what we learned to see years later—that she was lonely, and that she did not want to be coveted for the perfection of her skin or for the truly magnificent explosion of her bosom. When Helen Louise and J.D. began going around together we were astonished and insulted because Russell, in those days, was much more handsome than J.D., and Dave Zobrowski was twice as smart. All the same she looked at no else. Then he began leaving town on longer and longer expeditions. He would return wearing a southern California sport shirt or with a stuffed grouper he had caught off Key West. Helen Louise eventually went into the real-estate business.

He telephoned her at the office and they went to dinner at the Wigwam, which is now the swank place to eat. It is decorated with buffalo skins and tomahawks and there are displays of flint arrowheads that have been picked up by farmers in neighboring counties. The only incongruities are the pink jade ashtrays that, by midnight, seem to have been planted with white, magenta-tipped stalks to remind the diners that a frontier has vanished. And well it has. The scouts are buried, the warriors mummified. Nothing but trophies remain: a coup stick hung by the Wigwam's flagstone hearth, a pipe smoked by Satanta, a cavalry saber and a set of mouldering blue gloves crossed on the mantel, a tan robe laced to the western wall, a dry Pawnee scalp behind the bar. The wind still sweeps east from the lofty Colorado plains, but carries with it now only the clank of machinery in the wheat fields. The Mandans have gone, like the minor chords of an Iowa death song, with Dull Knife and Little Wolf whose three hundred wretched squaws and starving men set out to fight their way a thousand miles to the fecund Powder River that had been their home.

There is a gratification to the feel of history behind the places one has known, and the Wigwam's historical display is extensive. In addition, the food is good. There is hot biscuit with clover honey, and the old ham so mistrusted by Captain Lehmbruck of Brooklyn. There is Missouri fried chicken, spare ribs, venison with mushrooms, catfish, beef you can cut with a fork, wild rice and duck buried under pineapple sauce, as well as various European dishes. That evening J.D. asked for a certain Madeira wine and apparently was a little taken aback to find that the Wigwam had it. Travelers, real travelers, come to think of their homes as provincial and are often surprised.

Helen Louise had metamorphosed, as even we could see, and we knew J.D. was in for a shock. Through the years she had acquired that faintly resentful expression that comes from being stared at, and she seemed to be trying to compensate for her beauty. Although there was nothing wrong with her eyes she wore glasses, she had cropped her beautiful golden hair in a lesbian style, and somehow she did not even walk the way she used to. The pleasing undulations had mysteriously given way to a militant stride. Her concern in life was over such items as acreage and location. At the business she was quite good; every real estate man in town hated her, no doubt thinking she should have become a housewife instead of the demon that she was. But apparently she had lost her desire to marry or sublimated it. At the lunch hour she could be seen in an expensive suit, speaking in low tones to another businesswoman, and her conversation when overheard would be ". . . referred the order to me . . . Mrs. Pabst's opinion . . . second mortgage . . . bought six apartments . . ."

We guessed that J.D.'s evening with Helen Louise might be an indication that he had grown tired of wandering around the earth, and that he wanted to come home for good. Helen Louise, if no longer as voluptuous as she had been at twenty or twenty-five, was still provocative, and if she married was it not possible she might come to look very much as she had looked ten years before? But J.D had very little to say about his evening with her, and after he was gone Helen Louise never mentioned him.

"Did you know that in Cádiz," he said—because it was to him a fact worth noting, like the fact that in Lisbon he had lived on a certain plaza—"Did you know that in Cádiz you can buy a woman for three *pesetas?*" Whether or not he might have been referring to Helen Louise we did not know, nor did anyone ask.

"Once I talked with Manolete," he said, as though it was the first line of a poem.

"I've heard that name," Zobrowski answered. "He's a toreador, is he not?"

"I think 'toreador' was invented by Bizet," J.D. replied. "Manolete was a matador. But he's dead. It was in Linares that he was *cogido*. On the twenty-seventh of August in nineteen-forty-seven. At five in the afternoon, as the saying goes." And he continued, telling us that the real name of this bullfighter had been Manuel Rodriguez, and that after he was gored in Linares the ambulance that was taking him to a hospital started off in the wrong direction, and there was a feeling of bitterness in Spain when the news was broadcast that he was dead of his wounds.

"What you are trying to express," Zobrowski suggested, "is that this fellow was a national hero."

"Yes," said J.D.

"Like Babe Ruth."

"No," said J.D. instantly and with a vexed expression. He gestured helplessly and then shrugged. He went on to say that he happened to be in Heidelberg when death came to Manolete in the town of Linares. He looked around at us as if this circumstance were very strange. As he spoke he gestured excitedly and often skipped from one topic to another because there was so little time and he had so much to tell us. In a way he created a landscape of chiaroscuro, illuminating first one of his adventures and now another, but leaving his canvas mostly in shadow.

"One morning in Basel," he said, "it began to snow while I was having breakfast. Snow was falling on the Rhine." He was sitting by a window in a tea shop overlooking the river. He described the sunless, blue-gray atmosphere with large white flakes of snow piling up on the window ledge, and the dark swath of the river. Several waitresses in immaculate uniforms served his breakfast from a heavy silver tray. There was coffee in a silver pitcher, warm breads wrapped in thick linen napkins, and several kinds of jam and preserves; all the while the snow kept mounting on the ledge just outside the window, and the waitresses murmured in German. He returned to Basel on the same morning of the following year—all the way from Palermo—just to have his breakfast there.

Most of his ten years abroad had been spent on the borders of the Mediterranean, and he agreed with Zobrowski's comment that the countries in that area must be the dirtiest in Europe. He told about a servant girl in one of his *pensiónes* who always seemed to be on her knees scrubbing the floor but who never bathed herself. She had such a pervasive odor that he could tell whenever she had recently been in a room.

He said that Pompeii was his biggest disappointment. He had expected to find the city practically buried under a cliff of lava. But there was no lava. Pompeii was like any city abandoned and overgrown with weeds. He had visited the Roman ruins of North Africa, but the names he mentioned did not mean anything to us. Carthage did, but if we had ever read about the others in school we had long since stored their names and dates back in the dusty bins alongside algebra and Beowulf. Capri was the only celebrated spot he visited that surpassed all pictures of it, and he liked Sorrento too, saying that he had returned to the mainland about sundown when the cliffs of Sorrento become red and porous like the cliffs of the Grand Canyon. And in a town called Amalfi he had been poisoned—he thought it was the eggs.

All this was delivered by a person we had known since childhood, yet it might as well have come from a foreign lecturer. J.D. was not trying to flaunt his adventures; he described them because we were friends and he could not conceive of the fact that the ruins of Pompeii would mean less to us than gossip on the women's page. He wanted to tell us about the ballet in Cannes, where the audience was so quiet that he had heard the squeak of the dancers' slippers. But none of us had ever been to a ballet, or especially wanted to go. There was to us something faintly absurd about men and women in tights. When Zobrowski suggested as much, J.D. looked at him curiously and seemed to be struggling to remember what it was like to live in our town.

A number of things he said did not agree with our concept. According to him the Swedish girls are not in the least as they appear on calendars, which invariably depict them driving some cows down a pea-green mountainside. J.D. said the Swedes were long and gaunt with cadaverous features and gloomy dispositions, and their suicide rate was among the highest on earth.

Snails, he said, though no one had inquired, have very little taste. You eat them with a tiny two-pronged fork and some tongs that resemble a surgeon's forceps. The garlic-butter sauce is excellent, good enough to drink, but snail meat tasted to him rubbery like squid.

About the taxi drivers of Paris: they were incredibly avaricious. If you were not careful they would give you a gilded two-franc piece instead of a genuine fifty-franc piece for change, and if you caught them at it they became furious. But he did say that the French were the most urbane people to be found.

He had traveled as far east as Teheran and as far north as Trondheim. He had been to Lithuania and to Poland, and to Egypt and to the edge of the Sahara, and from the animation of his voice we could tell he was not through yet. While he was telling us about his plans as we sat comfortably in the cocktail lounge of the Pioneer House, a bellboy came in and respectfully said to Dave, "Dr. Zobrowski, the hospital is calling."

Without a word Zobrowski stood up and followed the boy. A few minutes later he returned wearing his overcoat and carrying his gray Homburg. "I'm sorry, but it's an emergency," he said to us all, and then to J.D., "Since you are not to be in town much longer, I suppose this is good-bye."

J.D. uncrossed his long legs and casually stood up.

"No doubt you lead an entertaining life," Zobrowski observed, not bothering to conceal his disapproval. "But a man cannot wander the face of the earth forever."

"That's what everybody tells me," J.D. answered. "It doesn't bother me much any more."

Zobrowski pulled on his yellow pigskin gloves and with a severe expression he began to settle the fingers as carefully as though he had put on surgical gloves. "In my opinion," he said suddenly and lifted his eyes, "you are a damn fool."

They stared at each other not with hostility, nor exactly with surprise, but as though they had never quite seen each other until that instant. Yet these were the two men who, about thirty years previously, had chipped in equal shares to buy a dog, a squat little beast with peculiar teeth that made it look like a beaver.

"From birth we carry the final straw," said Zobrowski at last.

J.D. only smiled.

Zobrowski's normally hard features contracted until he looked cruel, and he inclined his head, saying by this gesture, "As you wish." He had always known how to use silence with devastating force, yet J.D. was undismayed and did nothing but shrug like a Frenchman.

Zobrowski turned to Russell. "I had lunch with my broker the other day. He has some information on that Hudson's Bay mining stock of yours that makes me feel we should have a talk. Stop by my office tomorrow morning at eight-thirty. I have had my receptionist cancel an appointment because of this matter."

Russell's mouth slowly began to drop open as he gazed at Zobrowski. He never made reasonable investments and several times had been saved from worse ones only because he confided his financial plans, along with everything else, to anybody who would listen. Then, too, the making of money necessitates a callousness he had never possessed.

"That stock's all right," he said weakly. "I'm positive it's all right. Really it is, Dave. You should have bought some."

"Yes," Zobrowski said, looking down on him with disgust. And turning to J.D. he said, "Let us hear from you. Good-bye." Then he went striding across the lounge.

"Oh, God!" mumbled Russell, taking another drink. He was ready to weep from humiliation and from anxiety over the investment. In the past few years he had become quite bald and flabby, and had taken to wearing suspenders because a belt disturbed his intestines. He rubbed his jowls and looked around with a vague, desperate air.

"Whatever happened to little Willie Grant?" J.D. asked, though Grant had never meant a thing to him.

"He's—he's in Denver," Russell said, gasping for breath.

"What about Martha Mathews?"

This was the girl who rejected Russell, but J.D. was abroad when it happened and may never have heard. He looked astonished when Russell groaned. Economically speaking, she was a great deal better off than if she had married Russell. She had accepted a housing contractor with more ambition than conscience, and now spent most of her time playing cards on the terrace of the country club.

J.D. had been in love, moderately, in the abstract, with a long-legged sloe-eyed girl named Minnette whose voice should have been poured into a glass and drunk. Her mother owned a bakery. We usually saw Minnette's mother when we came trotting home from school at the noon hour; she would be standing at the door with arms rolled in her apron while she talked to the delivery man, or, in winter time, we would often see her as she bent over, pendulous, tranquil, somehow everlasting, to place chocolate éclairs in the bakery window while sleet bounced indignantly off the steaming glass. At such moments she looked the way we always wanted our own harried mothers to look. If the truth were known it might be that we found her more stimulating than her daughter, although this may have been because we were famished when we passed the bakery. In any event he inquired about Minnette, so we told him her eyes still had that look, and that she was married to the mortician, an extremely tall man named Kopf who liked to underline trenchant phrases in the little books on Success that you buy for a quarter.

Answering these somehow anachronistic questions stirred us the way an old snapshot will do when you come upon it while hunting for something else. Later on Russell was to say that when J.D. mentioned the yellow brick building where the four of us began our schooling he remembered for the first time in possibly a decade how we used to sit around a midget table and wield those short, blunt, red-handled scissors. We had a paste pot and sheets of colored paper, and when our labors were done the kindergarten windows displayed pumpkins, Christmas trees, owls, eggs, rabbits, or whatever was appropriate to the season. J.D. could always draw better than anyone else. When visiting night for parents came around it would be his work they admired. David Zobrowski, of course, was the scholar; we were proud to be Dave's best friends. Russell managed to remain undistinguished in any way until time for the singing class. Here no one could match him. Not that anyone wanted to. He sang worse than anyone who ever attended our school. It was as if his voice operated by a pulley, and its tenor was remotely canine. The class consisted of bluebirds and robins, with the exception of Russ who was placed at a separate desk and given no designation at all. Usually he gazed out the window at the interminable fields, but when it came to him that he, too, could sing, and his jaw began to work and his throat to contract, he would be warned into silence by the waving baton.

Going to and from the business district ordinarily meant passing this musty little building, which had long since been converted into headquarters for the Boy Scout troop, and which now related to us no more than the Wizard of Oz, but until J.D. spoke of it we had not realized that the swings and the slide were gone, and crabgrass was growing between the bricks of the front walk.

When we were in high school J.D. occasionally returned to wander the corridors of the elementary school. The rest of us had been glad enough to move on and we considered his visits a bit queer, but otherwise never paused to think about them.

These were the streets where we had lived, these the houses, during a period of time when today could not influence tomorrow, and we possessed the confidence to argue about things we did not understand.

Though, of course, we still did that. On winter nights we dropped away to sleep while watching the snow come drifting by the street light, and in summer we could see the moths outside the screens fluttering desperately, as though to tell us something. Our childhood came and went before we were ready to grasp it. Things were different now. The winged seeds that gyrate down from the trees now mean nothing else but that we must sweep them from the automobile hood because stains on the finish lower the trade-in value. Now, in short, it was impractical to live as we used to live with the abandon of a mule rolling in the dust.

In those days our incipient manhood had seemed a unique power, and our single worry that some girl might become pregnant. We danced with our eyes closed and our noses thrust into the gardenias all the girls wore in their hair, meanwhile estimating our chances. And, upon discovering literature, thanks to the solemn pedantry of a sophomore English teacher, we affected bow ties and cigarette holders and were able to quote contemporary poets with a faintly cynical tone.

On a postcard of a Rotterdam chocolate factory, sent to Russell but addressed to us all, J.D. scribbled, "I see nothing but the noon dust a-blowing and the green grass a-growing." If not contemporary it was at least familiar, and caused Zobrowski to remark, with a certain unconscious measure, "As fond as I am of him I sometimes lose patience. In a furrow he has found a feather of Pegasus and what should have been a blessing has become a curse."

Now J.D. was inquiring after one or two we had forgotten, or who had moved away, leaving no more trace than a cloud, and about a piano teacher who had died one sultry August afternoon on the streetcar. Yet his interest was superficial. He was being polite. He could not really care or he would not have gone away for ten years. He wondered whatever became of the bearded old man who used to stand on a street corner with a stack of Bibles and a placard promising a free copy of the New Testament to any Jew who would renounce the faith. We did not know what happened to the old man; somehow he had just vanished. Quite a few things were vanishing.

J.D. cared very little for the men who had once been our fraternity brothers, which was odd because in our hearts we still believed that those days and those brothers had been so extraordinary that people were still talking about them. Yet we could recall that he took no pride in being associated with them. The militant friendship of fraternity life made him surly. He refused to shake hands as often as he was expected to. We had been warned that, as pledges, we would be thrown into the river some night. This was part of learning to become a finer man. When the brothers came for us about three o'clock one morning, snatching away our blankets and singing the good fellowship song, we put up the traditional fight—all of us except J.D. He refused to struggle. He slumped in the arms of his captors limp as an empty sack. This puzzled and annoyed the brothers, who held him aloft by his ankles and who bounced his head on the floor. He would not even open his eyes. They jabbed him stiffly in the ribs, they twisted his arms behind his back, they kicked him in the seat, they called him names, and finally, very angry, they dragged him to the river and flung him in. But even when he went sailing over the bull-rushes he was silent as a corpse. Strangely, he did not hit the water with a loud splash. Years later he told us that he twisted at the last moment and dove through the river scum, instead of landing flat on his back as Russell did. They vanished together, as roommates should, but Russell was again audible in a few seconds—thrashing back to shore, where the brothers helped him out and gave him a towel and a bathrobe and a drink of brandy.

J.D., however, did not reappear. Even before Russell had reached the shore we were beginning to worry about J.D. There was no moon that night and the river had an evil look. We stood in a row at the edge of the water. We heard the bullfrogs, and the dark bubbling and plopping of whatever calls the river home, but nothing more. And all at once the structure of the fraternity collapsed. The last vestige of unity disappeared. We were guilty individuals. Some people began lighting matches and peering into the river, while others called his name. But there was no answer, except in the form of rotten, half-submerged driftwood floating by, revolving in the sluggish current, and, beyond the confused whispering, the brief, crying shadows of night birds dipping in wild alarm over the slimy rushes.

When we saw him again we asked what happened, but several years passed before he told anyone. Then he said—and only then was his revenge complete—"Oh, I just swam under water as far as I could. After that I let the river carry me out of sight." He swam ashore a mile or two downstream, and by a back road he returned to the fraternity house. Nobody was there; everybody was at the river searching for his body. The fraternity was almost ruined because of J.D.

Now he had climbed the Matterhorn, and we were not surprised. He knew what it was like in Venice, or in Copenhagen, and as we reflected on his past we came to understand that his future was inevitable. We knew he would leave us again, perhaps forever.

Russell, tamping out a cheap cigar, said boldly, "Eunice and I have been thinking about a trip to the Bahamas next year, or year after." He considered the nicotine on his fingertips, and after a pause, because his boast was empty, and because he knew that we knew how empty it was, he added, "Though it depends." He began picking helplessly at his fingertips. He would never go anywhere.

"You'll like the Bahamas," J.D. said.

"We consider other places," Russell said unexpectedly, and there were tears in his eyes.

J.D. was watching him with a blank, pitiless gaze.

"I think I'll go to Byzantium," Russell said.

"That doesn't exist any more."

Russell took a deep breath to hush the panic that was on him, and at last he said, "Well, gentlemen, I guess I'd better get some shut-eye if I'm going to talk business with Dave in the morning."

"It's late," J.D. agreed.

Then we asked when he would be coming home for good, although it was a foolish question, and J.D. laughed at it. Later, in talking about him, we would recall his reason for not wanting to live here. He had explained that the difference between our town and these other places he had been was that when you go walking down a boulevard in some strange land and you see a tree burgeoning, you understand that this is beautiful, and there comes with the knowledge a moment of indescribable poignance in the realization that as this tree must die, so will you die. But when, in the home you have always known, you find a tree in bud you think only that spring has come again. Here he stopped. It did not make much sense to us, but for him it had meaning of some kind.

So we asked when he would be coming back for another visit. He said he didn't know. We asked what was next. He replied that as soon as he could scrape together a few more dollars he thought he might like to see the Orient.

"They say that in Malaya . . ." he began, with glowing eyes. But we did not listen closely. He was not speaking to us anyway, only to himself, to the matrix that had spawned him and to the private god who guided him. His voice reached us faintly, as if from beyond the walls of Ávila.

ARCTURUS

Verweile doch, du bist so schön.
Linger awhile, thou art so fair.
Goethe

T HE CHILDREN, Otto and Donna, have been allowed to stay up late this evening in order to see the company. Now with faces bewitched they sit on the carpet in front of the fireplace, their pajama-clad legs straight out in front of them and the tails of their bathrobes trailing behind so that they look somewhat like the sorcerer's apprentice.

Outside the wind is blowing and every once in a while the window-panes turn white; then the wind veers and the snow must go along with it. Automobile horns sound quite distant even when close by. Aside from hissing, sputtering logs growing black in the fire, and alluring noises from the kitchen, the most noticeable sound is a melancholy humming from the front door. Otto and Donna are convinced a ghost makes this dreadful wailing and no amount of explanation can disprove it. Their father has lifted them up one after the other so that they can see it is only a piece of tin weather stripping that vibrates when the wind comes from a certain direction, and they have felt a draft when this happens, but their eyes are dubious; wind and metal are all very well, but the noise is made by a ghost. It is a terrible sound, as no one can deny, and upon hearing it Otto shivers so deliciously that his little sister must also shiver.

"What does company look like?" he inquires without lifting his gaze from the burning logs. And is told that company will be a gentleman named Mr. Kirk. Otto considers this for a long time, wiggling his feet and rubbing his nose which has begun to itch from the heat.

"Is he coming to our house?"

Otto's father does not answer. Lost in meditation, he sits in his appointed chair beside the bookcase.

Presently Otto sniffles and wishes to know why the man is coming here.

"To visit with your mother."

A cloud of snowflakes leaps to the window as if to see what is going on inside but is frightened away by the weather stripping. How warm the living room is! Donna yawns, and since whatever one does the other must also do, her brother manages an even larger yawn. The difference is in what follows: Donna, being a woman, does not mind succumbing, and, filled with security, she begins to lean against Otto, but he is convinced that sleep is his enemy and so he remains bolt upright with a stupidly militant expression that tends to weaken only after his eyes have shut. Though his enemy is a colossal one he accepts without concern the additional burden of his infant sister.

"Why?" he asks, and looks startled by his own voice. It is doubtful he can now remember what he wishes to know, but why is always a good solid question and sure to get some kind of response.

"Because your mother wrote him a letter and begged him to come see her."

Again follows a silence. The clock on the mantel ticks away while the good logs crackle and the coals hiss when sap drips on them. Otto is remotely troubled. For several weeks he has sensed that something is wrong in the house, but he cannot find out what. His mother does not seem to know, nor does the cook, who usually knows everything. Otto has about concluded the nurse is to blame; therefore he does whatever she tells him not to do. Sometimes he finds it necessary to look at his father, or to sit on his lap; there, although they may not speak to one another, he feels more confident. He is jealous of this position and should Donna attempt to share it he is prone to fend her off until orders come from above.

In regard to this evening, Otto has already gotten what he wanted. He does not really care about Mr. Kirk because the value of a visitor lies simply in the uses to which Otto can put him, whether it be staying up late or eating an extra sweet. All at once Donna topples luxuriously into his lap. His hand comes to rest on her tiny birdlike shoulder, but through convenience only. At the moment he is careless of the virgin beauty; her grace does not intrigue him, nor does he realize how this tableau has touched the heart of his father across the room. Somberly Otto frowns into the fire; almost adult he is in the strength of such concentration, though one could not tell whether he is mulling over the past or the future. Perhaps if the truth were known he is only seeing how long he can roast his feet, which are practically touching a log.

"Is he coming *tonight?*" Otto knows full well this is a foolish question, but there lurks the fear that if he does not show a profound and tenacious interest in the whole business he will be sent to bed.

With ominous significance his father demands, "Why do you think you two are up this late?"

Otto stares harder than ever into the fire. It is important now that he think up something to change the subject in a hurry. He yawns again, and discovers that he is lying down. He sits up. He inquires plaintively if he may have the drumstick on Christmas.

His father does not reply, or even hear, but gazes at the carpet with a faraway expression somewhere between misery and resignation and does not even know he has been spoken to by the cook until she firmly calls him by name.

"Mr. Muhlbach!"

He starts up, somewhat embarrassed. Cook wishes to know at what time the guest will be arriving. Muhlbach subsides a little, takes a sip from a tumbler of brandy, and is vague. "Ah . . . we don't know exactly. Soon, I hope. Is there anything you want?"

But there is nothing; she has finished all preparation for the dinner and now is simply anxious for fear that one delicacy or another may lose its flavor from so much waiting. She looks at the children on the carpet before the fireplace. Otto catches this look; he reads in cook's stern face the thought that if she were their mother she would have them in bed; instantly he looks away from her and sits quite still in hopes that both his father and the cook will forget he is even there. Seconds pass. Nothing is said. Cook returns to the kitchen with an air of disgust.

Now the suburban living room is tranquil once again, much more so than it was two hours ago. At that time there were tears and reprimands and bitter injustice, or so the participants think. Otto especially felt himself abused; he was the object of an overwhelming lecture. He did not comprehend very much of it but there could be no mistake about who was in disgrace; therefore he rolled over onto his stomach

and began to sob. Surely this would restore him to the family circle.
No one, he thought, could refuse to comfort such a small boy. It was a
fine performance and failed only because he peeked up to see its effect;
at this he was suddenly plucked from the floor by one foot. He hung
upside down for a while, gravely insulted, but found it impossible to
weep effectively when the tears streamed up his forehead, so after a fit
of coughing and bellowing he was lowered to the carpet. On his head,
to be sure, but down at any rate, and for some time after he occupied
himself with the hiccups. He still believes that his punishment was not
only too stringent but too prompt; one appreciates a few moments in
which to enjoy the fruit of one's evil-doing. Furthermore, all he did
was take a stuffed giraffe from his sister. It is true the giraffe belonged
to him; the trouble came about because he had not thought of playing
with the giraffe until he discovered she had it, and when he had wrung
it away from her he put it on the table out of her reach. So, following
the administration of justice, he was ordered to kiss his little sister on
the lips, a penance he performs with monstrous apathy, after which
the living room was turned into a manger for perhaps the twentieth
time and the father magically transformed himself into a savage dog,
growling and snarling, keeping everything for himself. Donna and
Otto are spellbound, so terrifying is their father in the role of a dog.
In fact he is so menacing and guards the cushions and pillows with
such ferocity that the point of the fable is invariably lost. On occasion
they have even requested him to be a dog so that they might admire
his fangs and listen enraptured to the dreadful growls. But perhaps
they are learning, who can tell?

Now the lesson is ended and, as usual, forgotten. The giraffe is
clamped upside down beneath Donna's arm; it is fortunate in having
such a flexible neck. She no longer cares that a visitor is on the way; she
does not listen for the doorbell, nor does she anticipate the excitement
that is bound to follow. By firelight her hair seems a golden cobweb,
an altogether proper crown. Blissfully asleep she lies, despite the fact
that her pillow is one of Otto's inhospitable knees. Barely parted and
moist are the elfin lips, while her breath, as sweet as that of a pony,
sometimes catches between them, perhaps betokening a marvelous
dream. She cannot be true, Botticelli must have painted her. Her
expression is utterly pious; no doubt she has forgotten her miniature

crimes. One hopes she has not dwelt too hard upon those miniature punishments that followed.

Now comes a stamping of feet just outside, an instant of silence, and next the doorbell, dissonant and startling even when one expects it. Company is here! Otto is first to the door but there, overcome by shyness, allows his father to open it.

Here is more company than expected. Kirk has brought along someone he introduces as Miss Dee Borowski, an exotic little creature not a very great deal larger than Otto, although she is perhaps eighteen. One knows instinctively that she is a dancer. She is lean and cadaverous as a greyhound, and her hair has been dyed so black that the highlights look blue. She draws it back with utmost severity, twists it into a knot, and what is left over follows her with a flagrant bounce.

They have entered the Muhlbach home, Sandy Kirk tall as a flagpole and a trifle too dignified, as though he will be called upon to defend his camel's hair overcoat and pearl-gray homburg. He has brought gifts: perfume for the woman he is to visit, its decanter a crystalline spiral. For the master of the house something more substantial, a bottle of high hard Portuguese wine. With a flourish and a mock bow he presents them both to Muhlbach. He apologizes for his lateness by a rather elaborate description of the traffic in the Hudson tube, and as if a further apology may bring a smile of pardon to Muhlbach's face he adds in an almost supplicating way that Borowski was late getting out of rehearsal. Immediately the dancer confesses that her part will be small; she is third paramour in a ballet production of *Don Juan*. Well, she is feral enough and will probably mean bad dreams for young men in the audience, but there is something ambivalent about her as though she has not quite decided what to make of her life. Her eyebrows, for example, do not grow from the bony ridge that protects the eye; someone has plucked the outer hairs and substituted theater brows that resemble wings. She pauses beside the lamp and a shadow becomes visible high on her forehead—it has been shaved. Now she has decided to take off her new mink jacket; underneath is a lavender sweater that clearly intends to molt on the furniture, and a pair of frosty-looking tailored slacks. Quite rococo she looks, and knows it too. But to complete this ensemble she is carrying a book of philosophy.

Replies Muhlbach, conscious that his own voice must be a mono-
tone, "My wife is upstairs. She will be down in a few moments. This
is our son and there asleep by the fire is Donna."

Kirk has been waiting for this introduction because he has presents
for the children. To Otto goes a queer little stick-and-ball affair, a
game of some sort. Otto receives the device without enthusiasm but
minds his manners enough to say thank you. For Donna there is the
most fragile, translucent doll ever seen. It is not meant for her to play
with, of course, being made of Dresden china, not for years yet. Kirk
places it on the mantel.

Miss Borowski has stooped a little so that she and young Otto look
at one another as equals. Otto wishes to appear self-sufficient but
despite himself he likes what he sees; then, too, she is considerably
more fragrant than his mother, who always has an odor of medicine.
He decides to accept the overture. They are friends in an instant and
together, hand in hand, they go over to inspect Donna, who has found
the carpet no less agreeable than her brother's leg. Otto does not
object to anyone's admiring his baby sister; there are times when he
discovers himself seized by the desire to tickle her ribs or her feet. He
does not know this is love. So much the better, for if he knew he might
stop. Nor is he unaware that she is the beauty of the house, though he
takes comfort in the memory of her astonishing helplessness. He fails
to understand why, despite his instructions, she cannot learn to put
on her shoes or even go to the toilet when necessary.

Sandy Kirk, meanwhile, has been appraising the home and he has
learned something: the supper table has been set. Only then does he
recall the invitation was for supper. Unfortunately he and the dancer
stopped to eat before coming over. Muhlbach hands him a cocktail,
which he accepts with a serene smile; he waits to see if there will be a
toast, but there is none. He notes that Borowski is giving the little boy
a taste of her drink and he sees Muhlbach frown at this.

Into the room, supported by a nurse, comes Joyce Muhlbach, and
the attention of everyone turns to her. She is unsmiling, clearly suffering deep pain. She is dressed but there is about her the look and the
fetid odor of someone who has been in bedclothes all day. Her eyes
are febrile, much too luminous. Straight across the room she moves,
clutching the nurse's elbow, until she reaches the invited guest. Kirk,
who is about to tap a foreign cigarette on the back of his wrist, seems

paralyzed by the sight of her. Her husband turns around to the fire and begins to push at a log with his foot. And the dancer, who is holding Otto by the hand, stands flat-footed with the prearranged expression of one who has been told what to expect; even so her greedy stare indicates that she is fascinated by the sick woman's appearance.

Joyce now stands alone, and while looking up at Kirk she addresses her son. "Isn't it about time for little boys to be in bed?"

Otto assumes that nasal whine which he feels the best possible for all forms of protest, but he knows the end has come. Still a token argument is necessary. He knows they expect one. He reminds his mother that he has been given permission to stay up tonight; the fact that it was she who gave the permission seems not especially cogent. With strangers present his pride forbids the wheedling and disgraceful clowning that is sometimes successful, so he is reduced to an obstinate monologue. He watches his father pick up Donna, who is quite unconscious; she could be dragged upstairs and would not know the difference.

All of a sudden Otto gets up from the corner where he has been stubbornly crouching since bed was mentioned, and the churlish whine disappears. He owns a rifle. It is on the top shelf of the hall closet where he cannot reach it; nevertheless it belongs to him, and if Miss Borowski has a fancy for rifles his father might bring it out. Otto has reasoned no further than this, indeed has done nothing but look crafty, when his father remarks that there will be no showing of the gun tonight. Otto instantly beseeches his mother, whom he considers the more sympathetic, and while his back is turned he feels himself caught around the waist by that inexorable arm he knows so well. His head goes down, his feet go up, and thus robbed of dignity he vanishes for the night.

There follows one of those queer instants when everything becomes awkward. Otto has taken away more than himself. Is it affectation that causes Dee Borowski to sit cross-legged on the floor? Time is running out on them all.

Joyce begins: "Well, Sandy, I see you got here."

The moments that follow are stark and cheerless despite the comfortable fire. A flippant answer could make things worse. One listens moodily to the poltergeist in the door. But Muhlbach reappears to save them, enters briskly with a cocktail shaker and says, while filling the dancer's glass, "A month ago my father died." And he proceeds to tell about the death of young Otto's grandfather. Nothing about Muhlbach suggests the poet—certainly not his business suit, not his dictaphonic sentences, least of all his treasury of clichés. His story unwinds like ticker tape, yet the visitors cannot listen hard enough. Even Borowski has forgotten the drama of herself, and if one should quietly ask her name she might reply without thinking that it is Deborah Burns.

And the urbane Sandy Kirk, who has found his way around half the world, by this recital of degeneration and dissolution he drifts gradually into the past, into profound memories of his own. Unlike the ingénue, death is not unfamiliar to him, death is not something one mimes on cue; Kirk once or twice has seen it look him sharply in the eye and finds he does not care for that look. As the story progresses he begins to empathize with Muhlbach; he is gratified that this man does know some emotion, and he wonders less why Joyce married him. When he read her letter, read the sardonic description of her husband, he was astonished to perceive that beneath the surface she was utterly in love with the man, a man who until now has seemed to Kirk like a shadow on the water. He did not much want to come for this visit because he is afraid of Joyce. Their relationship never brought them any kind of fulfillment, never carried them to an ocean, as it were, but left them stranded in the backwash of lost opportunity. Kirk has not been able to resolve his feelings about Joyce; he was never able to place a little statue of her in his gallery as he does with other women. No, the letter put him ill at ease; he did not want to see her ever again, but there was in her appeal such urgency that he could not refuse. However, he has come prepared. He has thought everything out. He has brought along this terribly serious little ballerina for protection. He has only to say the magic word, that is, he need only mention ballet or the theater and Dee Borowski will take over, destroying all intimacy without ever knowing what she has done. It is a shrewd device, one Sandy Kirk has used in other clumsy situations; all the same he knows that Joyce will not be deceived.

Now Muhlbach, seated like the good merchant that he is, shaking up his trousers so as not to result in a bulge at the knee, continues in his oddly haunting style, telling how young Otto was invited to the sick-room but was not informed he would never see his grandfather again. And they talked a little while, did the boy and the old gentleman who was dying; they talked solemnly about what Otto had been doing that afternoon. In company with two other neighborhood gangsters he had been digging up worms. At the end of this conversation Otto received a present all wrapped up in Christmas tissue, though Christmas had hardly come into sight. It turned out to be a primer of archaeology, and while Otto held this book in his hands there beside the bed his grandfather sleepily explained that it was a book about the stars. After a momentary hesitation Otto thanked him. Muhlbach, standing on the other side of the deathbed, was carefully watching his son, and many times since that afternoon he has mulled over a curious fact, the fact that Otto could recognize the word "archaeology" and knew its meaning. Indeed the book had been chosen for him because he had sounded interested in the subject; furthermore Otto has always had fewer qualms than a Turk about displaying his accomplishments. What restrained him from correcting his grandfather? It was a marvelous opportunity to show off. The father does not know for sure, but he does know that the boy is preparing to leave the world of childhood.

And so Muhlbach, without understanding exactly why either of them did what they did, hurried out to buy his son a rifle. In a sporting-goods store he handled the light guns one after another, slipped the bolt and examined the chamber, raised the sights, caressed the stock, and in fact could hardly contain his rapture, for he has always been in love with guns. To one side stood the clerk with arms folded and a mysterious nodding smile. "This is a twenty-two, isn't it?" Muhlbach asked, though naturally it was not a question but a statement. However he bought no ammunition because even pride must genuflect to reason.

From the bedroom comes the querulous voice of Otto, who has been abandoned, and he wishes to know what they are talking about.

"Go to sleep!" orders his father.

In the bedroom there is silence.

Every few minutes the cook has peered out of the kitchen, not to see what is going on but to announce her impatience. She has allowed the door to swing back and forth; she has rattled silverware and clinked glasses. She cannot figure out why people linger so long over a drink. She herself would drink it down and be done with the matter.

Kirk is now obliged to confess that both he and the dancer have eaten. Pretense would be impossible. He turns helplessly to Joyce with his apology and she feels a familiar annoyance: it is all so characteristic of him, the tardiness, the additional guest, the blithe lack of consideration. How well she remembers this selfish, provoking man who means so much to her. She knows him with greater assurance than she can ever know her deliberate and, in fact, rather mystic husband. She remembers the many nights and the mornings with a tenderness she has never felt toward Muhlbach. Thus Sandy Kirk finds her appraising him and he glances uneasily toward her husband: Muhlbach is absorbed by the snow clinging to the window panes.

It is decided that the guests shall sit at the table and drink coffee while dinner is served the host and hostess; there is no other solution. And they will all have dessert together. The cook thinks this very queer and each time she is summoned to the dining room she manages a good bourgeois look at the ballerina.

Around the mahogany oval they sit for quite a long time, Muhlbach the only one with an appetite. Once Joyce Muhlbach lifts her feverish gaze to the ceiling because the children's bedroom is just overhead and she has heard something too faint for anyone else, but it was not a significant noise and soon she resumes listening to Sandy Kirk, who is describing life in Geneva. He says there is a tremendous fountain like a geyser in the lake, and from the terrace of the casino it is one of the most compelling sights in the world. Presently he tells about Lausanne farther up the lake, its old-world streets rising steeply above the water, and from there he takes everyone in seven-league boots to Berne and on to Interlaken where the Jungfrau is impossible to believe even if you are standing in its shadow.

Muhlbach clears his throat. "You are probably not aware of the fact, but my parents were born in Zurich. I can recall them speaking of the good times they used to have there." And he goes on to tell about one or two of these good times. They sound very dull as he gives them, owing in part to his habit of pausing midway to cut, chew, and swallow some roast beef. It occurs to him that Kirk may speak German so he asks the simplest question, "Sprechen Sie Deutsch?" Conversation in German affords him a kind of nourishment, much the same as his customary evening walk around the block, but aside from his mother, who now lives in an upstate sanatorium, there is no one to speak it with him. Joyce has never cared much for the language and it appears that Otto will grow up with a limited vocabulary.

Kirk replies, "Nein. Spanisch und Französisch und Italienisch." To Kirk the abrupt question was disconcerting because he had fancied himself the only one capable of anything beyond English. He has come to this home with the expectation of meeting a deadly familiar type of man, a competent merchant who habitually locked his brain at five o'clock, and Kirk is trying to remain convinced that this is the case. Muhlbach admits to not having traveled anywhere dangerously far from the commuter's line, south of Washington, say, or west of Niagara, and it is one of Sandy Kirk's prime theses that a stay-at-home entertains a meager form of life. The world, as anyone knows, was made to be lived in, and to remain in one place means that you are going to miss what is happening somewhere else. All the same Kirk sports a few doubts about his philosophy and so he occasionally finds it reassuring to convince other people that he is right. He has a talent for evocation and will often act out his stories, tiptoeing across the room and peering this way and that as though he were negotiating the Casbah with a bulging wallet. Or he will mimic an Italian policeman beating his breast and slapping his forehead over the criminal audacity of a pedestrian. Very droll does Sandy Kirk become after a suitable drink; then one must forgive his manifold weaknesses, one must recognize the farcical side of life. Thus he is popular wherever he goes; it is a rare hostess who can manage to stay exasperated with him all evening.

He seems to present the same personality no matter what the situation: always he has just done something wrong and is contrite. He telephones at a quarter of eight to explain that he will be a little late to some eight o'clock engagement. "Well, where are you now?" they ask, because his voice sounds rather distant, and it turns out he is calling from another city. But he is there by midnight and has brought an orchid to expiate the sin. Naturally the hostess is furious and wishes him to understand he cannot escape so easily, but her cutting stare is quite in vain because he can no more be wounded than he can be reformed. One accepts him as he is, or not at all.

Now he has taken them through the Prado, pausing an instant in the gloom-filled upper chambers for a look at Goya's merciless etchings, gone on to Fez and Constantine and swiftly brought them back to Venice, where a proper British girl is being followed by a persistent Italian. She will have nothing to do with this Italian, will not speak to him nor so much as admit he lives, despite the most audible and most extraordinary invitations. Now a man must maintain his self-respect, observes Kirk with a dignified wink, so all at once the frustrated Italian seizes her and flings her into the Grand Canal, and wrapping his coat like a Renaissance cloak around his shoulders he strides regally off into the night. Such are the stories he tells in any of a hundred accents, and no one can be certain where truth and fiction amalgamate, least of all the narrator. He speaks incessantly of where he has been, what he has done, and the marvels he has seen. Oh, he is a character—so exclaims everyone who knows him. It is amazing that such a façade can exist in front of a dead serious career, but he is a minor official of the State Department and puzzles everyone by mumbling in a lugubrious way that his job is expendable and when the next election comes around they may look for him selling apples on the corner. Still, he travels here and there and draws his pay, rather good pay, no matter who is elected. It is suspected that he is quite brilliant, but if so he never gives any evidence of it: one second he is a perfect handbook of slang, the next he becomes impossibly punctilious. It is difficult to decide whether he is burlesquing himself or his listeners.

The Muhlbachs are content to listen, regardless, because there is little enough drama at home and this visitor floats about like a trade wind of sorts, bearing a suggestion of incense and the echo of Arab cymbals. His wallet came from Florence—"a little shop not far from the Uffizi," he will answer—and his shoes were made in Stockholm. They can hardly equal his fables by telling how sick young Otto was the previous summer, even though he spent several weeks in a hospital bed and required transfusions. It was a blood disease and they were fortunate that one of Muhlbach's business partners had contracted the same thing as a child and could supply the antitoxin.

Nor can they explain the curious pathos everyone felt over a situation the doctor created. It happened on the worst day of the illness, when they had at last come to believe he could not get well. While the doctor was examining him Otto became conscious, and to divert him the doctor asked how he would like to attend the circus that evening. Otto thought that would be fine and managed enough strength to nod.

So they agreed that the doctor should call for him at six o'clock sharp that they might have time to reach the grounds ahead of the crowd and secure the best possible seats. Otto then relapsed into a coma from which he was not supposed to recover, but one eye opened around five o'clock in the afternoon and he spoke with absolute lucidity, asking what time it was. There could be no doubt that the speaker must be either Otto or his reincarnation because he has always been fearfully concerned over the time. By five-thirty he was certain he should be getting dressed and by six o'clock he had begun to sob with frustration because the nurse prevented him from sitting up. When they sought to pacify him by means of a teaspoonful of ice cream he rejected it with pitiful violence. His father's promise of a trike when he got well was received with an irritated hiccup. In vain did they explain that the doctor had been teasing; Otto knew better. Any moment the door would open and they would all be dumbfounded. The clock ticked along, Otto watching desperately. The hand moved down and started up, and finally started down again. Then he knew for the first time those pangs that come after one has been lied to.

But perhaps it was not unjustified; they had thought he would leave them and he did not, and scars on a heart are seldom seen.

Meanwhile the cook has been acting superior. Around the table she walks and pours fresh coffee with her nose in the air as though its fragrance were offensive. She stumbles against Miss Borowski's chair, does this sure-footed cook. What can the matter be? And she is so careless in pouring that coffee slops over the cup into the saucer. It is true the cook apologizes, but her resentment is implicit and there follows a baffled silence at the table.

Joyce Muhlbach perceives the cause. The cook is jealous of the ballerina. But who can imagine the cook in tights? It would take two partners to lift her. Here is an amiable creature shaped like a seal, beloved of her employers and playing Olympian roles to a respectful audience of Otto and Donna, yet unhappy. She has found a soubrette at her master's table and is bursting with spite. She too would be carried triumphantly across a stage. Rather great tragedies may be enacted in the secrecy of the heart; at this moment something very like a tear is shining in the cook's artless eye.

Joyce again is listening to a sound upstairs. She is attuned to nothing with such delicacy as to the events of the nursery. Donna will cough only once, muffled by the pillow, yet her mother hears and considers the import. Is it the cough of incipient disease, or nothing but the uncertain functioning of babyhood? Accordingly she acts. To her husband everything sounds approximately the same, but that is the way with husbands, who notice everything a little late. Good man that he is, he cannot even learn how to tell a joke, but must always preface it with a hearty laugh and the advice that his listeners had better get set to split their sides. Of course it is all one can do to smile politely when Muhlbach, after ten minutes of chuckling and backtracking and clearing his throat, gets around to the point. Kirk would tell it with a fumbled phrase and be midway through another tale before his audience caught up with the first one.

She surveys them both as though from a great distance and knows that she loves them both, her husband because he needs her love, and Kirk because he does not. She half-hears the dancer asking if Sandy has changed since she knew him.

Again comes a stamping on the walk outside, but heavier than were the feet of Kirk. This is the sound of big men thumping snow from their boots. Everyone hears and looks through the archway toward the front door—that is, everyone except Joyce, who has instantly looked at her husband. Kirk from the corner of his eyes has taken in this fact and for the first time becomes aware of the strength of this marriage; no matter what happens she will look first at her husband and react according to him. There is something old and legendary about this instinct of hers, something that has to do with trust. Kirk feels a clutch of envy at his heart; when he and she were together she did not necessarily look to him whenever anything happened; he had always thought her totally self-sufficient. Now Muhlbach turns back to the table, frowning, and considers his wife, but when she cannot supply the answer he crumples his napkin, places it alongside his plate, and goes to the door. They hear him open the peephole, call someone by name, and immediately swing open the door.

Cold and huge they come in, two men. Duck hunters they are. One is John Grimes and the other is always referred to as "Uncle." Muhlbach, appearing overjoyed, insists that they come into the dining room, so after a few moments they do, though Uncle is reluctant. Both men are dressed in corduroy and heavy canvas. Grimes also wears a brilliant crimson mackinaw to which a few flakes of snow are clinging, and while he stands there boldly grinning the snow melts and begins to drip from the edges of his mackinaw onto the dining-room carpet. His pockets bulge with shotgun shells. His gigantic hands are swollen and split from the weather.

Behind him, away from the circle of light, stands Uncle, who is long and solemn and bent like a tree in the wind. His canvas jacket is open, revealing a murderous sheath knife at the belt; its hilt looks bloody. Dangling by a frayed strap over one of his bony shoulders is a wicker fishing creel, exhausted through years of use, from which a few yellowed weeds poke out. He has a bad cold and attends to it by snuffling every few seconds, or by wiping his nose on the cuff of his jacket. Obviously he is more accustomed to kitchens than to dining rooms, nor would he seem out of place in overalls testifying at a revival. He grins and grins, quite foolishly, exposing teeth like crooked tombstones, and when he speaks there is always the feeling that he is about to say something bawdy. But he is considered a great hunter; it is a rare animal or bird that can escape from Uncle. At present he is gaping at Miss Borowski. Uncle recognizes her as an unfamiliar piece of goods but is not altogether certain what. Borowski returns the stare with contempt.

Both hunters smell acrid and salty. About them wells a devastating aboriginal perfume of wood smoke, fish, the blood of ducks, tobacco, wet canvas, beer, and the perspiration of three inchoate weeks. Sandy Kirk got up slowly when they came in. No longer the center of attention, he stands with his napkin loosely in one hand and watches what goes on, making no attempt to join the bantering conversation. Astutely he measures John Grimes. With one glance he has read Uncle's book but this Grimes is anomalous: he might be a politician or a lawyer or some kind of professional strongman. Above all this duck hunter is masculine. The cumbersome mackinaw rides as lightly on him as does the angora sweater on Borowski. His very presence has subtly dictated the terms of the assembly: he rejects the status of guest and demands that he be distinguished primarily as a man; therefore Joyce and the dancer find themselves reduced to being women. By way of emphasis there looms behind him that sullen scarecrow known as Uncle with a few whiskers curling under his chin, in his awkwardness equally male.

The duck hunter feels himself scrutinized and swiftly turns his head to confront Sandy Kirk. For an instant they gaze at each other without pretense; then they are civilized and exchange nods, whereupon the hunter smiles confidently. Kirk frowns a little. Whirling around, Grimes makes a playful snatch at Uncle's chin as if to grab him by the whiskers. "Try to kill me, will you?" says he, and turns up the collar of the mackinaw to display a tiny black hole caused by a shot. At this Uncle begins to paw the floor and to protest but at that moment is petrified by an oncoming sneeze that doubles him up as though Grimes had punched him in the stomach. He emerges with a red beak and watery eyes and begins hunting through his filthy jacket for a handkerchief, which turns out to be the size of a bandanna.

John Grimes snorts and grins hugely. This further mortifies Uncle. The two of them look as though they can hardly restrain their spirits after three weeks in the forest and may suddenly begin wrestling on the carpet.

The cook has pushed open the kitchen door and is having a necessary look. Everyone is aware of her; she is not subtle about anything. She seems particularly struck by the fact that both men are wearing knitted woolen caps—John Grimes' is black as chimney soot and Uncle's is a discolored turtle green. It is curious what a cap will do. A cap is like a beret in that when you see someone wearing it you can hardly keep from staring. Cook has seen these men dozens of times but looks from one to the other in stupefaction. She is not unjustified because the headgear causes Uncle to appear even taller and skinnier and more despondent than he is; if ever he straightens up, the pompom of his cap must certainly scrape the ceiling. At last, conscious that she herself is beginning to attract attention, though she knows not why, cook allows the kitchen door to close.

But another rubberneck is discovered. Near the top of the stairs a pinched white face looks through the railing, and of course it is Otto come out to see what this is all about. He resembles a lemur clutching the bars of some unusual cage, or a tarsier perhaps, with his impossibly large ears and eyes wide open for nocturnal prowling. Like the cook, Otto finds himself on display; he becomes defensive and starts to back out of sight but is asked what he thinks he is doing up there.

"I want a drink," says Otto piteously and quite automatically. He has been on the stairs for ten minutes listening without comprehension to a description of the camp in the forest. He comes partway downstairs, holding on to the banister, and as the chandelier light falls upon him it may be seen that if there is anything on earth he does not need it is a drink: his belly is so distended with water that the front of his pajamas has popped open. Unconscious of his ribald figure, he asks, "Who are all those men?" He cares who they are, more or less, but the main thing is to turn the conversation upon someone else. While his mother is buttoning up his front he is trenchantly introduced to the hunters.

"Are they company?"

They are. The lack of repartee following his question implies he is unpopular, but Otto scintillates.

"What are they *doing?*"

It should be clear to anyone that the hunters are standing at the mahogany sideboard where the good cook has poured them each a cup of coffee. They are too wet to sit down anywhere. Otto studies them from top to bottom and says he thinks Donna needs to go to the toilet. Will someone come upstairs and see? The nurse is upstairs. If either of them needs anything the nurse will take care of the matter. Otto feels the balance of power swinging away from him; unfortunately he cannot think of anything to say, anything at all. He stands on the bottom step with his belly out like a cantaloupe and those dark eyes—the gift of his mother—wondering. There is nothing special on his mind when he complains that he wants to see the ducks; in fact he hardly knows what he said and is startled that it has gotten a reaction.

Grimes and Uncle have bagged a few over their legal limit, to be sure, but that is not the reason they have brought some to the Muhlbachs. At any rate two fat mallards are lying on the front porch and Otto is allowed to watch through the closest window while Uncle goes outside to get them. Otto mashes his hot moist face against the chilled glass and is quiet. They do not look like ducks to him, but that is what his father said; therefore they must be ducks.

Uncle stoops to catch each mallard by a foot. Already the birds are freezing to the step and when he pulls them up they resist; Otto sees that a few feathers remain on the concrete. The front door opens for a second while Uncle comes in, each bird hanging by one foot so that its other yellow web seems to be waving good-by. The heads swing underneath. The male looks almost a yard long—it cannot be that big, of course, but Grimes and Uncle, who is still snuffling, agree it is the biggest mallard they have ever seen. Around its green neck is a lovely white band; Otto reaches out hesitantly to discover if it is real. The neck feathers are cool and soft. The female is a mottled brown and buff, a small one, not much more than half the length of the male. They are dead, this Otto knows, but he is not certain what death is, only that one must watch out for it.

John Grimes takes each bird around the middle and everyone is a little surprised when the heads rise, just as though they had finished feeding, but the reason is simple: the necks have frozen. Grimes holds both mallards up high; he cracks the cold orange beaks together and smiles down at Otto.

"Quack! Quack!" blurts Uncle.

Otto knows who made the noise and pointedly ignores Uncle, but he cannot get enough of staring at the refulgent bodies. He has never seen anything so green or of such tender brown. The breasts are full and perfect; to find out what has killed them one must feel around in those feathers, parting them here and there with the fingertips, until the puncture is suddenly disclosed.

Otto is subdued, and when the episode of the ducks is ended, when they have been taken roughly into the kitchen and nothing more can be said of them, he must struggle to regain his plaintive tone. Now there is not a chance it will be successful, but he says he thinks Donna would like a drink. It is not successful. However, there are two big guns that Otto always keeps in reserve; one is that he believes he is getting a stomachache and the other is that he is afraid the stars are falling. He is no fool, this Otto, and realizes that if he tries them both on the same evening he will be found out. He studies his bare feet like a politician and estimates which question would be more effective, considering the fact that there are some ducks in the house and that his mother has been in bed all day. He begins to look wonderfully ill at ease.

"Are the stars falling down?"

Always that is good for an answer, a long melodious one, always. But tonight it is met by a grim stare from his father. He looks hopefully at his mother; she is not so ominous but equally firm. There is about the atmosphere something that tells Otto he might soon be turned across his father's knee. He elects to retreat and backs toward the stairway, wondering if he could reasonably ask for the dog-in-the-manger again. His father places both hands flat on the table, which means he is going to stand up. Otto abandons all hope, and, wearing a persecuted face,

goes up the stairs as rapidly as possible, which is to say in the manner
of a chimpanzee.

Almost immediately there is a crash in the upstairs hall followed by
the unmistakable sound of Otto falling. Once again he has forgotten
about the hall table. Originally there was a vase on this table but after
he destroyed it while hurrying to the bathroom they reasoned that
sooner or later he would take the same route; hence there is nothing
but a lace doily on the table. In fact, Muhlbach finds it a senseless place
to put a table, but his wife wants it there, though she cannot explain
why. Otto is bellowing. To listen to him one would be convinced that
in all history no individual has ever experienced such pain. He varies
pitch, rhyme, and tempo as he recalls the tragedy; it is a regular Oriental concert. The footsteps of the nurse are heard, and the matter of
her scientific soothing, but he will have none of this professional.

Joyce gets up from the table, but in passing behind Muhlbach's chair
an expression of nausea overspreads her face and she almost sinks to
the floor but recovers without a sound. Kirk starts to cry out, and
upon seeing her straighten up he emits a weird groan. Dee Borowski
and Muhlbach gaze at him very curiously.

Otto can still be heard, although the sincerity of his dirge may
now be questioned. At any rate he has been carried to bed, where the
nurse swabs his bumped forehead with mercurochrome and covers
it with a fantastic bandage that he seems to enjoy touching. Still he is
so exhausted by the hour, the splendor of the ducks, the strange men,
and the accident in the mysterious hallway that it is necessary to continue whimpering. This self-indulgence halts the instant he becomes
aware that his father has entered the room. Otto prepares himself like
any rascal for he knows not what judgment, and cannot conceal his
apprehension when his father draws up a chair and sits wearily beside
the bed. They talk for a while. Otto does not know what they are talking about. Sometimes they discuss his mother, sometimes himself, or
Donna. He industriously maintains his end of the conversation though
he feels himself growing sleepy, and in time he is neither displeased
nor alarmed to feel the hand of his father stroking his head. Somewhat
groggily he inquires if the stars are falling. In addition to being a useful
question, Otto is moderately afraid of just such a catastrophe. He did
not come upon this idea secondhand, but thought of it himself. The
first time it occurred to him he began to weep and though a number

of months have gone by so that he trusts the sky a little more he is still not altogether confident. One cannot be sure when a star is falling. Clearly there is nothing to hold them in place. Why should one not suddenly drop on his bed?

Countless nights, in winter and spring, autumn and summer, have Otto and his father gone out of doors, or sometimes driven toward the country far enough that the city lights were less obtrusive, and here, with the boy on his father's lap, they have considered what was above. At first there was a certain difficulty in communication. For example, Muhlbach discussed the planets and stars while Otto listened with profound concentration. Muhlbach was impressed until Otto, after a period of deep thought, inquired if Donna was a star, a question that might be answered in various ways, of course, depending. But with practice they began to understand each other so that after several months Otto grew familiar with the elementary legends and was apt to request his favorites, such as Andromeda, or The Twins. Or he might ask to hear that wonderfully euphonious index to the Great Bear, which goes: Alkaid, Mizar, Alioth, Megrez, Phecda, Merak, and Dubhe.

"What does the bear eat?" he asks, and this is certainly a question packed with logic. His father's faith is renewed; the lessons continue. Not far behind the bear—do you see?—comes Arcturus, its warden, who follows the animal about. This happens to be the father's personal favorite among the stars because it was the first one he himself ever learned to recognize, and was taught him by his own father, the very same who gave young Otto the archaeology book. Muhlbach hopes that Otto will learn Arcturus before any other. This is the reason he points to it first of all. He directs the flashlight beam toward this yellow giant, so many times larger than the sun, and though Muhlbach has searched the heavens with a flashlight numberless times he is yet amazed that this light appears to reach all the way.

We can never go there, Otto. It is too far. Muhlbach includes a few statistics and is again deluded by his son's intelligent expression because it develops that what Otto wishes to know is whether or not Arcturus is farther away than downtown. Still, hope springs eternal, and after smoking half a cigar Muhlbach has recovered from the blow enough to try again. Once upon a time—yes, this is the right approach—once upon a time Arcturus came flying straight toward the earth! What do you think of that? Otto is shaken by the premise; in his father's lap he sits erect and anxious, no doubt pondering what will happen when they meet, or met, since it is all in the past. Half-a-million years, for that matter, and Muhlbach, now savoring parenthood to the utmost, adds with a sportive air that the sole observers were troglodytes. Otto lets this pass. Now Muhlbach hesitates because he has pumped up his story; the full truth is that Arcturus was also drifting a bit to the side as if it approached and even now is passing us so there is not to be a collision after all. Fortunately Otto considers the telling of greater value than the tale. He is not much gripped by explanation or hypothesis; he would as soon just look. One would think he was gazing into a mountain lake. According to his father they can see perhaps three or four thousand stars in the sky; Otto again looks up and is stunned, though for a better reason. He is a pure voluptuary, a first-rate knight of the carpet. Sidereal time, relative motion, and years of light are all very well—astronomy, in short, can come or go, so Otto feels—but stars are magnificent. Briefly he is held by the constancy of Arcturus; then he loses it. There are a great many things in the sky. How shall he hold fast to one? When he is older he will distinguish more clearly but now a light is a light, each about as effective as its neighbor. Now he has been seduced by Mars. It seems bigger and more suggestive. What could he not accomplish if only he held it in his hand! As there is no moon, and Sirius is down, nothing can be more glamorous. How red it is! How wondrous bright! In vain does Muhlbach point out Pollux and Castor, Procyon, Regulus.

In his bedroom the little boy sleeps with one arm raised and a fist clenched as if in triumph, on his helpless face a stubborn look, his forehead all but invisible under the preposterous mercurochrome-soaked bandage. Muhlbach sits beside his son, watching and thinking. The bedroom is silent but for the breathing of the two children. The nurse has gone downstairs. After a while Muhlbach rises and walks soberly across the room to stand above his daughter; her pink jade lips are parted and it is clear her dream is a serious one. Muhlbach wonders if she will sleep until spring. He longs to pick her up, somehow to unfold himself and conceal her deep within, and he bends down until their faces are an inch apart.

He hears the front door close, the faint after-knock of the brass lion's head on the outside of the door. He moves on tiptoe to the window and looks down at his two friends, the duck hunters, who elect to tramp across the snowy lawn even though the walk has been shoveled. He looks at his watch to discover he has been up here almost a half-hour. He very much wanted to go hunting this year, possibly more than ever before; each time this thought comes to him he feels unutterably disgusted with himself.

Uncle and Grimes leave dark symmetrical prints on the snow and as always Uncle is one step behind. There is no reason for this; it is just the way they are. It comes to Muhlbach that John Grimes is leading his afreet by a chain round the neck. He watches them get into Grimes' car, sees the headlights flash and thus notices that the snow has stopped falling, and moodily he looks after the burning red tail lights until the street is again deserted. That snowy rectangle over which they walked oddly resembles the eight of spades; and now the half-moon comes floating above the rooftops as if to join in this curious game. Much higher—well along in the night—kneels the father image, Orion. While Muhlbach stands at the window the moon's light descends calmly upon his troubled face and reaches beyond him into the nursery past Donna's crib to the wall poignantly desecrated by paste and crayon scribbles. There a swan is in flight. Otto has seen fit to improve this wallpaper swan. What could be gained by telling him its elegance is perhaps impaired by the measles he has added? Muhlbach thinks over the shards remaining from his own childhood, but is conscious mostly of how much has perished.

Some time longer he stands there steeping himself in this restorative moonlight and looks around with approval at the knotty pine toy shelf he has knocked together and varnished, and again remarks the silence of this night which is counterpointed by the breath of his children. An unimpressive man he is, who shows a little paunch and the beginning of a stoop, though otherwise no older than forty warrants. People do not ever turn around to look at him on the street. At cocktail parties no feminine gaze lingers on him. When it comes to business there are men who find it worthwhile to seek out Muhlbach for an opinion; otherwise he is left alone.

Quietly but without disappointment he leaves the nursery, shuts the door, and descends the staircase hopeful that his wife has recognized the futility of this evening. It strikes him as incredible that she can maintain interest in a man she has outgrown.

When he enters the living room the nurse slips back upstairs. Sandy Kirk and Joyce are making no attempt to communicate; they sit side by side on the sofa but behave like strangers seated together at a movie. Borowski appears hypnotized by the embers; she has taken off her shoes and placed them neatly like an offering on the marble hearth. Muhlbach finds her naïveté wearisome and he thinks that if she does anything else ingenuous he will lose his manners and become rude. She does not even blink when he strides past; she does nothing but dully watch the subsiding flames, her mouth idiotically open. From his chair beside the bookcase he glowers at her, and it suddenly occurs to him that he is sick of the cook, too, and sick of the relentless nurse. He is sick to death of life itself and of the solicitous neighbors, and he has forgotten whatever is not despair. Too much is happening to him; all he wants is to be left alone that he may regain some measure of his inner strength. Even one hour, uninterrupted, might be enough. He thinks he cannot pretend much longer. His thoughts turn upon Goethe, from whom he is remotely descended, and he visualizes that man interminably searching himself for power while playing to his sycophants a stiff-legged excellence.

All at once his wife trembles; she bites her lip over some private thought, and looking at him she remarks, just loud enough to be heard, that John Grimes and Uncle left minutes ago.

Muhlbach, struggling against disorder, allows himself a few seconds before replying, "I know, I know."

Sandy Kirk rouses himself, picks up a magazine and fans his cheek as if only now he realizes how suffocating the room has become. Muhlbach, watching Kirk, is filled with hatred; it seems to him that never before has he encountered a man he despises so much.

"They missed you," his wife continues, "but I told them you'd go hunting again next year."

In this speech there is a note of self-pity that causes Muhlbach to shut his eyes and throw up his hands, though he does not say a word.

"I told them I was being selfish but I want you with me every minute of the time. Next year they'll have you the same as before." Having started she cannot stop; she turns swiftly upon Sandy Kirk and presses one of his limp hands to her breast. Her eyes fill with tears but except for this she appears peeved, resentful, and she talks compulsively. Words pour from her nerveless mouth without meaning and Kirk is obviously terrified. He stares at her out of the corner of his eye like a trapped animal; he is powerless to recover his hand. Muhlbach scowls at Dee Borowski who has turned around to watch, and he knows that she is aware of him, but she cannot get enough of the nauseating scene; she must look and look. Muhlbach springs out of his chair and rushes into the kitchen.

Sandy Kirk turns his head this way and that to avoid looking at Joyce. All the precautions he took, they were no good. She has not respected any convention; she has lunged through every defense and taken him. Even under the circumstances it was not decent of her to do that. She has always shocked him one way or another, even the first time they met. He had been a college student then and one afternoon was standing on a snowy bluff overlooking a river that had frozen close to shore. He had brought along a sled and was wondering if he dared coast down because the slope was studded with pinnacles of rock; furthermore, if he could not stop in time there was a very good possibility of crashing through the ice and drowning. Then he noticed this girl trudging up with a sled. When he warned her it was unsafe she replied, "Mind your own business," and without hesitation flung herself upon the sled, hurtled down among the rocks, and reappeared far out on the ice, wriggling to a stop not five yards from the water. That was the way she did everything. Now she is twenty-nine years old—an aged, wasted old woman who can scarcely walk without assistance. Her arms have shriveled to the bone and the veins are black.

Kirk is furious that Borowski has not reacted the way she was supposed to. When at last he had gathered the will to speak, to interrupt the horrible monologue, and pointedly mentioned *Don Juan*, the dancer only looked at him in stupefaction. So he has not distracted Joyce, she has still got him, hanging on, but then he recovers his voice, that familiar ally, and all by itself his voice starts to tell about something funny that once happened in Switzerland. Kirk waves his free arm and rolls his eyes comically toward the ceiling until at last, thank God, Muhlbach comes out of the kitchen. It is over, Joyce loosens her grip and he begins to pull his fingers away one at a time.

With an ingratiating tone Sandy Kirk addresses Muhlbach, who gives back a clinical stare and stretches out his hands to the fire. Seeing this calm gesture of self-assurance, seeing as it were, a true *Hofmeister*,

Kirk suffers a familiar malaise, for among diplomats and intellectuals, or artists of any description, he feels established, but faced with a solid pedestrian he loses confidence in his own wit and commences to doubt the impression he is making. It has always been so, though for the life of him Sandy Kirk fails to understand why. And this Muhlbach is indestructible, a veritable storm cellar of a man. No catastrophe will ever uproot him or confuse him, this man of the flatlands with a compass on his forehead. Kirk is envious, and also contemptuous. He is a little afraid of Muhlbach. He has finally managed to draw the captive arm away from Joyce, yet she clings mutely with her eyes. He feels sorry for her and wishes he could feel more, but there it is: she seems to him unreal and distorted, not the girl he once knew. This sick woman is distasteful. In the future he may feel some compassion, but this evening she has driven him backward till he has begun to grow violent. If she does not soon release him altogether he will throw a fit. He cannot stand being forced this way, being accustomed to having what he wants only when he wants it. During intolerable situations Sandy Kirk always envisions himself in some favorite locale thousands of miles away. It is a form of ballast. And now he decides to imagine himself in Biarritz seated regally on the hillside on his favorite bench. From there he would contemplate the Atlantic sun shining on red-tile rooftops, and after an expensive supper he might wander into the casino to luxuriate in the sound of clicking, rattling chips, and the suave tones of croupiers.

Otto has wakened; he can be heard talking to the nurse about something, no doubt vital. A jack-in-the-box will go down for the night more easily than will Otto. Recently he has taken to singing in the middle of the night; he disturbs everyone in the house with his pagan lament. "What are you singing about?" he will be asked, but he always refuses to answer.

Just then the phone rings. Who could be calling at such an hour? Sandy Kirk, like a doctor, must always leave word of his whereabouts, and so does the dancer, though with more hope than expectation. As usual the actual message is less exciting than the suspense. Joyce, whose call it was, returns to the living room almost immediately. She seems more vexed than she has been all evening and after resting for a minute she mimics the inquisitive neighbor.

"'I saw your lights were still on and simply thought I must find out if there was anything I could do.' She got a couple of ducks, too. Your friends are dreadfully generous."

Muhlbach makes no attempt to reply. He shakes his head as if he can endure nothing more.

Joyce Muhlbach's voice begins to rise unsteadily. "I told her not to telephone! I told that woman to let us alone!"

Borowski has emerged from her private reverie long enough to gobble this up, and Muhlbach, who was watching her, is again filled with loathing. Little by little everyone in the room becomes aware that a group of carol singers is approaching, and finally, in passing the Muhlbach home, their song is clear. The voices are young; most likely a group of students.

After they have gone Joyce slowly resumes twisting her wedding ring; it is loose on her finger and slides off easily, hesitating only at the knuckles. She takes it off and puts it on and all at once remarks that she has received an ad from a mortuary. In this there is something so ghoulish that it is almost impossible not to laugh. Her husband of course knows about the advertisement, but the guests have a tense moment. Joyce glances from one to the other in a malicious way, twisting her ring and sliding it off, waiting to see if either of them dare smile.

Borowski becomes flustered. "Sandy has told me everything about you." This gets no response at all. Borowski turns red and says that Joyce meant a great deal to Sandy years ago. Neither was that the proper speech, so Borowski glares at Sandy Kirk because it is his fault she has gotten into this situation.

Joyce is suddenly aware that Donna has wakened, and though not a sound comes from the upstairs nursery this same knowledge reaches Muhlbach a second later. Both of them wait. He glances across the room to her and she catches the look solidly as if she had been expecting it. Kirk guesses they have heard one of the children and he recalls that earlier instant when they reacted as a unit, causing him to sense how deeply they were married. He is a little injured that they mean this much to each other; he feels that Joyce has betrayed him. He knew her long before Muhlbach ever did. It is as if something valuable slipped away, disappeared while he was preoccupied. Now he thinks that he intended to come back to Joyce. They would have gone well together, and he knows that whatever Muhlbach may have brought her, he did not bring something she has always needed—excitement. This intelligent, sober, prosaic man escorted her into a barren little room, a cool study where she has withered. Kirk feels himself growing embittered over the way life has treated him. This woman was rightfully his own, even if she refused to admit it. There were instances, it is true, when she became tyrannical, but later she would always repent; and if he should abuse her he had only to hang his head until her eye grew milder. To his mind comes the observation of one of those lugubrious Russians: that from the fearful medley of thoughts and impressions accumulated in man's brain from association with women, the memory, like a filter, retains no ideas, no clever sayings, no philosophy, nothing in fact but that extraordinary resignation to fate, that wonderful mercifulness, forgiveness of everything.

The longer Kirk sits in the room with Muhlbach's wife the more does he perceive how terribly he is still in love with her. He has been afraid this would happen. She is one of those legendary creatures whom the French have so astutely named *femme fatale*. One does not recover. Kirk permits himself a furtive look at the husband. Yes, he has been stricken too.

What kind of a woman is she? One talks to her a little while of this or that, nothing remarkable is said, nothing in the least memorable, and one goes away. Then, all uninvited, comes a feeling of dreadful urgency and one must hurry back. Again nothing is said. She is not witty, nor is she beautiful; she is in fact frequently dour and sullen without cause. Periods of gloomy silence occur, yet no sense of emptiness, no uneasiness. She seems to wait for what is about to happen. It is all very confusing. Sandy Kirk broods, puzzles, gazes hopelessly into space for vast amounts of time thinking of nothing, unable to formulate questions worth asking himself, much less answer, feeling nothing at all but a kind of dull, unhealthy desire.

He steals another look at Muhlbach and discovers in that stolid face a similar misery, which makes Kirk feel better. He remembers with embarrassment certain phone calls during which he was unable to speak. "Hello," he will mumble, already despondent at the thought that she is listening. "Is that you?" And when she replies, sounding stubborn, or irked that he has telephoned at such an inconvenient hour, then every single thought explodes like a soap bubble. He waits anxiously to hear what she will say next, which is nothing: he is the one who has called, it is up to him to manufacture a little conversation. But he is destroyed by aphasia, he finds nothing humorous about life, not a thing worth repeating. What has he been doing? Well, quite a lot but now, thinking about it, what is worth the effort of describing? He summons all his strength: "What have *you* been doing?" He has just managed to mutter this. She replies in an exhausted voice that she has not done anything worth mentioning. This is impossible! He mumbles something about the fact that he has been thinking of her and called to find out what she was doing—what a stupid thing to say, he realizes, and discovers to his amazement that he is clutching the telephone as if he were trying to strangle it. The wire has been silent for five minutes. He prays no operator has decided to investigate this odd business or he will be locked up for insanity, and in a voice more dead than alive he demands, "Are we going out tonight?" He is positive she will say no, and that is exactly what she does say. Instantly he is filled with alarm and wants to know why not; she replies callously that she doesn't want to see him ever again but offers no explanation. He subsides. He leans against the wall with his eyes closed. He has not eaten all day but is not hungry. Minutes pass. Neither of them speaks. It is raining, of course; water splashes dismally on the window ledge and life is implacably gray. One cannot imagine sunshine, laughter, happiness. He staggers and understands that he was falling asleep. He whispers good-by and waits. She immediately answers good-bye. Neither hangs up. Love is not supposed to be like this. He announces his good-bye again with renewed vigor just as though he were rushing out to the golf course, but the mummery sickens him. There is no significant click at the other end of the line. What is she waiting for? Will she never release him? Can she possibly expect him to hang up first? Life is a wretched joke. He cannot abide the sound of his own name. Still she refuses to hang up the receiver, and it goes on and on, a long, dreary, stupid, incon-clusive affair. These calls have on occasion lasted a full hour or more, though neither of them said a good minute's worth. How desperate was the need to communicate, how impotent the message. So when he sees her he wants to know why she does not talk to him over the telephone, and she looks at him without a smile.

Kirk decides he is losing his mind. Has Muhlbach, that barn of a man, disgraced himself in a similar manner? Because normal men do not ignore their pride. Yet look at those tormented eyes! It is clear

that he, too, has fallen apart in front of her. There could be no other
explanation.

Kirk will never forget one night he went shambling through the
streets without enough energy to lift his head until all at once, as
though he had been handed a telegram, he started rapidly across the
city, rushed through Times Square with his eye fastened on Forty-
fourth Street, and just around the corner there she was! What fantastic
perception could account for this? And she seemed to be waiting—
expecting him! Yet she was anchored securely to the arm of some
nondescript man in a bow tie. As they passed each other he nodded
curtly and stalked into the crowd. What a lover does he make! What
happened to the celestial phrase? He is the sort of man who would
address the wrong balcony. Even his agony is fraudulent because he
is hoping everybody on the street notices his tragic face. He thinks
he could not be more obvious with the stigmata; still, nobody paused
when he strode somberly toward the river. Well, he has been through
no grimmer night than that one. It might have made sense if she had
been a famous beauty, but even in those days no one ever picked Joyce
out of a group. She never was quick on her feet, or had a musical
voice, nor did her skin ever take the light, as the artists say. And how
did they know—both of them—that they were destined to meet just
around the corner?

At this instant the cook appears, not in her black uniform but in a
rather shocking dress. She has finished every dish and emptied the garbage and now she would like permission to go home. Muhlbach calls
a taxi for her. Cook bids goodnight to everyone, to everyone except
the ballerina, and then she returns to the pantry where she will sit like
a monument on her favorite stool to brood until the taxicab arrives.
All have noticed her going upstairs a few minutes ago with a sweet
for the children. She wakes them up to feed them something that will
ruin their teeth; nothing can break her of this habit. Neither explanation nor threat of dismissal deter this cook, not even the formidable
nurse. Cook is of the opinion the children are her own and it is clear
that her heart would fall open like an overripe melon if Muhlbach ever
made good his threat. The nurse and the cook look upon one another
as hereditary enemies and neither questions that this should be so.
Nurse dislikes going into the kitchen and while there is apt to sit with
arms crossed and a severe expression. Cook feeds her without a word,

stinting just a little, and afterward scrubs the dishes quite fiercely. She has never seen this nurse before; who can tell how reliable the creature is? Cook believes this nurse is neglecting the babies and thus it is she sneaks upstairs at least once a night. That is why, when Muhlbach calls for something, there may be silence in the kitchen.

All at once comes the sound of a shot. Conversation stops in the living room. There are no cars on the street, so it could not have been a backfire, and besides it sounded as though it were in the house. Muhlbach is about to investigate when at the head of the stairway appears the nurse, dreadfully embarrassed, to explain that she has been listening to a gangster story on the radio. She hopes they were not alarmed. She just now looked into the nursery; the children were not awakened. No, they were accustomed to sounds like that. Machine guns and bombs are natural toys nowadays.

Well, so much for the shot; cook has not committed suicide after all.

Presently the taxi may be heard crunching up the street. One expects it to climb the little drive, but it does not, even though Muhlbach has sprinkled rock salt from the street to the garage. Cook expertly flickers the porch lights, but this taxi driver is leery of hillsides and does no more than blink his headlights by way of announcing that if she wishes a ride she must take the risk. That is the way of cab drivers nowadays; one must bow to their high-handed manner or simply do without. And should you fail to tip them they may slam the door on your fingers. Cook often tells about the friend of a very good friend of hers who lost a thumb just that way and almost bled to death. Oh, it is a gruesome tale indeed and always concludes with the cook nodding darkly, hands folded severely over her white apron. She believes in a day of reckoning with as much faith as she attacks her Sunday hymns in the kitchen. These hymns have made her a neighborhood celebrity; whenever she is mentioned someone invariably adds, "—the one who sings in the kitchen." The cab driver, ignorant of the future, states his position by lighting a cigarette, and at this the cook capitulates. She lets herself out the screen door—so useless in winter—and is heard walking cautiously down the icy steps. One can see her getting into the back seat of the cab. The door is closed and she is taken away, unhappy woman.

The children—"my babies," she calls them—are undisturbed that she has left. They are never sure whether they dream of her nightly visit or whether they really do wake up and eat something. No matter, they will see her the following morning. Just before noon she will arrive, lumbering and scolding without even waiting to learn what they have done wrong. If they have been really bad she will frighten them by saying she is going to California. Their eyes open wide. It is the word alone that Donna has come to fear; the sound of it is enough to make her weep. Otto knows it is a place far off in the direction of downtown where people go when they are angry, and he knows that no one ever returns from California, so he too begins to sob. Oh, there is no punishment worse than when cook starts packing her suitcase.

But they are sleeping now. Otto is a little boy, there can be no question of that, but Donna, what is she? She is so small! Can anything so tiny be what she will one day be? Will there come a time when she would abandon her father and her brother for the sake of someone they have never seen? Someone perhaps as impossible as Otto, or even more so? Surely no one more obstinate and militantly ignorant than Otto can lay claim to being human. Only wait and see! He will come for Donna with biceps flexed and a hat crushed on the back of his head. Most likely he will be chewing gum. He will converse like a cretin, yet how accomplished will he think himself. Will Donna think as much? Will she peer into her mirror and suffer anguish over the shape of her chin or the cut of her gown? She could not be more perfect yet she will despise herself because of him. Perhaps he will even be tattooed! He is so clever and so handsome, she thinks, how can it be that her father pokes fun at him? Well, her father has grown old and does not know about the latest things. In fact Donna is mortified that he chooses to wear the kind of collar and necktie he does; it might have been very well in Mother's day, but that was twenty years ago. "How just positively incomparable!" she cries at the sight of her girlfriend's new dancing slippers. By next month, though, every thing has become "beautific." Her father mulls over the expense he has gone to in sending her to a decent university. All in vain. She might as well have been educated by comedians. Yet how lovely she is! Muhlbach feels tears surging to his eyes, but of course nothing shows. Why not? Why is he unable to weep for beauty that is positively incomparable?

And he thinks of her mother, and when Donna twirls about the living room for him with flushed cheeks Muhlbach cannot trust himself to speak.

Who can say whether this will all come to pass? Is that the way it is to be, or will panic annihilate them all? Perhaps such horror will occur—bombs and irresistible rays not yet invented, a holocaust even the comic books have not conceived—that Donna will never be stricken by this ludicrous young god. In view of the damage he is sure to inflict perhaps it would be just as kind if she died in the wreckage of war. Well, they will all find out.

Now, this starry night, she lies serenely sleeping, a Botticellian morsel, the cook's beloved, an altogether improbable object, cherished above life itself.

Otto, being masculine, cannot afford to be so complacent as his sister, not even in dreams. His fists fly back and forth, he cracks his skull against the wall and does not feel a thing, he thrashes, mutters, climbs mountain peaks, vanquishes his enemies in a second, and above all else he frowns. Not for him the panacea of Donna's rag doll. A gun may be all right for a time, a puppy is even better, a picture book is good too, and attempting to climb the willow tree is a worthy project, but there seems to be no final answer. He must investigate one thing and then another, and in each he finds something lacking. Here he is scratching at the screen door again though he wanted to go outside not five minutes ago. His nature is as restless as the nose of a rabbit. No one can be certain what he is seeking.

He is wakened by something happening downstairs. The voices have changed. There is the sound of coat hangers rattling and of people moving around. Company is going. Otto looks groggily at the ceiling and tries to stay awake although he does not know just why. He would like to get up and look out the window but the room is cold; then too the nurse would probably come in and he does not especially like her. He has thought up some grisly tortures that he intends to try on the nurse, such as flooding the bathroom and when she runs in to turn off the water he will lock the door so that his father will think she did it. Otto has a great bag of schemes for the nurse. He is certain to drive her away. Meanwhile he must concentrate on the noises and so understand what they are doing downstairs. Donna is breathing passionately at the moment and Otto is annoyed by this interference; he props himself up on both elbows.

The front door opens and people can be heard talking outside. This is really too much; Otto is wide awake and out of bed, creeping to the window. There he crouches, his brilliant eyes just above the sill. The winter air makes his eyes water so he grinds his fists into them, the best remedy ever. And he shivers without pause. He has come unbuttoned again.

Muhlbach is following the guests down the icy walk to Kirk's car. Its windshield is a mound of snow and while the guests are getting into the car Muhlbach reaches out and brushes off the windshield. This is no instinctive action: for the past hour he has been thinking about this gesture. When he opened the door for Grimes and Uncle he noticed the snow still falling and saw that it was about to cover the other car. Not long after that he hit upon the proper method to end the evening, a simple act not only cordial but final. It should express his attitude. Now he has done it but too fast; Kirk was not even looking.

The engine starts up. The diplomat has fitted on his elegant gray gloves, settling each finger, and now pulls the overcoat across his knees while waiting for the engine to warm. Beside him the dancer is already beginning to look snug; she has drawn her rather large strong feet up onto the seat and tucked her hands deep inside the mink sleeves of her jacket. She is only waiting for the instant the wheels begin to turn, then she will lean her head against his shoulder and like the wheels she will roll toward a conclusion. She is always touched by this moment when the acting is done, the curtain comes swaying down, and life takes over. Each time, however, she is a little frightened, a little doubtful that she can survive.

Muhlbach, standing soberly beside the hood, brushes more snow from the edge of the windshield and receives a faint shock when Kirk acknowledges this by glancing out at him; for an instant the man looked older, much different, the hair on his temples appeared silver. Muhlbach is well aware that Kirk is eight or ten years junior, yet he cannot escape the eerie feeling that he saw a man distinctly older than himself.

Throughout the evening these two have avoided each other, and so it is destined to end. Circumstances have set the limit of their association.

They must be neutral forever. Sandy Kirk has divined the truth of this while Muhlbach was thinking it through. They nod. The car starts forward but immediately slips sideways into a rut where the wheels spin ineffectively. Kirk, tightening his grip, presses the gas pedal to the floor and Muhlbach realizes the man is a poor driver. The tires are screaming on the ice. Muhlbach waves both hands, shakes his head, goes around to look, and sees that he must get out his own car to give Kirk a push. In a few minutes it is done; they are safely away from the curb.

The visitors have gone. Muhlbach eases his car once more into the garage and closes the door, but despite the extreme cold he cannot bring himself to go inside the house right away. While he stands forlornly gazing down at his shadow on the moonlit snow he hears the voice of his son crying timorously into the windy night.

Muhlbach lifts up his head. "Go to sleep, Otto."

And the apprehensive Otto, peeping down from the nursery window, hears this faint reply. It is the voice of his father saying everything will be all right.

THE LAND WHERE
LEMON TREES BLOOM

M Y FATHER MET Mr. Wigglesworth somewhat by chance during the Second World War because a Nazi submarine torpedoed their ship. Mr. Wigglesworth was a member of the ship's company—at that time he was a baker—while my father belonged to an artillery unit en route to England. The fact that they scrambled into the same lifeboat surprised me a little, but they did, and during the next three days they became good friends. After the war their friendship continued. Mr. Wigglesworth lived in Seattle, where he worked as a baker for quite a few years but eventually opened a restaurant of his own. We lived in San Francisco where my father was a stockbroker. Several times he came to visit us, and to visit another friend named Cabot, whom he had known in the merchant marine. Mr. Cabot, who became an official of some labor union, would be invited to our home when Mr. Wigglesworth was in town. I looked forward to these occasions. I loved to stare at Mr. Cabot, a small digni- fied gentleman with flowing brown hair and a face like a horse, and I knew Mr. Wigglesworth would talk and talk and talk. Once in a while my father or Mr. Cabot would tell him to pipe down, but this never stopped him. On and on he went, on and on. I used to imagine him in the lifeboat, talking and talking while they floated over the waves.

My first memory of him was on Thanksgiving Day when I was five or six years old. I thought he smelled like cinnamon. He had merry blue eyes and pink skin and he was fat. In honor of the holiday he wore an orange vest. I remember him walking toward me and my sister. He was carrying a basket of fruit and he was grinning. Then all at once he fell down on the carpet. Mr. Wigglesworth is sick, I told my sister. She was four years older and she shook her head with her lips pressed together. No, she said, Mr. Wigglesworth is drunk. I was not sure what that meant, but because my sister was older I knew she must be right.

He had met Richard Nixon. That is to say, he had what might be called an encounter with Mr. Nixon, who was then Vice President. This happened in Seattle, and we heard the story every time he came visiting. Two secret service agents appeared at the restaurant and told him that the Vice President together with Mrs. Nixon and another couple would be dining there at eight o'clock on a certain date. The secret service agents wished to inspect the premises and they would like to select Mr. Nixon's table. Mr. Wigglesworth showed them around. They opened doors. They peered out windows. They examined the fire escape. They explored the kitchen. The restaurant was on the second floor with a nice view of Puget Sound, and they stood for a while at the top of the winding staircase. At last they decided where the Vice President's party would be seated.

Mr. Wigglesworth was flattered that his restaurant had been chosen, but he did not like Richard Nixon, and while telling about their meeting he would refer to the Vice President as a fascist, prefacing this noun with a hyphenated adjective if my mother was not present. Nevertheless, when the big night arrived he greeted the Nixon party and escorted them to their table.

At this point while telling the story he would pause. Although his listeners had heard it many times, Mr. Wigglesworth invariably paused before announcing that he himself took the Vice President's order. Then his face would begin to change color and his jowls would tremble while he furiously smoked a cigarette. I liked this part of the story. I always wondered if he would fall down on the carpet.

Do you know what that Mother ordered? he would ask with an expression of disbelief. Do you know? Do you know what that Mother ordered at my restaurant?

We knew the answer because he always shouted: 'Salisbury steak!'

The first time I heard this I asked in a shrill little voice what Salisbury steak was and my father explained that it was a fancy name for hamburger.

Whenever Mr. Wigglesworth talked about Richard Nixon he would

begin to shout and wave his arms. I thought he must be choking or
mosquitoes were biting him. His restaurant had been chosen because
it was one of the finest on the West Coast. My father had shown me
pictures of it in a magazine. It was a famous restaurant, but the Vice
President of the United States ordered hamburger.

The astounding tale continued. Mr. Wigglesworth told the Vice
President that his restaurant did not serve Salisbury steak.

Do you know what happened? Unbelievable! I couldn't believe it!
That fascist Mother looked at me and said: 'Manage it.' Mr. Wigglesworth lowered his voice when he imitated the Vice President: 'Manage
it.' Can you believe that? Listen, I'll tell you something else. Nixon's
eyes don't have any pupils. That Mother looked at me and his eyes
don't have any pupils. Unbelievable!

Next we would be told how he went to the kitchen to talk with
Octave, the chef. Octave had been carving something when Mr.
Wigglesworth asked him to prepare a Salisbury steak. Octave was
French and he was temperamental. When Mr. Wigglesworth asked
him to chop up a filet mignon, Octave began slashing the air with his
knife. At this point Mr. Wigglesworth's face would express terror
because he could not guess what Octave might do. Octave might rush
into the dining room and attack the Vice President.

That was the end of the story. I always felt disappointed. I wanted
Octave to chase Vice President Nixon out of the restaurant with a
butcher knife. I imagined Octave screaming French curses while
chasing Mr. Nixon down the spiral staircase and all the way through
Seattle, but it was not to be.

Mr. Wigglesworth usually ended the story by telling us that at least
Nixon didn't order cottage cheese. The first time he said this I turned
to my father because I didn't understand. My father said the Vice President loved cottage cheese with catsup and I almost threw up.

Another time the FBI wanted to question Octave, who was not a
United States citizen. This happened during the McCarthy era. Mr.
Wigglesworth's eyes would bulge and he would begin swearing when
he told us how he ordered the FBI agents out of his restaurant.

There were other stories just as familiar. We heard about the torpe-
doing whenever he came to visit. I liked the explosion and fire and the
ship sinking and soldiers and sailors jumping into lifeboats—which Mr.
Wigglesworth described with flailing arms and desperate cries—but

most of all I liked the submarine. It surfaced very near the lifeboat. A German officer climbed out and began to study the burning transport through binoculars. Then he lowered the binoculars. He had a monocle attached to a black ribbon around his neck.

A Prussian! Mr. Wigglesworth exclaimed. And he would stretch his face to show us what the German did. Can you believe it? That Mother had a monocle!

Next we would be told what the U-boat commander said while the lifeboat slid greasily up and down in the enormous deadly shadow of the submarine:

'Chentlemen, vich amonk you iss de kapdain?'

Nobody spoke until Mr. Wigglesworth stood up and claimed to be the captain.

The German officer stared at Mr. Wigglesworth for a long time. Finally he gave them a compass bearing to the nearest land. And just before submerging he called out: 'Chentlemen, Gott speed.'

I couldn't believe it! Mr. Wigglesworth always said. Unbelievable!

If a Nazi commanded the submarine they would have been massacred, but this was a middle-aged civilized Prussian.

Another favorite story was the affair with a mysterious Danish countess. If my mother was in the room he didn't tell it, and when I was very young my father would suggest that I go outside and play. This also happened during the war, some months after he had been torpedoed. He was in the South Pacific aboard a cruise ship requisitioned by the government, baking cakes and pies and frying doughnuts for American soldiers en route to Australia. Being a cruise ship, it quite naturally had a swimming pool, but the pool had been drained and filled with sacks of sugar. I remember thinking that a swimming pool full of sugar was an awful lot. I thought the United States might be planning to give a bag to everybody in Australia.

The countess shared a stateroom with three Army nurses. I asked why she was going to Australia. Mr. Wigglesworth belched. He leaned toward me and wrinkled his eyebrows. His head reminded me of a cantaloupe. She was a spy! he whispered. I thought he was teasing but I wasn't sure. I could smell whisky and tobacco and I thought he might be angry. I imagined those American soldiers bowing to the countess so I didn't understand how Mr. Wigglesworth got acquainted with her because I knew that bakers wore floppy white hats and always had flour on their hands. I was going to ask, but I could tell that my father and Mr. Cabot didn't want to hear any more.

He said he hollowed out a nest among the sugar sacks and invited the countess to join him for a little recreation. Dewey, that's enough, Mr. Cabot said. Mr. Wigglesworth went right on talking. He grinned and licked his lips and winked at me and all at once he hopped out of his chair while he pretended to be grabbing a woman's breast. Then he took off his jacket and rolled up his sleeve. There on his arm was a tattoo of a girl wearing a grass skirt. I thought I would get one just like it.

As soon as the maid announced supper he would jump to his feet and scurry toward the dining room. When my sister and I were little our family used to visit the zoo. I liked to watch the rhinoceros trot around clip-clop-clip-clop on those crusty little hooves and always said to myself there goes Mr. Wigglesworth to the table.

He liked to smoke during supper, which my mother hated. If he reached into his jacket for a cigarette I would look at her, but she was too polite to say anything. My father didn't like it either and he had told Mr. Wigglesworth. It didn't make any difference. One time he blew a cloud of smoke at a bouquet in the middle of the table. Then he said, Oh shit! and began flapping his hands at the smoke.

I didn't mind that he talked so much and I envied his adventurous life. It seemed to me that he had experienced just about everything. He had sailed to Norway and China and Guatemala and been torpedoed and made love to a countess on a sugar sack and he had looked Vice President Nixon in the eye.

That was not all. When he was a boy he met some Wobblies. During the great economic depression his parents would feed hungry men who tramped the roads looking for work and many years afterward somebody knocked at the door. There stood a man in a cheap suit, followed by half a dozen laborers. Sonny, the leader said, is your folks at home?

These were the Wobblies. They had come to repay a debt.

I shook hands with Big Mike Mulligan! Mr. Wigglesworth exclaimed while telling the story. Big Mike Mulligan! And he would show us the palm of his right hand. Big Mike! Unbelievable!

All of this came back to me when I saw Mr. Cabot on the street. He walked with a cane. His mustache and his long brown hair had turned white. His ears were bigger than I remembered. I didn't know how old he was. He could have been ninety. In one of my schoolbooks there was a picture of Alexander the Great on his noble steed Bucephalus and I suddenly recalled that whenever Mr. Cabot visited our home I thought of Bucephalus.

I introduced myself. He peered at me for several seconds. Then his expression brightened. Of course, he said in a voice like a barrel organ. Hello there, young fellow.

How about a drink? I asked because he loved Kentucky bourbon. He chuckled. No, the doctor had forbidden alcohol. A glass of fruit juice would be fine.

When we were settled in a coffee shop I asked about Mr. Wigglesworth.

Gone, Mr. Cabot said. His brother telephoned from Seattle. He was standing in line at the post office when down he went. He lived several days, babbling incessantly. Nobody understood a word. Gibberish. Now tell me about your father.

I said my father had died quite a while ago.

Mr. Cabot pursed his lips. A considerate man, he said with a thoughtful expression. Your father never failed to let me know if Dewey was coming to San Francisco.

When I was young I had heard my father say that both of them were Communists. I didn't know what that meant, but my father disapproved so it was exciting. I used to hope that Mr. Wigglesworth would talk about being a Communist. I knew Mr. Cabot wouldn't say anything. He didn't talk much.

I asked if Mr. Wigglesworth had been a member of the Communist Party.

For a time, yes. As was I. As were a good many working men in those days. Why do you wish to know?

He opened a very expensive restaurant. Isn't there a contradiction?

Oh, I think not, Mr. Cabot said. Dewey, like many of us, became disenchanted with the Party and struck out on his own while remaining sympathetic to the ideals of Communism. Contradictory? I think not. Capitalism has changed, to be sure. It is now less oppressive, but the struggle never ends.

I waited for him to go on.

He picked up the fruit juice with both hands and took a sip. You wouldn't remember, he said, but at one time if a fellow was suspected of being a Communist he might lose his job. His property might be vandalized. He might be unable to find work. I was turned away more than once and discharged from a jury without explanation. People in this country lost their wits. The Dies committee ran wild. And that McCarthy fellow. Quite a nasty episode. You would be too young to know about Hermann Goering.

I know who he was, I said.

Yes, of course. Well, when that bird was in the dock at Nuremberg he explained how to manipulate people. Scare them senseless. It isn't difficult. Tell them the nation could be attacked at any moment. Goering wasn't the first to understand this. What's disheartening is that it always works. Century after century. I saw it taking shape in the United States.

Mr. Cabot's teeth clicked and I realized they were not his own. He looked at me for an instant before continuing.

Well, sir, Dewey had no more than opened that place when the FBI showed up. They wanted to pin something on him. Mr. Cabot chuckled. Questioning Dewey was a mistake. Lord, Lord, how I wish I had been there. 'Boys, Dewey told them, 'I'm fireproof. I'm a capitalist. I own the joint.'

I asked what the FBI agents did.

Hah! Mr. Cabot said. Hah! They skipped out the door and never came back.

I asked if he was still active in union affairs. He said that occasionally he would attend meetings. Otherwise he passed the time reading, playing chess in the park if weather permitted, and reminiscing with a few old friends.

Did I know about the Hong Kong garbage?

I did. I knew that story by heart. The ship was tied up for several days to unload cargo and every evening just before sunset buckets of rotting feed and table scraps would be dumped overboard while sampans gathered at the stern.

Most unpleasant. Disgusting. Banana peels, mouldy prunes, bacon grease, chicken claws and guts, sour milk, rancid oil, fish heads, skin, bones—off the fantail it went, but those poor devils tried to retrieve whatever we jettisoned. They would dive into that scummy water for a biscuit. One evening Dewey and I were watching the scavenger hunt when he looked at me with tears in his eyes and said, 'What the hell kind of world is this?' Mr. Cabot folded his hands over the cane. Yes, he remarked almost to himself. 'Kennst du das land wo die citronen blumen?'

I don't speak German, I said.

'Know'st thou the land where lemon trees bloom?'

I don't understand, I said.

Oh, it scarcely matters, he said, looking beyond me.

I tried to imagine Mr. Wigglesworth with tears in his eyes. I could see him outraged by one thing or another, jowls quivering, blue eyes popping. I used to think he would explode like somebody in a cartoon. I remembered the orange vest and I could see him falling down on the carpet at Thanksgiving. I could almost hear him cursing and belching, but I couldn't imagine him about to cry.

I loved the stories, I said. That U-boat commander with a monocle and the swimming pool full of sugar. And those Wobblies—I thought they spun around and wobbled like tops.

Industrial Workers of the World. Their hearts were good, their methods a bit foolhardy. The movement had pretty well disintegrated by the time Herbert Hoover took office. Lord, how these years fly. Teapot Dome. Wobblies. Roosevelt.

I asked about the man who almost drowned in Cape Town harbor. Mr. Wigglesworth jumped in and held the man up until they were rescued. He claimed there were sharks everywhere.

Dewey could barely keep himself afloat, Mr. Cabot said. He lied, you know, as children lie, without quite understanding. I've no idea how many whoppers he told—oh, I expect he put Baron Munchhausen to shame.

What about the countess and the sugar sacks?

I was not aboard that ship.

Do you think it was true?

I've no doubt about a swimming pool filled with sugar. That sort of thing did happen during the war. As to the countess—poppycock! Vintage Dewey.

I wanted to believe it, I said. I did believe it.

After he told those yarns often enough he believed them himself.

How about the oil prospecting? He told me his father and a man called Ozark Jack decided to become partners but they argued about something so his father moved to Idaho and six months later Ozark Jack hit a big field near Tulsa. He used to wave his arms and shout: 'Six months! Six months! My old man gave up six months too soon!'

Yes, yes, Mr. Cabot said a bit impatiently. I heard about that fellow Ozark Jack from other sources. Dewey told the truth, I believe, for once in his life.

Those were boom years in Oklahoma, I said. Why would his father give up after drilling a few dry holes? Why move to Idaho?

Mr. Cabot sucked his teeth and gazed at the ceiling for such a long time I thought he had forgotten me.

Those days, he finally said. Those must have been exciting days. Much of the nation unexplored. People westering, moving along, following the sun, obsessed by they knew not what. Perhaps that is what drove Dewey's father to pull up stakes. What would he discover in Idaho? The Indians were unpredictable, the resources an enigma. He may have been something of romantic. Dewey inherited that.

Mr. Wigglesworth a romantic? How could this be? His stomach lapped over his belt like a roll of sausage. He didn't shave very often and a wet cigarette usually stuck to his lower lip. I remembered how he would lean back in his chair grinning and belching after he had eaten almost everything on the table. The jokes he told when my mother was out of the room were so blasphemous that I was afraid our house would be struck by lightning.

He admired those film toughs, Mr. Cabot said. Bogart. Cagney. That sinister fellow with slick black hair—what was his name? Raft? Yes. George Raft. And that author with a hairy chest.

Hemingway, I said.

Mr. Cabot nodded.

He told me a boxing promoter watched him spar with an Olympic champion and wanted him to turn professional.

Rubbish, Mr. Cabot said. Pish-tosh!

I asked about the Peruvian whorehouse. Mr. Wigglesworth liked to dance across the carpet of our living room snorting and grunting while he knocked down Peruvians right and left.

It didn't amount to much, Mr. Cabot said. We made port at Callao and eight or ten of us ended up late at night in that place. I don't recall just what happened, except that words were exchanged. There was a bit of shoving before things calmed down. In Dewey's mind it assumed Homeric dimensions.

He thumbed his nose like a boxer, I said. He pawed the air. He looked fierce.

Plum pudding, said Mr. Cabot.

I asked if it was true that a movie star wanted to marry him. She wore a sarong and was in a film with Bing Crosby.

Yes, yes. Exotic women pursued him to the ends of the earth. The daughter of a shipping tycoon. Some Bolivian heiress. British royalty. He fancied himself a roughneck Valentino. That movie goddess—that woman's name escapes me.

I thought it might have been Hedy Lamarr. I was about to ask, but Mr. Cabot appeared to be dozing off.

Then he straightened up. I considered strangling Dewey, he said. I was not alone.

Did you meet aboard ship?

No, sir. At the union hall where we waited for assignments. I tried to avoid the fellow because he never stopped talking. Some time afterward, as luck would have it, I found myself aboard ship with him. I recognized him at once. Indeed, it would be difficult to forget the man. I kept my distance as best I could, which isn't easy in tight quarters. One afternoon I heard him describing a story he had read. As you may know, there will be days at sea when you have time on your hands and a good many seamen tend to be readers. It's quite remarkable what some of them have read. No end of junk, to be sure, but you will find sailors who can discuss Flaubert, Aeschylus, Nietzsche, and so on. Well, this story Dewey had read was a Russian thing—one of those leisurely nineteenth-century tales having to do with a certain Captain Ribnikov during the Russo-Japanese war. Quite a long yarn. Ribnikov is a secret agent. Japanese. The Russians catch up to him in a brothel. He tries to escape by jumping out a window and breaks a leg. I had read the story years before. Kuprin, if memory serves. Yes. Alexander Kuprin. At any rate, Dewey couldn't remember the title and I spoke up. I recall being annoyed with myself because I didn't want to get into a conversation but I said Captain Ribnikov. Dewey looked at me in absolute astonishment. Probably he thought himself the only man aboard who had read it. You might guess what happened next. 'Captain Ribnikov!' he shouted. 'That's right! That's right! Captain Ribnikov!'

From then on, I said, you didn't mind the jabbering.

I managed to tolerate it, said Mr. Cabot.

I had never thought of Mr. Wigglesworth reading obscure nineteenth-century Russian stories. I remembered him blowing cigarette smoke across our dining room table while my mother pretended she didn't mind. And the wonderful orange vest. And flailing his arms and grinning while he boasted, telling one preposterous lie after another. I believed everything. I had never thought about long days at sea, men stretched out on their bunks with nothing to do. Now I thought about him falling down in a Seattle post office.

His brother spoke with the clerk, Mr. Cabot said. It appears that Dewey was holding a manuscript addressed to a publisher when he uttered a squeak and collapsed like a ton of bricks. The clerk went ahead and mailed it.

What? I said.

He was hoping to be published.

I thought I had misunderstood. What are you talking about? I said.

He wrote poetry. You wouldn't know, of course. I suspect I'm the only one he told.

Mr. Wigglesworth wrote poems?

He did. Yes, sir.

And the post office clerk mailed the manuscript?

After they hauled Dewey away. The package had been adequately stamped, so he mailed it.

I looked at Mr. Cabot to see if this might be a joke. He wasn't smiling. He was not a man who joked. Well, I said, did the publishing house accept the poetry?

Of course not, Mr. Cabot said. It was rejected immediately.

Did you read it?

Bits and pieces. Dewey wanted my opinion.

What was your opinion?

Trash. Execrable.

What did you tell him?

The truth.

I thought about asking how Mr. Wigglesworth reacted, but I could guess. He cursed and waved his arms and shouted. I wondered what kind of poetry he wrote. I thought it must have been about the sea, or his boyhood in Idaho, or maybe the Second World War. After all, nobody could write poems about the FBI or the restaurant business or Richard Nixon.

Mr. Cabot pulled a thick gold watch from his vest pocket. The watch reminded me of an earlier century. A great many questions came to mind, but the afternoon was fading.

CARIBBEAN PROVEDOR

AT FOUR O'CLOCK the sun was burning like a green lemon above the coconut palms. The ship's rail was too hot to touch. Koerner stood in the shadow of a lifeboat with a cigarette between his teeth and looked around. In the water alongside the stern some garbage was floating. On shore a few Negroes in straw hats sat on boxes in the shade of the customs house. Nobody else was in sight. There was no breeze, and not a sound except the hissing ball of the sun. Aboard ship nothing moved and there was a smell of hot canvas.

Koerner felt suddenly that his skull was as empty as a gourd. He looked at the deck to be sure that if he fainted he would not hit his head on a piece of iron. Then the feeling passed, but he thought it would be a good idea to go inside. A cold drink would be a very good idea. For almost eight hours he had been playing chess with the surgeon from Ohio. Neither of them had eaten since breakfast. They had played without stopping and were planning to continue until dinner time as usual, but the surgeon's wife got angry. After five days at sea the score stood 23 to 17 in the surgeon's favor, but he was going as far as Vigo and if his wife did not cause too much trouble there would be time enough to overtake him.

Koerner squinted at the shore to see if there was anything he might have missed but the town looked worse during the day than it had the previous night, and there had been nothing worth seeing even then. It was a port of call and they would leave in a few hours. The loading had been completed.

He dropped his cigarette into the water, stepped back inside the ship and descended to the lounge where he took a stool at the bar next to a fat man who was wearing a short-sleeved shirt. The fat man was stroking a little bottle of champagne as tenderly as though it were a cat and talking to the bartender in Portuguese. He stopped talking but continued playing with the bottle, wiping away the moisture with his fingers.

"Um Magos," Koerner said to the bartender.

The champagne was good and very cheap and it was cold and he thought he would be drinking a number of these little bottles while crossing the Atlantic.

"Are you on this boat?" the fat man asked in Portuguese.

Koerner nodded. The man was probably a merchant seaman, both of his thick hairy red arms were heavily tattooed. On his left wrist was a bright new watch which looked as though he had just that afternoon put it on.

"Are you a passenger?"

The heat, no lunch, and so much chess had been exhausting and Koerner did not want to get into a conversation. Besides, the man was anxious to talk and therefore probably did not have much to say. He began to roll the bottle between his palms and tried to remember when the ship was scheduled to arrive in Vigo.

"It's nice to be rich," the fat man said in a voice that was almost threatening. "I'm poor. I work for a living. I can't afford to go on a voyage."

Reluctantly Koerner looked at the man directly for the first time. He was about fifty years old, with a flattened nose and protruding lips and skin that burned but would never tan. Underneath the fat he was solid. He could have been a wrestler. Koerner noticed that the top of one of his ears was missing, sliced off quite cleanly.

"What do you do on this ship?" the fat man said.

"Not a thing."

"You don't do nothing at all. Is that what you tell me?"

"I play chess."

"Ah! You play chess, do you?"

"Every day. I've been playing this entire day since breakfast and I'm very tired."

"Every day. So you been on board a few days. You didn't come on board this ship last night?"

Koerner shook his head.

"I can't waste time playing around. I got a lot of work to do."

"All right," Koerner said.

"When you are not playing games what do you do?"

"I travel."

"That's all you do. You don't do nothing else?"

Koerner took a drink of champagne and then said, "Nothing else."

"You don't work on this ship?"

"No," Koerner said.

On a shelf behind the bar there were trinkets for sale. Portuguese galleons with billowing sails of filigreed gold, carved wood boxes inlaid with ivory squares, black lace Spanish fans, postage stamps from different countries in cellophane packages, flags, and miniature cork life preservers with the name of the ship. Some of the postage stamps were quite beautiful, especially the Japanese which looked like tiny woodcuts. There was snow on Mount Fuji, and waterfalls, and animals. He thought he might buy a package of them.

"I have business here. I'm the provedor," the man said. "I finished loading eight tons of food and drink on this ship. It's all done. I was working while you were asleep in your very pleasant cabin."

Koerner continued to look at the stamps.

"Now everything is on board so I'm having a drink. I'll buy you a drink, too."

"Thank you," Koerner said, "but I've already got one."

"I have been supplying this ship, all the ships of this line, and a lot of other ships for sixteen years. You don't know what it means to work hard like that. I have never done anything wrong. I have made friends all those years. Tomorrow I give the company my bill, then in a few days they pay me everything. Just sign the papers. I asked to buy you a drink. If you don't want to drink with me it's your business. I don't give a damn."

"Dois Magos," Koerner said to the bartender and took out his wallet, but the fat man pushed it aside.

"I can do this much," he said. "You don't get yourself in trouble drinking with me. You got nothing to worry about. Anyway, nothing worries you."

Koerner didn't answer.

"What's your name?" the fat man asked.

Koerner told him.

"That's what you call yourself. All right, if that's what you tell me it is. You say you're a passenger on this ship."

"I am."

"If you're a passenger on this ship where are you going?"

"Lisboa."

"Then you come back again?"

"Maybe."

"Traveling. That's what you said."

Koerner nodded.

"You work in Martinique?"

"I don't work in Martinique."

"You don't work for the French?"

"No."

"You look French, whatever your name is. Are you a tourist?"

The word was a little degrading, but Koerner decided to accept it. "All right, call me a tourist."

"Where do you live? You live in Lisboa?"

"No."

"You don't live on this island. I'm sure about that."

"You're right, I don't live on this island."

"In Curaçao?"

"No."

"I seen you once in Curaçao. A long time ago. Maybe three years ago."

"I was there once," Koerner said while he tried to remember when he had been in Curaçao. Then he remembered it had been about three years ago.

"In a café holding a newspaper, pretending to read. But you was watching somebody. I don't forget."

Koerner had not thought of it for three years but now he remembered sitting in a café with a newspaper, although he could not remember that he had been watching anybody.

"It was some English newspaper."

"Sure," Koerner said in English.

"Sure. Me too. Hell, yes," the fat man said in English but then continued in Portuguese. "I speak eight or nine languages. I don't know how many, maybe more than that. Spanish. German. French. Just about anything. In my work I got to. You didn't see me in Curaçao?"

"No."

"I can see you like a photograph. In Curaçao I could show you what table you was sitting at. I could tell who you was watching."

"You notice a lot."

The fat man stopped talking. Koerner drank some more champagne, then without turning his head he glanced at the wristwatch.

"You want it?"

"No."

"You want this watch I'll give it to you. It don't mean nothing to me." He was starting to unbuckle the strap.

"I don't want your watch," Koerner said. "I've got no use for it."

"Listen, whoever you call yourself, you know what my little girl said to me this morning? She said 'Papa, I know you have to go to work today because loading the ship means plenty of money for you, I know that.' Do you know what I said to her? I said, 'No, Sweetheart, the ship means you can go to school and it means nice things for you. It don't mean the money is for me.' That's what I told my little girl this morning. But you don't know what I'm talking about because you don't have no little girl. You don't have no idea at all what it means to bring a present to a little girl. A little ten-dollar watch from Switzerland. You don't know how much that means to a child. Something she can show her friends and tell them her Papa got this for her and it comes from Switzerland. A little ten-dollar watch. A ten-dollar watch! But you don't care about these things. They don't mean nothing to you."

Well, now, Koerner thought, I believe he's going to smuggle that watch past customs.

"You want it? You want this watch, I'll take it off and give it to you if that's all you want," the provedor said. He was breathing heavily.

"Keep it. I don't need it."

"A man like me works from the day he's born, but he don't get very rich. What do you want?"

What is he saying? Koerner wondered.

"I don't forget you, not for one minute. A long time ago in Curaçao I told myself, 'There he is. That's him.' I feel sorry for you, William Koerner, if that's what you tell me your name is. I feel sorry for anybody like you that goes around like you do, doing what you do. Not having any wife to come home to, not having a little girl throw her arms around your neck when you get off work. Eating by yourself every night. It don't make no difference to you, I know that, but I feel sorry for you. I'd rather be in my place."

Koerner waited to hear what the man would say next.

The provedor shrugged his shoulders. "A cheap watch. What difference does it make? Who cares? It don't hurt nobody. You want another Magos?" he asked in a voice that tried to be friendly.

Koerner shook his head.

"A man like me. What am I? All my life I work hard, but I don't amount to nothing. Maybe you're important. Probably that's what you think you are. You're proud of yourself, but I don't envy you. I don't want to trade places with you."

He realizes I know about that watch, Koerner thought, and he's afraid I'm going to tell the customs officer. But why should I? It's no business of mine. He can smuggle half the watches in Switzerland for all I care. I don't work for customs. He knows that.

Or does he?

And then everything the man had said gradually began making sense.

He believes I'm an inspector. This man thinks I work for the shipping company or for some government. He doesn't believe a word I've told him.

"Maybe you like what you do," the provedor was saying. "Maybe you don't. You do it just for the money? If that's what you do it for nobody's going to care if you live or die. A man like you could get killed and nobody cares. What good does money do? Sure, plenty of things. A lot of things. I know. I know that. But what kind of a life have you got?"

Suppose I were an inspector, Koerner said to himself, and suppose I had just now caught him with this watch. At the moment he's not guilty of anything because he hasn't taken it ashore. So why is he worried? I don't understand. Suppose that in a few minutes he does try to take it through without paying duty and he's caught, what would happen? Nothing. They wouldn't let him keep the watch, that's all. I can't understand why he's worried. Of course if he'd made a habit of this, if he'd been smuggling things ashore for sixteen years that might be a different kind of horse.

So that's it! Not just a wristwatch this afternoon, my fat friend, you've got a business going on the side. Coming aboard and going ashore day after day, one ship after another, for all these years. No wonder you're worried. I would be, too. And you don't know who I am, do you? If I were in your britches I'd be scared to death.

It mounts up, doesn't it? Sixteen years multiplied by how many ships? How many people do you deal with? And what do you bring ashore? What were you and the bartender talking about when I walked into the lounge, and why did you stop talking? Will there be a few cases of cognac hoisted ashore late tonight? That ten-dollar watch is nothing. That's a peanut, isn't it, my friend? You've finished work and you feel so good you decided to wear it ashore right past the customs officer, right past his nose because you feel so good. Ordinarily you'd slip it into your pocket and nobody would search you because you're the provedor. Everybody knows you. After all, you've been here sixteen years.

Yes, indeed, it does mount up, doesn't it? But something else mounts up too, my friend, my ambitious businessman. Every day you've got to worry, like every other ambitious businessman. And you wait, and you wait, because you've juggled the accounts, and each day the waiting is a little harder. But you've got to keep on because you're not quite strong enough to let it go. Just one more time. One more time. Then suddenly I'm here.

Koerner put his elbows on the bar and smiled.

"William Koerner," the provedor said, "if that's what you call yourself, I feel sorry in my heart for anybody like you. Nothing makes any difference to you. I got to pity you."

"Ah," Koerner said, and shrugged.

"Sure," the fat man said, "you can be like that. How many people you hurt don't mean a thing in the world. You don't care for nobody. You got no family. No little girl waiting at home asking her Mama when you're coming in."

He loves his daughter, Koerner thought. She's the only person or thing on earth this man loves.

"Why don't you get married?" the provedor asked. He was trying to pull his face into an expression of intimacy, but he could not get rid of the fear. "When a man gets married he knows what's worthwhile. He don't run around hurting people."

Whenever I please, Koerner told himself, following the idea slowly, as though it was a speared fish pulling him through the water, I can destroy this man. I can ruin his life. I can destroy his business, his reputation, and probably his marriage. Whenever I want to, from now on. I can do it because he thinks I can. He himself gave me the power, which means he can't possibly doubt it. I'm powerful because he thinks so. And whatever I want to do with him, I can do. If I order him to go ashore and wait for me, he will. If I stand up and beckon to him he'll follow me like a toy on a string.

"Give me a cigarette," he said.

The provedor picked up the package and offered it; Koerner took one and waited and the provedor lighted it for him.

So this is how it feels, Koerner thought, this is the way it feels. I'd never have guessed. I can actually destroy a man and I can hardly keep from laughing. I can put an end to a man's life and I feel a kind of elation. I feel as though I'd like to do something nice for this man. I don't know why, but I rather like him.

"What do you call yourself?" Koerner demanded, and smiled.

The provedor gave him a curious look, almost of surprise, or of some deep and sudden confusion.

"Oh, come on now," said Koerner, trying to control his excitement.

The provedor continued to look at him with a speculative expression, but finally said, "I am Hans Julio García."

It had been a stupid question, Koerner realized too late.

"Ah," he said, turning his face aside, "for some reason that sounds familiar. Did we meet in Curaçao?"

The provedor didn't answer.

Koerner looked into the mirror behind the bar. He could see the fat man's ear. The top of it appeared to have been taken off with a razor swipe, and he remembered his first impression of the provedor, of how solid he was under the creases of fat. It occurred to him that Hans Julio García probably was a very dangerous man, and that he had been threatening this man.

I wonder what might happen, he asked himself, when this man decides I'm not who he thinks I am. I don't know. What happens probably will depend on how he feels about me. If he thinks I never suspected the truth he won't have any feelings about me and he'll forget me. No, not that. He won't forget this afternoon, or me, for a long time. I'll be the tourist he talked to in the bar.

But if he thinks I did suspect the truth? If, let's say, he thinks I've guessed. What then?

I don't know that either. I don't want to think about it. I don't know how I got into this but I don't like it. I feel like I've put my hand inside a jar full of spiders. I didn't realize what I was doing. This could get ugly. I don't know how it got started. It was that watch. I noticed the watch because it was new and it didn't belong on his wrist, his wrist is too big for it. Then I looked at it again because I was hungry and wanted to know how soon I could eat but he didn't know that. I should have asked the time instead of trying to see the dial, but I didn't want to talk to him. How was I to know this would happen?

But if I go on pretending to be an inspector, how could he find out I'm not? He's afraid of me; he's quit asking questions. He's pretending more than I am. Sorry for me, he says. I pity you, he says. He doesn't pity me; he hates me. He's terrified. His hand was shaking when he tried to light my cigarette. He thinks I know everything about him. By God, why couldn't I turn him in? Why not? I didn't ask for this; it's his fault. I came here to get a drink, that's all, and now he's involved me with his guilt. Damn this man's soul, Koerner thought, and felt himself becoming angry. I could see this man in Hell! Why should I care what happens to him? He means nothing to me. Nothing! All right, by God, let him suffer! He deserves it—the lousy thief!

But could I do it? Say I have the power, can I use it? If I ruin him, who else is ruined? His daughter, for one. His wife. I don't have any idea who else. What difference does it make to me? For all I know they're both as rotten as he is. Yes. The little girl, too. And how do I know she exists? Because he talked sentimentally about "my little girl" and what she'd said to him this morning. How do I know it's true? How many lies have I heard since he started talking?

Koerner had been leaning on his elbows, rocking the stool slowly backward. He glanced at García. The fat man was gazing at him very seriously.

He's waiting. I've got to make up my mind. Suppose on the other hand I let him off. But how? He's never admitted anything. Just the same he's guilty and he knows I know it. He's waiting to see what I do. Suppose I've decided to let him go. What do I say? "I feel sorry for you, Hans Julio. I pity you. I don't want to hurt your daughter. I'm not going to do to you what I thought I would." Oh yes. He'd believe that on the day he'd believe my name is William Koerner. He'll believe me only when I act the way he expects me to act, whether it's false or not. And if I've come here to get him I'd never let him go, not unless I was corrupt.

Suppose I hinted about a bribe. And say he agreed to pay me. What's to stop me from being twice as corrupt? Turn him in as soon as I get the money. Or come back later. Bleed him again and again.

I must be out of mind, Koerner thought and shook his head. I'm trying to figure out whether I can untangle this mess by accepting a bribe. I must be going mad. This is a dangerous man beside me who assumes I'm somebody that I'm not. If he ever finds out how much I've guessed he might kill me. Right now he's wondering. He knows I've learned something and he realizes that I'm playing with it. He's about to lose control. He thinks he's already lost, he has no more to lose. This man is brutal, he could put a knife into me. He's almost ready. I can feel it. I've got to do something, there's not much time. I can't take a bribe. As stupid as I've been so far, that would be worse. The ship leaves tonight. He has people on board who will know about me.

What's left? If I try to turn him in, exactly what do I do? Go ashore with him following me like a sick bulldog and present him to the customs officer? "Look here, officer, just have a look at what I found!" Oh yes. Sure. We're at the bottom of the world and I've cornered a man who thinks I'm Death. He's waited for me. He's been waiting all these years. Once he saw me in Curaçao and he believed I was Death. Oh yes, we understand each other. There's no need to speak. But at this moment what's he thinking? I don't know. All I know is that he believes in me and therefore he must hate me. It was he who gave me this authority, yet he hates me because I have it.

Koerner went over the situation carefully with himself.

I have an authority that I don't want and I'm not able to give it away. I'd throw it in the water if I could, there's nothing I want less. What do I do?

Say I can't accept a bribe, and say I don't dare to let him go. I've made one false move already; one more and he'll sense the truth. I'm no actor. Why hasn't he found me out already? Because he wants so much to believe, that must be it. And because I made no effort to persuade him, which makes it hard to doubt.

All right, say that's the case, yes, and I couldn't possibly turn him in. Supposing I did act well enough to lead him off the ship, where's the proof? There's none. Only what I've guessed. He'd get rid of that watch in a minute. And maybe the customs officer is his partner, I don't know. It doesn't matter. I can't finish him. I should never have started this. But I didn't; he was the one. He built this into what it is. The fault's not mine; he can't blame me. When I learned what was going on I helped a little, but not much, and I didn't think it would come to anything like this.

I'm trying to be logical, but I can't think. My head's full of mice scrambling in every direction. How much longer will he believe? He must have told himself I wouldn't be here unless I had him trapped. He imagines I have every exit blocked. He imagines he can't escape unless I allow him to, which is the reason for the servility and fright and the lies dripping and sliding from his lips, yes, and the threats I heard.

Koerner had been gazing almost stupefied at the Japanese stamps, at the waterfalls and the tiny white cone of Fujiyama. He blinked and looked at himself in the mirror and was relieved to see that he appeared unconcerned. He picked up the bottle, poured out the rest of the champagne and drank it quickly. The champagne was warm and he knew he was beginning to get drunk.

Either I make use of what I know or I don't, he said to himself, and I think I'd rather not. I'd rather back out of this without getting my skull crushed or a knife in the ribs. I'm not a hero with celluloid teeth. When we get to Lisbon I could talk to somebody who might be interested. I don't know who, but somebody ought to be interested. I could do that much, although I doubt if anybody will listen. But I can't break this up by myself.

"You're just traveling," the fat man said. "That's what you told me."

Koerner nodded.

"You said you were on vacation."

Koerner shook his head.

"That's right," García said, "you didn't tell me that. I forgot. If you're not on vacation, what kind of work do you do?"

"I work at a desk."

"In Lisboa?"

"New York."

"I don't know what kind of work you do," the provedor said finally. "I never got a chance to have a job like you, so I could go traveling around playing games. I work hard."

Koerner listened carefully.

"You got friends on this island?"

Koerner knew instantly that he must not hesitate about answering, or show the slightest caution.

"No," he said, "in fact I couldn't give you the name of anybody within a thousand miles of this place."

"No? Who do you play games with?"

"Right you are! I do know somebody's name."

Hans Julio García smiled.

"You told me your name, too, a while ago," he said, "but I forgot."

Koerner told him again.

"Sure. I got a bad memory." And suddenly García began to laugh. "You're not Poigt," he said. "Okay, Mr. William Koerner, I want to buy you a drink. I'm going ashore, but I'll buy you another drink."

"It's almost time to eat. I didn't have any lunch."

"That's right. You're a chess player," said Hans Julio García, laughing.

Koerner grinned.

"Well, you go eat dinner," said the fat man. "Good-bye, whatever your name is."

"Good-bye," Koerner said.

He walked out of the lounge and went up on deck instead of into the dining salon. The deck still smelled of hot canvas but the late afternoon air seemed not so deadly. Beyond the breakwater the Caribbean lay dark blue-green and slightly broken like a stained-glass window.

So somebody exists, he thought, whose name is Poigt, or who calls himself Poigt, who causes the fat provedor to wake up in the middle of the night. It's for him that Hans Julio García waits. And one afternoon Poigt will step into the lounge as quietly as I did. Yes, the day will come. Or maybe it won't. It might never. What a shame, I'd like to know. Not that it concerns me very much, but still I would like to know.

He wandered to the other side of the deck. The sun looked larger and was wedged between two palm trees like an orange or a pome-granate. A few gulls were soaring above the ships in the harbor. On the quay some people were getting out of a taxi. He put his elbows on the rail and waited. Presently he saw the fat man go ashore. The watch was not on his wrist.

It must be in his pocket, Koerner decided. Isn't that curious. He's not so sure of himself anymore. I took the edge off his confidence. In fact I believe what I may have done was make things more difficult for Poigt. My fat smuggler is going to be much more cautious from now on. I hadn't expected that.

The provedor waved to somebody in the customs office, then walked through the gate and into a warehouse.

OCTOPUS, THE SAUSALITO QUARTERLY OF NEW WRITING, ART & IDEAS

F OR AT LEAST twenty-five years the retired ferryboat *Sierra* had been sinking into a Sausalito mudflat. It listed to the left, the decaying prow rode several degrees above the stern, various cats lived somewhere within the hull, and at high tide the ancient side-wheeler moved a bit as though struggling to rise from the muck and live again those glorious days when it ploughed majestically across the bay to Oakland. A fat Greek artist named Philiátes leased the front end of the *Sierra*. Philiátes was seventy or eighty years old with a pair of green olives for eyes and a pockmarked nose that nearly met his chin and he loved to give parties.

During one of these parties, according to what I was told, Willie Stumpf decided to explore the rotting bowels of the ship. The interior was gloomy and Willie was drunk, but after stumbling around for a while he emerged at the stern, which offered a spectacular view of San Francisco Bay. From the stern he climbed a ladder to the quarterdeck, where he was rewarded with an even more dramatic view. He inspected the captain's cabin. Despite mildew, gull droppings, spider webs, and the remnants of a dead cat, he thought it would make a suitable office for the literary magazine he intended to start. His intended editor-in-chief, Cal Bowen, happened to be at the party, so Willie described what he had found. Bowen, clutching a bottle of vodka, followed Willie on a tour of the wreck and declared everything to be perfect, after which they seated themselves on the collapsing fantail to discuss the future. The magazine would be called *Octopus*. It would be published four times a year. Willie suggested that when circulation reached 100,000 they could publish six times a year. Bowen thought that sounded reasonable. Later, as circulation increased, Willie said, they could go monthly. All right, said Bowen. *Octopus*, said Willie as he reached for the vodka, what a great name! Absolutely a great name!

The captain's cabin was hosed down and fumigated. New plumbing was installed, worm-eaten wood and shattered windows replaced, everything repainted. Willie bought ads in the trade journals announcing that a vibrant innovative West Coast literary quarterly, *Octopus*, welcomed submissions from new or established writers and graphic artists.

Manuscripts began to arrive not long after the editorial office opened. Manuscripts continued to arrive. Every day the postman dropped off another heap. Willie was subsidizing *Octopus*—paying the rent, utilities, and so forth—but he was less than rich. When the first issue was ready to go to press he would have to buy paper, etc. In other words, as Bowen explained the situation to me, there would be no money to pay an associate editor if someone wished to become an associate editor. In other words, I said after thinking about this remark, you are asking if I would like to work on the magazine without being paid. We might have a drink and discuss that, said Bowen. Let's go to O'Leary's.

There's one problem, he said after we had spent a while at O'Leary's and I had agreed to become the associate editor. The problem is Willie. Willie considers himself an editor. He thinks of himself as the new Max Perkins, the new Cowley, the new Mencken.

He's the publisher, I said. He's the businessman. He's supposed to take care of business. You are the editor-in-chief and I am the associate editor. We decide what's going to be published. Why don't you tell Willie to keep his hands off the manuscripts?

I did, said Bowen. I told him to stay away from my desk and stop picking through the manuscripts. I reminded him I was the editor-in-chief.

What did he say?

He said he was the publisher and I was a word man.

A word man?

That is correct, said Bowen. How long have you known Willie?

Maybe a year, I said.

Long enough, Bowen said and took another drink. The main thing, however, is that he can't tell *Moby Dick* from the latest potboiler. In other words, he is about as discriminating as a high school freshman. He thinks the magazine should have lots of cartoons.

I resign, I said.

You can't resign, Bowen said. You promised. Besides, he does have some good ideas. Not very many, but once in a while.

For example, I said.

He thinks that after we get the magazine off the ground we should expand into book publishing. He says there's a market for worthwhile books. He thinks we should publish books of high literary quality.

That's not a good idea, I said.

Well, said Bowen, it's Willie's money. Have I told you about the swindler?

The swindler, he explained, had mysteriously appeared on the ferryboat with a briefcase that was never opened, an engaging smile, and a proposition. He, the swindler, although that was not how he referred to himself, would, in exchange for five thousand dollars, obtain stock certificates worth one million dollars from a bank in Los Angeles. These stock certificates he would lend to Willie, who could use them however he wished—as collateral, for instance, to borrow money to finance the development of this exciting literary venture. He, the swindler, was enthusiastic. There was every reason to believe, he told Willie, that the *Sierra* could become the pulse and heart and soul of a highly profitable publishing empire. All it required was capital. With the money that could be borrowed on stock certificates worth one million dollars the sky was the limit—although that was not the expression he used.

Willie's scared to death, Bowen said. He wants to get his hands on those stock certificates but he's afraid the guy is a crook.

What's your opinion? I asked.

Well, said Bowen, this crook gave two references—a company in New York and another in Florida. Cheryl called them both. The New York number is disconnected. The company in Florida never heard of him. Also, this crook doesn't know where he lives.

I asked who Cheryl was and he explained that she was a graduate student at Berkeley. She came in three times a week to empty wastebaskets, take packages to the post office, type rejection letters and so forth. She wanted to get into publishing and thought *Octopus* would be a wonderful place to learn what it was all about. She would be listed on the masthead as an editorial assistant.

Let's get back to the swindler, I said. Why doesn't he know where he lives?

That's an interesting question, Bowen said. He told us he bought a house but he can't remember what street it's on because he just moved in.

If you want my opinion, I said, it sounds as though he could be a swindler.

That's possible, Bowen said. He's coming back tomorrow and they're going to sign the agreement. Willie agreed to advance him one thousand so he can drive to L.A. and pick up those stock certificates.

We had been drinking at O'Leary's for quite a while and it seemed to me that certain fundamentals of a logical conversation were being neglected. The swindler doesn't know where he lives, I said, but Willie intends to give him one thousand dollars. Or do I misunderstand?

You are beginning to get the idea, said Bowen.

Let's talk about something else, I said.

Working on the ferryboat is not like working in an ordinary office, Bowen said. It's picturesque. For instance, you know when the tide comes in because pencils roll off the desk. Also, if the tide is high you see lots of cats on the quarterdeck, especially if the moon is full. The other night I was reading manuscripts when I got this peculiar sensation so I went outside to look around and there were all these cats and a suspicious object floating in the moonlight near the stern. I almost called the cops, but Willie doesn't want cops or fire inspectors or health inspectors on board. For one thing, the wiring is bad. He did some of the electrical wiring himself to save money and that ship might be a hundred years old.

I considered this. You are telling me the *Sierra* might go up in flames? Is that what you are telling me?

Bowen looked thoughtful. Well, he said at last, even if it did you wouldn't be in much danger. The bay isn't deep so you could jump off the stern. If the tide happened to be out you'd land in the mud.

Suppose we talk about the manuscripts, I said.

There's one thing I ought to mention before I forget, Bowen said. We've been having a little problem with this crazed photographer. Maybe you know him. Lucky Pizarro. He cruises around San Francisco on a motorcycle and takes pictures of accidents. He carries a gun and last year he shot out half a dozen streetlights on Lombard. He got ninety days or something. It was in the *Chronicle*.

I remember, I said. I didn't realize he was out of jail. What's the little problem?

He brought over a portfolio of his pictures and wants us to publish them.

Accidents?

Accidents, Bowen said. All of them. There were about a hundred. He said if we didn't publish his pictures we might wish we had.

I think he got the wrong magazine, I said. Did you explain to him that *Octopus* is a high-quality literary magazine?

Willie talked to him. Willie said Lucky said we'd better publish those pictures.

What are you going to do? I asked.

We can't publish them, Bowen said. I couldn't finish looking at them. I almost threw up.

He might torch the *Sierra*, I said.

That's conceivable, Bowen said. I hadn't thought of it, but you could be right.

Are there any other problems? I asked. I get the feeling you haven't told me everything.

Nothing important, he said. I told you the union was threatening to picket us.

No, you didn't tell me, I said. Why is the union threatening to picket us?

Willie hired a non-union printer who charges about half as much as union printers.

You could get Lucky Pizarro to take a picture of the *Sierra* after the union goons have trashed it, I said.

That's very funny, Bowen said. You were asking about manuscripts. The truth is, I wasn't expecting much because we don't pay anything, but three or four really good things have come in, which is encouraging. And Willie says after we start making money we can pay the contributors.

When we start making money does the associate editor get a salary?

I wouldn't care to speculate, Bowen said.

I asked what he had in mind for the first issue. He summarized a few stories that sounded worthwhile and said he had accepted five etchings by a Stinson Beach artist. There were other possibilities: an excerpt from a novel about Chicano gangs in Bakersfield, some nature poems by a Salt Lake City schoolgirl, a scholarly essay on the evolution of German opera. *Octopus* would not be doctrinaire; nothing would be predetermined, nor would its embrace be limited. All that mattered was quality. I doubted if that kind of a magazine could sell 100,000 copies or anything like it, but you have to respect idealists; and besides, as Bowen had pointed out, it was Willie's money.

One thing does make me uncomfortable, he said. Willie thinks we should publish the memoirs of Philiátes.

I knew Philiátes only slightly. There were endless rumors about him and no doubt he had led a remarkable life, but listening to him talk was like listening to somebody who had been marooned on an island for fifty years. If he wrote everything down, I said, maybe it would make sense. On the other hand, maybe not.

As a matter of fact, Bowen said, Willie thinks if *Octopus* published the memoirs in Greek it would attract a lot of attention.

He's absolutely right, I said.

He's right, Bowen agreed, but ten pages of Greek would be suicidal. Maybe I can talk him out of it. Actually, not all of Willie's ideas are bad. He thinks we ought to publish recipes—recipes by well-known painters and sculptors and novelists and poets. As far as I know, that hasn't been done. We might have a page of recipes in each issue.

I thought about this. It was unexpected. However, as Bowen insisted all along, nothing would be predetermined. We would print whatever we chose to print. Willie's next idea was equally odd, but again, it was unusual enough to be worth considering; he had told Bowen that we might devote one entire issue to the artwork and writing of criminals.

He met some guy from Oklahoma who's out on parole. This guy did a stretch for holding up a hot dog stand in Tulsa. He wears shiny wingtip shoes and a pinstripe suit and slicks his hair straight back. He reminds me of somebody—Pretty Boy Floyd or Dillinger.

Listen, I said. With a bona fide swindler financing us and Lucky

Pizarro and Pretty Boy Floyd and one issue devoted to criminals, that ferryboat is going to be visited by more than a Sausalito cop or a wiring inspector. What does this pinstripe stickup artist want?

Strangely enough, Bowen said, he doesn't seem to want anything. Willie wants him to represent us on campus.

I'm not going to believe any of this, I said, but go ahead.

Bowen explained that Willie thought *Octopus* could become the favorite magazine of college students everywhere. It would be sold in campus bookstores and coffee shops and on newsstands. He envisioned students from Harvard to East Quackenbush State discussing the latest issue, eagerly buying subscriptions, urging their classmates to buy it, mailing it home to their parents. And this ex-stickup artist from Tulsa would travel from campus to campus in his pinstripe suit and wingtip shoes to promote it. I tried to imagine our representative heading out of Sausalito in a station wagon loaded with copies of the first issue featuring a scholarly essay on the evolution of German opera, etchings by a local artist, ten pages of Greek, and some recipes.

What's his name? I asked.

Fingers.

Fingers. That's all?

That's what he told us to call him. Just call me Fingers, he said.

Does he remember his address?

I can't answer that, Bowen said. All I know is, Willie told me he's from Oklahoma.

I wondered about the connection between Fingers and a criminal-man issue, but by this time it didn't seem important. I had very mixed feelings. On the one hand, Bowen was serious about publishing a respectable literary magazine and I thought that with two hundred and fifty million people in the United States there might be two or three thousand who wanted more than drivel. On the other hand, there was Willie. I was impressed by Willie's confidence and energy and by the fact that he would subsidize such a precarious venture, but then I would think about him calling his editor-in-chief a word man. He had been joking, but I felt uneasy. I asked Bowen if we had received any subscriptions.

Eight, he said, counting my dotty aunt.

Eight, I thought. Eight subscribers. Still, the first issue hadn't come out and the advertising campaign was just getting started. It was impossible to predict what might happen. Quite a bit would depend on the first issue.

Bowen plucked an ice cube out of his drink and began sucking it. I suspected from his expression that he had something to tell me but wasn't sure how to phrase it. Finally he scratched the tip of his nose and asked if I knew Babydoe Slusher. Only by reputation, I said. And then he told me she had given Willie a list of people who might subscribe or who might help subsidize the magazine. This made no sense. I wondered why she would do that. For one thing, everybody on the list would deny knowing her.

Maybe she has an ulterior motive, Bowen said. Anyway, Willie's decided to put her on the masthead as a contributing editor.

Babydoe? I said. Babydoe Slusher will be on the masthead?

Willie thinks it's a smart move. He says she's on what might be called intimate terms with practically all the men in California—movie stars, bankers, lawyers, civil rights leaders, congressmen, scoutmasters— just about everybody.

Congressmen, I said. Listen, I don't know if I want this job. I'm having very serious second thoughts. What about the guy from Oklahoma? Will he be on the masthead?

Presumably, Bowen said. I presume Fingers will appear on the masthead. Also, Willie is drafting letters to some big names in contemporary literature—critics, major novelists, poets, artists. He says having them associated with *Octopus* will give us prestige.

I thought about a critic for the *Times* looking down the masthead and finding himself squeezed between Babydoe Slusher and Fingers somebody.

Willie can be persuasive, Bowen said. I was skeptical about a Sausalito literary magazine, but he talked me into it. I wouldn't be surprised if he talks some of those big names into joining us. By the way, did I tell you that Spook will be a contributing editor?

Spook?

He comes in here once in a while—sad little guy with sleepy eyes and a Fu Manchu mustache. You may have seen him.

I've seen him, I said. What will Spook contribute?

That's an interesting question, Bowen said.

What does he do? I asked. Is he a journalist?

Bowen gazed dustily toward the ceiling. I believe Spook is a small-time drug pusher. That's what I've heard. He's very polite. You hardly know he's in the room. Did I tell you about Doc Arbuckle?

I'm not sure I want to hear about Doc Arbuckle, I said. Who is Doc Arbuckle?

He's from New York. Willie says he's a hotshot advertising sales-man. He used to work for one of those Madison Avenue agencies. He's going to be our advertising representative.

Why did he leave Madison Avenue?

Actually, I have the impression there may have been a scandal, Bowen said. I met him a couple of days ago. He's all teeth and hair.

Doc Arbuckle, I said. That sounds like an alias.

According to Willie, Doc is a firecracker. According to Willie, Doc will put us on the map.

It occurred to me that *Octopus* was going to be on the map with or without Doc Arbuckle. Maybe what we should do, I said, is run a photo of Babydoe Slusher in the buff on the cover.

It's curious you should mention that, Bowen said. You won't believe what Willie has in mind.

I'd rather not know, I said. Let's get back to this Madison Avenue hotshot. Has he sold any ads?

Bowen didn't answer. He was looking at the door and there was a strange expression on his face.

What's wrong? I asked.

Bad news, he said. Lucky Pizarro. I'm afraid he's seen us.

Listen, I said. I'm not sure I have time for this job. To be honest with you, I have serious reservations about a number of matters concerning the magazine and besides I've got a lot of things to do. I resign.

Now don't be hasty, Bowen said. Think it over.

ELECTION EVE

PROCTOR CYRIL BEMIS, emeritus CEO of the securities firm that bore his name—Proctor Bemis, grossly fat, not yet altogether bald, cheerful when undisturbed by gout, sat beside the fire as a fat man likes to sit, with fingers laced across his belly, jowls at rest, and thought about Costa Rica while his wife sorted the mail. He thought he would enjoy a visit to Costa Rica. Sunshine, gentle waves lapping sugar-white beaches, palm fronds dipping in the breeze, carioca music or whatever it was, pretty girls smearing oil on their legs, deep-sea fishing, rum, ocean-fresh lobster—oh yes, Mr. Bemis thought, twirling his thumbs on his belly. No drizzly, threatening overcast. No winter storm watch. No schoolboys in black trenchcoats gunning down classmates. No lunatics blowing up federal buildings. No hillbilly militia. No politicians braying platitudes. Costa Rica ought to be just fine, yes indeed. He dropped one hand into the silver bowl of cashews, scooped up a handful, and tossed them into his mouth.

How many people want money? he asked.

His wife looked at him over the top of her spectacles and he thought she was going to say something about the cashews. Then she turned through the envelopes.

Democratic National Committee, addressed to you. HOPE. CARE. Bread for the World. Alligator Refuge. I think that's all, except bills.

How many bills?

One, two, three, she said. Three. No, here's another.

My God, said Mr. Bemis.

Here's a note from Robin. I do hope they're enjoying the trip. Let's see, what else? This looks like an invitation from the Wibbles.

He watched her open the envelope. I don't want to go, he said.

Now isn't this tricky! A masquerade party the night before the election. They'll have presidential masks. George Washington. Lincoln. Eisenhower. Nixon. Jimmy Carter, who wasn't one of my favorites. Harry Truman. Gerald Ford. You can take your choice.

No, Mr. Bemis said. No.

You could be Grover Cleveland. He weighed three hundred pounds.

I don't weigh three hundred, Mr. Bemis said. I won't go. Absolutely not.

She opened the envelope from their daughter. Well, my goodness! Mark won a prize at a carnival.

What did he win?

A statue of Donald Duck. He loves it. Melanie skinned her elbow. Ed has a touch of flu. Oh, my word! Somebody broke into their car and stole the radio. They'll need to see the insurance company. Otherwise, everything's fine.

I'm glad they're having a good time, Mr. Bemis said. Now listen, Marguerite. I am seventy-three years old. My knees hurt. My back hurts. I don't want to stand around listening to Thornton and Stu and Betsy and Cliff and all the rest. I know their opinions on everything from school vouchers to nuclear bombs. Let's go to Costa Rica.

You were seventy-five last March. I'm going to phone Renée and tell her we'll be delighted.

I will throw up, Mr. Bemis said. I will kick their damn Siamese cat.

Ooma isn't Siamese. She's Persian. She's just adorable. And you needn't have a fit. The party isn't for another month, three weeks from Monday.

Monday? Mr. Bemis asked with dismay. That's football night. I think the Chiefs and Broncos are playing.

I'll be right back, she said.

Mr. Bemis threw a cashew into the fireplace and wondered how he might talk her out of it. He remembered going to costume parties when he was a child. He had worn a red devil mask and remembered looking through the eyeholes. Witches, goblins, clowns, all sorts of games—pin-the-tail-on-the-donkey, blindman's-buff, spin-the-bottle—little girls shrieking, balloons popping, parents watching, candied apples, licorice whips, paper hats, ice cream. It had been fun.

However, those days were gone. I don't want to bump into Charlie Hochstadt wearing a Reagan mask, he thought. Lord, what have I done to deserve this?

Reagan. Mr. Bemis threw another cashew at the fire. Why hadn't the man been dragged out of office by the heels? Ollie North funneling weapons to the Contras from the White House basement but El Presidente knew nothing about it. Smacking his lips when he was questioned, pretending to think. Let me see, now, that must have been some time back, some time ago. Smack. Yes, sir, a while ago. Smack. Smack. Well, now, I'm afraid I don't quite recall.

Mr. Bemis grunted and opened the newspaper. Oil prices rising. Electricians vote to strike. Light planes collide. Drought in Oklahoma. Post office worker shot dead. Charlton Heston looking less and less like Moses, more like Madame Tussaud's lover. Another religious cult swallows poison. Mutual funds merge.

He glanced up when his wife returned from the telephone.

Renée and I had the most delightful chat. Everyone is excited. It's going to be gobs of fun.

Somebody will put on a Truman mask and play the piano, Mr. Bemis said. Somebody will be FDR and wave a cigarette holder. Some jackass will do Nixon, hunch the shoulders and give us that V sign. Let's go to Costa Rica. Call that nice young woman at the travel agency and book us a flight.

I cannot bear it when you behave like this, she said. Will you please stop whining.

I only whine if there's a reason, Mr. Bemis said. I'm not as fat as Grover Cleveland.

Stop eating those cashews. All you get from now on is grapefruit juice.

Mr. Bemis glared at his left foot, which had begun to ache. He thought about the palm trees and sandy beaches and pretty girls in bathing suits. He looked out the window. It was raining, almost snowing.

AS THEY WERE being chauffeured to the party on election eve he remembered how much he despised Reagan. The man had spent the war in Hollywood and never heard a live bullet but he could not stop saluting. He saluted and saluted and saluted. He would snap off that Hollywood salute to a flagpole or a fireplug. He would salute a dachshund if there was a photographer nearby.

Proctor, stop that, his wife said.

Stop what? he asked.

You're grumbling.

I'll keep it to myself, he said.

How long have we been married?

Mr. Bemis thought about this. Why do you want to know?

I know perfectly well. But even now, after so many years, I cannot for the life of me understand you. At times you might as well be a complete stranger. She leaned forward. Phillips, do you have trouble seeing the road?

Phillips answered in his pleasantly neutral voice. No, Madam.

You will be careful, won't you?

Phillips replied that he would be careful.

Mr. Bemis watched snowflakes dissolve on the window and thought about trying to explain, but it would be difficult. She had voted for Reagan. She voted for Bush and Dole and Nixon. If she had been old enough she would have voted for Landon and Hoover and the Whigs. She hated Kennedys, all Kennedys, including wives and fifth cousins, and thought they contaminated whatever they touched. She disapproved of modern art and welfare and foreign aid. She did not like immigrants. She subscribed to newsletters warning that liberals had weakened the armed forces. The United States could be destroyed at any moment. Crazed, malignant letters oozing poison. Absurd theories. Libelous charges. Implausible conspiracies. Rhetorical questions. Secret societies. Jewish bankers. Communist armies in Montana. Letters concocted of hate and fear. Doomsday letters. Nourishment for the paranoid.

We'll have oodles of fun, she said, patting him on the knee. Just you wait.

I do not intend to wear a mask, he said. I like who I am.

Renée told me that several husbands objected. You can be yourself. I wouldn't expect anything else.

What about food?

There'll be a nice buffet.

Itty-bitty pinkie sandwiches and cheese dip, Mr. Bemis said. I wish we were going to Costa Rica.

However, the Wibble buffet was sumptuous, imperial, a whopping tribute to an exemplary bourgeois life. Mr. Bemis gazed with satisfaction at the roast beef, sliced breast of duck, venison, platoons of shrimp, a giant salmon, lamb chops sprinkled with herbs, prosciutto, crisp little sausages, and more. Rosy red tomatoes stuffed with something creamy. Butterfly pasta. Mushrooms. Mr. Bemis gazed at the beautiful mushrooms. Asparagus points, juicy pickles, gargantuan black olives. Nor was that all, oh no. Desserts. A perfect regiment of seductive desserts. Lemon tart. Mince pie topped with hard sauce. Blue and white cheeses. Chocolate mousse. Peaches. Pears. Melons. Petits fours. Nuts. Strawberries. A silver compote of mints. Fancy bonbons individually wrapped in gold foil. Nor was that all. Mr. Bemis clasped his hands.

Good to see you! boomed a familiar voice. Mighty good! I am counting on your vote, sir!

There stood Quint Huckleby disguised as Abe Lincoln.

Hello, Quint, said Mr. Bemis.

Lincoln is the name, sir. Abraham Lincoln. May I take this opportunity to remind you that our great nation stands at a crossroads. Tomorrow we decide. Shall we permit ourselves to be hornswaggled? Or do we fulfill our grand and glorious destiny with the Grand Old Party? Should I be fortunate enough to earn the confidence of the American public I shall propose to Congress that we chase those Democrat scalawags out of town. Tar and feathers, sir! That's the ticket!

Huckleby shuffled into the crowd, bowing to ladies, clapping men on the shoulder.

Mr. Bemis looked around and saw Marguerite chatting with the Vandenhaags. He looked again at the buffet. An olive, perhaps? One or two little sausages? What harm could there be in a slice of duck?

He noticed Speed Voelker loading a plate. Voelker never seemed to change. Year after year a bulky, menacing presence in a tailored pinstripe suit. Broken nose. Massive, sloping shoulders. Neck like a tree stump. Diamond ring. Hair slicked back like a hoodlum in some gangster film. Big as a water buffalo.

I hear you and Dodie went to Europe, Mr. Bemis said.

Voelker nodded. The whole shebang. Tower of London. Norway. Copenhagen. Swiss Alps. Berlin. Venetian gondolas. You name it. Europe costs like the elephant these days.

Uncle Sam gave me a tour, Mr. Bemis said. Didn't cost a cent. France, Belgium, Rhineland. Mostly on foot.

Voelker grinned. I was a lieutenant in Patton's outfit. Like to froze my nuts off. Mud, rain, C rations, bugs. I saw that old fart once, close enough to touch.

I saw Ike, Mr. Bemis said. He drove by in a Jeep.

McCarthy deserved a medal. Ike didn't do squat about those Commies at State.

Yankee Doodle and all, Mr. Bemis thought.

Voelker pointed his fork at the dessert table. Eisenhower was reaching for a chocolate mousse.

He ought to be here. Straighten out the lefties.

They watched Eisenhower pick up a few bonbons.

Tomorrow we kick butt. Dump the goddam liberals. They ought to move to Russia if they don't like the U.S.A.

Enemy headquarters, Mr. Bemis thought. He watched Voelker stab a slice of beef and tried to remember how long they had been acquainted. Norman Voelker. Star athlete. Captain of the high school football team. Honor roll. Class president. Speed to his friends. And what was I? Corridor guide. Nothing else after my name in the yearbook. I didn't know how to catch a football and if I tried to jump a hurdle I'd have broken my neck. He never spoke to me. Not once. Not once in four years did he say hello. Now here we are, high-priced attorney and ex-stockbroker, members of the same country club, almost equal. Almost. Not quite.

Jerry Ford, Voelker said.

And there he stood, jaw protruding, vacuous, amiable, shaking hands with Lucy Waldrop.

He played at Michigan. Pretty good lineman.

Mr. Bemis munched a spear of asparagus and thought about Ford pardoning Nixon. Twenty-five flunkies went to jail, maybe twenty-six, but not Tricky Dick. Everybody thought the republic would collapse if Richard Milhous wore prison stripes. In fact, the republic would be better off if Nixon had spent a couple of decades mumbling and raving in the jug. No man is above the law, we told ourselves. What a lie. The time has come to put this matter behind us, declared his faithful subordinate who by the grace of God and a terrified Congress inherited the office.

Those eighteen minutes of tape. What skulduggery did they preserve? Jimmy Hoffa. Mr. Nixon, high priest of law and order, scourge of corrupt unions, pardoned Jimmy Hoffa, who strolled out of prison and dropped from sight as if he had walked the plank. Was he squashed inside an old Chevrolet? Why did Mr. Nixon intervene? Rosemary Woods deserved a medal for loyalty, if nothing else, trying to demonstrate how she accidentally erased those eighteen minutes, almost twisted her back out of joint. Meanwhile the world's greatest investigative body, the FBI, couldn't figure out what happened.

Mr. Bemis grunted, heard himself make some disrespectful remark and observed Voelker light up with rage.

Norman! Marguerite exclaimed. What a pleasure! It's been ages! You look marvelous! Ida Mae tells me that you and Dodie treated yourselves to the Grand Tour. That must have been a thrill. Did you see the fountains of Rome? Proctor and I are so jealous.

She went on talking while Mr. Bemis considered the situation. People were gathering around Voelker. They wanted to be seen chatting with him. That being so, why not slip away to the buffet? Nobody would notice. Why not two or three of those tasty little shrimp? Prosciutto? Of course. Mushrooms? Yes, indeed. Another pickle? Maybe a soupçon of pasta?

He found himself at the table. He spoke cheerfully to the Armacosts, recommended the mushrooms. He said hello to Woody Schenk, discussed the Wyandotte Hills Country Club renovation. He nodded to Virginia Tyler, whom he did not like very much, spread anchovy paste on five crackers, reached for some olives, and moved along. He walked around the table for another slice of duck. Then he paused.

Missouri Waltz, he said.

Sure enough, Harry was thumping the piano. Beside him stood Jimmy Carter theatrically beating time.

He thought about Jimmy's struggle with the rabbit. Nobody except Bosch or maybe Lewis Carroll could have dreamed it up—March hare bent upon murder swimming crazily toward the President, planning to bite his ankle. Jimmy in that canoe flailing away with a paddle. The rabbit finished him. Inflation got out of control, which was serious.

And that hostage fiasco, American helicopters on a cloak-and-dagger rescue mission lurching around the desert like injured bats, that was humiliating. But the rabbit did him in. The President fighting a loony rabbit, that was too much.

Nancy Reagan should have been there, he thought as he slipped a cracker into his mouth. The newspapers said she carried a pistol, itty-bitty derringer or some such. Blap! No more bunny. Mr. Bemis stopped chewing. Why did she carry a pistol? He tried to remember if she had been in any of Reagan's films, maybe the dance hall girl in some Wild West horse opera. What could happen in the White House? He imagined her leading a gaggle of tourists. They pause to admire a portrait of John Adams when out pops the masked intruder from behind a marble bust of Spiro Agnew. Stick 'em up! Your purse or your life! But the First Lady is prepared. Not so fast, young fellow! Just you wait till I find my derringer. Let's see. Kleenex, aspirin, nail file, sunglasses, eye shadow, lipstick, mascara, brush, comb, tweezers, cold cream, lotion, scissors, hairspray, compact—I know it's here someplace.

He thought about Charlton Heston brandishing an eighteenth-century musket for the benefit of photographers and gung-ho patriots. Moses defending life, liberty, and his Beverly Hills mansion from the redcoats. Why not an assault rifle? Why not wave a Saturday Night Special?

I do believe, murmured a voice from the past, I know this handsome dog.

Mr. Bemis turned around and there beneath a ragged brown toupee resembling a smashed bird nest, decades older than when last seen, was Howie—the same Howie Price-Dodge who got so drunk he tried to climb the Spanish-American War memorial and served heroically in the OSS and married a Chicago stripper and demolished the family fortune.

Get yourself a plate and let's talk, Mr. Bemis said. In fact, I'll join you.

Howie explained that during the Vietnam War he went back into service. He had been a liaison officer stationed at the Pentagon. He knew McNamara. He attended high-level briefings. He shuttled between Washington and Saigon and learned quite a bit. He knew

Westmoreland. He had ridden in helicopters while enemy soldiers were interrogated and saw them pushed out.

This world is no place for idealists, he said.

On the contrary, said Mr. Bemis.

Howie squinted, adjusted his toupee, and went on talking while Mr. Bemis thought about the days when they agreed upon almost everything from politics to women to beer. It was strange that so much time had gone by. He looked around the room at familiar faces and it occurred to him that this was where he belonged. Yes, he thought, I'm one of these people. I've lived a solid Republican life. I earned money the good old-fashioned way selling stocks and bonds, lots of money. I joined the best country club. Marguerite and I have a couple of fancy cars and a very expensive home. I drove myself to the office for at least a hundred years while Marguerite took care of everything else. We've done our work, toted that bale. We deserve what we have. Yes, I belong here. The trouble is, I feel like an Eskimo.

Howie was explaining that America could have won the war if it hadn't been for draft dodgers and the liberal media. And while Mr. Bemis listened to Howie justify Vietnam he remembered the ugliness. Even now, after all this time, it festered like the Nixon pardon, provoking arguments, refusing to heal. The flesh of the nation was raw. The photograph of that naked child seared by napalm running toward the camera screaming in agony, that image would not fade. And he reflected that he had frequently touted E. I. Du Pont, which manufactured napalm. Du Pont, as everyone knew, was a substantial corporation with good earnings, a secure dividend, and offered the likelihood of capital appreciation. A dollar invested with Du Pont was a dollar prudently invested.

Mr. Bemis examined his plate. Celery. Two olives. One radish. Not much. Howie was interpreting the disaster, explaining why the security of the United States depended upon Southeast Asia. Mr. Bemis munched an olive and looked around. Next to a flattering oil portrait of Cope Wibble in a ponderous gold frame stood Emmajane Kathren, Democrat, chatting with the Altschulers while holding a shrimp impaled on a toothpick. Beneath the glowing chandelier stood Monte and Lorraine Fordyce, Democrats both, listening to Joslyn Upshaw. We're not many, he thought. Oh, not many. What's to become of us?

Half a century from now will we be extinct? And as he considered this it did not seem implausible.

Is that Speed? Howie asked.

Mr. Bemis nodded. Voelker was holding DeWitt Simms firmly by one elbow while talking to his wife.

Lord God, Howie said, I'll never forget the way he flattened that Rockhurst defensive back. Everybody in the bleachers whooping, then you could hear a pin drop. What was that kid's name?

It happened sixty years ago, Mr. Bemis said. McNabb, McNee, McGee, one of those names.

Paralyzed, Howie said. Just a kid. Hell of a note. I still see that ambulance on the field.

They watched Simms try to pull away. Voelker ignored him.

Built like a piano. Give him the ball and Katie bar the door.

Harry Truman was plunking out "Sewanee River." A woman laughed insanely. Voelker—arrogant as a Babylonian king—held Simms captive, demeaning the man in front of his wife. A Texas voice boasted about upholding law and order with a noose. Two masks collided and all at once it seemed to Mr. Bemis that he had entered a madhouse where the inmates were performing a macabre dance.

Voelker approached casually but rapidly, sapphire-blue eyes fixed on Howie. Almost at once they were discussing Vietnam, why it was necessary, how the war could have been won.

Voelker gripped Mr. Bemis by the elbow. What about you, sport? Tell us what you think. Did you support our troops?

I mistrusted the government, Mr. Bemis said.

Tell us about it, soldier. We want to know what you think.

You want to know what I think? I remember how Ike tiptoed into that swamp and Kennedy followed. The best and brightest had no more sense than Hogan's goat. And I remember LBJ plunging ahead like a goddamn rhinoceros. I remember Nixon after everybody got sick of the war telling us he had a secret plan for ending it. He told us delicate negotiations were under way. My grandfather's banana. Nixon kept it going past election day because he wanted another term in office. You want my opinion, lieutenant? I didn't salute.

Mr. Bemis jerked his arm away from Voelker.

He had addressed the office staff on various occasions, but this was different. It occurred to him that he should have chosen public life. He saw himself on the floor of the Senate addressing misguided colleagues, instructing, ridiculing, exhorting, convincing. Persuasive arguments came to mind, burning rhetoric, soaring imagery.

No doubt you gentlemen recall the domino theory. No doubt you recall the days when half the citizens of this country thought we should turn Hanoi into a parking lot because if we didn't stop the Communists over there we'd have to stop them on the beaches of Hawaii. If not Hawaii, the beaches of California. Do you remember when schoolchildren were taught to crouch underneath their desks? Keep away from windows. Pull down the shades. Atomic bombs are dangerous. Do you recall the backyard bomb shelter? Of course you do. We were advised by our government to dig holes in the ground. Furnish the hole with toilet paper, matches, bottled water, spinach, dehydrated beef, Graham crackers. Newspaper delivery may be suspended. Magazines and phonograph records may help to pass the time. Moonstruck madness, gentlemen, if I might borrow a phrase from the great John Milton.

Mr. Bemis discovered that he had an audience. People were staring. Obviously they wished to know more.

Ladies and gentlemen, while destitute citizens rummage through garbage cans and prowl the streets, what does our government do? It sheathes the Pentagon in gold. I submit to you that we could at this moment vaporize whatever creeps, crawls, flies, walks, hops, slithers, or jumps. I submit to you that we could do this thirty times over. Meanwhile, Republicans wring their hands, claiming we are defenseless, ill prepared, at the mercy of two-bit tyrants. In fact, no eight countries on earth allocate as much to the splendid science of war as we do, yet conservatives argue that we need a Maginot Line in the sky. As Mr. Reagan explained it, a missile shield will protect us from nuclear attack just as a roof protects a house from rain. The simplicity of this man's logic astounds us.

Mr. Bemis realized that his voice had risen. He patted his brow with a handkerchief.

May I remind you that when Isaac Newton was president of the Royal Society he caused a newly designed cannon to be rejected. Why? Because, Sir Isaac said, it was a diabolic instrument meant only

for mass killing. Our culture, ladies and gentlemen, is altogether
different.

What do people in other countries think of us? he asked. How do
they regard us?

This was a provocative question, so he paused significantly before
continuing.

They see a nation steeped in righteousness where guns are as easy
to buy as lollipops. A nation that executes criminals without spilling
one drop of blood. A nation of hypocritical preachers with the brains
of pterodactyls and politicians who would sell their daughters for a
vote. But I digress. Let me say a few words about our teflon President.
He informed us that pollution is caused by trees. Many of us did not
realize that. He told us that a Nicaraguan army could march from
Managua to Harlingen, Texas, in two days. Yes, two days. Honduras,
El Salvador, Guatemala, Mexico. Quite a march. And once across the
Rio Grande, what would these Nicaraguan Communists do? Burn the
Harlingen County Courthouse?

Folks, I'm just getting started. Dutch opened his presidential campaign in Philadelphia, Mississippi. He did that for a reason. He went to
that town where three civil rights workers were lynched and declared
that he stood for states' rights. Every good ol' boy from Tallahassee to
Kalamazoo got the message.

Nor should we forget those Marines in Beirut. The Joint Chiefs
advised pulling out of Lebanon. Mr. Reagan knew better. What happened? Some Lebanese kid drove up to Marine headquarters in a truck
loaded with TNT. Two hundred and forty-one dead Marines.

It occurred to Mr. Bemis that he might have talked long enough,
but there was so much to be said.

Ronald Reagan secretly attempted to overthrow the elected government of another country and what did Congress do? Renamed the
airport in his honor. Fifty years from now people will wonder what
kind of dope we were smoking.

Mr. Bemis took a deep breath. He felt encouraged. People were
attentive.

He heard himself speak of George Bush whose nose kept growing—
longer, longer, and longer. He spoke of the oil in Kuwait, of April
Glaspie. He spoke of Jesse Helms, of Joseph McCarthy, J. Parnell

Thomas. He pointed a finger while speaking of the National Rifle
Association. Ladies and gentlemen, he said, some things about this
country turn my innards upside down. Politicians claim they trust
the judgment of ordinary people. Well, sir, I do not. Athenian citizens
condemned Socrates to death. So much for the perspicacity of John
Q. Public. Did I mention Roman Hruska?

He noticed that his audience was dwindling. He looked around for
his wife. There she stood, her face a deathly mask, arms crossed.

Are you satisfied? she asked. Dodie and Norman left in a huff.
Norman was livid.

Mr. Bemis felt tired. It was late and his knees ached. He wanted
to go home. He saw that it was snowing and wondered if they might
have trouble on the Sycamore hill.

All at once people stopped talking because somebody outside had
fired a gun. Several men walked uneasily toward the windows.

ON THE WAY home Marguerite abruptly threw up both hands like an
opera singer. I do not believe, she said, enunciating each word, that
ever in my life have I felt so embarrassed and ashamed.

I thought I did quite well, said Mr. Bemis.

Proctor, what in the name of sense? What on earth? I cannot imagine what got into you. Oh, I could simply expire.

It just happened, he said. It felt good.

That speech was utterly incomprehensible. April Glaspie! J. Parnell
Thomas! Nobody had the faintest idea what you were talking about.

I did, said Mr. Bemis.

Roman Hruska! I haven't heard that name in fifty years.

I didn't like him, Mr. Bemis said. There were a lot of people I didn't
get around to. J. Edgar Hoover. Thurmond. Rusk. Laird. I could think
of plenty.

Proctor, do you realize what you've done? We won't be on anyone's
guest list. Never again. Never! Never! Never!

That wouldn't be the end of the world, said Mr. Bemis.

She put one hand to her forehead. Oh, this has been a perfect night-
mare! I can just see Eunice Hupp telling everyone under the sun. And
let there be no mistake, Proctor, I certainly want the United Nations
out of our country. Foreigners have no business telling us what to do.

If those foreign bankers get their way they'll take every cent we have. Every last cent. Furthermore, you know quite well that the Trilateral Commission is bent on enslaving America.

We've gone through this a hundred times, said Mr. Bemis. And how many times did we quarrel about Vietnam? he wondered.

I think I'm going to cry. It was such a nice party. Socrates! I have not the remotest idea what goes on inside your head. There are times when I think I married an alien.

That's interesting, Mr. Bemis said. That hadn't occurred to me.

Everybody was having so much fun. I'm just sick. Honestly, I wanted to sink through the floor. Phillips, she said, raising her voice, are you able to see the road?

Yes, Madam, Phillips replied.

It looks awfully snowy. Shouldn't we take Leimert?

I believe we can make it up Sycamore, Phillips replied in the same neutral voice. We could take Leimert if you prefer.

Mr. Bemis grinned. Phillips didn't want to lose his job. Who are you pulling for? he asked. The elephant or the jackass?

In tomorrow's election, sir? Both candidates seem qualified.

He's afraid I'll fire him, Mr. Bemis thought. I wish he'd speak up. All of us had better speak up.

Phillips looked straight ahead, gloved hands on the wheel, attending to business.

I know who I'm voting for, Mrs. Bemis said. I am unbearably tired of scandal. One thing after another. It's time we restored decency to government.

Mr. Bemis considered mentioning Nixon, but that was a long-dead horse. Decency in government. What an oxymoron. Both candidates seem qualified. One of them can't remember how to button his shirt and the other would lick dirt from a voter's boots.

As he reflected upon the evening he felt pleased with himself. I blew that party to smithereens, he thought. Hoisted the Jolly Roger—not that it will do any good. And the shot. Sooner or later everybody will find out that Speed blasted a snowdrift or a tree or punched a hole in the sky. Nobody will be able to make sense of it. Ha!

What a blessing Ronald Reagan wasn't there, she said as they waited for a traffic light.

That fake, Mr. Bemis said. I needed another twenty minutes.

Ronald Reagan was a President we could admire and trust. He won the Cold War and cut taxes and set us on the road to prosperity. He made us feel good about ourselves and he brought back morning to America when many people thought we were on the verge of night. Those tax-and-spend Democrats want to give our money to black people.

She heard that on the radio, Mr. Bemis thought. Some right-wing gasbag. She believes whatever they say. She's a true believer and she's terrified. She gets up in the middle of the night to pray.

I just hope the Republicans win, she said.

Mr. Bemis folded his hands across his belly and considered the invasion of Grenada. A sleepy tourist island near Venezuela. Reagan ordered the attack without consulting Congress, probably without consulting anybody except Nancy's astrologer. Why? Because the Prime Minister was liberal and the airport runway was being extended. Soviet bombers would be able to land and refuel en route to the United States. True enough, if they flew the wrong direction a couple of thousand miles. Reagan never looked at a map in his life. If he did, he couldn't understand all those numbers and squiggly lines. So what happened? U.S. Navy planes bombed the Grenada mental hospital. They didn't mean to bomb a hospital, but they did. An international court of justice at The Hague condemned Reagan. Nobody cared. Millions want his face on the ten-dollar bill. Millions want him on Rushmore. All right, there's room enough if we get rid of Lincoln.

People forget, he said. They ought to be reminded.

You certainly don't forget. And I do not wish to be reminded of anything else. I have heard more than enough, Proctor. More than enough.

She had almost divorced him because of Vietnam so he decided to keep quiet. He thought about Howie, who seemed a bit uncomfortable with himself. Years at the Pentagon. Policy wonks. Alice in Wonderland briefings. Light at the end of the tunnel. Somewhere along the way they got him.

Now what are you grumbling about? she asked.

I wasn't, he said.

I thought you would never stop eating. I was so humiliated. You made four trips to the buffet.

Three, Mr. Bemis said, holding up three fingers.

Eunice Hupp was watching me while you made a fool of yourself.
Oh, Proctor, how could you do such a thing? I'll never live it down.

I took one small step for mankind, said Mr. Bemis.

I do not understand what possesses you. We have so much to be
thankful for. We have a nice home in the loveliest neighborhood. We
have everything we could possibly want. Everything.

She was right, of course. And yet, he thought, she's wrong. Is there
anything I want, he asked himself, that I don't have? I don't know. I'm
a success. I ought to feel satisfied.

Phillips drove carefully up the Sycamore hill. Streetlights through
falling snow reminded Mr. Bemis of a village in France when he had
been a private in the Army. He tried to recall the name of the village
but it was gone. He touched the window with one finger. The glass
was warmer than he expected and the snow was turning to slush. He
wondered how he could be seventy-five years old when he had been
a young soldier just yesterday.

Marguerite, he said, I'm hungry.

What little of her face could be seen above the collar of the fur coat
proved that he had not been forgiven.

You are imagining, she said. You couldn't conceivably be hungry.

That was an hour ago, he said. What's in the fridge?

She refused to answer.

He thought affectionately of the buffet—gorgeous black olives,
anchovy crackers, lamb chops, venison, duck, salmon, lemon tart—
and heard a familiar rumble in his stomach. He considered the evening
while Phillips drove them homeward and something from Aristophanes sifted like a snowflake through the years. What heaps of things
have bitten me to the heart! A small few pleased me, very few.

That was not the whole of it, but he could not remember what came
next. For now, that was enough.

St. Augustine's Pigeon

Too late loved I Thee, O Thou Beauty of ancient
days, yet ever new! too late I loved Thee! And
behold, Thou wert within, and I abroad, and
there I searched for Thee! deformed I,
plunging amid those fair forms which
Thou hadst made . . .

MUHLBACH closes the book sharply. How long must this continue? he asks of himself. Everywhere and always this theme
recurs, spirit opposing flesh. I'd thought I would escape,
but as Augustine would say, Alas! Yes, indeed, alas. Here am I dressed
up for the twentieth century, affluent, reasonably affluent, stuffed with
trivial comforts, with a home in a borough, two children, and my wife
is dead. The pain of deprivation subsides neither more nor less quickly,
I suspect, for me than it did for him; and the body's flesh does not care
for sentiment more now than in past millenniums, conscious only that
it has been deprived. What is more selfish than the body's appetite?

He taps the book with his index finger, a bit didactically, and puts
it on the shelf. Rising from the depths of his green leather reading
chair, he walks to the window; there he stands for a long time with a
meditative and dissatisfied expression. From across the river Manhattan confronts him.

It's possible, he says aloud, that I ought to acquire a mistress. I've
said to myself that I should live moderately, which I have done, but too
long. My spirit is suffocating. I've all but forgotten the taste of pleasure. It's as though I'd eaten plain bread for a year. What is ordinarily
sweet and natural to other men seems as exotic to me as frangipani
or a glimpse of Zanzibar. My senses are withering. My fingertips have
memorized only the touch of paper. I need to court an Indian dancer

with bells strung to her ankles, I need to go out shooting tigers, smoke hashish, explore the Himalayas. God knows what I need.

He turns from the window and looks critically at the room where he spends so much time. It is a comfortable room, this study he has established, a sanctuary, a rectory filled with books, a few photographs, records, a humidor, the substantial chair—yes, and it has become odious.

Muhlbach suddenly clasps his hands as though he were about to drop to his knees before an idol and offer up some passionate supplication. There are times a man must liberate his soul, otherwise he's in for trouble.

If I do not, he says, but persist in guiding my life, the reins of it beneath my thumb—well, who knows? It is not moderate or reasonable to live as immoderately as a demented anchorite plucking thistles for a shirt, suffering voluptuous hallucinations. A woman could save me from myself. And surely it should not be difficult to find one, not if I proceed logically.

Just then Mrs. Grunthe, that paragon, that archetype of sense and logic, brusquely raps at the study door.

Eight o'clock. Supper's on the table.

Whereupon she departs, muttering. But Mrs. Grunthe always mutters, whether the day has been good or bad. The plink of mandolins sounds no different to her than the crash of lightning; in fact it would be alarming, thinks Muhlbach, if her disposition improved.

Eight o'clock, he says softly. I'm sure it is. Exactly eight. This, too, is my own doing. How many times has Mrs. Grunthe laid out supper at eight? The hour does suit me, the emanations of the day are gone, it all seems natural. The children are ravenous by six and I'm never home by then, so we eat separately. It's as though I have no family any more. Yes, I'm exiled from delight, he thinks, opening the study door.

And what do we have for supper? Chicken à la king with peas. Hardly a banquet. Mrs. Grunthe for some reason likes to prepare chicken à la king. We have it too often, I wonder if I should let her know. The problem is, she's not good at taking hints. What was last night's supper? He pauses, napkin half unfolded, and tries to remember what he was given to eat twenty-four hours ago, but cannot.

I believe I'll have a little wine, Mrs. Grunthe.

This isn't Sunday, she answers, Sunday being the day he is in the habit of opening a small bottle; nevertheless she plods off to fetch it.

This isn't Sunday, he remarks when she's out of hearing. Has my life sunk to such a pattern? I ask for a bottle of wine on Saturday night and my housekeeper comments. She may even tell her friends about this strange occurrence. Next thing you know, Bertha, he'll take to drinking on Monday and Tuesday and Wednesday and every other blessed day of the week. You can go a long way to hell with little steps.

And furthermore, Muhlbach announces silently when she reenters with the wine, I intend to go to hell, Mrs. Grunthe—very quickly, if I may say so. I'm planning to catch myself a little something, Mrs. Grunthe. What d'you think of that, eh?

Will you be wanting anything else?

Muhlbach is startled. The wine, of course, that's what she means. Will I be making any other odd demands, that's all. She wasn't reading my mind. And he is tempted to ask: Why? Are you going out? For a moment the thought has come to him that Mrs. Grunthe is about to take a lover. She's going to slip away from the kitchen and run barefoot through the night, one hundred and eighty pounds of nymph, to the eager arms of Salvador, the mechanic. Salvador has been seen drinking coffee in the kitchen when he should have been flat on his back on a dolly beneath an automobile at Sunbeam Motors; God knows what intrigue has been prepared.

No, no, nothing else, Mrs. Grunthe. How are the children?

Both quiet. Donna's gone to sleep. Otto is in his room building a model airplane.

That's fine. Oh, by the way, Mrs. Grunthe, I'll be going to the city for a little while this evening.

No response.

Muhlbach feels a trifle let down; after all, when one is setting out to discover a mistress, and gives a hint, it's justifiable to expect some curiosity. He pushes his fork at the creamed chicken and eats without appetite. It is not the stomach that's hungry.

When he has finished eating he doesn't linger with a cigarette but immediately goes upstairs to Donna's room. She is thoroughly asleep, too beautiful to be real. No doubt she is dreaming of princes and castles and white horses with flowing manes.

Otto in his room is just as quiet; he is gluing an insignia on the airplane and cannot be distracted by much conversation.

I'll be going out for a while, Otto.

Okay, says Otto.

I won't be late. If you want anything, Mrs. Grunthe will be here.

Okay, I know it, says Otto.

Incidentally, have you finished your homework?

At this Otto looks bemused, as though he has never heard of any such thing.

Speak up. Is it done?

Practically, says Otto, and quickly adds that he can do it tomorrow. But the rule is that he does his weekend homework on Saturday because he tends to disappear on Sunday.

I think, says Muhlbach, you'd better do it now. A short, fierce, querulous discussion follows, which ends with Otto sighing heavily.

Okay, but it's nothing except some stupid decimals and junk that any moron could do with one hand tied behind him.

In that case, my friend, if you are such a mathematical prodigy, why did your last report card show a C minus in arithmetic?

But to this there is no answer. Muhlbach does not insist. The horse has been flogged enough. Otto is on his feet with a gloomy expression rummaging about for a textbook.

So the house is in order, the inhabitants making their usual rounds, and Muhlbach considers himself free to do what he pleases. He heads for the shower, thoughtfully, fingering his bald spot. I'm going out to attract a woman, he thinks, and not by the use of my wallet; that may not be easy, I do look a bit professorial, but still it's true that women aren't so fussy about appearances as we are. And I'm not ugly, it's just that I look uncommunicative, as though I had a briefcase full of government secrets. I wish I didn't always look so stiff, but what can I do? Maybe I should try to smile more often, my teeth aren't bad. Well—step up, ladies! One insurance expert in average health, slightly bald, slightly soft at the hip, more perceptive than most, but also more constrained than most, seeks passionate and exotic companion between ages of eighteen and—now really, let's not be absurd!

Begin again. Between ages of twenty, no, twenty-three, for instance, and, ah, thirty-five. Thirty. Twenty-six. Must be, ah, sophisticated and, umm, discreet. Abandoned. Lascivious. Dissolute. The more dissolute the better. Everything that I am not but would like so much to be. A young lady experienced in each conceivable depravity, totally intemperate, unbuttoned, debauched, gluttonous, uncorked, crapulous, self-indulgent, drunken, and preferably insatiable. Never mind if it is an adolescent dream, never mind. There may be no such woman this side of Singapore, but I won't settle for less. Not for a little while. What about Eula?

Thank you, I believe not, he says to himself in the mirror, cautiously parting his hair and frowning. Eula Cunningham is comfortable as a pillow is comfortable, which at times is quite enough, but sometimes is not. Eula is yesterday's bouquet. Eula is a loaf of bread, unleavened and thirty-eight years old, if I'm any judge. Thirty-two, she claims. Maybe. She gives me the feeling of thirty-eight. I don't say she's stale or hard, no, no, it's just that she's like any domestic beast, or a geranium on the windowsill, and let the metaphors fly where they choose.

Straightening up, he draws a long breath and studies his chest. It is not impressive. He exhales. No, it is not impressive at all.

He turns the shower handle, tests the water with one hand, shivers and wraps a towel about his pale shoulders. There he stands meditatively naked, curling his toes into the fluffy blue rug while he waits, a sight to inspire terror in nobody, the image of no feminine dream. He thinks again of Eula. Madame Everyday, that's what she is. Eula has the instincts of Mrs. Grunthe and fifty million others. Proper sisters, all of them. Eula won't be pinning an orchid in her hair or shimmying across the room, not now, not ever, because she never has, because it would attract attention, would be rather flamboyant, cause eyebrows to lift. She won't fly away to Las Vegas to play roulette, she won't practice the Lotus position. She is, in fact, just like me, reason enough to catch a cat of another color.

Muhlbach flings away his towel and thrusts himself beneath the shower as though he were plunging into a waterfall.

Mrs. Grunthe is downstairs waiting, arms folded, when he descends. Miss Cunningham has telephoned. What about? Mrs. Grunthe didn't ask, obviously doesn't care. I'm expected to call, he thinks, Eula's hoping I'll return that call, but I won't. I have other plans. Tonight I hope for the taste of Hell.

Good night, Mrs. Grunthe. If Miss Cunningham calls again, you can say that I'll get in touch with her soon.

Ten minutes later, underground and attached to a metal loop, it seems that he is already halfway to Hell. Rocking through the tunnel, he reflects once again that the professional aestheticians have been wrong, utility does not equal beauty. Some opposite dictum may lie closer to the truth. What is most useless or inefficient, say, is most appealing. What is more wasteful and extravagant, for example, than that epitome of sexual allure known as the chorus girl? But again, how is sex identified with beauty? It's a knotty problem.

Emerging from the subway, he sees just ahead, or thinks he does, a familiar profile. It's difficult to be positive, the crowd is gathering, shoving through the turnstile, and she is gone. He hurries a few steps further, stands on tiptoe, looks and looks, then turns around, searching every ramp, but she's disappeared. He goes to the phone booth.

Yes, she's listed in the book. In fact, she is listed twice. Blanche Gershman on East Seventy-third, Blanche Gershman on MacDougal Street. Which Blanche is real? Which is the red-haired Blanche with the poise of a lacquered mannequin whose husband killed himself? Chances are that she would not be living on MacDougal, not with her taste for elegance. He studies the number on Seventy-third. Here is the opportunity. Of course, the opportunity is not new; it is just that he's never thought of calling her, she has seemed so Continental and gelid, distant and expensive and bathed in rumor, a mistress of shadows. She is a figure in a French novel and he could not visualize himself with her. She must think of him—if ever she does think of him—as an office grub who has yet to recognize the exceptional perfumes of life. Persuading a woman that she has been mistaken can be a tedious process. Muhlbach hesitates.

If it was indeed Blanche getting off the subway, then ipso facto she can't be at home and therefore to call her now would be a waste of time. On the other hand, she probably doesn't ride the subway, ever. She might be home. Still, it's Saturday night, very unlikely that she's there, she's more apt to be at somebody's penthouse. He cannot make up his mind. But then suddenly he puts a dime in the slot and dials. The telephone rings just twice. A male voice answers.

I think there must be some mistake, says Muhlbach. What number do I have?

The voice reads off the number he has dialed.

I'm calling Blanche Gershman. Is she at home?

The voice asks who is calling Blanche.

It occurs to Muhlbach that this would be a good point at which to hang up. Something is wrong. If a man answers, hang up, that's the classic advice. But it has never happened to him—he has never called a woman without knowing the circumstances—and he finds that the idea of simply hanging up the receiver is both rude and cowardly. It smacks of being in some woman's home and dashing out the back door while the husband comes in the front. It's a bit farcical. He wants no part of it. Blanche is single, so far as he knows, a widow with whom he is acquainted and whom he has every right to call. He cannot bring himself to hang up, although he is certain that he has the correct number and also that Blanche's situation has changed. The male voice has such a proprietary sound.

He introduces himself to the unknown, explaining that he is acquainted with Blanche. Then he listens, expecting a congenial response, and hears nothing but hoarse breathing.

Is this by any chance her husband? he inquires, for it's possible that she has remarried.

The owner of the voice evidently is too confused or annoyed to speak. The receiver at the other end of the line is clumsily dropped in its cradle; Muhlbach, at once a little surprised but yet not too surprised by this treatment, is left holding a dead instrument. He feels insulted by such tactlessness and for a few moments does not hang up. However, there's nothing else to do. Nor would there be much point in calling again. Does Blanche have a new husband or a lover? He suspects it is the latter, and this is oddly gratifying. All right, she has found someone, so will he.

Out of the phone booth, he pauses to settle his hat and straighten his tie before the mirror of a chewing gum machine, then briskly walks up the steps toward the surface world. Blanche might not have been an appropriate mistress in any case. Probably she wouldn't. It's just as well. He feels a bit relieved. Talking to her could have been quite awkward; no doubt she would have thought he was calling in regard to her policy. And for a woman she's tall, close to being a flagpole. She's graceful and sensuous, true, her movements are feline—she knows what men are all about. Isn't it a pity that this experience couldn't be housed in the satin corpulence of Eula Cunningham—that amiable Venus of Willendorf, steatopygous as an Upper Paleolithic figure. Now there would be a woman, thinks Muhlbach, there would be something!

Exactly what sort of a mistress should a man have? The possibilities are infinite. A ballet mouse, agile and quiet and seldom noticed? Or a more heroic piece of goods? One of the great madams, say, regal and unforgettable, with a cold eye and a bank account and scattered parcels of real estate, supporting her amplitude behind black corsets like a formidable gift from faraway provinces. Or an actress dressed up in hats and veils. A society girl?—somebody you could introduce to senators. Well, he thinks, who or what's waiting for me? My shoes are polished and there's money in my pocket. Not a great amount, but enough for tonight. I'm ready for adventure. Now, let's see, where shall I find it?

He stops walking and looks around, for it occurs to him that he doesn't have a plan in mind and has allowed himself to be carried half a block by the crowd. Well, the logical place to begin hunting for an available woman is in the middle of town, is it not? Yes, all right. What happens next?

I'm going in this direction because of the people alongside me, he reflects, but this is foolish. Suppose I work my way into the con-trary stream, where will that lead me? What should I do? I ought to do something, I ought to make a positive gesture. Take the ferry to Staten Island? That doesn't seem appropriate; if I should meet a strange woman on the ferry she'd be apt to have a book tucked under her arm. She'd wear spectacles and her hair would be in a tidy bun. No, no, I've come to Carthage for the sizzling and frying of unholy love. I won't go to Staten Island.

He studies a billboard advertising a musical comedy on which there is a chorus girl fifteen feet tall. The corner of the billboard is streaked with birdlime. This does not add to her appeal, but it can be overlooked. What sort of mistress would she make? Avaricious she is, there's that look in her wickedly tilted eye. But also there's little doubt that she is passionate, probably given to illegal practices. This, he thinks, is the sort of woman I'm after, the question being merely how she's obtained. Must I buy ticket after ticket to the same seat and endure this loutish entertainment for God knows how many weeks until she can't help but notice me? Is she worth all that? Six dollars for each performance. It would cost a hundred dollars before she so much as recognized my face.

If not a chorus girl, what? A cigarette girl, possibly. That would not be so glamorous, but after all I won't be taking her to Sun Valley or the Riviera where she would need to be introduced. And philosophers tell us that one's like another, attraction is where we find it. What about a model? A Tintoretto creature living in a cold-water flat, whose friends are intellectual and consumptive? That might be stimulating, a substitute for the youth in Paris that I never had. It's not too late. I'm just past forty, and artists and their kind are notoriously indifferent to age, among other things. Yes, that might do. Well now, I could pay a visit to Washington Square and see what's going on. I don't want a receptionist or a secretary or a teacher or a female executive or Eula Cunningham. What I require is something in spangled tights — a cocktail waitress, for example, who works at some extraordinary place with a shadowy reputation, where they ring a bell and girls come sliding down a fireman's pole. That sort of thing. Something on that order. Yes, or a flamenco dancer from Valencia.

Where does one meet these women? They exist, one sees them on the stage, sees their pictures in magazines or in the Sunday supplement as a result of some affair under the most bizarre circumstances, hears of them having leapt naked into the Tivoli fountain. But otherwise, where are they concealed? Why are they not more available? Are there not enough of them to go around? Do they live secluded in Hollywood harems and in Fifth Avenue apartments with gold plumbing? Occasionally one does see them on the street near the entrance to Saks, say, or in the lobby of an elegant hotel. But they are unapproachable. They are guarded by watchful eyes, by the very mystique of their existence. They are not for the man who works conscientiously in his office at Metro Mutual, now and then removing his glasses to pinch the bridge of his nose and wonder where life has gone. They are not for him, they are not seen with men who carry briefcases and who ride the subway hopefully reading the *Wall Street Journal* for news that a moderate investment is prospering.

I have forty-five shares of General Motors, says Muhlbach to himself, and I have sixty—thanks to the split—of Allied Potash, plus several bits of this-and-that. It's a tidy egg, for years I've watched it hatching, but there's a certain type of woman who'd gobble it up. I must remind myself to be careful. Yes, I'll be cautious.

It seems to him that already he has compromised his security, and quite possibly Mrs. Grunthe suspects him of squandering funds that must be kept safe for Otto and Donna. But Mrs. Grunthe, he reflects, has assumed more significance than she deserves. A housekeeper she is, that's all, yet she functions like a guardian of virtue, implacable, honest, devout in her brutal Anglo-Nordic way, and a terror to every spot of grease, every germ that seeks to invade the house. Mrs. Grunthe is priceless, of course, but her rectitude is stifling. No doubt the germs expire as much from guilt as from the incessant and terrible roar of Mrs. Grunthe's vacuum cleaner.

It occurs to Muhlbach that he needs a drink. At home he customarily has a daiquiri before supper, and because he did not have one this evening he thinks he will have it now. There is a nice place that he remembers on Lexington so he turns in that direction, and presently is seated at the bar with the daiquiri between his fingers. The place is busier than he remembered, he has not been here for almost a year, and it has been remodeled. He observes the comings and goings through a gilded mirror and sips his drink. Then, because nobody is looking at him, he has a look at himself. It is luxury for a man to gaze at himself in public; women are allowed the privilege, men are ridiculed. Well, he decides, women are also ridiculed, but with affection. There's a difference.

He glances from side to side. Nobody's noticed, so he continues to study the image in the mirror: it appears to be that of a man who is either ill or exhausted. The lips are compressed. The eyebrows lean toward each other. And at this moment, Muhlbach thinks, I could not possibly smile. My head feels moulded, each feature set. I do believe I'm made of papier-mâché.

Just then two Hollywood people walk directly behind him and are ushered to a table. The woman's face and body are recognizable, although he cannot recall her name and does not think he has ever seen one of her movies. She is wearing a white leather trench coat open halfway to the navel and may not be wearing anything else. Of course it's impossible not to stare at her and inevitably their eyes meet. She looks at him boldly, for so long that he feels the blood rising to his face and is relieved when she looks away. Was there some meaning to this look? Can it be that she is tired of the pudgy director or producer, or whatever he is, and has issued a discreet invitation? Could it happen?

Muhlbach again stares into the mirror; the actress obviously is bored, she is yawning. Her lips are tinted not red but white, and have been outlined with a pencil; there is something inordinately sensual about this, the hollow of her mouth is suggestive.

She is offered a cigarette. She leans forward, the leather coat bulges, parts at the breast, two broad soft globes of flesh come pouring into view and rise slowly rather like poached eggs against each other. Down that phenomenal bosom the crease deepens and lengthens until, thinks Muhlbach, one could mail a letter in the slot.

Desperately he watches her preposterous body. She is not amusing, however ludicrous. Grotesque she may be, but amusing she is not; only fools, hermaphrodites, and jealous women pretend to find her so.

Quickly he steps down from the bar stool and avoids glancing at her while he makes his way to the street. She will having nothing to do with him; if she stared at him with such insolence and challenge it was merely what she had taught herself to do; she would return any man's gaze.

But what he has seen cannot be forgotten and he strides along angrily, sober and baffled. It seems to him unjust, unjust that he must spend his life and energy among women such as Eula, ordinary women—unimaginative, average, modest women. It is not right. He feels obscurely cheated; it seems to him that if he were given the chance he could prove himself with the half-mad actress in a way that he has never proved himself before. He clenches his fists, halted by a red light at the corner.

Indemnities, cordial handshakes, briefcases, promises, raincoats, percentages, statistics, a drink before supper—too many years of it, too many years, he thinks bitterly, and discovers that he is walking along Fifth Avenue. There's a bus approaching; he realizes that he has been intending to get on this bus and go to the Village. All right, why not? He has not been to the Village in years.

He rides down the avenue with a fixed, irritable expression. He sees nothing. He does not know who is sitting next to him. He thinks again of the actress, of her flesh and the white leather coat. He has been on the periphery of another kind of existence, one infinitely more exciting, one that he is not privileged to share. He has not enough money to buy himself into it, does not have any creative talents that might win a place for him, nor friends who already belong. He is excluded, he can come no closer to this actress than imagination will take him; it is no good saying to himself that she is stupid and vain, that within a decade she will be meaningless. It is dry comfort every night to turn a book's thin pages.

He is surprised that the bus has stopped. The driver is looking at him strangely. Everybody else has gotten off.

Muhlbach steps down and brushes against a young girl in black leotards and a turtleneck sweater who is dismounting from a motor scooter.

Alors, she cries, prenez garde, s'il vous plâit! But the accent is American.

I'm sorry, says Muhlbach, I should have watched where I was going.

Just then an odd-looking youth appears, dressed in a cape and a plumed hat, takes the motor scooter, and wheels it away; apparently it belongs to him and she had borrowed it for a ride around the square.

Sale cochon! exclaims the girl, snapping her fingers at Muhlbach.

He looks down at her with annoyance. The insult is nothing, the fatuous expression of youth, but he is irked by her pretense. She's not French, he doubts that she has been farther from home than the Cloisters. She is not more than seventeen, undeveloped, with delicate rebellious features. On her flat breast hangs a chunk of turquoise at the end of a leather thong. Very well, she has chosen to play at being what she is not, so will he.

Et vous-même, ma petite? Est-ce-que vous êtes si propre? he answers crisply, gratified that he has not forgotten everything learned in school. He sees at once that she is startled; her assumption had been that he would not understand. Now she gazes at him respectfully and he guesses that she has exhausted her knowledge of French. Her Village sophistication is badly torn, she may be even younger than she looks.

Are you a Frenchman? she asks, a bit derisively; but it's plain that she wants to know. She wants to believe that he is. She wants to believe that he has just arrived from Paris.

I'm twice as French as you, says Muhlbach.

Dad, you're too much! she replies, suddenly at ease. I mean, like, you're making the scene!

Muhlbach flinches slightly at being called Dad. It's true there's considerable difference in their ages. Well, it is true that chronologically he might be her father, but still she shouldn't call him that.

As a matter of fact, yes, says Muhlbach, since you put it in those terms, I am making the scene.

Well, dig, dig, Daddy.

Is she suggesting that he leave, or what? Maybe she's wishing him a pleasant evening.

Comment t'appelles-tu? he inquires.

Je m'appelle Rouge, she grins.

Rouge? That can't be your name.

She shrugs, very French.

Could this be an invitation? What does she mean?

Rouge settles the question. You got some wherewithal? I mean, like, cheesecake at the Queen's Bishop, dig?

Fine, says Muhlbach. She means to take him somewhere. He will be expected to buy her a piece of cheesecake. All right, fine, why not? He feels exhilarated. He is being picked up. A tough little Bohemian in Greenwich Village has picked him up. For the first time since leaving the house he smiles. Let's go, Rouge, lead the way. Take me to the Queen's Bishop, whatever and wherever it is. I'll buy you a wedge of cheesecake, Rouge, I'll buy you the whole pie if you want it.

Across the square they go. Muhlbach glances at each passerby to discover whether or not he is making a fool of himself, meanwhile half listening to Rouge, who's more talkative than he suspected. He cannot understand everything she says; she speaks an ephemeral dialect. If he could recall the patois of his own youth, which at the moment he cannot, would she comprehend? He thinks that when they are settled in the Queen's Bishop he will try to remember a few expressions and will try them on her.

The Queen's Bishop, what sort of place could that be? And then, as they walk by the last benches in the park he notices the chess tables. Of course! Coffee, cheesecake, sandwiches, interminable discussions about God, Communism, Art, Free Love, and a chessboard for the asking. That's the sort of place it will be.

Rouge, talking enthusiastically, as though they had known each other for at least a week, leads him down one street and up another and finally down a flight of worn stone steps to a basement with a brightly painted door.

In they go, and the emporium is quieter than he'd anticipated. There are no loud discussions, no arguments. It's like a library with everyone bent over chessboards instead of books. There's an Italian coffee urn on the counter, a case of pastries, a door leading into what appears to be a little kitchen, travel posters on the wall, and the proprietor—a dwarf wearing an apron and a checkered vest—carefully sweeping the floor with a broom taller than himself.

Bonsoir, Rouge, says the dwarf.

Bonsoir, Pierre, says Rouge.

Good evening, says Muhlbach, and takes off his hat.

Monsieur, the dwarf replies courteously, but goes on sweeping the floor.

So, the Queen's Bishop is very much as I guessed, he thinks, pleased with himself; and though he is not hungry he joins Rouge in a slice of cheesecake—which is delicious. He tells her so.

The most, Pop.

Muhlbach looks about the Queen's Bishop and wishes that he had not worn his business suit. With an old pair of slacks and a sweater he wouldn't feel so out of place; he might even have passed for an artist. But it's too late now, and if Rouge does find his suit rather bourgeois she has not yet commented on it. Anyway, this is the Village where unnatural couples are common enough.

How about a game? he asks.

She hesitates, glances narrowly across the table at him, and Muhlbach's heart beats heavily. What has he said? Does "a game" have special significance?

Man, says Rouge, nobody's going to believe this!

I'm pretty good, Muhlbach answers. How about it?

Rouge measures him. She has not decided. Well, she might agree to play chess, at least she has not said anything altogether negative, so he signals for the dwarf, who brings over a board and a cigar box filled with chessmen.

The game's not free, however. Thirty cents per hour, per player. Muhlbach pays, amused. One hour with Rouge for sixty cents, change that one might leave for the bartender uptown. Has he ever found a better bargain?

He takes a pawn in either hand, shuffles them, holds out his fists side by side, and Rouge taps one.

White.

She arranges the white pieces while Muhlbach, having glanced about the Queen's Bishop and found no one watching, begins to set up the black.

Rouge opens King Knight to Rook 3.

Highly unorthodox. What has she in mind? He bends his attention to the board, fingers in a steeple.

Hey, wow! she whispers.

He discovers that she is staring with admiration at his hands. They are strong, neat, graceful hands; he is proud of them and has himself often looked at them and thought that he should have become a surgeon. These sensitive hands of his seem wasted when they have nothing more to do than shuffle papers, zip and unzip a briefcase, button a stiff white collar. Yes, it's a waste. They're the hands of an artist, of a musician, of a philosopher.

You do tricks? she asks, and he realizes that, incredibly, she is wondering if he is a magician. A magician! If only I were, Rouge, if only I were.

I sell insurance, fire insurance mostly, he says, and waits.

Too much, she answers.

Muhlbach opens his defense with pawn to King 4.

That figures, she remarks, nodding.

Does she know me so well? he wonders. Am I that conservative? He's tempted to recover the pawn and start again, but too late. She moves quickly, Queen Knight to Rook 3, and Muhlbach stares at the board. What's the significance of this curious ploy? An expert counterattack would make short work of such a beginning; its weakness will soon be quite evident. But he hopes that she will somehow strengthen her position. He is indifferent to winning or losing, so long as the game lasts—it's playing with her that counts—and while he pretends to concentrate on the board he imagines a crumbling apartment on Bleeker Street where roaches climb up and down the rusty pipes and the odor of gas seeps from a blackened stove, and the blankets on a sagging iron bed are worn through and frayed. Late Sunday morning, he thinks, we'd have orange juice, coffee, and croissants, if that would please her. Read the *Times*, listen to Mozart. If I seem elderly and repugnant, Rouge, I'll give you a present.

She has moved again; he answers.

The game proceeds, pieces are deployed, taken, and dropped in the cigar box. But Muhlbach does not play with much enthusiasm. He is depressed by lecherous fantasies of Rouge; and that she resembles his niece is mortifying. Furtively he stares at her. She doesn't notice. She squints and glares at the board, savagely gnawing her lips.

He has felt, meanwhile, crawling over and around his feet, a small living object that demands attention. Rouge's foot? Could that be? With infinite tact beneath the table, concealed from the rude eyes of other chess players, has she sought him out? Her little foot, slipped loose from its sandal, creeps across his shoe, rubs affectionately against his ankle. He feels a gentle tug at his trousers, deft and knowledgeable, not the blind, clumsy tug of a human foot—there's a beast down below. He bends down to look. There is a hamster nibbling at his cuff.

Does this belong to you? he asks.

Rouge doesn't answer. One of her pawns is threatened.

Go away, whispers Muhlbach, go away, go away, you silly animal! and he nudges the hamster, which pays no attention. He discovers that it has eaten a series of little holes in his cuff.

Queen, says Rouge thoughtfully. En garde, Pops.

Muhlbach surveys the board. The attack is obvious, has been so for the past six moves. Check, he replies, a bit reluctantly because he doesn't want the game to end; but she has obliged him to close the trap. He leans down again and pulls the hamster off his foot, worried that he may receive a nasty bite, but the hamster patiently returns to its task. Muhlbach hisses at it, thinking that perhaps it is frightened of cats. But the hamster with beady eyes fixed on his trousers cannot be alarmed.

With a sigh Muhlbach returns his attention to the game. The cuff already is ruined, another few holes won't make much difference. He tries to ignore the gentle weight on his foot and the soft, persistent tugs. If only I had a piece of lettuce, he thinks; and says aloud to Rouge as he moves a pawn, Check. And, I'm afraid, Mate.

She doesn't give up. She has one move left, that's true. It's inconsequential, a bit embarrassing. She should have the grace not to insist on making it, but she does, she retreats grimly. He realizes for the first time that this game has meant something to her; it must have been important that she defeat him. Well, it's too late. He can't possibly lose, there's just no way to lose, none at all. He searches the board. Perhaps he could pretend that he was working on a more intricate and aesthetically satisfying Mate and thus justify the forfeit of a piece.

He looks up, aware of two spectators. They have come out of nowhere and now stand one on either side of the table, ragged and solemn, the natural companions of Rouge. One is the boy who owns the motor scooter, still wearing his cape and plumed hat, and smoking a stogie. The other, who appears to be about Muhlbach's age or a little older, is a bearded Negro with a beret and a snaggly grin. Why are they here?

Muhlbach cautiously picks up the enemy bishop, replacing it with his own. There's no need to speak. Rouge looks at him for just an instant; she is cold with rage. He attempts to smile; he feels guilty.

Cha-boom! murmurs the Negro.

The boy in the plumed hat removes his stogie and puffs a row of tiny smoke rings.

Thank you for the game, Rouge, says Muhlbach.

Cool the crap, says Rouge.

Cha-cha-cha! exclaims the Negro. Ba-zoom-ba!

Rouge, still peeved, introduces the visitors. They are named Quinet and Meatbowl. It seems they would like to sit down; in fact, without being asked, they do, and Muhlbach finds three pairs of eyes trained on him. Something is now expected of him. What can it be? He looks from one to the other. Quinet clears his throat and inspects that magnificent cigar. The Negro, who is humming and tapping his fingers on the table, does not once remove his gaze from Muhlbach. Nor does Rouge. They're waiting. But for what?

Muhlbach begins to feel uncomfortable. After a few moments he takes off his glasses, wipes them with his handkerchief, holds them up to the light, carefully hooks them on again. It is almost as though he were being initiated.

Perhaps—could it be? Has he been accepted? The defeat of Rouge might be significant. Yes, now that he thinks it over, no one in the Queen's Bishop paid the slightest attention until the end of the game was near, until it was plain that Rouge couldn't win. It was only then, he recalls, that a few heads began turning their direction. Everyone in this place must be acquainted; they come here every night and have learned to communicate with each other as mysteriously as bees or ants; they've known what was going on. Rouge isn't a good chess player yet she must hold some position of authority here and I've made a spot for myself by defeating her! For a moment he imagines himself coming to the Queen's Bishop night after night, growing bolder, being less concerned with appearances, imagines himself in a beret and a suede jacket, with a mustache and goatee, saluting Quinet and Meatbowl and Pierre with casual familiarity.

Muhlbach realizes that he is smiling, first at Rouge, then at her two rococo companions, for no reason except that they have welcomed him to the sanctuary of the Queen's Bishop. It is flattering, really. Do these people care about his business, his habits, his background, whether or not he has money? No. No, they are interested in him for himself alone.

He sees that Meatbowl is grinning; Quinet grins, too, if not as pleasantly. Just then Pierre arrives, his head on a level with the table. Pierre is carrying a dented aluminum tray on which there are four large bowls of minestrone and some crackers. Obviously this is the rite, the moment when he becomes a catechumen. Now they are to break bread. Muhlbach feels powerfully moved; he feels within himself something that he has virtually forgotten—a flow of love toward his fellow man. And that he should have rediscovered this community at such a humble crossroads! His eyes are moist with tears; he is tempted to reach over the table to take Meatbowl and Quinet by the hand. It is all so unexpected.

He blinks, looks down at the steaming minestrone. He is not hungry, and as a matter of fact the minestrone does have a doughy appearance, but he will eat it and love it because this soup is symbolic.

When he lifts his head he finds the dwarf standing at his side, gazing at him attentively with one hand outstretched, palm up, ready to be crossed with silver.

The silence is profound. Every chess game has stopped.

At this instant many things become clear to Muhlbach, just as chemicals in a beaker of liquid turn instantaneously to one great glittering shard of crystal. Life is as it is, not as man wishes it to be. He has entered this house, which is not his own, which he had no prerogative to enter, and has been promptly recognized. I've been false, he thinks, and they have known it from the first. They knew me before I knew myself.

Now he is docked for this audacity, for having intruded. Now he must pay.

The dwarf is waiting.

No one speaks. Muhlbach wonders how he could have been so stripped of sensitivity. He, alone, is out of place. Even that old man in the corner who has not said a word to anyone, but has sat motionless with a tattered overcoat buttoned up to his chin and speckled arthritic hands folded over a cane—that old man belongs to the Queen's Bishop. The gangling boy in denim work clothes and flowered cowboy boots who is sipping coffee at the bar, with a guitar case at his feet—he is part of it. The fat girl in a muumuu who is absently reading a newspaper and scratching herself—she is welcome here. Even the two lesbians with crisp silvered hair and masculine suits, withdrawn, hostile, frightened—yes, they are made to feel at home here, they are given refuge from the terror and confusion of the outer world. Why am I different? he wonders. Why am I not welcome? Why is it that I represent the enemy? What do these disparate people communally own that I do not share? Is it poverty? No. That must be subsidiary, it's not the principal. These people are like odd patches on a quilt, how curious they won't accept another. Well, what do I stand for? A nation's hypocrisy? The tribes of Philistia? Can they despise me as an individual because I am dressed like a bureaucrat? Am I the corporate executive gorged on stolen figs who never serves a sentence? Is it not hurtful to be accused by outcasts?

So his thoughts chase each other over and under with the alacrity of tigers in a circus.

And she has signaled these two—Quinet and Meatbowl, he thinks angrily. That leaves the sourest taste. The question now is whether to accept the imposition and pay for everybody's minestrone, or not. To do so is to avoid embarrassment, but at the same time to acknowledge a personal ignominy. Either way, I lose. If I object and complain that I've been taken for granted, if I point out that no one consulted me, say to the dwarf what he knows perfectly well—that he and they are in league to pluck me cleaner than a squab, just as they've plucked other innocents, no doubt—if I do raise my voice, what's gained? What's to be saved? Well, two dollars, but what else? Self-respect? Is this a thing that strangers are qualified to evaluate?

He looks at the dwarf's untrembling hand, the right hand of iniquity. In the Tenth Book of Augustine it is written that our fellow citizens must be also our fellow pilgrims—those who have walked before equally with those who are on the road beside us, and with those who shall come after us. We are meant to serve them, if we elect to live in the sight of God; to them we are meant to demonstrate not what we have been, but what we are and continue to be. But neither are we to judge ourselves.

Muhlbach reaches for his wallet.

Daddy, says Rouge, this gruel's the greatest. Quinet nods approvingly. The Judas kiss. Ba-boom-boom! says the feeble-minded Negro.

All of them are sure. They never doubt.

And when they have finished spooning up the soup, when the last noodle has disappeared, the final bean devoured, without one further word they get to their feet and go. He is left to reign over the table, over four bowls—three of them as empty as the day they were lifted from the potter's wheel—four bowls and the mock ivory pieces of a lengthy intellectual triumph. The flesh—the flesh he coveted—is gone. Everything considered, it's been not unlike a vision in the desert.

Tell me, what's your name? he hears himself inquire again. Not Rouge, what's your Christian name?

That's it, she seems to say. Like what else is there, you know? A chick's got a short time and then it's night, you dig? So, like, express it uptown, Pop.

But are not the senses of our bodies mutual, he wonders, recalling Saint Augustine, or is the sense of my flesh mine, and the sense of your flesh yours? If we are not the same, how could I perceive all that I do, even though we have our separate organs?

Muhlbach disconsolately picks at the flaking table. His strength is gone. If he were at home he would fall into bed exhausted. How long he sits at the table he does not know. When he walks out of the Queen's Bishop no one looks up.

A warm wind is blowing through the trees. An ice cream vendor waits at the corner. An artist who paints bucolic scenes on colored velvet stands hopefully beside his merchandise in the light of a theater marquee and the reflections from a thousand automobiles.

Muhlbach sits down on a bench in Washington Square. Through the arch he sees the flow of traffic. He hears, as though from a considerable distance, the noise of the city. He feels slightly chilled, as though he had been without food all day. It is a weakness of privation, abstinence that chills to the bone. The sickness is deep. It will pass, of course, and it's not fatal. Yet the cure is absurdly simple. The body of a woman, that is all. That is all.

I'm both parts of a man, he reflects, body and soul. I think that the interior of me is the better, but it is also the weaker. How does any man resolve the conflict that continually rages between the exigencies of his body and the burning pod of the soul? I am famished for love and I despise myself, although it is much too easy to call myself dust and ashes. I know that there are things about myself that I do not know. Certainly now we see through a glass darkly, not yet face to face.

After a while he gets to his feet and walks to the curb where he waits for a taxi. He feels as though he has been mildly poisoned, or has had a quart of blood withdrawn; he sees his wife again, as though in a mirror, her taut body stretched across his own, her mouth yawning with excitement; but he cannot summon her warmth, and the weight of her thighs is no heavier than dust.

A taxi veers aside and stops. Muhlbach climbs into the back seat and orders the driver to take him to some nightclub—any one that's close by—so long as there are women in the show.

The taxi swerves and lurches through the Village, the driver cursing, and turns north.

Very soon he finds that he is being delivered to the Club Sahara. Apprehensively he considers the fluorescent sign, the doorman costumed as a sheik, and wishes that he were not alone. The club looks ridiculous but also a trifle dangerous. He has not been in any such place as this for several years.

Effendi, says the doorman, bowing and making a vaguely religious gesture with one hand. Don't miss the harem dancers. Exotic entertainment once seen only by caliphs in the privacy of the seraglio!

Muhlbach gives him a quarter and marches up the staircase to be met by another sheik. There's an admission charge, after which the curtains are drawn aside and he steps into darkness. The show has begun. On stage sit four musicians, each wearing a tasseled red fez.

This way, effendi, says a voice. Muhlbach discovers that he is standing next to a figure in a white burnoose.

He is led to a table in a corner. The stage is partly hidden by a post. He shifts his chair, is nudged by some invisible party whose view he has blocked, and so resigns himself to what he has. The table interests him; he has never been seated at a table so small. It is round and is about the size of a pancake griddle. A slave girl arrives by flashlight to take his order.

Meanwhile, to the wicked clink of finger cymbals, Nila, direct from Beirut, Lebanon, has undulated into the spotlight. Muhlbach polishes his glasses, settles them on his nose, and after crossing his arms he prepares to watch the dance; just then the slave girl reappears with his drink. One dollar and fifty cents. He is a bit shocked. Considering the admission fee, this is too much. However, there's nothing to do but pay. She goes away to get change for the bill he has given her and returns almost immediately.

I'm afraid you've made a mistake, says Muhlbach when he has counted the change she holds out on a platter. It was a ten I gave you, not a five.

The slave answers that it was a five.

It was a ten, he knows, because he is meticulous about such things. He does not make mistakes of this sort, he never has. He remembers having looked at the denomination of the bill when he handed it to her. For a moment he wonders if he should simply give up and go home. The night to this point has been nothing if not a disaster. At best it has been a disappointment and at worst he has suffered humiliation enough to last the year. He looks helplessly at the ruins of his ten-dollar bill.

Will there be anything else, sire?

Not at the moment, thank you. For the time being this is quite enough.

Very good, sire. The slave girl switches off her flashlight and steals away.

On the stage Nila is swaying like a viper to the music of oud and darabukka. Flutes are wailing, cymbals clink. Her costume, which may or may not be authentic, consists of loose transparent pantaloons tied at the ankle, a gilded halter with loops of coins that dangle to her navel, and a Cleopatra bracelet squeezing the tawny meat of her upper arm. She dances as sinuously as though she were remembering the pasha who came to visit last night, and Muhlbach finds that he enters into the soul of her dance: America becomes distasteful—an insensate, vulgar, flatulent, bloodless subway nation of merchants, thugs, Protestants, and barbers. He considers giving up his position at Metro Mutual and moving to Lebanon.

Nila melts to the floor, heavy strings of brass coins flowing. Her pale orotund belly possesses a life of its own. The jewel in her navel winks at him. Truly it is a wondrous belly—throbbing, heaving, pulsing, quivering. It trembles, it palpitates, it almost weeps, and then mysteriously vanishes but soon returns larger than ever, rolling languorously from side to side. Muhlbach is quite fascinated; he leans forward.

However, the slave girl is at his table. Would he like another drink?

No, he replies, but changes his mind. Yes, do bring me another. Mindful that money disappears in the Club Sahara as if it were dropped on a shifting sand dune, he searches his pockets to collect the exact amount, nothing extra. Not a surplus peso, not a drachma, no gulden, no dinar, no yen, no reis—in brief, not a pfennig.

When she comes back he is prepared for an ugly scene, but having collected for the drink, the slave girl slips away into the night without saying a word, so there would seem to be an arid truce between them.

Will she serve me again? he wonders. I suppose I'll be ignored from now on, or possibly bounced. We'll find out soon enough.

A new harem dancer is on the stage. Lisa from Port Said, direct from a triumphal tour of the capitals of the Middle East, the personal favorite of Sheik Ali Bey. She is slender and charming, with a sensitive face. Muhlbach feels himself half in love with her. She's as delicate as a fawn. Her eyes are edged with kohl. A jeweled pendant glitters on her forehead. He is positive that she is looking toward him while she dances; it seems to him that she is entreating him to go with her. They will go together, hand in hand, back to the days of King Solomon; they will live in a whitewashed hut, or a tent, and mind a herd of goats. Anything becomes possible when Lisa dances. Anything. The ringing of her tiny cymbals destroys him; he does not know if he can stand this passion. She is calling him to Paradise.

Lisa, ladies and gentlemen! Lisa! A nice round of applause for the little lady.

Lisa bows, smiles like the carnival courtesan she is. As she walks into the wings she peels off the diadem.

And still, thinks Muhlbach, she's what I need. Maybe she was born in the Bronx and has no more danced in triumph through the capitals of the Middle East than I have been shot out of a cannon or gone parachute jumping, but I need her. If there's a God, a God with compassion, He knows. I cannot help it if I lust after the favorite of Sheik Ali Bey—who's probably better known as Mick, Abe, or Louie, who at this moment is lounging at her dressing table paring his nails with a switchblade knife. Yes, each inordinate affection becomes its own torment.

The question no longer is one of aesthetics or of sensibilities. The question is: how do you acquire a belly dancer for a mistress? Do you send a note concealed in a dozen roses? How should it be addressed? Do you ask the slave girl for the dancer's true name? Then what do you write? Dear Lisa Goldberg, et cetera, et cetera, signed Your Faithful Admirer. This must be ancient fiction; furthermore it would necessitate coming back again to occupy the same table, becoming a spectacle yourself, the butt of obscene jokes. Suppose that is the procedure. Consider the implications.

I can't do it, he thinks. I cannot do it. Suppose she replied, and told me to wait for her outside the stage door, in the alley, among the trash cans and mewing cats. The truth is, I simply don't understand how these things are accomplished. I just don't know how. I'm pricked and urged along by this degrading appetite and I drag after me a great load of doubt. I know that what I'm following is not happiness, or even satisfaction, but a state in which I am free of my mortal goad. This is the simulacrum of content. I think that I would settle for it. At least, thank God, I am not altogether ignorant of my ignorance.

Another dancer's on the stage—Riva, she is called, the toast of three continents, direct from Istanbul for an exclusive engagement at the Club Sahara. She, too, has a tender belly possessed of demons that she sets about to exorcise, but the slave girl has come around again and Muhlbach is distracted; not knowing whether to say yes or no, he orders a third drink. Or is this the fourth? What difference does it make? He does not feel well. He inspects the rim of the glass and wonders if he has swallowed a little something that he did not pay for. Riva fails to interest him—excepting the magic belly, which he observes with remote concupiscence. Otherwise he is not moved, she lacks the grace of Lisa, she is not half so Byzantine, has not the deep conviction or felicity. Riva does not promise much.

Just then like an evil flower blooms the thought that perhaps he could attack some unknown woman. Incredible! Muhlbach adjusts his glasses, as though he might be able to see the origin of this insane conceit. He tries to remember if some previous thought has brought up such a criminal idea from the depths of himself, or if he has overheard or seen anything that nourished it. Nothing. Nothing. The woman swaying on the stage has summoned it, but why? Already the idea has become unreal, impossible. Of course I never would, he reflects, but at the same time how interesting that I should think of it! Yes, very interesting indeed. So in spite of my intelligence I'm not much different. There, spattered across the front pages of the tabloids, but for the grace of some inherent power go I—good God! Good God, are we so near the precipice, each one of us?

He squints against the smoke, realizing for the first time just how crowded, uncomfortable, and perfidious the Sahara is. And to say that it is expensive is to put it courteously. He looks at the leader of the four musicians, at the great beaked avaricious nose and snapping black eyes, the trimmed mustache, the tassel on his fez. Abdul Somebody. Abdul, nodding and smiling rather like a crocodile, leads the authentic Arabian band while Riva slithers around the stage to a flute obbligato of sorts. She is barefoot, with fingernails like the talons of the phoenix and the profile of a hawk. She is fierce and she is mean, there's little doubt; also, she looks dirty, as though she had spent her

life in the back rooms of the club. He thinks again of Lisa: no matter
if she's a fraud, her lithe body was altogether genuine, and because
he will never enjoy that body—and he knows he will not—he wishes
he had never seen it.

The lights go on, the musicians put away their exotic instruments.
The next show will begin presently, but Muhlbach decides he will not
be there. He joins the crowd struggling through the curtained exit
and while he is being jostled and elbowed and struck in the back, and
perhaps fondled, he asks himself what he has gained by coming here.
Nothing, of course, except a clearer knowledge that his temptation
has not ended.

Once outside the club he asks himself what to do next. He is standing on the corner with his hands clasped tightly behind his back when
someone speaks to him—a naval officer, a stoop-shouldered lieutenant commander with a Southern accent, and Muhlbach recognizes the
adult face of the boy who used to be his closest friend, who had been
his college roommate twenty years ago.

Puig, for that is his name, insists that they have a drink together.

He'll ask what I'm doing, thinks Muhlbach, if I'm married, if I have
a family, and so forth. I know every question he's going to ask.

What is it that's disappointing about Puig? Is it that he's changed so
little? He does look older, yes, and his face is still disfigured by those
hairy brown warts. He looks somehow depraved, the cold agate eyes
blurred by a hundred barrels of sour mash bourbon, the ribbed stomach of youth collapsed and grossly distended. Puig's khaki uniform
is wrinkled, the little black shoulder boards are perched askew. His
cap is set too far back on his head and he is perspiring. And he's so
delighted, Muhlbach reflects, that we've run into each other after all
these years.

The longer he looks at Puig, the more it does appear that Puig has
changed, but still, the first thing he'd noticed was not any outward
modification but that, apart from having physically aged, he might still
be mingling with college boys. There's been no inner growth, merely
this deterioration of the surface. Muhlbach remembers that Puig had
been very fond of music, particularly of Victor Herbert and Sigmund
Romberg; now he guesses that although twenty years have elapsed,
Puig's not yet graduated. He loved the jingles and the macabre stories

of Poe; probably he still does. Puig reached his highest point of sensitivity with Rodin. That's real carving, he used to say.

Any old port in a storm, Puig is saying.

Muhlbach follows him across the street into a dank saloon, and there they sit on high leather stools. Puig insists on paying for the drinks, then he swivels back and forth and talks and appraises every woman that walks by. He's married and has four boys. He's executive officer of the U.S.S. *Huxtable*, which dropped anchor only last night. After the war ended he stayed in the Navy, it seemed the simplest thing to do; now the pay is good, there are benefits, and when he's not at sea he gets in quite a few rounds of golf. Life's all right in the peacetime Navy, not really bad, claims Puig.

Well, probably it's neither more nor less satisfying than the insurance business; and certainly to be based in Casablanca one year and on the other side of the world the next is far more stimulating than year after year in the dust-free, odorless, subdued, and regulated neutrality of Metro Mutual.

Just then with a lecherous little squeak Puig slides off his stool and whispers that he will be back in a moment.

Muhlbach nods and remains at the bar, contemplating his drink. He is envious of Puig, who has no scruples, who has never been concerned with dignity. Puig is at home in the gutter because he does not recognize it as such; if asked, he might very well admit to being in the gutter, but of course to identify a place or a condition of the soul doesn't mean that it's been recognized.

Minutes go by. Muhlbach has finished his drink. What's become of Puig? Foul play? Is he stretched out unconscious in a back room? Not likely. His uniform implies that the total weight of the United States Navy would fall on any malefactor unwise enough to despoil its wearer. Whether this is true or not, Puig never was the type to be victimized. Wherever he is, and whatever he's doing, he's all right. It's almost certain that during these past twenty years nothing unfortunate has happened to him, nor will anything damage him more than temporarily until the day of his death; even that he may turn to some account—triple indemnity taken out the day before, something similar.

It is this blithe ease and fortune of Puig that annoys Muhlbach, that causes him to turn restlessly on the leather stool; because Puig is so average, so direct and ponderous, and because tonight his snuffling chase is similar to Muhlbach's own, equally discreditable. This is not comforting.

Both of us suffer the muddy cravings of the flesh, he thinks, the bubblings and foggy exhalations that demean the spirit. Only he is not aware of how he has fallen; he sees nothing despicable or ridiculous in his acts. The truth is that I must be considered inferior to him because whatever it is possible to corrupt is inferior to what cannot be corrupted. Whatever cannot be damaged or lessened is undoubtedly preferable to what can be, just as whatever suffers no evident change is better than what is subject to change.

Restless in his weariness, Muhlbach can do nothing but wait.

Puig returns, but not alone. He brings Gertie, with the inevitable shiny black handbag. She is as drunk as the grape can make her.

You're all alike! shrills Gertie. No good sons-of-bitches, every blessed one of you. Always after the same thing, by Christ! Only one thing ever on your mind! I should've listened to my first husband. He's got the number of guys like you! Who needs you? Answer me that! Triumphant in her rhetoric, she leans soggily against Puig, who has trouble holding her upright.

Stand by, Gert, we're casting off. See you, buddy, murmurs Puig, somewhat apologetically. Together they go leaning out the door.

What about me? thinks Muhlbach, once more abandoned. I was hoping he would invite me to go with them. I'd share her, God help me. I would have, if I had been invited. Then he looks around—for the first time seeing the bar in which he has been seated—and realizes with amazement that he's been descending: it resembles the entrance to a sewer.

He does not know how he got here, but what alarms him is not that he has reached this low step but where the next might take him, since he has not descended deliberately; some inner force has been diligently at work, a despotism too deeply buried and silted over to be uncovered. Realizing this, he believes he should be able to control it, but is not sure.

Immediately he gets off the stool and walks out.

The city air is not clean, and it seems to have become much warmer during the past hour; it is almost uncomfortable, as though summer would begin again. A polluted river breeze hangs in the soot-blown street. His suit feels thick, the collar tight.

There's a taxi parked at the curb. The driver, like a messenger from above or below, is looking directly at him.

Times Square, says Muhlbach without enthusiasm and climbs into the back seat. I've got to get off these dark avenues, he thinks. I've been too long at the periphery. Other people are finding happiness, they evidently know where it is; strange that I don't. And stranger still, I've the feeling that I too could have found it, if I'd been able to recognize the form it takes. Doubtless the saint was right in telling us that those things are not only many but diverse that men witness and select to enjoy by the rays of our sun, even as that light itself is one, in which the sight of each one beholding sees and holds what pleases; so, too, there may be many things that are good, and also differing aims of life, out of which each chooses as he will. Now, in matters of the flesh, it's said that whatever you perceive through the flesh you perceive only in part, and remain ignorant of the whole, of which these are parts; yet still these parts do delight you.

Times Square, says the cabbie, taking off his yellow hat to scratch his skull.

So soon? Muhlbach is surprised. He sits forward, blinks in the artificial light, and reaches for his wallet. However, his pocket is empty. Never, in fact, has a pocket felt so absolutely empty. The wallet has been stolen. He is positive of the moment when it was stolen—as he was jostled by the crowd leaving the Club Sahara. He remembers that in the bar with Puig he started to reach for it but Puig caught his wrist; the last time, therefore, that he touched it was in the Sahara. But this is merely the deduction of the conscious mind, which is a useful tool but a blunt one; the wallet was lifted by somebody in the crowd, and now that he has been informed by the emptiness of his pocket that it is gone he realizes that the perpetually vigilant self within himself has been trying to notify him ever since it happened.

To placate his incredulous brain he methodically feels through all of his pockets, then, with the cabbie's assistance, searches the back seat. The wallet's not found, of course.

The cabbie is prepared for a struggle, since nothing's half so important as being paid. You want to go back?

No, says Muhlbach, take me to the Tyler Plaza. I'll cash a check.

You know somebody there?

I do. The manager's a friend of mine.

You better hope so, pal.

There's more insolence than sympathy in this remark. Why did I attempt to justify myself? Muhlbach asks while the taxi works its way through the crowd. What business is it of the driver who I know at the hotel, or if I know anybody at all? That's not his concern. He'll be paid. I'm stripped of my money and all at once I'm as insecure as a schoolboy. As for going back to the club, I'd rather lose a dozen wallets. I'll telephone and ask, I can do that. But I couldn't walk up those steps again. This has been a wretched night. Good God, I've been robbed. Robbed!

The cab driver follows him into the Tyler Plaza.

May I please speak to Mr. Sproule, says Muhlbach to the clerk.

Mr. Sproule, according to the clerk, is not there; he's at home sick in bed with the flu. Could Mr. Ascagua be of any assistance?

I need to cash a check, says Muhlbach. Sproule is a close friend of mine. I'm sure it will be all right.

Just let me speak to Mr. Ascagua, suggests the clerk, who is unctuous enough to run a mortuary. He then disappears for ten minutes. Finally it develops that, most unfortunately, Mr. Ascagua has stepped out for a little while.

What time do you have? asks Muhlbach.

Almost two in the morning.

Call up Sproule and I'll talk to him.

The desk clerk is afraid he couldn't do that.

Then you give me the number because I cannot remember it, and I'll damn well call him.

Reluctantly, peevishly, and with a look of insane discomfort, the clerk agrees. So the call is made.

David, says Muhlbach, I'm sorry about this. It's a long story and I feel like an imbecile. Somebody took my wallet and here I am. I need help. He listens, nods to the cabbie, and hands over the telephone to the clerk.

Yes, sir, of course, begins the clerk, I'll be glad to. Yes, sir! Right away, sir!

Muhlbach has no difficulty visualizing Sproule propped up in bed, eyes bulging, mustache and jowls aquiver with indignation.

No trouble at all, sir. Certainly, sir. Not a bit, sir! I certainly will do my best. And a different breed of clerk comes off the telephone.

By the way, says Muhlbach, are there any rooms left? Because I think I'll stay overnight, provided you can locate something away from the street.

The clerk is positive that he will be able to find a very nice room, meanwhile the cashier will be delighted to take care of Mr. Muhlbach's check.

In a few minutes the cabbie is paid and tipped and goes on about his nocturnal business; and Muhlbach with a modest roll of bills lodged carefully in his trousers pocket feels somewhat better. He calls home to tell Mrs. Grunthe that he has decided to spend the night in town.

Mrs. Grunthe is not asleep as he had supposed she might be; she is wide awake. He is oddly touched by this, but also slightly irritated. She has been sitting in her favorite chair, watching television and knitting and every once in a while no doubt lifting her eyes to the clock on the mantel.

How are the children? he inquires. They're asleep, naturally. Everything is under control; as usual, nothing is ever much out of control while Mrs. Grunthe is present.

I'm tired, he explains. I don't feel like riding the train back at this hour. I've decided to stay overnight, that's all.

Mrs. Grunthe does not take to this idea; she suspects something. Muhlbach remembers that she now and then preaches against the wickedness of gambling; probably she thinks he has become involved with a bunch of card-playing Italians. She always has been suspicious of Italians. Puerto Ricans, Greeks, Negroes, Chinese, they're very much the same, they are not devils, however foreign; but Mrs. Grunthe knows that sinfulness dwells in the Italian breast.

So be it. Good night, Mrs. Grunthe. Dream of Salvador.

Now there is only one call to make, and it will be futile. He calls the Club Sahara, explains that he was there earlier and that his wallet is missing. Just by chance has it been found? No answer. He hears the clink of glasses, laughter, remote voices, and once more the music of oud and darabukka inscrutably beckoning him across the wire. Time goes by while he holds the receiver and blinks his eyes to keep awake. Finally, without explanation, somebody at the other end of the line hangs up.

This insult is one too many. He had planned to go to bed but now, after this, there is only one possible resolution to the night—he will get drunk. He has not been filled to the brim since his wedding day and that was fourteen years ago. Now seems like a good time. No doubt the time was long past. Probably a man's anguish and his troubles are best washed away once in a while, since they are bound to return. In any case, where's the nearest cocktail lounge and how fast can it be achieved? He calculates that half a dozen ought to finish him, after which he'll get a good night's sleep. It may be joyless, that's not the point. I'm half out of my senses, he thinks, with grief and shame and mummified passion. I'm a coward and a celibate. I don't have guts enough to approach a kootch dancer, I don't have either the brains or the sex to interest a Bohemian girl. I'm a fake, a pompous ass, a stuffy bourgeois pedant, and a—well, what's the use? I could go on and on. And a blessed son-of-a-bitch not the least of these. Oh, but I am miserable! How miserable I am.

This causes him to feel a little improved. He heads grimly for the cocktail lounge. To his surprise it's nearly deserted. There are a few lonesome men at the bar, who look around as he comes in, a waitress, and two bartenders. The thought of joining his fellows on a stool is disagreeable; he selects a table in the darkest corner.

The waitress begins walking toward him. She does not wear a dress but red mesh stockings to the hip, a black Merry Widow, and a marvelous blonde wig.

Muhlbach knows that he is staring at her like a provincial, but he does not care. Frustration, disgust, anger, disappointment, the badly stained and spattered image of himself, mauled dignity—whatever the night and this impossible city have proffered is wrapped up and tied in one vulgar bundle which he might throw away if he can bring a light to the eye of this steamy wench. Pride and confidence may then be restored, may grow and flourish. He knows in the midst of his dejection that such a thought, such hope, is madness, that he will fail again. Yet he is a man, no matter what else: lecherous and unrepentant in the depths of exhaustion; desirous of much more than can be reckoned; muddied by concupiscence; made wild with shadowy loves; halted by the short links of his mortality and deafened by conceit; seldom at peace; adulterous and bitter; stuck and bled by thorns on every side; rank with imagined sin; exiled forever and yet ever returning, such he is. Brambles of lust spring up on all sides while he plots the course. He learns that Carmen is her name.

As she walks away her fat thighs torment him and he is heavily swollen by lascivious plans. With a dull, furious gaze he follows the gathered pink chiffon decorating her extravagant rump like a rabbit's flag and wonders if he will explode from passion before she comes back. Jesus, oh Lord! I've been taken prisoner by this disease of my flesh, he says to himself, and of its deadly sweetness, and I drag my chain about with me, and I dread the idea of its being loosed.

Carmen doesn't wear a ring, he notes when she returns. He introduces himself, but she replies with a shrug.

He mentions that she could be the sister of someone he used to know years ago in Washington. She doesn't say a word.

Well then, says Muhlbach, tell me, what time is it?

She doesn't know.

I'll be wanting another drink as soon as you can get it, he says, leaning back against the cushions, and is grateful that she goes away without so much as a glance at him. He swallows most of the drink and looks around. The lounge is not uncomfortable, in a rather calculated way, as though it had been designed to solace defeated men. Muhlbach shuts his eyes. It's true that Carmen does remind him of somebody in Washington; he tries to remember but cannot. He remembers that he had been attracted to whoever it was, but then, just as now, nothing came of it. The reason was the same, as it is invariably the same. It never will be different.

I'm trapped like a bird in a loft, he thinks.

Carmen is returning and it occurs to him that she, too, is a bird—a glorious bird of the jungle with plumage as indescribable as a tropic dawn. When she bends over to serve him he seizes her wrist. She utters a little cry and draws back; there is a momentary struggle before he lets go, more shocked than she.

Porfirio! she calls.

That one word brings out of some gloomy recess in the lounge a dapper, swift, and unmistakably dangerous Latin with a diamond stickpin on a white silk necktie. He stares at Muhlbach through tinted glasses and inquires if he may be of service, although this is not why he has come to visit. He conveys a very different message.

Muhlbach, shaken doubly by his own conduct and by the implied

threat of violence, has difficulty answering. Exposed to Porfirio's pitiless gaze, he takes out his handkerchief and weakly pats his face. He
is glad that Carmen has gone. If anyone must witness his shame, it
should be another man.

I'm afraid I feel a little sick, he says.

You had enough for tonight, says Porfirio, not unkindly.

Muhlbach nods, perspiring.

You make it to the door by yourself?

In a few minutes I will. Let me sit here until I recover.

Take your time, says Porfirio, and sidles away.

Oh my God, asks Muhlbach during his moments of grace, what
has become of me?

Before getting up he reminds himself that he is seriously drunk, at
least that is what the evidence suggests, and if he has not acted nobly
anywhere else tonight, he will manage somehow to leave this place
unassisted. I'll do that, he says, if I drop dead one step beyond the
arch.

Cautiously he gets up. He walks with unspeakable dignity past the
piano and the bar and so into the lobby to the desk where he asks for his
key, while the meditations of Saint Augustine sing loosely through his
head. There is no place that I can rest, he thinks; backward or forward,
there is no place. I have dared to grow wild and touch a multiplicity
of things in order to please myself, but each consumed itself in front
of me because I exceeded the limits set for my nature. But is there
not attraction in the face and body of a woman that is very great and
equal to the face and body of gold? For the flesh has like every other
sense its own intelligence.

Holding the key in both hands so that he will not drop it, he heads
for the elevator. He does not know what time it has become, except
that it must be quite late; and he is amazed by the determination of
his body, which does not care whether it is three or five or twelve but
would as soon walk out again into the street.

In the elevator he is relatively certain that he is going to vomit; he
concentrates on other matters in the hope of deceiving his stomach,
and once inside the room he does not feel quite so sick. In fact, after a
very few minutes, there seems to be no reason he should not refresh
himself with a shower and go out. Really, a man's luck changes. Yes,
of course, things should improve.

But this is the voice of the Devil—that wheedling tone is familiar.

Muhlbach refuses to listen. He sits down on the edge of the bed to examine the cuff of his trousers. The hamster has eaten more of it than he thought. Tomorrow he must buy a new pair of pants. But tomorrow is Sunday. All is wretchedness and cross-purpose.

The softness of the bed soon affects his body. He lies down but immediately gets up and walks back and forth, wrestling with the devilish proposal. He mutters, squeezes his hands, turns around, explains to himself that it is all a fabulous absurdity. Some time later, fully dressed, not able to sleep naked if there is no other body for companionship, he stretches himself on the floor. Hours pass. He sleeps nervously, aware that he is alone; it is as though the troubled evening continues.

By morning the night phantoms have not been vanquished; at breakfast he scarcely tastes his food but sits gazing through the window of the coffee shop at the sensual movements of women on the street. Even their shadows on the pavement suggest and hint at Babylon. The morning is brilliant, and morning is reflected everywhere, but he cannot enjoy its splendor. This is Sunday, he reflects, a time for Christian worship, but I am obsessed. This is the seventh day, yet I am unable to rest.

Then, whether it is a hallucination or not, he believes that he sees Rouge across the street, accompanied by Meatbowl and Quinet. If he is not mistaken, and he wonders, they are standing outside a bookstore. Quinet and Meatbowl are gesticulating—stock characters in an old folk comedy—while Rouge, like Columbine, perhaps invisible to mortal eyes, stands just apart as though waiting for Harlequin. Now imploringly she looks toward him; she has discovered him at his table. He cannot remain where he is. He quickly pays for his breakfast and hurries out.

Yes, they are there. They do exist, all three of them, outlandish spirits. And has Rouge truly seen him? Is she beckoning? Is there something that she wants? A book, a meal, a game of chess, a diamond to exchange for a night of love? No matter, he will give it to her. How different from the pains of youth. Here is no thought of pressed flowers, moonlit walks along the beach. Here is the meaning of the body's work, its need; the rest is wasted time.

Impatiently he waits for the light to change, worried that Meatbowl and Quinet will wander off and she will follow and be lost forever.

But Columbine is there, looks up with great grave eyes at his vigorous approach. Bright indeed is this morning, fortunate are those who have found each other. Is not the very air filled with clapping wings?

So the deus ex machina, a pigeon, one gray pigeon otherwise quite nondescript and indistinguishable from the millions, unaware or indifferent to the magnitude of its act and to the finality with which it will score a human life, possibly two lives, briskly cocks its head, winks once, and without a ruffled feather sends down from Heaven the fateful message.

Muhlbach, in mid-stride, hears the liquescent thunder against his hat. He takes it for a distant earthquake because the sky is blue. But no! Informed by Rouge's insane shriek of laughter, by the looks of horror, sympathy, and stupefied amusement from passersby, as well as by his own desperate inner certainty, Muhlbach takes off his hat. One glance certifies the pigeon's mighty blow. After this, what can befall a man?

With the hat held upside down in one hand as though he were collecting coins he stalks up Broadway. Perhaps, he thinks, this is for the best. I've hoped for what was never meant to happen. I have spent one whole night attempting to distort the truth that was born in me; now I have learned. Whatever I touch henceforth—whether it is the body of the earth or the air itself—I must be sure that it is within my province and does not belong to any other. But still, knowing this was not meant to be, does not, nor ever shall diminish the yearning. I know this, as I know that seven and three are forever ten.

BOWEN

HE CAME OUT of a skeletal midwestern town beside the Mississippi and his favorite novel was *Huckleberry Finn*. Instead of floating down the river on a raft he joined the merchant marine, but until the day he stripped himself naked on a cliff overlooking the Pacific and just after dawn stepped forward to eternity he imagined himself as Huck—only more sophisticated and intelligent, maddened by genius. I never knew the source of his romanticism, which had about it the appealing innocence of another era. Sternwheel paddleboats roiled the Mississippi not long before he was born and perhaps he could hear them churning around the bend.

I first saw him in Paris, seated on an old-fashioned trunk in the hotel suite of a famous Southern author, grande dame of American literature. He had begun writing a novel about his voyage to New Guinea aboard the freighter *Pelican* and he had come to pay homage, perhaps to divine the secret of her eminence. I remember that he sat motionless on the ancient steamer trunk and his eyes were crystal gray.

Three years later I saw him in California. *Voyage of the Pelican* had been published with unusual success. Reviews were excellent. He had been interviewed on radio and television. A movie producer was going to option the book. Several paperback houses were interested in reprint rights. He told me it was selling better than anybody expected. He had married a porcelain English goddess named Felicia, they were buying a little house in a eucalyptus grove near the Golden Gate, and he believed his days as a merchant seaman were over.

About that time he met another dislocated midwesterner, Willie Stumpf, in O'Leary's bar and grill. Stumpf had inherited a few thousand dollars, he admired Bowen's novel and thought the two of them should publish a literary magazine. He would be the publisher. Bowen could be editor-in-chief. They discussed it until O'Leary's closed. Bowen said the magazine should be called *Octopus* because nothing escapes the grasp of this remarkable creature, and they ought to publish it quarterly. Willie Stumpf said that was a great idea, he would rent an office. They shook hands. Both of them were very drunk.

Marriage turned out to be more expensive than Bowen anticipated; he learned that women require all sorts of things. Then, as if by magic, Felicia became pregnant. He was astonished and dismayed. It seemed to him that life was happening too quickly. Next, the Hollywood producer rode off into the sunset without a word of explanation, as movie producers tend to do. Bowen had started another novel and after contemplating the situation he decided to ask his New York publisher for an advance. The publisher agreed, although with some reluctance, and the advance was rather stingy, considering those good reviews. Then Willie Stumpf discovered that because *Octopus* would cost quite a lot to print, there might not be enough left over to pay the editor-in-chief's salary. Bowen cursed the universe with particular emphasis on Hollywood producers, New York publishers, and Willie Stumpf, after which he got drunk as he often did when fortune showed her ugly face, and concluded that his days as a merchant seaman were not over.

Aboard the oil tanker *Gulfport* somewhere west of Jalisco he missed a step on a gangplank and fell to the deck with such force that he split a kneecap. When I saw him next he was limping, but cheerful. Insurance had taken care of the medical bills, he and Felicia now had a charming daughter, Willie Stumpf had promised $300 a month as soon as *Octopus* showed a profit, and a national travel magazine had commissioned him to write about the San Francisco waterfront. As if this were not enough, *Voyage of the Pelican* would be translated into Swedish. It was strange and wonderful how one's luck could change.

He wrote a colorful description of the waterfront for which he was handsomely paid, so he got drunk and bought a dog. Every now and then somebody who had read the novel or the waterfront essay would compliment him. Once in a while a stranger asked for his autograph. His name appeared in newspapers. A columnist said he was the best writer in California. The public library asked him to give a reading. Felicia was happy. Day by day their tiny daughter Aurora grew more beautiful. Except for the fact that he was having trouble with the second book, life could hardly be better.

The first novel had almost written itself so he did not understand why *Harvest* should be difficult, but the longer he worked on it the more dissatisfied he became. Ideas evaporated. Words would not fall into place. No sooner did he write a line than he scratched it out. The narrative had no logic. Emotions that he tried to evoke seemed false. He began to wonder if he might be arguing against himself, if consciously he might be opposing his unconscious. He remembered a comment by Jung to the effect that a faulty interpretation encourages feelings of stagnation, opposition, and doubt. This, he said, was exactly how he felt, and he thought a change of scene might give him a new perspective on the novel. Unexplored streets, unfamiliar faces—if he could get away for a couple of weeks he might interpret the problem correctly.

He went to Mexico. In Oaxaca he rented an airy whitewashed room with a big overhead fan, a view of the plaza, and a window screen to keep out mosquitoes. He decided to stay for a month because it seemed like a perfect place to work on *Harvest* and life south of the border was cheap.

Oaxaca, he discovered, was full of pleasant surprises. Scarcely had he gotten settled when he met a Sacramento kindergarten teacher on vacation with the result that he did not get very much sleep and found it hard to concentrate on the manuscript. Then, during the second week, Oaxaca turned unpleasant. Eighty dollars vanished from his duffel bag. He suspected the chambermaid because she had a key to the room and she avoided looking at him. After a few more days, exasperated and restless, unable to work on the book, he came home. Although he had lost eighty dollars he did receive something in exchange—a stomach disorder that would afflict him the rest of his life.

The first issue of *Octopus* appeared with the title of an essay on Baudelaire printed upside down. Nobody could understand how this happened. The printer claimed it was not his fault. The proofreader said everything had been rightside up when she went over it. The poetry editor, Troy Dasher, said he had nothing to do with printing the magazine, he merely accepted or rejected poems, so he was innocent. Wendy, the part-time associate editor who scanned unpromising manuscripts, wrote letters of rejection, and made coffee, said she had nothing to do with it. Willie Stumpf accused Bowen, who, as editor-in-chief, must have neglected his duties. This annoyed Bowen, who said he had done everything expected of an editor-in-chief. Besides it was the publisher himself who had delivered final proofs to the printer. Why hadn't the publisher bothered to look at what he was delivering?

All of them adjourned to O'Leary's bar where the argument continued. After enough drinks Willie and Bowen vowed to settle the matter outside, so everybody marched across the street to a parking lot. O'Leary's bartender telephoned the police station, which was not far away. A policeman walked over to investigate. The publisher and the editor-in-chief, between insults, had begun shoving each other, so Troy Dasher attempted to separate them just as the policeman arrived and mistook Dasher for the cause of the trouble. Unlike most poets, Dasher was heavily muscled. When somebody grabbed his arm he flung the assailant against a parked car. The entire staff of *Octopus*, as well as the printer, was then escorted to the police station where the publisher, editor-in-chief, and poetry editor were charged with fomenting a public disturbance.

Not long after this incident a small paperback house bought *Voyage of the Pelican*, which was good news, although Bowen had been expecting a sale to one of the international giants. The first printing would be 10,000 copies instead of perhaps ten times that many, but the size of the printing was unimportant. If the paperback drew a large audience they could go back to press.

Meanwhile he continued to work on *Harvest* and he predicted that it would do even better than the first book. It was going to be a very long novel about midwestern America with dozens of significant characters. Because of the length and complexity there were technical problems, but he felt confident that he would soon have everything under control. In order to receive the advance he had signed a contract, but he wanted his agent to negotiate with the publisher for better terms. This novel, he said, might very well be a classic.

Bad luck came visiting once again. Outside of O'Leary's one night he was stopped by a derelict who asked for money. He responded by calling the bum a bum, and for declaring an obvious truth got his nose smashed. Nature had endowed him with a beak in place of a nose and the assault crumpled it. However, on his craggy midwestern face it did not seem inappropriate. He never had been vain, not in the usual sense, and except for the humiliation he felt at having his nose bloodied in a street fight the grotesque encounter meant very little. He was vain only of his talent.

The technical problems, whatever they might have been, were at last resolved and he mailed his second book to New York. The manuscript probably weighed as much as a metropolitan telephone book because he said it was almost nine hundred pages long. He looked forward to an excited call from his agent, but she did not finish reading it for nearly a month. Then she sent a note explaining that the office had been swamped and she would let him know as soon as there was any news from the publisher.

After a long silence he heard from New York. It had been accepted.

By coincidence, the publication date of *Harvest* was his twenty-ninth birthday. A celebration seemed like a good idea, and O'Leary's bar the logical place. Bowen invited everybody and told the Canterbury Bookshop to provide a stack of copies, which he would autograph.

He began drinking before the party started. In the past he had been able to drink throughout an evening with amiable sobriety, but he had done it too often. His body could absorb no more. His eyelids drooped and his mouth hung open. In a display of arrogance or contempt he propped his feet on a table, patted his crotch, and mumbled that he had written a superb book, a masterpiece. Among the guests was another writer he had always liked; but now, focusing on him, Bowen deliberately belched.

Harvest failed to attract much notice. When the first book came out he was identified as a promising young writer, but not this time. Reviewers were disappointed. One or two offered tepid praise and expressed hope for his next work. When I saw him a few months later I asked if there had been any movie interest. He said an important director was reading it.

He was angered and puzzled by the reaction to his second novel. He had visited a number of bookstores to discuss it with the clerks and he urged them to promote it. He suggested window displays, and he autographed every copy in stock so that none could be returned to the publisher. He telephoned book critics to complain that they had not understood what it was about. He said they were fools who could not appreciate anything more complex than a children's story with a moral set in italics. Originality befuddled them. He explained all of this while slumped in a corner of O'Leary's patio drinking beer. Finally the waitress asked him to hold his voice down and keep his boots out of the flowers.

When another issue of *Octopus* rolled off the press everything was rightside up, but Willie Stumpf felt dissatisfied. He thought more copies could be sold if the magazine had cartoons and Bowen told him he should be marketing codfish instead of literature. As a result, the next issue was indefinitely postponed.

Still, the planets must have been aligned in Bowen's favor. A philanthropic organization dedicated to helping artists, writers, and musicians awarded him a three-month fellowship at a bucolic retreat in southern California. He had not applied for it; indeed he had never heard of the organization that awarded these fellowships, but he saw no reason to decline a gift. The fellowship did not provide for wives or children, so Felicia and Aurora would stay at home.

When I next saw Bowen he was asleep in a Santa Monica hospital. He had told me to call the foundation if I happened to be in the neighborhood, so I did and was informed that he had been taken ill. At the hospital they directed me to his room. The door was open. When I saw him lying on his back with his face the color of parchment and his hands folded on his chest and that broken beak of a nose jutting from the blanket like the prow of a sunken ship I thought he had died. I hurried down the corridor and talked to a nurse. She said he was asleep. I said he might be dead, or almost dead, and perhaps she ought to have a look, but she insisted he was taking a nap. I went back to the room. He had not moved and he resembled a corpse, but I could hear a gentle snoring.

A few days later he was out of the hospital. I found him in a rustic cabin where he was busily typing up a short story. Life in the cabin had stimulated him to write stories, he said. As for the illness, an ulcer had developed during his tenure as editor-in-chief of *Octopus*, but it didn't amount to much. It gave his stomach something to think about other than the mysterious Mexican ailment.

He wrote five or six stories while he lived in the cabin. His agent had sold one to a men's magazine for a respectable amount by the time Thanksgiving came around, but the others were gathering rejection slips. An excerpt from his celebrated first novel had appeared in a textbook on the art of writing, which was complimentary, but payment was meager, and royalties had declined to the point that Bowen referred to them with amazement. His ulcer muttered, his entrails bubbled with the Oaxaca flux, and the bank had warned him about overdrafts. He no longer sounded cheerful.

He told me that he had a recurrent dream of silver dollars littering the beach while he floated indolently from one shining heap to the next. He said it was a marvelous dream. Awake, he dreamed that some New York literary panjandrum would discover his neglected second novel, catapulting it to the peak of the best-seller list where it stayed month after month. He imagined Hollywood executives wondering if he could be persuaded to write a movie script. Telegrams from Lotusland offered rich contracts, each proposal more extravagant than the last. His career had opened like a morning glory. Why should it fade? He compared himself not unfavorably to Conrad and Melville.

Felicia handed him a cigar on Christmas Day. Bowen was not thrilled. I heard that on the day after Christmas he sold a pint of blood.

And I heard about his affair with the olive-eyed Eurasian girl, Wendy, part-time associate editor of *Octopus*. She had come to the golden state of California looking for adventure. She was in her twenties, although she seemed no more than fifteen, and she must have become pregnant not long after Felicia.

Felicia learned about Wendy. I do not know what she said to Bowen, but he moved out of the eucalyptus grove and into Willie Stumpf's apartment where he was less than welcome. After a series of drunken arguments during which Bowen called his host an illiterate huckster, a mediocrity, a bumpkin, a cultural adolescent, a cartoon-lover, an undergraduate intellectual with a tin ear, and whatever else came to mind, he was evicted. He then lived for a while in the vacant garage of another friend where he started to write an existentialist novel about his experiences aboard the tanker *Gulfport*. His duffel bag and a few other possessions lay on a shelf alongside some camping equipment, a used battery, assorted wrenches, sections of pipe, garden hose, and a sack of fertilizer. His desk was a packing crate. The author himself could be observed seated in a canvas chair on the oil-soaked concrete, fashionably dressed in dungarees, moccasins, and a San Francisco Giants baseball cap. On warm days he typed without a shirt, exhibiting a flaccid paunch for whoever cared to look.

Occasionally he interrupted work on the novel to write a travel essay, which he could do without much effort by recalling the odors and sounds and activities of distant ports and by describing in humorous, picturesque language the human flotsam he had met. And he wrote sketches of small town life, affecting the style of Sherwood Anderson. A few of these sketches sold to midwestern journals, but they reeked of plagiarism. What animated Bowen to write at a level beyond understanding was the mythic quality of life at sea.

Felicia at last relented, so he moved back into their untidy little house among the trees. When they were first married she had attempted to cook and she had managed to keep the house reasonably clean, but now the center of what had drawn them together was sliding askew. She had put on fifteen or twenty pounds that sagged like tallow from her delicate bones and her English porcelain face was beginning to wrinkle. Somebody described her as a premature grandmother. Day and night she served spaghetti, Bowen said, and she was feeding Aurora peanut butter sandwiches. He could remember what he had loved about her once upon a time, but it no longer affected him. He, himself, was noticeably less attractive. He had lost a front tooth and in order to save money he did not have it replaced; or perhaps he took pride in his raffish appearance—the reincarnation of Huck.

Now and then some newspaper asked him to review a book, usually a novel about the sea. When *Voyage of the Pelican* was first published he had been called upon frequently, and because he knew the subject his criticism was perceptive. But little by little his reviews grew venomous, as though he resented competition. Then he began to mention his own work while commenting on the work of someone else so that calls for his service had become less frequent.

However, the gods of Olympus look indulgently on poets and dancers and sculptors and scribblers. Bowen must have been a favorite because he was offered the position of writer-in-residence for a year at a distinguished New England college. Living quarters would be furnished, he would be required to teach a workshop once a week, the rest of the time would be his own. Felicia, Aurora, and the baby could go with him. It sounded like an easy job, the salary would more than pay his bills, and campus life was relatively civilized. He remembered his days at the state university—tweedy professors and sycamore trees and football games and bonfires and pretty girls everywhere—so it did not take him very long to decide. Most of all he liked the promise of so much free time. He hoped to complete his *Gulfport* novel before the academic year ended.

Bowen's reign as writer-in-residence did not go well. It did not begin auspiciously, nor did the situation improve. At a cocktail party intended to welcome him and the new artist-in-residence he got drunk, he neglected to zip his fly after a visit to the men's room, he attempted to kiss a glamorous young teacher of Romance Languages, and he called the artist-in-residence a comic book illustrator who couldn't paint a catsup bottle. At another ceremonial affair he again drank too much and called the wife of the Dean of Admissions a babbling frump. And it was said that he became involved with one of the girls in his literary workshop. The college no doubt was relieved when he went back to California.

A few months later Felicia stabbed him. According to what she told friends, he used vulgar language and threatened to strangle her so she picked up a bread knife to protect herself but he paid no attention, which is how it happened. Bowen's account was different. They had argued, so in order to get away from her he went for a walk in the eucalyptus grove. When he got back to the house she came at him with a steak knife in each hand. Whatever happened, Felicia called the police, who dispatched an ambulance to the scene of the crime and Bowen was rushed to the hospital because he did not have very much blood left.

When I saw him he looked better than he did in Santa Monica. He was flat on his back again but he sounded optimistic. He did not blame Felicia. Neither did he blame himself. I asked how he was getting along with *Gulfport*. He stared at the ceiling with a thoughtful expression and licked his lips as though anticipating a drink. Oh, he said, there were a couple of problems, nothing important. And the ulcer? Oh, nothing to worry about. On the doorstep of middle age with a bad kneecap, watery entrails, fading eyesight, a missing tooth, an explosive stomach, quite possibly a damaged liver, and now a couple of stab wounds, he seemed to think himself invulnerable.

Bowen's publisher rejected *Gulfport*. He was shocked. He had been expecting a large advance. Thousands in the bank would solve nearly all of his problems. There would be no more arguments with Felicia about paying the bills. He would buy a roll of tar paper and fix the leak in the roof. He would visit the dentist. He would pay off the mortgage. He would get a new muffler for the car, which thundered and smoked like an old diesel and swayed through the eucalyptus as though the tank had been filled with whisky. He might even get a new car. Thousands in the bank would restore his confidence, which had been unspeakably abused. *Gulfport* was a major book, he insisted, maybe the best novel written in America during the past fifty years. The rejection made no sense. And he disparaged a recent novel that had been critically praised, saying the author had a tin ear and the critics should be reviewing science fiction.

The longer he thought about being rejected, the angrier he became, and having worked himself into a rage he decided to commit suicide. His death should be a lesson not only to the idiots at the publishing house but to all the newspaper hacks who had dismissed his second book. After he was gone they would realize their mistake. He pointed out that *Remembrance of Things Past* had been rejected by an editor with a tin ear.

So, one night when the moon was full, he wandered away from the house with a bottle of whisky, a bottle of sleeping pills, and a copy of the scorned manuscript tucked under his arm. When he came to an appropriate site overlooking San Francisco Bay he seated himself and uncorked the whisky. Some time later he opened the bottle of sleeping pills, washed them down, and stretched out with *Gulfport* clasped to his breast. He would not be found until the next day, which was unfortunate because his death would seem more tragic if searchers discovered his body beneath a full moon, but it couldn't be helped. Next day a peaceful corpse would be found among the towering eucalyptus. News that Bowen had killed himself would stun the literary world. It would be the subject of intense discussion from Greenwich Village to Beverly Hills, and posthumously his novel would be published to enormous acclaim.

He awoke on a bright sunny morning with birds twittering through the eucalyptus grove and found himself covered with vomit. The pills had made him sick. The pages of his manuscript were scattered. He crawled around collecting them and then he decided to read the opening of *Gulfport* to see if it was as brilliant as he thought. The first page proved that he had not been mistaken. He read the next page, and the next, and he did not stop until he had finished the opening chapter.

It was good. Here and there a few lines might be improved but they were easy enough to fix, so he went back to the house, took a shower, and started to work.

The bungled suicide left him disgusted and humiliated. I don't even know how to kill myself, he said. I can't do anything right.

He resembled the youth with crystal-gray eyes who sat on a steamer trunk in a Paris hotel, but it was no more than a resemblance. His eyes appeared rheumy, as though something inside had been melting. He wore glasses for reading. The fine tawny hair was a disorganized cobweb. Occasionally his lips twitched.

The god of misfits looked upon Bowen with pity, or maybe it was the god of malice. *Voyage of the Pelican*, by now half-forgotten in the United States, was sold to a Dutch publisher. But a short time afterward Bowen's agent called to explain that there had been a misunderstanding. The terms were not as generous as first believed. In fact, the advance against royalties would be little more than a gesture.

He vanished. He had done this before when he was discouraged or enraged, so Felicia paid no attention. Somebody told her that he was loitering around the waterfront wheedling drinks and money from strangers, but she merely shrugged.

When I saw him again he wanted to talk about the town where he had grown up. He ran the fingers of one hand through his uncombed hair and said the town lay on a marshy point thick with osier. He described the Methodist church and a feed store and chicken coops behind the houses and a Bible with gilt edges. He could remember antimacassars on the sofa in the parlor where shades were always drawn against the afternoon sun, willow branches touching the river, red-winged blackbirds, an old steamboat landing at the foot of Main Street. He talked about people gathering to watch a channel dredge that groaned and thumped and spouted sandy mud. In August the creeks ran dry, he said, and his grandmother would sit on the porch swing with a rag dipped in camphor tied around her head. He remembered whippoorwills and wild geese and the south wind and a clock ticking in the public library. His mother belonged to the Epworth League, she had a pink conch shell that gave out the roar of barbarous foreign seas. His father worked as a Rock Island brakeman. And while I listened I had no idea what he meant. He was talking to someone else—some biographer commissioned to preserve each fragment of his mosaic. I understood that he was trying to explain something, but only he knew what it was.

Then he said he might ship out again. He thought he would write another realistic novel like *Voyage of the Pelican*. His stomach lapped over his belt.

Nobody was surprised when Felicia divorced him. Bowen himself was not surprised; he cheerfully admitted that he had not been a faithful husband, that he drank too much, that he had not earned enough. What seemed to trouble him most was the failure of literary critics to understand the significance of his work and public indifference to everything he had written since that first novel. He mentioned Hart Crane plunging into the Gulf of Mexico.

That was the last time I talked with Bowen. Considering the number of beer bottles he left on the cliff he must have spent quite a while up there. Just when he made his decision is a mystery because he was alone. Sometime after dawn he took off his clothes and folded them. In each moccasin he placed an empty bottle and before the final step he put on his glasses. When I heard about the glasses, which lay on the sand near his body, I wondered why he had worn them; but of course he wanted to see where he was going.

ASSASSIN

KOERNER TRIED to remember everything he knew about Harlan. Considering how long they had been acquainted, not much. Harlan grew up in Kentucky or Tennessee, some flyspecked coal mining town where broken machinery rusted in vacant lots and old men wearing bib overalls sat in front of the general store like tombstones, that sort of place. All across America were towns like that. He had a gaggle of sisters and brothers, maybe six or eight. He played in the high school band, trumpet or trombone. Koerner remembered him joking about the band. He had never gone back to visit. If so, he didn't mention it. He was a stubby, bald-headed man, solid as a fireplug, with reptilian eyes. People were surprised to learn that he enjoyed singing because he looked like a wrestler. "Danny Boy," "The Rose of Tralee," "Shenandoah," the songs of Stephen Foster, and Christian hymns were among his favorites.

Soon after LBJ committed the United States to Vietnam, he joined the Army. Now he limped, his right hand was disfigured, and his wife Lucybelle said he kept a leather pouch stuffed with medals and ribbons. Also in the pouch was a human ear.

He and Lucybelle had been contentedly married, so far as anyone knew, for at least thirty years. A son and a daughter, both married, and a son just out of college who lived with an older man.

Lucybelle, a queenly figure at fifty-something, had grown up in New Orleans and continued to favor bourbon drinks laced with Coca-Cola, pack after pack of cigarettes, a black velvet choker, and tarantula perfume. Everything about Lucybelle hinted of social pleasantries distinguishing the affluent from the rabble, colored servants, private schooling, muggy Southern nights, dances where young ladies wore white gloves. Koerner thought she had inherited money, perhaps quite a lot. Harlan, who showed a long nose for California real estate, what to buy, when to sell, probably added more than a few banknotes to the family fortune.

However it came about, they enjoyed life in baronial comfort on an exclusive hillside north of the Golden Gate, reassured by the occasional sight of a security guard cruising by. Ships from everywhere coasted beneath the famous red bridge. San Francisco sparkled like Byzantium. Across the bay, sometimes obscured by fog, Oakland and Berkeley pursued altogether different dreams.

Koerner, agreeably stuffed after a catered Oriental supper, took another sip of wine and looked around the table. At opposite ends Harlan and Lucybelle presided. Otherwise, Nelson, the vastly rich neighbor, with his sulky companion Bryce—a Renaissance prince with a gynandrous consort. Gussie and Marsha, interior decorators who lived in a Telegraph Hill penthouse. Then there was Wallace, oddly resembling a squirrel, whom Koerner had not seen before.

Bryce seemed more peevish than usual. Quite obviously he preferred to be someplace else. He might be very different when he and Nelson were alone, but then again, maybe not. The yellowish cheesy face suggested a decadent angel.

Harlan was describing a raft trip down the Colorado River. He needed a doctor's approval because of his age and because it would be a strenuous hike from the plateau to the river. The doctor decided he could make it. Harlan never doubted he could make it. There would be four inflatable rafts guided by local river rats. They would emerge from the canyon on Lake Powell above Hoover Dam. Lucybelle refused to go.

When I was a teensy thing, she said, and stopped to cough, Daddy took me fishing. Now I tell you I just plain hated each and every single minute. I enjoyed myself right here, thank you.

Harlan laughed. He said the food wasn't bad, not bad at all. He expected ten days of hardboiled eggs, stale sandwiches, and canned peaches, but the river rats turned out to be pretty good cooks. Fried chicken one night, sirloin steak another night. Shishkebab, trout, lamb stew, barbecued pork. Soup, salad, dessert. The only thing he didn't like was drinking river water. They purified it with tablets, so nobody got the Aztec two-step, but it looked and tasted like mud.

You won't believe this, he said. You know who else went on that trip? A bunch of college girls in bathing suits—fifteen or sixteen at least. Blondes, brunettes, a couple of redheads.

I'm glad I stayed home, Lucybelle said. I just know you made a fool of yourself.

Harlan asked one of the river rats if they got paid to escort half-naked girls down the Colorado. Aw, man, said the river rat, this is nuts. Usually it's old Mormon families.

On the fourth night beneath a spooky red moon a herd of wild burros stampeded through their camp. Harlan didn't know what scared the burros or where they came from. Prospectors used to look for gold in the canyon during the nineteenth century and sometimes a burro got loose. Probably that was how the herd originated.

Figured it might be the Last Judgment, he said. Burros raising hell, girls running around shrieking in the moonlight.

Nelson and Lucybelle pretended to listen. Bryce inspected his fingernails. Wallace attempted to hide a yawn.

Harlan kept going. He described how they would paddle ashore for lunch. He talked about mid-afternoon rain showers, navigating rapids, exploring side canyons, rock-climbing, listening for echoes, searching for Indian petroglyphs. He described how one of the river rats fell overboard while trying to impress the girls by doing a headstand. He described clouds. He described a vulture.

Let's go home, Bryce said to Nelson.

For heaven's sake! Nelson whispered.

Gussie and Marsha exchanged significant looks. Koerner thought they had learned to communicate without speaking.

You don't appreciate me, Bryce said. You never have.

Nelson turned to Harlan. I'm so embarrassed. As a rule he's sweet. I didn't expect this.

You found somebody else, Bryce said. I can tell.

Nelson sighed, tossing his hands in a delicate gesture of impatience or frustration. We've been together three years and five months almost to the day. From the moment we saw each other—fireworks! Isn't that true? he asked, smiling at Bryce. Come now. Be yourself.

You listen, both of you, Lucybelle said. Dessert is a surprise. Chocolate boysenberry trifle with meringue, oodles of pecans, cashews, and peppermint sprinkle. It has so many calories you'll never speak to me again.

Oh, you devil! Nelson exclaimed. Lucy, you are! How I wish we could stay, but this dear child is on the verge of throwing a fit.

Wallace, leaning forward, smiled across the table at Nelson. I'm told you have a gorgeous estate. I should love to see it, if that wouldn't be an imposition.

Nelson glanced at Bryce, who pursed his lips.

Please join us, Nelson said.

Marsha and Gussie decided they would share a trifle, although they must be leaving soon.

Lucybelle frowned at Koerner. Baby doll, you are not leaving! I forbid you to leave.

I love chocolate, Koerner said. I'll eat three or four.

Fairies! Harlan said when the door closed.

Honeybunch, Lucybelle said, you like Nelson. You know you do.

Fags and dykes! Harlan said angrily. Why don't they keep that Nellie business to themselves? Why do they advertise? God, they make me want to puke!

He had been toying with a pair of chopsticks, now and then pretending to snatch a fly out of the air. Koerner recognized the scene from an old samurai film. The famous warrior is eating when killers burst into the room. The samurai ignores them. They advance, threatening him, scowling ferociously. He does not seem to be aware of them. He reaches out with the chopsticks, catches a fly. The demonstration terrifies them. They look at the sword resting on a mat beside him. In half a second he could leap to his feet and slice off their noses. They nearly fall over each other in a desperate effort to escape.

Koerner thought about the first time he saw the chopsticks. Harlan, wearing a black satin kimono, clicked the chopsticks, waggled them, and said he felt pretty sure the owner wouldn't be using them anymore. Then, too, he had played the role of samurai plucking a fly out of the air. Gotcha! he whispered. Koerner understood that he had killed the man.

Last time in the city we went to Emilio's for lunch, Harlan said. Lucy got up to visit the ladies' room and you know what? Some fairy patted me on the ass. I should have wasted that sucker! What the hell is wrong with those pansies?

Well, goodness, Lucybelle said.

Koerner looked at the head and skin of a bear hanging on the wall in back of Harlan's chair. He had shot it with a bow and arrow not long after returning from Vietnam. He had parted the fur to expose a ragged puncture. Mean mother, he said, and laughed. Sucker just about did me in.

Who had skinned the bear? It wasn't important, of course. Or perhaps it was. Skinning the enemy used to be important, like taking a scalp or displaying the enemy head on a pole or shrinking the head until it became a toy, or keeping a Vietnamese ear in a leather pouch. Not so many generations have passed since men huddled around campfires in Ice Age caves, wore animal pelts and danced and sang, pretending to be deer or bison or tigers or mammoths.

If they make you want to puke, Koerner said, why do you invite them to your home?

Harlan did not move. What's that supposed to mean? he asked.

This is absurd, Koerner thought. He understands the question. He and Lucybelle very often invite gays to dinner parties and he couldn't be friendlier. This makes no sense. Why does he pretend? I never thought he would fake anything, not Harlan. There was always some hardscrabble honesty about him. I respected that. I respected him for that as much as anything. Now he's evasive. The expression is false. Those eyes are cold as glass. He looks like a prehistoric hunter in a museum exhibit.

Suddenly it occurred to him that Harlan was frightened. This did not seem possible, not after three years in Vietnam. The injuries and medals told it all. If trouble hopped out of the bushes, nobody would ask for more dependable company. It might be easier to frighten a fireplug than to scare this man. Now, afraid of a question, Harlan sat without moving beneath the totemic head of a wild animal.

Koerner understood that he could only wait for this moment to pass. Whatever he might say or do would make things worse. In the menacing silence he reflected that perhaps it was true, the mind is a world of streaming shadows.

MRS. PROCTOR BEMIS

MRS. PROCTOR BEMIS—lineal descendant of a Revolutionary War general, wife of a Kansas City merchant prince, mother of two boys and a girl who would inherit the Bemis fortune as well as the farm implements company founded by grandfather Suddarth—Mrs. Bemis, in spite of her social eminence, distinguished lineage, prominent husband, attractive children, and stately home, was exasperated; and what further exasperated her was the knowledge that her husband did not share this feeling. He, on the contrary, looked as complacent as an overfed dachshund.

Mrs. Bemis, angrily watching her husband while he lounged in his favorite chair beside the fireplace reading the *Kansas City Star*, thought about General Benjamin Suddarth—friend and neighbor of George Washington—whose gold-framed portrait by Rembrandt Peale hung in the dining room like a religious icon. It seemed to her that if General Suddarth were alive he would do something about the violence and liberalism that threatened to destroy society. General Suddarth would insist upon capital punishment for dangerous criminals instead of patting them on the wrist. General Suddarth would sweep the streets clean of beggars, thieves, drug addicts, vandals, prostitutes, alcoholics, and pornographers. He would restore pride and dignity to the United States. He would abolish the food stamp program. He would crush welfare cheats as though they were insects. And the graffiti was awful. General Suddarth would do something about that.

Mrs. Bemis, vexed by the lack of expression on her husband's face, demanded to know how he was able to sit there reading the paper.

Mr. Bemis did not find this question unreasonable. They had been married a good many years and he was seldom disconcerted by anything she said even when he could make no sense of it. He peered over the top of his spectacles as he waited for her to continue.

In the grocery, Mrs. Bemis said while trying to restrain the anger she felt, I saw a young couple buying everything they could put their hands on. They paid for most of it with food stamps.

Mr. Bemis waited attentively because he expected more, but that was all she said. He nodded, cleared his throat, and returned to the newspaper.

Mrs. Bemis thought about going to the dining room to speak with General Suddarth. Large areas of the Midwest were flooded because there had been weeks of rain. Television showed vast tracts of midwestern farmland inundated. The Mississippi, Missouri, Ohio, and any number of tributaries were overflowing, thousands of people had been driven from their homes; yet this young couple, without a care in the world, had bought imported cheese and wine. They had been laughing while they rolled the grocery cart up one aisle and down another. Mrs. Bemis had followed them and had seen them pick up whatever appealed to them; she had followed them to the checkout counter and had seen the young man give food stamps to the cashier. He appeared to be in perfect health, perfectly able to work for a living. So was the girl. Why were they entitled to food stamps?

This outrage reminded Mrs. Bemis of the President. She had been willing to give the man a chance, despite the fact that his private life was a disgrace and everybody knew what would happen if he was elected. Now, of course, taxes were being raised. And how would this money be used? To support loafers and chiselers.

Chrysler plunged two-and-a-half, said Mr. Bemis. I don't like the way things are shaping up. That damn Fed chief. I'd better give Eliot a call.

Is he a Democrat? Mrs. Bemis asked.

Is who a Democrat?

Whoever you were talking about.

The chairman of the Federal Reserve? I have no idea. Why?

I was just wondering, Mrs. Bemis said. She closed her eyes and lightly massaged her temples while she thought about two young Negroes she had seen drifting around the Plaza. Apparently they belonged to a gang because they wore baggy trousers and nylon jackets with some kind of insignia and baseball caps turned backward. They had no business on the Plaza. The police should have questioned them, but the police did nothing. Once upon a time the Plaza had been charming. People were well dressed and polite. Now it was unsafe. Shoppers had been accosted by alcoholic beggars and shabby eccentrics—which was the reason Mrs. Bemis carried a whistle in her purse. If someone had suggested a few years ago that she carry a whistle she would have been puzzled, but times had changed. Now there were mysterious symbols and ominous messages spray-painted on park benches and trash cans and mailboxes. Kansas City had been quite different while she was growing up. Of course there had been a certain amount of vandalism and crime—burglaries, an occasional murder in the North End—but nothing serious in the Country Club district.

The situation on the Plaza has become just intolerable, she said. Almost anything could happen.

Her husband did not respond.

Mrs. Bemis frowned as she thought about the colored boys. They had a legal right to be on the Plaza, yet there was no good reason for them to be there. They did not intend to buy anything. She had followed them and knew they did not intend to buy; they were loitering, gawking at displays in the shop windows. They might have been planning a burglary. They might have been armed. They were not the first Negroes she had observed in the Country Club district, but these two were by far the least presentable. Obviously they did not care how they looked. Years ago they would have been rounded up and warned not to come back, otherwise they would be arrested as vagrants. Their attitude said all too clearly that they would go where they pleased, and their presence in an area where they did not belong was menacing. Mrs. Bemis had carried the whistle in her hand while she followed them.

Mr. Bemis abruptly lowered the newspaper. Marguerite, he said, what could happen on the Plaza?

There have been so many incidents. Just the other day Helen Gamble saw a man loitering near the entrance to Swanson's.

Why don't you carry a gun? That tin whistle wouldn't scare a chickadee.

This annoyed Mrs. Bemis. In case of emergency she would be able to alert bystanders to what was happening, but she did not want to carry a gun. A man should protect his family so it was appropriate for a man to carry a gun, but it would be inappropriate for a woman. Besides, he was joking. Nancy Reagan reportedly carried a pistol and for some reason he was amused by this.

She decided to think about how nice Kansas City had been when she was a child. How very secure she had felt. How pleasant and comfortable everything used to be. She thought about her parents. She thought about her brown and white dog Hopscotch. She remembered one Sunday in April when all of them got into the car, including Hopscotch, and they drove to Swope Park for a picnic. She had made a collar of dandelions for Hopscotch and a butterfly landed on the potato salad. Now everything was different. So much was unfamiliar. Movies used to be entertaining, but now they emphasized violence or sex. Popular music was romantic and couples danced together, but now the young musicians seemed to lunge and shout while people danced alone. Artists painted women with lopsided faces. What did it mean?

I feel sick about Robin moving in with that boy, she said.

Ah, said Mr. Bemis from behind the paper and it sounded as though he had yawned.

What they are doing is indecent. If they live together they should get married. He is taking advantage of Robin.

Umm, said Mr. Bemis.

Why is she supporting him? Why doesn't the boy get a job?

Alex wants to paint and Robin tells me she doesn't mind working.

I realize that times change, Mrs. Bemis said, but I cannot begin to tell you how much I disapprove of this arrangement. It is immoral.

They're happy, said Mr. Bemis. Let them alone.

Mrs. Bemis plucked anxiously at her necklace. It isn't right, she said. If they are in love they ought to get married and Alex should look for work. What will happen if she becomes pregnant?

Mr. Bemis sighed.

I don't care for his paintings, Mrs. Bemis said. I don't pretend to be an art critic, but I think they are hideous. Who on earth would buy them?

Why ask me? said Mr. Bemis.

He hasn't sold a single one. Do you think he's a Communist?

Ten years ago, Communism.Today, enlightenment. Alex and Robin probably eat carrots and meditate.

We never behaved like that when we were young.

You didn't know me when I rode a motorcycle, said Mr. Bemis.

Well, I do not approve, Mrs. Bemis said. I thought Robin would marry Tyler Pence. They went around together for such a long time. I felt sure they would become engaged.

Mr. Bemis rustled the paper. Marguerite, listen to this. Members of the school board in Tavares, Florida, wherever the hell that is, after reciting the pledge of allegiance to the flag, voted to teach Lake County students that American values are superior to all others. New policy shall include and instill appreciation of patriotism, free enterprise, freedom of religion, et cetera. One board member says teaching supremacy will make the boys enthusiastic about going to war.

Don't you think America is worth defending? Mrs. Bemis asked.

I certainly do. And anybody who burns our flag ought to be prosecuted.

That's what Hitler thought.

I do not care what Hitler thought. This isn't Germany.

Madame Chairman of the Tavares board objects to deep-breathing exercises, which could induce in the student an altered state of mind. Also, they figured out a way to save money—dropped sex education program for retarded kids.

There is no reason for sex to be discussed in school, Mrs. Bemis said. It encourages children to experiment. Nothing but trouble can result. She twisted her wedding ring and frowned, wondering if the colored boys were retarded. That would explain why their shoelaces were untied and why they shuffled aimlessly around the Plaza. It was a shame the Negro district didn't have better schools. The boys might be able to make something of themselves if they received a good education, so it wasn't altogether their fault. America was not perfect by any means. Colored people were discriminated against, which wasn't right; they should have the same opportunities as everyone else. But it did seem that at times they went out of their way to cause trouble. The boys had been encroaching and they knew it.

She remembered a big Negro who passed her on the sidewalk while she was going to the post office. He brushed by so closely that she could smell him. He had almost touched her. She had been afraid that he might follow her. Inside the post office she spent more time than necessary, and before going outside she took the whistle from her purse. Of course he might have meant no harm, but he did come unusually close—as though he intended to frighten her.

Why is it, she asked herself, that so many colored people were changing their names? And why did some pretend to be Muslims? They were Christian, probably Baptist, so why should they adopt outlandish Arabic names and pretend to be what they were not? Supposedly it had to do with resentment over the way their ancestors were treated, which was understandable. But what did they expect to accomplish by changing their names? Apparently they were determined to make an issue of the past.

Then—just as vividly as if they were on a movie screen—Mrs. Bemis saw the welfare cheats. She watched the young man select a bottle of wine and saw him roll his eyes at the girl, who laughed. It was quite obvious what they intended to do. And who would pay for their enjoyment? At a time when taxes should be cut, what did this administration want? Middle-class citizens who did not ask for government help were expected to support idle young men, unwed mothers, the United Nations, socialized medicine, career criminals, foreign aid programs, missions to Mars, and whatever else appealed to the left wing. Mrs. Bemis angrily drew in her breath and closed her eyes. What earthly reason could there be for supporting the United Nations? Foreign governments had no business telling America what to do. General Suddarth would put a stop to such nonsense. However, ultra liberals controlled the media and Congress and now they had gotten into the White House. Nobody should be surprised that taxes were going up or that good manners had become a thing of the past. Conservative values were ridiculed or ignored. Abortion had been legalized, although it was a crime and a sin. Pornography was displayed on magazine racks. Homosexuals boasted of their unnatural acts and lobbied for special privileges. Homosexuals. The word itself was disgusting. Why would a normal person decide to become homosexual? Mrs. Bemis shook her head. Nothing made sense. America was no longer one nation under God. School prayer had been prohibited and children were taught evolution because the textbooks were written by secular humanists.

I'll be damned, Mr. Bemis said. Get this. Two kids in upstate New York killed a swan. Broke the bird's legs and stabbed it forty times. Forty times! Cut off the head. Swan's legs snapped just like twigs, according to the younger kid. Umm, they left the bird's head on the steps of a police station.

Mrs. Bemis grimaced. Why would anybody want to kill a swan?

Mayor of the town says people demand maximum punishment for the kids. Death threats and so forth.

How old are they?

Fifteen. Seventeen. Father of one kid says he can't understand the big brouhaha. "All this over a duck," he says.

But why did they do it?

Drinking. Jumped a fence, caught the swan, broke its legs, stabbed it. Younger kid told police he blacked out, claims he doesn't remember much.

Proctor, in Heaven's name, what is happening? Has the world gone mad?

Umm, said Mr. Bemis.

Well, Mrs. Bemis remarked after a long silence, I agree with the townspeople. Those young hoodlums ought to be paddled within an inch of their lives and locked up until they learn to behave. Alcohol is no excuse.

It occurred to her that instead of being punished the boys probably would be released on probation. No doubt a psychiatrist would testify that because they had been drinking they should not be held responsible. That happened so frequently. No matter what crime had been committed there would be a psychiatrist to explain why the offender was innocent. What he had done wasn't his fault because he had been unable to control his emotions. In fact, so they argued, the criminal himself was a victim because he suffered from depression or multiple personality disorders, or drug withdrawal symptoms, parental abuse, alcoholism—one thing or another. It was infuriating. Criminals ought to be imprisoned and they should not be released. Most crimes were committed by a small percentage of the population so it would make sense to keep those men in jail, but they always seemed to get out. Again and again and again they were pardoned or released on parole, which only encouraged them to continue robbing and murdering. No sooner was one locked up than some psychiatrist or clever attorney or liberal judge would find a reason to let him out. This was wrong. If the prisons were crowded, which might well be true, why not build more? Tax money was wasted on all sorts of ridiculous social programs. Why should the federal or state government subsidize artists, for example, when ordinary citizens were afraid to walk the streets? Why not use that money to build prisons? The federal government ought to maintain the armed services and the interstate highway system; everything else could be left up to individual states and local communities.

Teamsters, Mr. Bemis muttered. Picketing the Fairfield assembly plant.

I do not approve of picketing, Mrs. Bemis said. They should settle their differences some other way. Those strikes usually end in violence.

She had expressed her feelings about pickets and strikes quite a few times in the past, but it was worth repeating. Unions were legal and the law must be obeyed, even though union members themselves frequently violated the law. Of course nobody should be forced to join a union. If a laborer decided to join, that was his privilege, but those who did not wish to become members should not be denied an opportunity to work—which happened quite often. Union members blocked the entrances to factories, jeered and threw stones, overturned cars, and attacked people who wanted to work. This was not right. Everybody knew this was not right, but the union leaders did not care about anything except getting their way. And most of them were corrupt.

I wish General Suddarth were alive, she said.

Umm, Mr. Bemis replied. Ha! Star Wars budget reduced. Reagan's Maginot Line in the sky could be kaput.

Proctor, that makes me simply furious! Liberals waste our tax dollars coddling criminals and Heaven knows what else when the money ought to be spent on national defense. We could be attacked at any moment.

By whom?

This exasperated Mrs. Bemis; she waved the question aside. We ought to be prepared. Russia cannot be trusted. Stalin was worse than Hitler. We've got to remain on guard. Is there anything in the paper about tax reduction?

Not likely, Mr. Bemis muttered. Well, well, another JFK book.

That's one I can do without, Mrs. Bemis said. Why must they glam-
orize him? He should have been imprisoned.

Why not the whole bunch?

The Kennedys?

All those humbugs we put in the White House.

I thought you meant the Kennedys.

JFK and Bobby worried folks, no doubt about it. More than once
I've heard somebody say Oswald deserved a medal.

I don't approve of assassination, Mrs. Bemis said, but I most certainly do not approve of immoral conduct. That is one thing I find
inexcusable.

Mr. Bemis gave her a peculiar look and she turned away. John
Kennedy had been promiscuous and she could remember what she
felt—along with shock—at the news of his death. She remembered
feeling that he had gotten what he deserved. His behavior was disgusting. And he had been Catholic just like all the Kennedys. They might
not be Jews or atheists, but neither were they true Christians.

I admired President Nixon, she said.

Tricky Dick, said Mr. Bemis. Nine lives.

The liberal press was always after him. It made me so mad. He
was one of the first to point out the threat of Communism. He and
Senator McCarthy. I suppose that's why the liberals were out to get
him. They hated him because they knew he wasn't afraid to stand up
for America. He should never have been forced to resign. I wish he
could have remained in office forever. I always believed he was telling the truth about Watergate. And of course he did put an end to the
Vietnam war.

She tried to remember when the war had ended. The draft evad-
ers would be middle-aged by now. A few of them probably were still
living in Canada and it would be just as well if they never came home.
They had given aid and comfort to the enemy. They were traitors.
The United States did everything imaginable to help South Vietnam
and if the country had remained united behind President Nixon the
war effort would have been successful. But Communist sympathizers
had organized riots and protest marches and the liberal media supported them. How many American soldiers died because North Vietnam thought those protesters represented America? And somebody
in the Pentagon had stolen classified documents. Mrs. Bemis tried to

think of his name, but could not. Whoever he was, he had made the situation worse.

She thought about the long-haired filthy students taunting President Nixon, the subversive peace symbols, the caricatures and horrid photos—the naked Vietnamese girl seared by napalm, the televised execution of a handcuffed prisoner, the embarrassing helicopter escape. And at these memories she felt almost as irritated as she had felt during the war.

What we did was right! she said bitterly. We have nothing to be ashamed of. We were trying to help.

Ancient history, Mr. Bemis remarked. Vietnam sounds like the Peloponnesian War except when some farmer trips over an old mine or an unexploded bomb.

He was referring to a television special. The pictures of mutilated children and peasants had been horrifying. Mrs. Bemis gazed out the window. I suppose all they can do is watch where they're going, she said. But don't you agree that our intentions were good?

I do, I do, he agreed, although his tone indicated that he would prefer to read the paper.

Mrs. Bemis, with hands folded in her lap, reflected on the amount of time she had spent watching newscasts and listening to various analysts explain why North Vietnam would lose the war. It would be impossible, they had explained, for a small impoverished country like North Vietnam to defeat the most powerful nation on earth. She thought about the pictures of huge bombers dropping what appeared to be tiny sticks on Hanoi. Emaciated little captives—none of whom seemed to be more than five feet tall—were guarded by brawny American soldiers.

Mrs. Bemis suddenly realized that her husband was talking about a Presbyterian conference in Minneapolis. Two thousand women had convened to discuss and celebrate feminine religious beliefs.

Ritual affirming the sensuality of women, he said. Shared milk and honey. Laughed at patriarchal traditions. Methodists there, too. Well, well. "Our maker Sophia, we are women in your image. With the hot blood of our wombs we give form to new life. With nectar between our thighs we invite a lover." So on and so forth. Warm body fluids remind the world of its pleasures and sensations. Revolutionary way of perceiving God.

Everybody has gone insane, said Mrs. Bemis.

Sophia a personification of God found in the Book of Proverbs. "I was set up, at the first, before the beginning of the earth"—whatever that's supposed to mean. Conference organizers insist the meeting was a thoroughly Christian effort to dramatize a feminine Biblical metaphor. Ha! One speaker invited lesbian, bisexual, and transsexual women to join her on stage. Denounced as blasphemous by evangelical wing of the church. Ha! I'll bet!

Mrs. Bemis, with lips pursed, wondered about the women in Minneapolis. That they should publicly celebrate their immorality seemed not just vulgar but a deliberate attempt to offend and shock respectable people. They were nearly as perverted as men. She remembered a poetry festival on television where an old man with a white beard chanted about his love for adolescent boys. Now, of course, those homosexuals were diseased and ought to be quarantined. Why were they permitted to infect other people? Negroes and Communists and homosexuals and every other minority under the sun insisted upon their so-called rights, but what about the rights of decent men and women?

It isn't fair, she said.

Her husband did not reply and she discovered that he had left the room. Perhaps he had gone to call Eliot about the stock market. She closed her eyes and imagined Kansas City as it had been many years ago. She thought of a green bicycle she got for Christmas, and Hugh Puckett who gave her an orchid, and her best friend Chessie. She remembered pedaling around Mission Hills with Chessie, who had a blue bicycle. One afternoon they stopped beside a pond to watch some boys who were fishing. After a while they tossed pebbles at the boys and rode away as fast as they could. She thought about the neighbors and the colored maid, and Francisco who came around once a month during summer to cut the grass. She remembered vacations at Lake Quivira when the children were small, and the time Robin sprained her ankle. The time Peter was arrested for speeding. Mark's beautiful wedding. None of it seemed so terribly long ago. In those days Kansas City was quiet and safe. People were courteous. Nobody used drugs. Maybe some of the colored people did, and perhaps a few Italians in the North End, but drugs had been unknown in the residential area. There were no lesbians, bisexuals, or women masquerading as men. There weren't any male homosexuals. There had been two or three effeminate boys in high school and one of them was chased into a vacant lot by some football players and given a bloody nose, otherwise the sissies were ignored. Most of the boys had been nice. Several of them drank and drove too fast, but none of them carried knives or guns. There wasn't much vandalism, except at Halloween. There weren't any beggars in the Country Club district. There weren't any armed guards in the banks or television cameras or security guards in the shops.

Mr. Bemis grunted. Mrs. Bemis opened her eyes and noticed that he had returned with a drink.

Immigrants, he said. Boatload of Chinese got ashore near San Francisco. Scattered like rats.

I do not understand how that can happen, Mrs. Bemis said. How many were there?

Who knows? Dozens. Hundreds.

Can't anything be done?

Pai gow, fat chance, Mr. Bemis said. They probably had fake identification cards before they jumped ship. Relatives in Chinatown. How do you catch them?

Immigration laws ought to be enforced, Mrs. Bemis answered in a determined voice because it seemed to her that the Coast Guard had not done its job. Possibly the Coast Guard didn't have enough ships, but somehow these illegal aliens ought to be stopped, otherwise more and more would arrive and the economy would suffer. Mexicans waded across the Rio Grande, boatloads of Negroes sailed up from the Caribbean, and hordes of Orientals—Chinese especially—managed to elude the Coast Guard. It was not right. They knew they could earn more money in the United States so what they did was understandable, but they ought to be stopped. Immigration laws meant nothing to them; all they cared about was getting in. Quotas were necessary because there must be limits, and the law should be obeyed.

Couple of juveniles found a corpse near the railroad tracks, Mr. Bemis said. Can you guess what they did? Reported a body to the cops? Wrong. They toyed with it—poked it with sticks—invited their pals to have a look.

Mrs. Bemis sighed. Proctor, what is going on? What is wrong with those children?

Where are they leading us? Mr. Bemis asked.

The educational system is to blame, Mrs. Bemis said. Discipline
has become a thing of the past. And as she considered this it seemed
undeniable. The lack of discipline in schools was appalling so the children did as they pleased and neglected their studies. They learned
almost nothing. Permissive educational policies were devastating.
High school graduates scarcely knew how to spell. Few of them could
put together a coherent sentence. Some of them would be unable
to find the United States on a map of the world. Some could not do
elementary arithmetic. They had no manners, no ambition, no education. European schools might be just as good as American schools,
possibly better. Yet these rude, self-indulgent, hostile American children would be awarded diplomas because the liberals did not believe
anybody should fail.

Mister Softee murdered.

What? said Mrs. Bemis.

Philadelphia. Ice cream truck driver robbed and murdered. Customers laughed while he bled to death.

You are making this up, Mrs. Bemis said.

First came familiar music of the truck, then an argument. Gunfire
while the music tinkled on. Word spread that Mister Softee was shot.
Iranian immigrant with three kids, first week on the job. Undisclosed
amount of cash stolen. Group of teenagers improvised songs about
the dying driver. Sounds like a ghetto neighborhood.

We need more police, Mrs. Bemis said. We need more and more
and more police, that's all there is to it. This sort of thing seems to
happen day and night.

Send for the Marines, Mr. Bemis said. Swamp the country with
gung-ho leathernecks.

That might not be a bad idea, Mrs. Bemis said, although I'm sure
the ACLU would object. Why do they wear beards?

Mr. Bemis lowered the paper. Beards?

Every single one of them. I realize that during the nineteenth century it was normal for a man to have a beard, but we do not live in the
nineteenth century. I assume they are attempting to make some kind
of political statement, but they look silly.

Who are we talking about?

You know perfectly well who I mean. Those ACLU lawyers. All of them wear beards and they always stand up for the troublemakers.

And this reminded Mrs. Bemis of how she despised socialists. She remembered Harry Bridges, who had come to the United States from Australia and was forever organizing strikes on the West Coast, just as Eugene Debs and other socialists had tried to overthrow capitalism early in the century. They were not satisfied unless they caused trouble and most of them secretly belonged to the Communist party. They should have been deported or imprisoned. Instead of being grateful to America they attempted to destroy it. They had no respect for private property, they did not want anybody to succeed. They wanted to take everything away from those who were willing to work and give it to those who did nothing. And there had been Roosevelt to back them up. And then more Democrats—which resulted in more government interference with the lives of ordinary citizens. Now the middle class was being taxed out of existence. Why should those who had worked hard throughout their lives be expected to subsidize abortions for lazy unmarried colored women? The minute those women got out of the hospital they became pregnant again because they knew the government would provide. And some of them already had five or six children but no husband. Why should decent citizens pay for the rehabilitation of drug addicts who had nobody to blame except themselves? Why should respectable people be obliged to support idlers and cheats who had no self-respect? But of course that was what liberal socialists wanted and if they got their way the nation would go bankrupt. Liberals were anxious to spend every cent. Tax and spend. That was how they reasoned. But why not use tax money sensibly? Marijuana and other drugs were grown in South America and smuggled into the United States, so why not cancel offensive programs such as the National Endowment for the Arts and use that money to curtail drug production? It should not be difficult to locate the fields and it should not be difficult for the Air Force to bomb them. That ought to teach the drug dealers a lesson.

Proctor, Mrs. Bemis said, when the United States invaded Panama didn't it have something to do with drugs?

Mr. Bemis cleared his throat. As I recall, the problem would be solved if we could apprehend Noriega.

But it seems to have gotten worse.

That's right. Our troops accomplished their mission and now you can buy heroin from your friendly neighborhood dealer.

Well, Mrs. Bemis said after thinking about this, I'm sure President Bush knew what he was doing.

Mr. Bemis nodded and murmured to prove that he was listening. Pre-dawn vertical insertion, he said a few moments later.

What?

Panama reminded me of Grenada. According to the Pentagon, Reagan's attack on Grenada was a pre-dawn vertical insertion.

Mrs. Bemis realized that she had practically forgotten about Grenada. She frowned, trying to remember. There had been some American medical students on the island who asked to be rescued—or was that right? And it had been necessary to bomb a mental hospital. Or was the hospital bombed by mistake? In any case, it happened quite a while ago and no longer mattered; President Reagan had taken care of the situation. She tossed her hands in despair. At times, Proctor, I believe you go out of your way to provoke me!

Umm, he said. Nasty situation in Walla Walla. State decided to hang somebody, but the fellow wouldn't cooperate. Struggled. Had to spray him with pepper and strap him to a board. Strapped to a board—ye Gods! Sprayed with pepper? Death penalty supporters outside the gate whooping and cheering. Prison authority complained, said an air of decorum should prevail. Two hundred and forty-first execution since capital punishment resumed in 1976.

I have no idea what the man did, Mrs. Bemis remarked, but I'm glad he wasn't paroled. He got just what he deserved.

Another one in North Carolina. Gas chamber. Cyanide. Fellow dressed in diapers and socks. Socks? Damned if I understand the socks. Sounds like a fraternity initiation. Face covered by leather mask. Screams continued five minutes.

I don't believe that, Mrs. Bemis said. The man does not feel a thing. After one breath he simply goes to sleep.

Supreme Court earlier rejected argument that gas chamber is cruel and unusual. Harry Blackmun dissented.

Both men should have received lethal injections, Mrs. Bemis said. Lethal injections are painless and merciful.

Mr. Bemis silently turned a page.

Capital punishment was a deterrent. Common sense proved this beyond a doubt and there was no reason the sentence should not be carried out at once. Why did murderers have a right to appeal? A person convicted of a terrible crime had absolutely no rights. Sooner or later there would be more justices like Blackmun. Then, of course, one vicious criminal after another would be pardoned or paroled in order to attack somebody else.

Proctor, she said, what do you suppose will become of the middle class?

Ah, Marguerite, he said, that's a provocative question.

Do you know the answer?

Mr. Bemis reached for his drink. No, he said. No, I don't.

You are so blasé. You can be utterly maddening.

Mr. Bemis swirled the ice in his glass.

Proctor, she continued in a firm voice, the time has come for us to sell our stocks. Every single one.

Mr. Bemis was astonished. What? Why? For God's sake, Marguerite, are you losing your mind?

I think we would be safer owning gold.

If the market crashes it'll recover.

But I just don't know what might happen. I dreamt of General Suddarth.

Ah, said Mr. Bemis. And how is the old boy?

You think I'm overwrought. You think there must be something the matter with me. Do you find nothing wrong with gangs of hoodlums roaming the streets and pornographic films and drive-by shootings and child molesters and drugs and soaring taxes and a President whose personal life is a national disgrace? Do you think I am hysterical?

Not in the least, Mr. Bemis said. We're going to hell in a handbasket. As he said this he glanced across his spectacles and felt surprised because the face of the woman he had known intimately for so many years conveyed something unexpected. It seemed to him that he was looking at a confused, terrified child. The dangers of the world—dangers both real and imaginary—had overwhelmed her. She had withdrawn. In the wrinkled face of this woman with whom he had lived for such a long time were the eyes of a child wakened by a threatening sound in the night. He felt touched and dismayed by her anxiety.

Mrs. Bemis covered her face with both hands. I'm so upset, she whispered through her fingers. I'm afraid to have lunch on the Plaza.

Yes, well, he said uneasily.

I want Hopscotch.

What? he asked. You want what?

NOAH'S ARK

I N THE BOOK of Genesis it was written that a man ought not to be alone—he should have a helpmeet. Tessie often thought about this while vacuuming the carpet or washing dishes and the idea troubled her. She tried to imagine what it would be like to marry one of the boys she had known while growing up on the farm. Some had been nice enough, yet they always pressed her to go for a walk with nobody else around; they wanted to kiss her on the mouth and fondle her body, which would be indecent. So she had been polite to them when they invited her to dance or go to the movies, and once in a while she had permitted her hand to be held, but nothing more, because according to First Corinthians it was not good for a man to touch a woman. And she recalled the passage from Deuteronomy that said that when a man has taken a wife, if she finds no favor in his eyes then he can write a bill of divorcement and send her out of the house. This was painful to think about. However, since she had moved to the city and gone to work for Dr. and Mrs. Stocking it seemed to her that she had been excused from marriage. Surely the Lord understood what was in her heart and would not be angry if she went through life alone. Still, this meant that some young man would have no helpmeet. The whole thing was a puzzle. She wondered if the Lord might be watching with a displeased expression.

Whenever Tessie thought about Dr. Stocking she wagged her head. Dr. Stocking was a skinny little psychiatrist with a shrill voice and the face of a chipmunk. In the hall closet he kept a gorilla costume and every so often he would put on this costume and take a walk around the block, which set the neighborhood dogs to barking.

Mrs. Stocking was just as peculiar. She taught Religious Studies at the college but she paid no heed to the Holy Bible, nor did she go to church. Usually she sat on the porch smoking French cigarettes and reading. Books—some written in foreign languages—were scattered upstairs and downstairs, all over the house. Tessie was annoyed by this because books ought to be arranged neatly on shelves, but Mrs. Stocking had told her to let them alone.

Days never seemed long enough. If it wasn't Tweetwee the canary needing attention, or the guppies' aquarium, or Scraps the fox terrier who needed a bath, there was the laundry, or shirts to be ironed, or the grocery list, or a delivery boy ringing the bell, or the gas meter reader, or the postman with a package. Then, likely as not, Gigi would arrive in a terrible rush, even though she didn't have much to do. If she wasn't begging money from her parents she wanted something tucked away in the attic or the basement—phonograph records, clothes, pictures from her school days. A sweet child and playful as a kitten, Tessie said to herself, but she married so young. Well, who am I to judge?

Now and then as she went about her chores Tessie would pause in the breakfast room where half a dozen colored glass bottles decorated the windowsill. There she would stand admiring the colors and chatting with Tweetwee, who sang to the sunshine from his green wire cage or fluffed his feathers or crept from side to side on his wooden perch and cocked his head with such impudence that she could not help laughing.

Oh, goodness! What a naughty fellow! Dirtying your paper! Don't you know I got more than enough to do without changing your paper again? Such a rascal! You want more seeds? I expect you do. If it ain't one thing, it's another. Mrs. Stocking will be after me for not finishing the carpet and what am I supposed to tell her? Answer me that, will you? And what about the guppies? The poor little things take sick if I don't look out for them. That moss just keeps growing. Now what are you up to? First you hop off your perch and then you hop right back up on it. Goodness, you are a trial! And where is that Mr. Scraps? Chasing all over the neighborhood, I imagine, barking at delivery boys and getting his feet muddy. I declare he is the feistiest dog a person ever saw. Now I've got to get on with my work. I ain't dusted upstairs and then it'll be time to fix lunch.

In the evening after she had cleared the dinner table and washed and dried the dishes and put them away, Tessie climbed the dark narrow staircase to her room in the attic. There she turned on the electric fan or the heater, according to the season, pulled off her shoes, and settled in the rocking chair beside her bed. From here she could look at the trees in the backyard through a little round window resembling the porthole of an ocean liner. Sometimes she gazed at television or listened to gospel programs on the radio before going to sleep.

Every Sunday night she listened to Reverend H. L. Hunnicutt whose program emanated from Chattanooga, and one night Reverend Hunnicutt spoke on the Book of Revelation. Tessie listened drowsily to his powerful voice while rocking in her chair. Gog and Magog were at this moment preparing to wage battle against the kingdom of the Lord. Led by Satan, loosed out his prison after one thousand years, these enemies of God whose number was as the sand of the sea were girding their loins for combat. And was not the dreadful hour imminent? Was it not fast approaching? O yea! Was not Heaven itself alight with shooting stars? Were not the silhouettes of four horsemen visible at dawn? Had not the very moon suffered eclipse? Were there not devastating floods? Volcanic eruptions? Hurricanes? Tidal waves? O yea! O yea! cried Reverend Hunnicutt. And the sea shall give up the dead that were in it. And death and Hell shall deliver up the dead that were in them. And on that fateful day shall every man be judged according to his works.

Monday morning while doing the breakfast dishes Tessie thought about what Reverend Hunnicutt had said. Later as she was dusting furniture she thought about it again. And just before noon while she stood at the kitchen sink peeling apples she looked out the window and saw Mrs. Stocking in the garden with a trowel and shears and the sprinkling can. Tessie frowned because Mrs. Stocking wore dirty old slacks, one of her husband's cast-off shirts, and a ragged straw hat.

Far be it from me, said Tessie. After drying her hands she straightened her apron, walked out the back door and marched across the lawn to ask if Mrs. Stocking knew when Gog and Magog would threaten the world.

You appear disturbed, Mrs. Stocking said. Or could it be my imagination? Is something wrong?

There shall be earthquakes in diverse places and famines and troubles, Tessie replied in a stubborn voice. Heaven and earth shall pass away, but the word of the Lord shall not pass away.

Mrs. Stocking was on her knees beside the rose trellis. She took a deep breath and said: Oh, dear.

The number of God's enemies is as the sand of the sea.

Mrs. Stocking smiled politely. Yes, I'm sure that must be so. Tessie, what would you think of a hearing aid? Dr. Stocking and I have discussed the matter and both of us believe it might help. Naturally we would take care of the bill.

After a few moments Tessie returned to the house. In the kitchen she picked up an apple and the paring knife but discovered that she could not see very well because her eyes had filled with tears. She put the apple and knife on the drainboard, climbed to the attic, and sat in her rocking chair. Through the round window she could look down on Mrs. Stocking trimming the rosebush.

Wasn't no cause, she whispered. She sniffled and blew her nose. Then she began to sob because Mrs. Stocking had been rude.

Underneath the bed was an old suitcase that served as home for packets of Christmas cards and letters from long ago neatly tied with colored ribbons, a leatherette album containing snapshots of the farm, a plaster bluebird she had won by tossing rings at the county fair, a baby's shoe coated with bronze, a tiny pair of mittens, the eighth-grade report card when she got a B for spelling, and her mother's cameo brooch. There, too, slumped cheerfully in the suitcase—his brown button eyes shining with mischief—was a rag doll named Sailor Boy. His puffy hands were soiled and his cloth face was stained because she had so often held hands with him and had kissed him goodnight so many times. Here and there Sailor Boy had split at the seams, but she had sewn him together again.

With the doll clasped to her breast she rocked gently beside the bed while talking about the end of the world. What do you think, little fellow? How much longer you expect we might be around? Lord alone knows. We just best hope. Well, now, if you ain't a rascal—sailing everyplace under the sun! A person couldn't never guess what you been up to. You been good? And don't you fib! Them as speaks the truth got nothing to fear. Only sinners stand to be punished.

Then she remembered what Mrs. Stocking had said. Wasn't no cause to talk like that, she told the doll.

Gigi arrived one afternoon while she was making fudge cake.

Fudge cake! Gigi cried, and tap-danced across the floor. Is Mother home?

This is Wednesday, said Tessie. What's wrong with your mind?

Right! She teaches until three. I always forget. Gigi stooped to pet Scraps, who dozed beneath the kitchen table with his muzzle on his paws and his ears twitching.

That dog, Tessie said. He all but took a bite out of the postman yesterday morning. He does and his name won't be Mr. Scraps no more, it'll be mud, let me tell you. I give him a bath not three days ago but would you just look. Goodness, what a trial.

Gigi laughed. When I was here last week I saw you talking to Raymond. Why don't you go out with him?

Raymond?

Sure. You might have a jazzy time. After that, who knows? Maybe a passionate flaming insane romance.

Oh, my! Tessie said and tried to keep from smiling.

Don't you think about getting married?

Can't say as I do.

Weren't you ever in love?

Years back, said Tessie. There was a fellow named Sylvester Voss. But he drank. Then he'd chase around half the county shouting and breaking things. Scared the life out of folks. I wouldn't choose to marry that sort of fellow.

But you must get lonely. I mean, night after night.

I'm fine, Tessie said while peering into the oven. Just fine, thank you.

That's weird. When I was a kid you used to tell me how much you wanted children.

That's so. There was a time.

Gigi grew thoughtful. You must have wanted to smack my bottom more than once. I always asked for something different. If Mother and Dad were going to have pancakes for breakfast I'd ask for a waffle just to be different.

Children love to fuss, Tessie said. You had your share of tantrums.

You know what used to make me feel sad? We'd be eating dinner together at the table and you'd be in the kitchen all by yourself. I used to leave the table and come out here to talk to you. Mother didn't like it.

I recall.

I was afraid you felt neglected. It didn't seem fair.

Now Gigi, don't you make me cry.

I wanted to invite you to sit at the table with us, but I couldn't.

Now stop, Tessie said. You run along.

I thought you were really special. You never criticized me or tried to improve me the way Mother did. Her big mission in life was to make me perfect. What a laugh!

She wanted to bring you up right. You ought to be grateful she cared.

Gigi made a face. Teaching meant more to her than I did. She was always reading and taking notes. She never had time for me.

What's got into you? Tessie asked.

That's how I felt, Gigi said. I can't help it. You were the one who taught me how to sew and bake. All those girl things I learned from you. I remember watching you fix those goodies at Thanksgiving and Christmas. I used to watch you basting the turkey and wondered if I'd ever learn how to cook. And once when I got sick you held me on your lap and told me stories about what it was like on the farm when you were a kid my age. Mother just put her hand on my forehead to see if I had a temperature and then went back to her desk.

Now you know she loves you more than anything in the world.

Sure, I know it, Gigi said. Once for my birthday you made a red flannel nightgown with angels on the collar. I was thrilled.

You looked cute as a bug.

And one morning you invited me up to your room and told me to guess what was in the tree, so I looked out the window and I could see right into the robin's nest. There were those little pale blue eggs. They were simply darling. Do you remember?

I do. You wasn't but maybe nine.

I was eight. I'll never forget. And Saturday nights we'd watch the Lawrence Welk show. Wow, did you have a crush on him!

Goodness, Tessie said. Why bring that up?

One time I asked if you'd marry Lawrence Welk and you clapped your hands and said, "The minute he asks!"

That's so, I did. He had a real nice smile.

Listen, Gigi said after tasting the fudge cake, why don't you give Raymond the eye? He'd invite you out.

You scamp! I couldn't never do a thing like that. I wouldn't know how.

Get Myra to show you.

Myra?

I've seen how she ogles the delivery boys and telephone linemen and Jehovah's Witnesses and anything else in pants, especially when the Fitzgeralds aren't home. She's a hot number.

Shame on you, Tessie said. Shame on you for such talk.

But what Gigi had said was true. Myra did flirt. And this was strange because Myra had a mustache like a twelve-year-old boy and her left arm was two or three inches shorter than her right arm. Well, Tessie thought, the Lord does move in mysterious ways.

Now you best run along about your business, she said. I've got more than enough to do.

Gigi laughed and hugged her. You're so shy! Get Myra to fix you up on a double date. You spend all day doing housework and then hibernate in the attic like a nun. You don't ever go out.

I'm not missing a thing, Tessie said. In case you forget, young lady, I attend Bible class twice a month.

Bible class, said Gigi. Bible class. Okay, it's your life.

Gigi was right, Tessie thought. Still, there was no sense going out just to be going out. And there was no reason to make eyes at Raymond or any other man. It would seem forward. Raymond was decent enough. When he came around to do yard work he was always polite, but spending the evening with him would be different. He might get ideas.

A few days later Tessie was in the dining room polishing silver when Mrs. Stocking returned from the college with a satchel full of books.

Oh, good for you! she exclaimed. Silver does tarnish, doesn't it?

Tessie nodded.

A while ago, Mrs. Stocking went on in a careful voice, I sensed that something important was on your mind. I felt that perhaps you wanted to have a talk. I could have been mistaken, but are you in difficulty?

I hear fine, Tessie said.

Of course you do, Mrs. Stocking went on in the same voice and placed her satchel on a chair. I've simply been wondering if—well, you've mentioned that you contribute to a radio ministry.

Reverend Hunnicutt, Tessie said and began to polish the soup tureen.

What you do with your money is your own affair, but Dr. Stocking and I have discussed this. Frankly, we're concerned. We haven't the slightest idea how much you contribute, or how often. Your donations may be appropriate. Nevertheless, some of these radio evangelists can be remarkably persuasive.

The kingdom of God is nigh, Tessie said and continued polishing.

After a few moments Mrs. Stocking said, Well, I've no wish to intrude. She glanced at her wristwatch. We're going to a cocktail party at the Woodruffs and I should get ready. My hair is a fright. If there's anything you wish to discuss, please don't hesitate. You know you're almost a member of the family.

Tessie decided to ask about Gog and Magog, but when she looked up Mrs. Stocking had disappeared.

Sunday night after clearing the table and washing the dishes she climbed to the attic, shut the door, and arranged herself comfortably in the rocking chair to wait for Reverend Hunnicutt's broadcast. On the dresser between a tinted photograph of her parents and a pink glass angel with lace wings stood a little globe filled with water. Inside the globe was a miniature Swiss chalet surrounded by tiny evergreens.

Hearing aid, Tessie said with contempt. She picked up the globe and gave it a fierce shake. The evergreens and the chalet vanished in a blizzard.

After the opening hymn of his broadcast Reverend Hunnicutt pointed out that the cost of keeping his ministry on the air had been rising steadily and he urged those who believed in Jesus to express their love. This meant a pledge. He described those listeners who were contributing ten percent of their income as soldiers in a growing army of the Lord that daily girded itself to battle Satan. Beyond doubt Jesus heard the prayers of these generous listeners. But would not the Lord listen yet more closely to those who found in their hearts the charity and wisdom and love to contribute twenty percent? For what is charity? Reverend Hunnicutt inquired. What is charity if not the Holy Spirit?

Twenty percent, Tessie murmured. Gracious, wouldn't that be a sum?

Yea! O yea! sang Reverend Hunnicutt. Blessed are the charitable! Blessed are the generous!

Whenever Tessie mailed an offering, no matter how small, she received a gilt-edge postcard assuring her that the Lord would not forget. Twice she had enclosed a note asking when to expect the Second Coming, but Reverend Hunnicutt had not answered. She reminded herself that he must get thousands of letters.

Now, as she listened, she felt that he had mysteriously entered the room and was stroking her hand, comforting her. With Sailor Boy on her lap she rocked dreamily and whispered to the doll: Where are you sailing, precious thing? Where will you sail this evening, precious child?

Dear friends in radioland, Reverend Hunnicutt continued, do you know the story of Noah's Ark? Of course you do. You have heard it told and retold. But let us take a moment to reflect upon the significance of this instructive story. Ask yourselves, each and every one of you, what it means. What does it mean? Dear friends, the meaning is clear. Almighty God saw that this earth was corrupt and filled with violence and therefore He vowed to destroy everything that He had created, both man and beast, yea, and the creeping things and the fowl of the air. God saith I will bring a flood of waters upon the earth to destroy all flesh, and everything that is in the earth shall die. But with thee will I establish my covenant, and thy wife, and thy sons and thy sons' wives. So saith the Lord God. And the Lord commanded of Noah to make an Ark of gopherwood to the length of three hundred cubits, of breadth fifty cubits, of height thirty cubits. And when Noah was six hundred years old this flood lay upon the earth, but the Ark was lifted above the earth—it went upon the face of the waters. And the waters prevailed. The waters prevailed, dear friends, for one hundred and fifty days. And when the windows of Heaven were stopped and the waters assuaged, the Ark came to rest upon the mountain that is called Ararat. Yea! It came to rest.

Reverend Hunnicutt paused. Whenever he did this Tessie felt

surprised and thrilled; her eyes widened with pleasure. She felt that she had known him all her life and it seemed that he was speaking to her alone. His reassuring voice was that of someone who kissed her forehead while she was falling asleep many years ago. Her eyes closed. Precious, she sighed, dear child. Drowsily she waited for him to continue.

Praise the Lord, he said. Dear friends, all of you in radioland, how I wish we might clasp hands on this glorious occasion because there is good news tonight. O yea, let us praise the Lord because the news is great. Alleluia! The Ark of Noah unseen by any mortal eye since God threw open the windows of Heaven—that Ark which came to rest upon the mountain of Ararat when the waters were assuaged—the Ark of Noah has been found! Alleluia! Praise the Lord!

Next morning after breakfast Tessie stayed in the kitchen until Dr. Stocking left for the office. Then she returned to the breakfast room with a dish towel in her hands and told Mrs. Stocking what Reverend Hunnicutt had said.

At first Mrs. Stocking did not answer. She was working a crossword puzzle in the newspaper. After a while she took off her reading glasses and looked at Tweetwee, who chirped merrily in his cage.

Not again, she said.

The Ark lies buried deep in snow high upon the slopes of Mount Ararat, Tessie said.

Mrs. Stocking took a sip of coffee and gestured at a chair. Do sit down. Is this what you've been wanting to discuss?

Tessie obeyed reluctantly because it did not seem proper. She spread the dish towel across her knees and waited.

I hardly know how to approach this, Mrs. Stocking said almost to herself. Tessie, dear, we don't take the Bible literally. For instance, the wife of Lot didn't turn into a pillar of salt—not really. Nor did the Pharisees actually swallow camels. You understand the impossibility of such a thing. Nor did the Red Sea roll apart for the Israelites. As a matter of fact, we believe this passage might refer to the Gulf of Suez rather than to the Red Sea. Be that as it may, no power on earth can negate the laws of physics. In other words, Biblical anecdotes should be regarded as a source of profound philosophy and quite marvelous poetry.

The Lord rained fire and brimstone upon Sodom and Gomorrah,

Tessie said. He overthrew them cities in which Lot dwelt. His wife become a pillar of salt. Genesis nineteen.

Mrs. Stocking tapped her pencil on the newspaper. Finally she said, Both of us—and Gigi, of course—all of us are so fond of you. And we do respect your faith. However—oh, really, I find this quite distressing.

The waters prevailed one hundred fifty days.

You can be so obstinate, Mrs. Stocking said. You are positively medieval. I'm sorry. Please excuse me. Mount Ararat rises seventeen thousand feet above sea level. Seventeen thousand feet! Oh, never mind.

They seen the Ark, Tessie said.

Who has seen the Ark?

This man from Dothan, Alabama. Reverend Hunnicutt he read a letter this man wrote over the radio. It was during the war. He was in the Army over there someplace and he made friends of this family and one day they took him up the mountain to show him where it was at. He seen it. He seen pictures about the Flood in this cave they went into high upon the slopes of Mount Ararat.

Pictures, you say. Murals?

I beg pardon?

Tell me about these pictures. Who painted them?

Tessie considered. I expect it was likely Noah or the sons of Noah. His sons was Shem, Ham, and Japheth.

Yes, Mrs. Stocking said. Can you describe the Ark?

It was of a piece until the beginning of the war, according to this man from Dothan. There was these cages inside. He seen little cages for the birds and big cages for lions and tigers and elephants. Also, there was a good many hammers and ancient tools from the days of Noah. No mortal eye has beheld them tools since the days of Noah. Also, there was ice because it was high up on the mountain. And there was pitch. He seen all this pitch.

The seams had been caulked?

I didn't catch what you said.

The cracks between the boards were filled with pitch?

Tessie nodded. Rooms shalt thou make in the Ark, and shalt pitch it within and without with pitch. I expect it's up there. This man from Dothan he seen it.

I do not question the man's sincerity, Mrs. Stocking said. Now, has

Reverend Hunnicutt suggested that in exchange for—oh, the entire business is utterly exasperating! I hesitate to ask, but is this evangelist selling splinters from the Ark?

Tessie's mouth tightened.

Mrs. Stocking twirled the pencil between her fingers. Tessie, are you familiar with St. Bernard of Clairvaux? I assume you are not. St. Bernard informs us that no creature can be intelligent save by the aid of reason. In other words, it is prudent to reflect critically—I might even say skeptically—upon what we are told.

Tessie considered the dish towel on her knees and discovered a loose thread. She snatched it out.

For example, Tessie, are we not informed that Noah took into the Ark clean beasts by sevens? Yet we have been told also how they entered two by two. Perhaps a firm editorial hand was needed while the Bible was being assembled! Mrs. Stocking laughed crisply. Or take Jesus—was he crucified at the third hour, as related by Mark? Or about the sixth hour, as related by John? And what about Saul's daughter Michal, who had no child until the day of her death, according to Samuel. Yet she bore five sons, this also according to Samuel. And we have been assured in Paul's first epistle to the Corinthians that when the trumpet sounds the dead shall be raised incorruptible. Yet we read in Isaiah how the dead shall not live when they are deceased—they shall not rise. Well, then? Which are we to believe?

Three times six is the sign of the Beast.

Mrs. Stocking pretended not to hear. What about the Deluge? Similar legends abound in the folklore of such diverse people as American Indians, Fiji Islanders, and Australian aborigines. Or, should you choose, ignore this diffusion but reflect on the chronology. The tradition of a catastrophic flood antedates Christianity by quite a while. In 1872 the British philologist George Smith deciphered the inscription on some baked clay tablets from the ruins of Nineveh. These tablets relate the adventures of a hero named Gilgamesh who, seeking eternal life, spoke to one of his ancestors, Utnapishtim—the only survivor of a gigantic flood. The tablets tell us that a ship at last came to rest on the mountains of Nizir. And what do you suppose happened next? A dove was sent forth, but could find no resting place, so it returned. Then a swallow was sent forth, but it too returned. Then a crow was released and did not return. In other words, despite variations in detail, what we have is a version of the Deluge from the library of King Assurbanipal who reigned seven centuries before Christ. What do you make of that?

It wasn't no crow, Tessie said. It was a dove. Noah sent forth a dove. And the dove came in to him in the evening; and, lo, in her mouth was an olive leaf pluckt off: so Noah knew that the waters were abated from off the earth.

You have a remarkable memory, Mrs. Stocking said.

I can recite the presidents of the United States, said Tessie.

All of them?

Every single one, Tessie said. And she began, but Mrs. Stocking interrupted.

All right, all right. I believe you. Now where were we? Let me think. What I was attempting to point out is the antiquity of the flood legend. It is much older than the Assyrian tablets. Scholars have traced the Gilgamesh epic back five thousand years. So what does this mean? Quite possibly the persistence of such a tale expresses our search for understanding in the face of catastrophic disasters.

It wasn't no crow, Tessie repeated. It was a dove. Genesis eight.

Mrs. Stocking gazed at the crossword puzzle. Then she picked up the newspaper, but immediately put it down with a look of annoyance. Let's start over, she said. The Bible tells us the water was fifteen cubits deep, which is about twenty-six feet. Now, Tessie, in 1929 the famous archaeologist Sir Leonard Woolley probed a layer of silt in Mesopotamia that had been carried down from the upper Euphrates galley and beneath this residue he found traces of reed huts dating from the Erech dynasty. According to Woolley's calculations, this flood must have been at least twenty-five feet deep. The implication is unmistakable. Our famous Christian legend originated in a prehistoric Mesopotamian flood. Wouldn't you agree?

The time draweth nigh, Tessie said. The beast come up out of the sea having seven heads and ten horns and upon his horns ten crowns and upon his heads the name of blasphemy.

Revelation? Mrs. Stocking asked.

Thirteen, said Tessie.

I don't doubt you for an instant. Be that as it may, the legend occurs also in Greek mythology. Deucalion, the son of Prometheus and Clymene, ruled over a kingdom in Thessaly and when Zeus resolved to inundate the earth Deucalion constructed a ship for himself and his wife Pyrrha. Now, when the vessel came to rest on Mt. Parnassus, Deucalion was instructed by the oracle at Themis to cast the bones of his mother behind him. But how should this be interpreted? Deucalion concluded that his mother was the earth. Therefore he and his wife cast stones behind them. The stones hurled by Deucalion became men, while those cast by Pyrrha became women. I think that's an exquisite parable. Don't you?

Tessie winked at Tweetwee, who cleaned his feathers and trilled happily in the warm sunshine.

Mrs. Stocking spoke rather sharply. According to the Koran, the wife of Noah is Waila. This woman attempted to convince people that her husband was out of his mind. Do you find this amusing?

Tessie gazed at her like a tombstone.

After a long silence Mrs. Stocking said: Dr. and Mrs. Joggerst will be here for supper next Friday.

Dr. and Mrs. Joggerst?

Dr. and Mrs. Joggerst. Surely you remember them? They raved about your coconut meringue pie. Do you suppose you could make coconut meringue pie for us next Friday?

Coconut meringue?

Coconut meringue. They'd be delighted. I—it's simply that—oh, I've got to run, she continued after a glance at her watch. I've a class at ten.

After Mrs. Stocking drove off to the college Tweetwee cocked his head in such a funny way that Tessie could not help laughing. She wagged a finger at him. What are you up to, you rambunctious thing? Two of your ancestors was in the Ark, did you know that? Yes, sir! In the seventh month on the seventeenth day the Ark come to rest upon the mountain of Ararat. My goodness, how you scatter them seeds! You are a caution! Well, I can't waste half the day chattering with you. But Mrs. Stocking she don't have no right to poke fun.

That afternoon Myra whistled, which meant the Fitzgeralds were not home. Tessie was at the sink washing lettuce. She dried her hands and went out the back door so they could talk across the hedge. And no sooner did she begin telling Myra what Mrs. Stocking had said than she started to cry.

Myra frowned. Lordy Lordy, you do gush worse than my grandma. What was it she called you?

Medieval. She got no cause to say such a thing.

Medieval. Why, that's a compliment, Myra said while tapping ashes from her cigarette. Medieval means you can work miracles.

I don't care, Tessie said. It ain't nice.

Stop blubbering, Myra said. Holy Maloney!

Well, it ain't, Tessie said, and pulled a handkerchief from the pocket of her uniform and wiped her nose. What kind of miracles?

Why ask me? Myra said. I don't know. Probably any kind.

To work miracles a body needs faith.

That's true, Myra said. But you got faith enough for ten ordinary people.

I believe in the Lord.

I do, too, Myra said. Only not as much as you. I never saw anybody with more faith. I expect you could work a miracle.

That would be a calling, Tessie said.

Myra released a perfect smoke ring. Likely if you set your mind to the matter you could do it. I expect if you prayed hard enough you could be touched with the power. I wouldn't be surprised but what the Lord might bless you.

Tessie caught her lip in embarrassment and looked away.

Well, I don't see why not. Give it some thought. Only for Pete's sake stop blubbering. Seems like somebody always hurts your feelings. You do beat all. You want some gum?

Gum? No, thank you.

I believe I will, Myra said, if you don't mind. She stripped the paper from a stick, bent it double, and began chewing. Guess what! I got a chain letter.

You got what?

Chain letter. Now if you ain't the limit! Everybody knows what a chain letter is. It's where somebody sends you a letter with the names of these five other members included. So you send this first member a dollar and pretty soon other people they send you a dollar. Then after a while this list gets around all over the country—maybe all over the world—and all these members they send you a dollar. That's how it works. You get millions of dollars. Of course some people they break the chain so you don't normally receive that much.

Millions of dollars?

So they say. Emmaline who works for the Knapps in that white brick house with the Airedale—I helped out there at a party and she told me her aunt got twenty-six dollars in three weeks!

Twenty-six dollars?

Yeah, Myra said. I'd buy me a new pair of shoes. These is killing my bunions. Anyhow, what was we talking about?

Chain letters.

Myra chewed thoughtfully. No, before that. Oh! It was miracles. Well, a month or so back you was telling me you seen devils fly out of people's mouths. Now is that a fact?

People use bad words, devils fly right out.

Real ones? Horns and wings and a tail and so on?

Real as can be.

Now that's amazing, Myra said. That truly is amazing. I never could figure out what devils looked like except them pictures you see. Bats. That'd be my guess. You ought to squash a couple. That'd show you got the power. If you could do that you could work miracles all right.

It's something to think about, Tessie said.

Myra coughed and began to adjust the straps of her brassiere. Now would you just look at them pretty white clouds! Couldn't hardly be a nicer afternoon. What you got in mind for vacation?

Vacation? I hadn't give it much thought. Vacation don't come round till next summer.

I'm going to Colorado Springs, Myra said. I'm going up Pike's Peak. I always did want to go up Pike's Peak.

Colorado Springs. That must be a distance.

Colorado Springs here I come! Myra said. You never know, I could meet somebody on top of Pike's Peak.

You just might find yourself in a nasty fix.

I sure hope so, Myra said. I'm rusting away like some old tin can. Hey, let's us go to Danceland.

Danceland?

Saturday a week ago I was there and met this fellow Purvis. We did some stuff, if you know what I mean, but I didn't appreciate his attitude. He kept grabbing things and telling me let's get married and how much he loves me, but I heard that before.

You best watch out.

I don't get buffaloed, Myra said. I look out for number one. Hey, let's you and me go. I love to dance. I just hope that Purvis don't show up.

Oh, Tessie said, them fancy twirls and steps these days, I wouldn't scarcely know which way to turn.

I could teach you. Nothing to it. Also, it helps to lose a few pounds of flesh. I notice you have a tendency to put on weight. Besides, I'm dying to try out this new mascara I got called Queen of Sheba.

A place such as that don't sound decent.

You're so proper! You and Mrs. Fitzgerald. Hey, we could go bowling. Bowling alleys is full of men.

Tessie glanced at Myra's shriveled arm.

Foo! said Myra. That don't stop me. You don't need but one. Let's us go some night.

Most likely it would cost a peck.

Myra rolled her eyes. I declare I never did see the equal. One extra penny in your purse and you send it to that preacher.

Reverend Hunnicutt he serves the Lord.

Excuse me if I step on a few toes, only it wouldn't surprise me none if he lives in some big marble mansion and rides around in the back of a limousine with a chauffeur. They do, some of them. I'm not saying he's like that, if you follow me. Only some of them, they do.

Reverend Hunnicutt he spreads the Word.

Now that's a good cause, Myra said, except you don't spend nothing on yourself.

Oh, well, Tessie said. Ain't much I need.

Myra aimed a plume of smoke at a butterfly. Seems to me you'd ought to do more for number one.

Judgment is nigh. The armies of the devil is assembling this very minute at a place they call in the Hebrew language Armageddon.

Now how do you know? I believe as much as the next person, but there's stuff nobody can't be sure about such as Adam and Eve, and that's a fact. I mean, just taking the first example that come to mind, how do you know what he looks like?

Does who look like?

Myra coughed and pointed upward. What color of beard has he got? Likely gray or white, at least that's my opinion.

This annoyed Tessie. God had a beard, but talking about it did not seem right. She frowned and replied in a determined voice: His only begotten son come down to earth on our account.

I ain't about to deny that, Myra said.

The Lord is our savior even unto the end of the world.

Suppose he's watching us this very minute, how does he know what's going on over there in China? Or what them Eskimos is up to? Myra was triumphant.

That ain't none of our business. You got no cause to ask.

It don't hurt to wonder, Myra said. That's my opinion. Anyway I sure hope he's merciful because there's things I ain't too proud of. A while back there was this fellow Stanley. Him and me got acquainted at the Silver Saddle and he had this tie clip like a horse head and this diamond in one ear. I didn't treat him too nice, if you know what I mean. He was a Polack and religious as all holy Maloney—talking to God whenever he run into trouble. Anyhow that's what he told me and I felt like asking what language was it. I mean, how is God going to talk Polack?

That is just plain blasphemy, Tessie said with a severe expression.

Well, a party does wonder, Myra said. I expect I shouldn't ought to mention this, but has he got that thing? You know, the Bible says how men was made in his image, and men they got that thing. What do you figure he does with that thing all by hisself?

Shame! Tessie cried. Watch your tongue, Myra! The trumpet is fixing to sound.

Myra wagged her head. Well, if you ain't the voice of doom, I swear! You and Mr. Fitzgerald. Listening to you a person would think if it ain't Judgment Day or Satan's army it's earthquakes or floods about to drown us in our tracks or the sky falling down like some old circus tent or killer bees flying up from South America to sting us all to death or whirlwinds or I don't know what. I never in my life met anybody so full of doom as you—except Mr. Fitzgerald. With him it's the Democrats. He got more money than you could poke a stick at, only he turns red as a beet and yells how the Democrats is trying to put him in the poorhouse. He all but has hisself a stroke at the word.

He's Republican, ain't he?

I hope to tell you that man is Republican. He got so many guns in the game room I'm scared to go near. Nothing he cares more about than shooting—aiming them guns every which way. He's still mad about that Vietnam War, you know, how some of the boys run off to Canada. He says they'd ought to be shot because they was traitors to America. He's fixing to set up a flagpole over there by the barbecue pit.

Dr. Stocking, he says Mr. Fitzgerald ought to be put away.

Is that how psychiatrists talk?

I heard him. Clear as a bell.

I'm surprised, Myra said. I truly am surprised. You just never know.

The way he goes on about Republicans, if he was my little boy I'd clean his mouth with soap.

The two of them don't hardly speak, I notice. What kind of car is that he drives?

Now it ain't Buick, Tessie said. I believe it come from Italy.

Myra nodded. I supposed as much. I said to myself the minute I saw that automobile there's a Democrat. I bet him and Mrs. Stocking don't even watch television. Mr. Fitzgerald swears the both of them is Communists.

Communists, Tessie said. That would be a thought.

I never did see one—not to my knowledge. Anyhow, Dr. Stocking best take care when he dresses hisself in that gorilla suit or Mr. Fitzgerald will shoot him. I like to suffered a heart attack first time I seen it. Maybe he's the one ought to be locked up. What kind of normal person puts on a gorilla suit? Answer me that! Myra tapped the ash from her cigarette. I wouldn't mind borrowing it, though. I sure could scare the lights out of that Purvis. Hey, you want to see the moose Mr. Fitzgerald shot? Ugliest thing that ever was. He got the head stuffed or whatever they do and stuck up over the fireplace.

I don't care for such things, Tessie said. Thank you anyway. My little brother Gaius, he was a hunter, always bringing home squirrel and rabbit.

I never did taste squirrel. Rabbit braised in wine is real tasty, though. Gaius, there's a nice name.

He's a sailor.

So you told me. You told me one day he packed up and left the farm without hardly a word. Is that right?

Good-bye and off he went. Gaius, he was the quiet one.

A sailor. Fancy that.

He's been just about everyplace on earth, I expect. China and I don't know where all. He sent me this picture postcard of some heathen temple. Did I show you?

Twice, Myra said impatiently. I wished I had a brother, but there wasn't nobody in the family except me. Sailing around, that's what I'd do if I was a man. I wouldn't stop for nothing. Anyhow, I ain't, so that's that.

The Lord knows best.

I suppose, Myra said with a gloomy expression, but it don't seem right men get all the fun. I bet anything Dr. Stocking can go a hundred miles an hour at least in that automobile. Boomer, sometimes he lets me drive his Ford pickup.

Who's Boomer?

I guess you never met. I'll introduce you when we get better acquainted. Myra stopped chewing and stood on one foot. I might slip off these shoes if you don't mind. Them bunions is murder.

Feel free, said Tessie. I do the same.

Thank you, Myra said, and stepped out of her shoes. Excuse me for getting personal, but is Tessie your real name? I was always afraid to ask because it ain't none of my business, only now seemed a good time. I don't mean to pry.

It's Therese.

Therese. That's real pretty. I wish I had a pretty name.

Myra's pretty.

It's common—like I wasn't nothing.

Well, you're not common. You're very special. I think you're a very special person.

Thank you. I could call you Therese.

Oh, now, Tessie said, that ain't necessary.

I don't feel like my name ought to be what it is. I do feel special, though. Thank you. Nobody before ever told me I was.

What do you feel your name ought to be?

Jacqueline.

That's pretty, too.

I ought to of been named Jacqueline. I can see pulling up to Dance-land in one of them automobiles with a convertible roof and the men, they'd be crawling over theirselves like I was the queen bee. Myra shuddered. "Oh! Oh!" they'd say. "Here comes Jacqueline!" You know what I'd do? I'd honk the horn and drive off. Leave them standing there bug-eyed, every last one. That's what I'd do.

Tessie thought about this with her lips pursed.

Hey, how much you suppose that automobile cost?

That automobile? I don't have no idea, Tessie said. Quite a sum, though.

I expect, Myra said while smoothing her eyebrows. Dr. Stocking, he must do right well listening to all them lunatics.

Tessie frowned. The Lord Jesus can heal. Folks as bring their troubles to the Lord got no cause to spend a dime.

I sure wish the Lord would fix this arm, Myra said. I used to pray when I was little, asking Jesus to make me like everybody else, only nothing happened so I quit. I mean, there's got to be certain things beyond the Lord's power.

Jesus is Lord, Tessie replied in a confident voice. Ain't nothing beyond His power.

Well, foo! Ask the Lord to make me no different.

That'd take a miracle.

You got the faith. Give it a try.

Tessie looked doubtful. Somehow that don't seem right.

Myra lifted her withered arm. See if you can do it. What have I got to lose? And at that instant a ray of sunshine broke through the clouds.

Jesus! Tessie screamed. Jesus God!

What's going on? Myra asked.

Tessie clasped her hands. Sweet Jesus! Come round to this side, Myra! The Lord is here!

Myra slipped on her shoes, opened the gate and walked through the hedge.

He is here, Tessie whispered. Do you feel His presence?

I don't know, Myra said. I guess so.

Praise Him!

Praise the Lord, Myra said. Are you sure?

Tessie whimpered and trembled. Lord! I got the rapture! She pointed at Myra's arm.

What's happening? Myra asked.

Lift up thine eyes!

Myra squinted at the clouds.

Kneel down! Tessie shouted.

Boy oh boy, Myra said, this is nuts.

Tessie gripped her arm with both hands and started to pull.

Ouch! Myra said. That hurts!

Thy will be done! Tessie cried.

Let go, said Myra.

Don't it feel longer?

For the love of Pete, Myra said. The spirit sure enough got you. Let go.

How does it feel?

About as usual, Myra said. Anyhow, that's enough. Let go.

Tessie was breathing passionately. Can't you feel it? Don't it feel longer?

Sweet gooseberries, Myra said. Do you know what you're talking about?

Alleluia, Tessie murmured with her eyes closed. Oh my! Oh dear me! Thank you, Jesus! Dear Lord, thank you! Through the open window of the breakfast room she could hear Tweetwee chirping.

I believe! Tweetwee sang. I believe! I believe!

All at once Tessie understood that she was able to speak a marvelous foreign language. A torrent of strange words poured unexpectedly from her tongue and when she gazed upward she saw God on His throne looking down with approval.

PUIG'S WIFE

MUHLBACH LISTENS uneasily to the droll French wit of Huguette Puig. He tries again to interrupt, but she's too quick; she's waiting for him to say only one thing and until he says it she will not stop talking. He looks at the clock on his desk. Eight minutes. Eight minutes with scarcely a pause. In the outer office the Hanover agent is waiting, so is somebody else.

But of course, Huguette is saying, you must understand that you would become involved with une vrai femme du monde. . . .

All right! All right! Muhlbach finds himself laughing. He knows he will agree to whatever she wishes; she knows it too and immediately stops.

It's nearly five o'clock now, he says. I expect I could be there by six-thirty.

Marvelous! I shall put on my black peignoir. . . .

So, having given in, having agreed to a closer look at the apple, Muhlbach hangs up the telephone and rocks back in his chair with a thoughtful expression. Is she joking, or is she not? What if she does indeed open the door dressed in a black peignoir? Then what? How far do you carry a joke? And what time does Puig arrive? Muhlbach tries to remember. He remembers asking, but she was vague. Something about eight o'clock, but she was quite vague. Muhlbach frowns and taps his fingertips together. She's joking, of course. But of course! As she would say. Just the same, he thinks, I suggested twice that we meet in the cocktail lounge and twice she kept on as though she didn't hear what I said. I don't like it. I should have said I'd meet them later. I don't like this situation.

The green light on his desk winks importantly; he stares at it for a moment, wondering again how such a simple device could cost so much, and also why he bought it. Then he leans forward and touches the key.

Yes, Gloria, what is it?

The Hanover agent has left because he had another appointment; Mrs. Fichte called a few minutes ago and wants you to call her as soon as possible; a Mr. Arnauldi would like to see you about a new filing system.

There's more. Muhlbach listens without much interest. Finally Gloria runs out of news. Hanover will be back tomorrow or the next day, never fear. About Mrs. Fichte, I'll get in touch with her. I'll see Mr. Arnauldi in a couple of minutes—I want to call home first.

Is it okay if I take off a little bit early?

I suppose, Muhlbach answers, but don't overdo it. Now get my house, will you?

At home Donna answers the telephone and suddenly Muhlbach wishes that Mr. Arnauldi would go away and that the Hanover agent and Mrs. Fichte would elope to Persia with Mr. Fichte in mad pursuit, and Huguette Puig, yes, and Gloria and whoever it was from Chase Manhattan and the briefcase salesman and everybody else on earth would somehow disappear. A world has been shattered by the sound of Donna's voice. But before he has time to answer he hears a light scuffling and an argument and next, inevitably, the asthmatic Scandinavian accents of Mrs. Grunthe lugubriously informing him that this is Mr. Muhlbach's residence.

Mrs. Grunthe, I won't be home for supper tonight.

Ooh?

Muhlbach is just able to keep from echoing this noise. Sooner or later, he thinks, I'm going to do it. Then she's going to feel insulted and quit.

Not coming to supper, you say?

That's right. An old friend of mine is going to be in the city. I've decided to have supper with him and his wife. His name is Commander Puig. I won't be late. I expect I should be home by ten or eleven. If you want to reach me before then, they're staying at the Murray. Commander Puig. That's spelled p-u-i-g. At the Murray Hotel on Sixth Avenue.

He waits, knowing that she has been setting down this information carefully, every bit of it, even the fact that Puig is an old friend.

Now, let me talk to Donna.

Mrs. Grunthe replies that Donna has gone outside to play.

Don't bother her, I just—oh, never mind. What's Otto doing?

Otto is somewhere in the neighborhood playing basketball.

When he comes in, remind him of his homework. His grades could certainly stand improvement. Muhlbach pauses, but can think of nothing more. Goodnight, Mrs. Grunthe. You needn't wait up, although as I say I don't expect to be late.

Now there is Arnauldi to deal with; next there is somebody else and somebody else, then mysteriously the office is quiet. The telephone no longer rings. The white-plastic hood has been drawn over Gloria's typewriter. As to the demon secretary herself, at this moment where is she? Muhlbach tries to remember where Gloria goes for the evening parade. The Golden Lion? Slattery's? Not that it matters, doors open everywhere very much the same. In she will swagger and promptly be appraised by the men at the bar as though she were a piece of livestock. That's how she wants it, so all's right with the world. Like Donna, she's gone outside to play.

He stops a minute near the window, gazes down on the evening rush, listens to the remote honk of taxicabs, whistles, small voices shouting. Another day ended. Nothing much accomplished. A reasonable amount of money was earned, enough to get by and a few dollars more. It's necessary, nothing to be ashamed of, no reason to feel dissatisfied. After all, no intelligent man can spend his life on a Polynesian beach gathering driftwood. And unless you were born with an IQ of 200, say, or a voice that would make people forget Caruso, or—well, unless you're somehow exceptional what's left but to put in the days of your life like this?

Muhlbach answers the question by sharply tapping the window with his index finger, then turns and goes out the door and rings for the elevator. It, too, is empty. Silence. Emptiness. He looks at his watch and is surprised. Already past six-thirty. He realizes that he's been wasting time, but why? Of course the puzzle's not very intricate. Huguette. How much safer it would be to take the subway home, telephone her and apologize. That's what I'd like to do, he thinks, but I can't. I'm going to see her. I'm cursed with this Protestant conscience that forces me to do what I say I will do, and I hate it. What I want right now is to go home to my children and Mrs. Grunthe's casserole.

That's just about all I want. Not that I like casserole so much, at least not every single Thursday. Why on earth doesn't she try something different? But in a way the certainty of it is reassuring. In fact I suppose the certainty of casserole on Thursday is worth the monotony of eating it. What reassuring habits I have. I'm afraid of them and yet I can't give them up. I dislike the strain of defending myself against the unexpected. I suppose I must be getting tired as I grow older. Tonight I don't want to exert myself, I just want to go home. Instead of doing that I'm on my way to see Huguette. I don't look forward to sitting in that hotel room with her, defending myself against whatever she has in mind. I really don't want to sit there for an hour trying to balance a loaded drink until Puig arrives. If he's late I'll be forced to have a second drink, and somehow I think he's going to be late.

Muhlbach looks at a woman getting on the bus. She resembles Huguette—that sharp French profile suggesting both the bulky provincial shopkeeper's wife and the arrogant Madame of the seventeenth-century chateau. The history of a nation, he reflects, is in that face, even to the untidy hair. Other than the profile, what is it about her that reminds me of Huguette? Her coat? The way she stands? The packages? I can't be sure. How long since I've seen Huguette? Two years? No, longer than that. I don't understand why she called. Did I make such an impression? That's a flattering thought, but not likely. Puig must have told her to get in touch with me. But why was she determined to see me alone? Why did she insist that I come to the hotel so early? If he told her to invite me for supper—well, I can't make it out. There's no sense to it. I just don't understand what she wants. I can't believe the obvious, that would be grotesque. Whatever it is, I should have refused, told her flatly I couldn't get there until eight.

He stoops to look out of the bus, finds himself nearly face to face with one of the stone lions in front of the library and straightens up. He looks again at his watch. Another ten minutes, then a long block to walk. Thirty minutes late, at least. Forty if the lights are red. Meanwhile she's drifting around that hotel room in a black peignoir. If she's not decently dressed, he says almost aloud, I won't go into the room. I'll tell her to put on some clothes and meet me downstairs. I should have made it clear on the phone. I'm not an explorer and after so many years I've realized the fact, thank God. Why didn't I make it clear? I should have been firm, but she kept talking. I didn't have a chance to

explain. Now I've gotten into this ridiculous situation. Well, I won't
go in, no matter what she's wearing.

Huguette, in a short pink bathrobe and slippers, opens the door as
soon as he knocks.

You're late, she scolds, pulling him firmly into the room, but then
so am I you see! I went shopping, little idiot that I am. . . .

Muhlbach notices that she scanned the corridor while greeting
him, a cold survey more revealing than the bathrobe. He feels a nearly
forgotten astonishment at the lies women tell. And the most unbelievable
able part of their role is that they expect to be believed. Of course
they don't, not completely, but at the same time of course they do.
He almost laughs.

And how have you been? Huguette is saying. So good to see you! Sit
down, I won't bite you, at least not yet. Sit down. You haven't changed.
But as for me—oh la! pauvre Huguette. . . .

Seated opposite him on the couch she continues talking while she
pretends that something is wrong with her slipper. She leans forward
and he is gradually presented with a deep, snowy bosom. The act is
outrageous, but instead of smiling he finds himself gazing solemnly
at the delicate weighted flesh. For a moment it is not Huguette that
he sees but the marvel of a woman entering the beautiful middle age
of womanhood.

She goes right on talking, perhaps unconscious of what she has
done, but just then a white and rather bony knee pops out as though
to see what's going on. She covers it and sits erect.

La! she exclaims, patting the knee. Le cinéma, alors.

This invitation to discuss her knee is a bit too direct; Muhlbach
clears his throat and takes a sip of the drink she has poured. It tastes
like a drug. She must be desperate, he thinks. Why did I come here?—I
knew it was a mistake. Now I've got to juggle this woman for an hour.
By the time Puig gets off duty and gets to the hotel my tongue's going
to be thick as a paintbrush. Why did I let her talk me into this?

But almost as quickly as the question comes the answer. Yes, he
thinks, I know why I'm in this room. All these years of hating Puig
for what he did to me and now I've got the chance to pay him back.
There's no other reason. She didn't persuade me, I wanted to come. I
might as well be honest about it. Both of us have been pretending but
she's more honest than I am—she's not deceiving herself. She wants

another man and decided I might be available. I knew that. I knew it right away, I knew it after the first minute on the telephone, and I was willing to accept but pretended that I wasn't. So that's why I'm here, to use his wife. The timeless insult. These years of waiting for revenge, not quite admitting how much I've hated him. I'd have gone along another twenty years without making a move against him because I didn't really know how I hated him until she called. Now I can use his wife. I can take her in a moment, or put it off a while, just as I please. She's mine. She's told me half a dozen times already that she's mine. Puig's wife! Puig's wife, Muhlbach repeats to himself, tasting it like an oyster in his mouth.

He glances directly into her eyes; she looks back without the least embarrassment.

Do I want her now? he asks himself. Do I want this woman now? Now while the offering is fresh? Or should I wait? Let the sea fruit ripen. When would it be sweetest? Now or later?

But the pleasure of the thought becomes a little sickening; he shifts around on the couch as if the cushions were uncomfortable. Then an ugly thought obtrudes and he glances at her again. How much does she know? Did Puig ever tell her what happened? Probably not. No, probably not, because to him it was never a matter of much importance. He won and I lost, so for him it ended. Ended successfully and therefore insignificantly, so I doubt if he told her about it. In fact, he's probably forgotten. He forgets easily. I was always the one who remembered. Sometimes it seems I don't forget anything that happens to me, Muhlbach thinks bitterly. Not anything. Twenty years and what he did is almost as humiliating now as it was then. Why can't I forget?—throw it away somehow. My God, I've bottled it up and I've smelled it ever since. Twenty-three years it must have been, because that was our second year at college. He laughed about it afterward and he kept waiting for me to laugh, I can still see his face. He thought the whole thing was a joke. Maybe so. Maybe he was right and sensible and I was wrong. Anyway, he's forgotten. He'd forgotten about it long before he got married and all this time I've never once referred to it. There'd be no point in telling her even if he did remember, so this can't be a plot against me. Besides, the winner doesn't plot against the loser. I read too much into everything. She didn't lure me here so Puig could jump out of the closet and catch us in flagrante delicto.

What's wrong with her is no great mystery—her husband's been at sea for several months and she's made up her mind to punish him for leaving her, it's that simple. She wants to injure him at the moment of his return. No, a moment before he returns, meaning she won't let him know that he's been punished. And as long as they live together she won't tell him what took place. She loves him, she doesn't want to hurt him; at least she doesn't want to destroy him.

How intricate women are, thinks Muhlbach while he listens to Huguette talking, and yet how naive. This one, for instance. What did she expect her husband to do? Was Puig supposed to call up the Chief of Staff and say he'd rather stay home than go on duty with the fleet? She didn't think about it, not as a man would, she merely had a Feeling. My husband is leaving me alone, so when he comes back I'm going to get even. I'll teach him not to treat me like that! How obvious, yes, but at the same time how extremely curious. So I'm here—I'm here not because she was attracted to me. I'm here to provide a service. And afterward, of course, the three of us will go out to dinner. I can even guess just how she'll look—delightful! As talkative as usual, brightly witty, the charming continental wife. There would sit Puig full of ignorance at her right hand while I sat full of guilt at her left. And she'd insist I be there. Absolutely. Very curious, Muhlbach reflects as he takes another drink.

Huguette is chatting as though nothing of any consequence was on her mind. She is Mrs. Puig who got home late from shopping; she is entertaining her husband's friend for a few minutes before excusing herself to get ready for dinner.

Muhlbach pokes the ice in his glass and avoids looking at her. He wonders if she will give up, if she will in fact ask to be excused so that she may put on some clothes. It would be awkward if Puig came in just now and found them sitting this close together, with her suggested nudity. He remembers an unpleasant scene not so different from this—visiting a relative, taking off his coat and rolling up his sleeves because the evening was warm, talking with the wife while they waited, at last the door opening and then that sudden suspicion like an evil jewel glittering in the night. Remembering this makes him uneasy; he stands up and wanders around the narrow room while Huguette goes on talking.

Presently the telephone rings, but she doesn't answer. Again it rings, and again. Huguette is almost reclining on the couch, her lips pursed, her expression vague and troubled, and Muhlbach begins to wonder if she is insane. It occurs to him that he knows practically nothing about her. Huguette Fanchon. A war bride out of some obscure Breton village, she's been married to Puig for a long time, nearly a full generation. But that's all I know, he thinks. I don't know anything else about her.

With an impatient gesture Huguette reaches for the telephone. Allo? Yes?

Muhlbach stares at her face, at the profile so totally French, as though etched by the needle strokes of some icy French master. Ingres. David. She will always be French, not American. She is still a Breton woman, oddly transported and far from home.

He realizes that she is speaking in French, completely absorbed by the telephone. She listens, her expression changes, becoming no softer yet unmistakably relieved. She's talking to a man, but not to her husband, who's no linguist.

Muhlbach turns away, slightly embarrassed at having stared, embarrassed that he must listen to the conversation. He sees himself reflected in the window—standing alone near the center of the room, a tall and consciously dignified businessman with a drink held safely in both hands, and it occurs to him that he himself could be the insane party, as mad as any creature beyond the Looking-Glass.

Plus tard! Pas maintenant! Comme j'ai déjà . . .

Quite obviously she is not talking to her husband. But then who is it? and what's the conversation about? Hearing only what she says is rather like trying to read through the slots of a stencil. Is it somebody in the hotel? Muhlbach can hear the man's voice, rising as if he was getting angry. Huguette offers a peculiar hissing noise, sighing between her teeth.

Restlessly Muhlbach walks toward the far end of the room and stands gazing across the city. A short distance away in space his reflection stands gazing into the room with an irritated expression. Then the severe features of the phantom are broken by a smile. He studies himself sardonically. What are you waiting for out there? Are you waiting for a woman to stop talking on the telephone or are you waiting for the end of your life? Which is it? You've been standing around for a long time, why don't you do something? When was the last time you simply did something instead of trying to make up your mind about it? Quite a while. Quite a long while.

I'm too sensible and always have been, Muhlbach decides. I'm too cautious. I can't behave like a simpleton even when I'm drunk; I only double into myself. It doesn't seem fair. Here I stand in a hotel room with a woman who for all I know may be a whore, but I'm too sensible to make a move. I've been talking decorously with a half-naked strumpet. Why? Why is that?

What are you doing? asks Huguette. Are you planning to jump out in order to escape from me? She walks toward him without pulling the robe across her breast. I'll get you something fresh to drink, she says, draws the glass slowly from his hand and walks away.

Not a word about that call, he thinks as he watches her putting ice into the glass. Not that she owes me any sort of explanation, but an American wife would probably say something, even if it was a lie. But not a word from this one. How long has she been in the hotel? I wonder. I wonder. I assumed she got here this afternoon, but I wonder if she might have been here several days. If men are calling while you pretend to wait for your husband, is he ever coming? Dear Huguette, is my friend Puig really on his way? Or am I one more on your list? Then other questions begin taking shape, questions that previously had seemed not worth asking.

Why didn't I hear from Puig himself? He's been at sea for quite a while, yes, but the fleet must have stopped at any number of ports—he could easily have sent a postcard letting me know he'd be here. When she telephoned why didn't she mention that Puig suggested we get together? But she didn't mention it. She's hardly mentioned her husband. Is he coming? Is he? And if he isn't how soon will she tell me the truth! Yes, that also could explain the phone call. Somebody else wanted in this room, but two men at once is one too many. Isn't that so, Huguette? Or is it? Maybe three at once would suit you!

The implications multiply. Is she—is she a whore? Does she come to NewYork every so often in order to work here? Maybe that's what it's all about. Muhlbach feels his vitals begin to contract. When she hands him the second drink he accepts it reluctantly, as though the glass was contaminated, and continues to look out the window. It seems to him that her hand is the hand of a whore. The shape of her ankle, the whiteness of her skin. Whatever she says. Each gesture. The open suitcase. Cigarette stubs in the ashtray—how many men have been in this room? The closet door is not quite shut; he can see one of her dresses and maybe that too is not without meaning, meant to excite him. Many significant facts that had seemed as unrelated as the stars now appear to form a constellation. The room key lying on the desk, why is it there instead of in her purse? Why did she look up and down the corridor so efficiently? And he begins to remember the items in the newspaper—women caught in raids, jailed, the men sneaking away guiltily. He begins to feel obscurely frightened. He knows that his feelings do not show on his face, or in his movements, not as they would have shown twenty years ago; nor is he as frightened as if he was a college boy locked in some carpeted suite. But still he feels anxious, tense, and irritated with himself because of it. All in all, how much better it would be to be at home eating Mrs. Grunthe's casserole or playing with the children. Where would they be now? Otto is probably in his room working on another airplane that soon will be hanging by a thread from the ceiling. And Donna? Where is she? Muhlbach feels himself softening. He blinks, looks around, and discovers Huguette gazing at him expectantly. She has asked something. Would you like to sit down?—was that what she asked? He tries to recall her words but can't.

I'm sorry Huguette, I'm afraid I wasn't paying much attention. I was thinking about my children.

Oh! You're excused, she laughs. And do you know that we have four boys? Four!

Muhlbach notices that he is being led to the couch again. Why does she keep pulling at me? he wonders. Doesn't she ever get discouraged? I can't understand why she's so persistent. What does she expect me to do? Do I have to tell her I don't want any part of it? This is ridiculous, and pretty soon I'm going to look like a fool. If I keep on resisting she's going to say what's wrong with him? She'll decide that there really is something wrong with me and then how do I convince her that there isn't? It's what she'll think, I know it. It's what every woman thinks when a man doesn't come bounding toward her at the signal. He's inadequate. He's nothing. But what am I supposed to do? pull out my wallet and give her some money? Then do I simply get undressed? Is it as simple as that? I should have learned how these things are handled years ago, I should have gone to a cathouse at least once. I wouldn't feel so ignorant. Now I don't know what to do. I've walked into this by myself but I don't know how to behave. She thinks I understood the situation from the very beginning. Probably there were some clues she gave me on the telephone and I accepted them without knowing what I was accepting, now she can't figure out what's wrong. Good Lord, how bizarre! She must be thinking it was a waste of time to call me—I suppose that's it. Yes, because she's one of them. The Murray Hotel. The Murray. It sounds familiar. There were some professionals in this place, I'm sure of it. Flushed out a few months ago.

Huguette is talking about her boys; Muhlbach takes a long swallow of his drink and gazes at her. To be what she is, that's not amazing, but to sit there on the couch with her bathrobe half-undone and talk about her boys. It's incredible. And Muhlbach has no more doubts, she's a professional. He is deeply surprised, not that such whores exist but that he should find himself in the company of one. Then, too, the fact that she is married makes it all the more unbelievable. Housewives, secretaries—there's no longer a division. The old order has collapsed. Life used to be a reasonably simple business. There were certain things you did and things you didn't, or if you did—well, then, at least you realized what you were doing. It was as plain as the painted line in the middle of the highway, you stayed in one lane or another and if you crossed over you were blind not to know it. But now? An officer's wife! By day a housewife in New Jersey, the wife of Commander Puig. Neighbors see him coming home and they see him when he leaves, wearing the uniform of a United States naval officer. The neighbors know, therefore, that Puig and Puig's wife must be respectable. That's so. It must be so because it must. But is it? What about Puig himself? What does he do when his ship drops anchor at Marseilles?

Muhlbach realizes that he wants to see Puig again. Until this minute it hadn't mattered very much. He had looked forward to Puig's arrival merely because it was expected, with no particular enthusiasm, as if an old movie was returning to the neighborhood, or as if somebody was giving him a book he'd read years ago; but now he does want to see this man who had once been his closest friend. Thinking about the past they shared revives in him the affection he once felt for Puig. Four years of college life, sleeping in the same room practically side by side and waking up together, eating together, shaving one right after the other, borrowing and lending—the proximity seemed convincing, yet was it? Was it really? Puig no doubt will seem as real as ever when he walks in the door, although not what he used to be. When he comes in will he stir up the quietly mouldering leaves? or have they flaked and crumbled? so that he will walk in with nothing but some canvas baggage of the present. Muhlbach wonders. How intimately did we know each other? Perhaps not as well as both of us assumed. Since then how many times have I seen him? Four times. Five times, maybe. The world has gone through another war since we were in college, affecting us in more ways than we could imagine. That, too, was an experience we shared several thousand miles apart, just about as equally as we shared the end of our adolescence. How does he feel about the war? We've seen each other since it happened, but never talked about it. I'll ask him. He must have liked the Navy, otherwise he wouldn't have stayed in. Or is that true? The last time we met—let's see, he talked mostly about playing golf. He got every Wednesday afternoon off and went out to the course. Talked about a set of clubs he'd bought. Except for that—I can't remember but I'm pretty sure he enjoys the Navy. The peacetime Navy, that's what he called it. Yes, he does like it. But how much longer is it going to be a peacetime Navy? I'll ask about that, too. Another war seems to be on the way. Powers forming. We do our part to promote it, testing all possible enemies, trying to make up our minds whether or not to fight, and who. Aim one way, then another, like a bunch of kids with BB guns, but maybe the indecision is better than any possible decision. Puig might know what's going to happen, he's worked his way high enough that he ought to have some idea. I'll find out what he thinks. It's strange I don't already know what his opinions are. Strange I know so little about him. Suppose somebody asked me about Puig, what should I say? Married to a Frenchwoman and they have four children. Been in the Navy since the war. Likes to play golf. What else?

That's all! Muhlbach thinks with astonishment. I've assumed I know practically everything about him, but the truth is I couldn't explain to anybody how he's felt or what he's done during the last twenty years. If anybody had asked me how well I know him I'd have said I know him better than anybody else does, except his wife. Yet this is what it comes to. Married, with four children. A career in the Navy. And that's all I know. What does he look like? Well, he's medium height, sandy reddish hair getting thin, a melon face that used to look like the face of a boxer. And his eyelashes turn white during summer. At least I think they do. It seems to me that every summer he turned red and white instead of brown. After those hours on the sun deck I looked like a Mohawk but he came down like a piece of veal or fish. Covering himself with unguent, wincing, grunting. Yes, I could answer if somebody asked what Puig looks like, but that really tells nothing about him. His wife is what tells about him. Huguette Fanchon. Madame Puig. Madame Huguette Puig.

Muhlbach realizes that he has been tipping the glass and rattling the ice cubes more than he intended. In fact, there's not much left of the second drink. His stomach, however, feels receptive; he decides he might even have a third drink before they step out for dinner, unless Puig shows up very soon. He smiles at Huguette and reaches across in front of her to pick up a cigarette. She lights it for him, holding his hand warmly.

She's beginning to get drunk, Muhlbach thinks. I can tell from the way she's been rambling along talking about nothing of any importance. However, let her talk, I don't care. Reflectively he looks around the room. The situation doesn't seem as ominous as it did half an hour earlier.

Oh la—the time! Huguette exclaims, and claps her hands. You know I should be dressing. If we are going out. . . .

Muhlbach looks at his watch. After eight o'clock! He lifts the watch to his ear with an expression of concern. The watch sounds all right. But seven minutes after eight! That doesn't seem possible. And where's Puig?

Huguette is examining her fingernails. The bathrobe somehow has managed to slip aside and expose one of her shoulders, yet she isn't aware of this. He wonders if he should mention it. But how do you express a thing like that? It would be a good idea to let her know, but what do you say? "Huguette, pull yourself together!" or "Huguette, what's going on here?"

Muhlbach frowns at her shoulder and decides to say nothing. She's old enough to look out for herself. Then, too, there's always the chance that she knows exactly what's going on. They're usually aware of these things, they know how much is exposed. He looks with interest at the curve of her breast—a large amount. Just then the robe slides another inch, still she hasn't noticed. And the way it slipped—Huguette didn't move a muscle but the robe fell down anyway.

Muhlbach clears his throat. The time has passed when he could decently have spoken of the matter; to say anything now would be embarrassing.

What in the world has become of your husband?

Huguette shrugs.

I suppose he'll walk in any minute.

Oh yes, any minute! She appears to be dissatisfied with one of her fingernails. She squints at it, turns the finger around, and sighs.

Muhlbach gets up and walks around the room gazing at the pictures on the walls. How splendid if Puig should open the door and find them seated together like that. It would make a nice tableau. Very nice indeed!

The telephone rings again. This time she answers without hesitation and Muhlbach suddenly understands that there has been an arrangement. Puig has told her that he would call at eight o'clock. That explains why she didn't want to answer the telephone an hour ago—she didn't know who it was. Or maybe she did know but didn't want to talk to him, whoever he was. It also explains why she's been in no hurry to get dressed—she knew Puig wouldn't get here at eight.

Muhlbach listens. Yes, she's talking to her husband.

Only after the call is finished does he realize that he has been listening for some reference to himself, in fact that he had been half-waiting for Huguette to beckon him over and give him the telephone. But she talked to her husband as though she were alone.

He says he will be a little late. . . .

How late? Muhlbach interrupts. What time did he say he would get here?

Huguette looks up in surprise. She explains that there has been an accident aboard the ship. A sailor was injured, that's why Puig will be late, but he will be on his way in a few minutes.

Why do you stare at me? she asks. Have I done something wrong? and she stands up and comes close to him.

Muhlbach feels excited and angry. There's no doubt she is waiting for him to untie the belt of her bathrobe.

What a strange man you are! Talk to me, please. Do say something.

I don't like you when you behave like this. She reaches for his hands as though to squeeze them.

He turns away but knows that whatever she is, she's not a whore. Something she has done—something she's said—something he couldn't quite perceive has proved she's not. What was it? What proved her innocence? Innocence! Innocent of being a professional, that's all. She's innocent of very little else. "I don't like you when you behave like this!" Could that be it? Or the moment when she got up from the couch instead of smiling and leaning back. She seemed distressed, worried—he shakes his head, not certain what to believe. If it isn't money she wants, what does she want? Because I can't be what she's after. She hasn't seen me for the past two years, so why should she want me? I know how cold I look. Even if she told me that she thought I was attractive I wouldn't believe it. Well, then, is she simply auditioning lovers? Was somebody else here at five o'clock? And after I'm gone who will it be?

He turns toward her and sees that Huguette's face is the face of a woman obsessed—not fixed and professional. Her eyes are luminous. Her eyes remind him of someone else. For a few seconds he stands in front of Huguette, stricken by those eyes, trying to remember, then he thinks of his grandmother as she lay dying. There was that same look a few hours before her death. Nothing else he has ever seen resembles it. The brilliant gaze of an old woman finally emptied of all pretense.

Why do you look at me so?

This is how they ask, but Muhlbach doesn't answer. Plainly she is offering her body, not as a gift, but in exchange for the use of his, a cold bargain. He tries to estimate how much he wants her. The fact is, not very much. When she telephoned the office he first assumed she wanted to buy some insurance, that's how little she means. Not once has he thought of her these past several years except as Puig's wife. Now, tonight, almost inexplicably she shows this naked willingness; instead of a wife she becomes a woman and displays the queer values of women.

If I were twenty I wouldn't hesitate, he thinks. Or would I say to myself that she's too old? She must be at least thirty-five, maybe older. She could be forty. If I were twenty again, how would I be looking at her? Not as I do now. I'd think she was a joke. I'd see myself telling about it in the fraternity house. I never had an adventure like this when

I was young—it was always somebody else who did the telling—but I
know what it would have meant to me. Now? Now is it amusing?

Muhlbach realizes that he is still gazing at her and that she is trying
to interpret his gaze. Why has she arranged this? he wonders. What's
happened between her and Puig? and suddenly he's convinced that
Puig is impotent. There can't be any other explanation. The endless
boasting, chasing after one college girl and then another—nobody
doubted that Puig was nailing them to the cross. In the Navy it must
have been the same. So many conquests, but all of them too obvious,
too apparent. How many were actual and how many did Puig invent?
Or were all three hundred of them invented? No, Puig's not that
empty. Maybe a few have been so real that Huguette's disgusted.

Well, whatever's the cause, thinks Muhlbach, I'm not going to play
my part. I can almost read the script: we're no sooner in bed than
the door opens, the husband enters, hangs up his hat, and announces
cheerily that he's home. Well, Huguette, I'm not very good at farce,
so I think I can do without that royal scene. I'm not going to spend ten
minutes as your leading man, thank you just the same. Find yourself
another actor. Revenge is what you want. I don't know why. I don't
know what he's done to you, or what you imagine he's done—I don't
know why you're disappointed but look somewhere else, not at me.
I'm not the man.

Eh bien. . . .

Somehow she has understood. Muhlbach knows that somehow she
has understood his thoughts well enough. It's over. "Eh bien!" As if she
has compressed the history of her sex in a phrase.

And because it's over and he has ended it by doing absolutely
nothing—exactly as so many other affairs of his life have ended at the
beginning, because he has done nothing—he feels his head swelling
with anger. What's the matter with me? he demands. Puig's wife is
here! Mine for the taking. And I hate him. Christ how I've despised
him all these years. So take her! Use her! Use her like the bitch that
she is!

But of course the moment has gone, and the anger he feels is toward
himself. Once again he has caught up with life too late.

It occurs to him that maybe they should talk the whole thing over.
She might like to know how he feels. But she already knows, at least
it's probable; she seems to have sensed the situation. The best thing

might be to let the curtain drop and simply wait for Puig. Muhlbach shuts his eyes for a few seconds and imagines himself at home in his old green leather chair, the children running around upstairs while Mrs. Grunthe plods back and forth from the kitchen to the dining room as she sets the table. That's where I ought to be, he thinks, that's where I ought to be!

Opening his eyes, he discovers Huguette bending down patting a pillow, her great box-like hips solidly in front of him. He looks at her hips in despair. He feels crushed and ruined, and decides angrily that he will go over, throw his arms around her waist and see what happens next.

Just then somebody turns the handle of the door. Puig's voice calls through the gilded panel—he's locked out. Huguette goes to let him in, but before opening the door she pulls her robe together and tightens the belt.

Puig, discovering Muhlbach in the room, is quite obviously dumbfounded. He can't believe what he sees; he remains on the threshold with a Navy overnight bag in his hand and the remnants of a husbandly smile on his peeling face—it's plain that he has been in the sun recently, his nose is bright pink and looks extremely tender. He glares at Muhlbach and breathes hoarsely through his mouth; but Huguette is already at work and within a very few minutes Puig is inside, has taken off his garrison cap and is comfortably seated with a drink in his hand, still confused but gradually accepting the situation—as much of it as she has chosen to tell.

It's been a long time! Puig exclaims. A long time!

Muhlbach agrees.

I didn't expect to see you here, says Puig.

Huguette points out that it was meant to be a surprise.

Jesus! remarks Puig without much sign of humor.

Muhlbach asks where the fleet will be going next. Puig doesn't know or claims he doesn't; he adds that he has been in the Mediterranean for the past few weeks.

How tired I am of winter! Huguette exclaims. Why didn't you take me? I'm so sick of this cold weather! Snow! But then it snows again. . . .

Puig soon stops listening to her. He loosens his tie and speaks to Muhlbach. When was the last time we met?

You'd just recently been transferred from the *Huxtable*.

Oh yeah, what a scow. And the old man nuts for Navy regs. That was one tour I won't forget. He talks about this for a while and when he has finished Muhlbach asks if he has been playing much golf.

Sure. Every chance.

You should be in the low seventies by now.

Nope. Hooking off the tee, same as usual. I got a weak wrist, that's what kills me. High seventies. Low eighties. He looks thoughtfully at Huguette, who gets up without a word and goes into the bathroom and shuts the door.

How about you? he continues. You still play?

Nope, haven't held a club in my hands for ten years, Muhlbach answers, conscious that he is beginning to sound like Puig.

At school you had a pretty good swing. Pick it up again and see what you can do. You ought to break ninety.

I might. I might start playing again. Being behind a desk most of the day I don't get much exercise. They say it's a good game for us at our age.

Puig laughs unpleasantly. I'm not old. If I had time for a couple of weeks at the gym I'd be as fast as I was in college. Don't make any mistake. I can still handle myself.

Muhlbach looks at him curiously. It's as though Puig is hinting at something, and has switched from golf to boxing.

You weren't bad, Puig goes on in a condescending voice. One time at Lakewood you tied me on the front nine. Both of us shot a forty-three. I had a thirty-six on the back, you had a forty-eight. My shoulder was stiff that morning. It took a while to get warmed up.

Muhlbach remembers, and remembers Puig mentioning his shoulder for at least a month after that day.

I guess I never told you how much it bugged me, you tying me. You never appreciated how competitive I am. I hate to get beat. I couldn't stand losing marbles when I was a kid. I felt like killing the other kid, get him down in the dust and pound hell out of him. Puig laughs and begins unbuttoning his coat. Now how about you? What've you been up to since I saw you last?

Business. I'm never up to anything else.

Whose fault is that?

You say it's a fault. Well, maybe it is. Maybe it is. My days are practically identical. No variety. Lack of excitement. So you could be right—fault's the word.

Muhlbach listens to this lordly pronouncement and decides he has had enough to drink. My own voice, he thinks, but I've lost control of it. Somebody inside me is talking. However, I'm not mimicking Puig any longer, there's that much to be grateful for.

Variety! Puig answers with an ice cube in his mouth, and spits the cube back into the glass.

He's tired, Muhlbach thinks. Or is it nervousness? He hasn't said anything about what happened on the ship. He could just possibly have been responsible for the accident. He's upset, but what about?

I might as well tell you, Puig remarks as though the thought had communicated itself, finding you here doesn't make me too happy.

The remark is almost impossible to believe. Muhlbach tries to believe he has imagined it—Puig didn't actually say that. Yet he did.

I've been gone such a long while. Cruising around. Storing it up inside. Then I come back and open the door expecting to find Huguette by herself. Forget it, he adds, scratching his jaw with one finger. Don't pay any attention to me. I'm in a bad mood. You were about to say something. Go ahead. I interrupted. What's on your mind?

I shouldn't be here. Huguette—that is, since you didn't know. You weren't expecting me. I thought you were.

What about Huguette?

The challenge in Puig's voice is unmistakable; with bright watery eyes he watches the wall an inch above Muhlbach's head.

I'm asking again: what about Huguette?

Muhlbach realizes that there have been other scenes like this. Puig suspects her. He suspects every man who comes near her. He has never seemed dangerous so the idea of him in a jealous rage is rather funny, but he is tense and this might not be an appropriate time to laugh. Muhlbach considers how to answer. Puig is waiting. The answer begins to seem important.

Such a violent age! Muhlbach says carefully. How violent we are these days.

Amen! Puig answers, squinting with annoyance.

At that moment Huguette turns on the shower. She has been

listening. Puig, however, hasn't noticed; he leans back, rolling his head from side to side as though he was in pain.

Individually, but also as nations, Muhlbach continues, cautiously pulling at the conversation. I've been wanting to ask. Apparently another war is shaping up, but for some reason we can't recognize the enemy. Yesterday we thought it was Russia. Today, China. Now what about tomorrow? Name tomorrow's enemy. What would be your guess? India?

Puig doesn't turn his head; he looks across his nose to see if this is a joke.

Four years together—four years! but what makes you tick I'll be diddled if I know. I never could understand you. You used to sit in the library annex with a gooseneck lamp curled over a book. I used to look at you and ask myself what you were really like inside. What makes him go? I asked myself. Is it money? I figured you must want to earn a lot of money after you graduated. Maybe you did. I have the impression you're doing all right.

Let's trade jobs.

Puig laughs and settles more comfortably into the chair. On account of money? We get benefits, sure. Dental work. Cut-rate movies at the base. Except for that it's nothing much. You don't want to trade with me.

Not on account of money. On account of the travel. I'm rotting away behind a desk. At certain times I catch myself trying to guess where you are—envying you because you're somewhere on the other side of the globe. I imagine the fleet anchored off Ceylon. If you've ever gotten there or not I don't know, it doesn't matter. I stop by the fountain in the office for a drink of water but just then I see you in Marrakesh, or walking along the esplanade at Palma. Maybe you're two thousand miles from there, that doesn't matter. I see you in these places.

Hell's bells, says Puig with a cheerful expression, if you want to go why don't you go? Lock up the shop for a while and go! You sit on your butt and complain, just like you always did.

I don't think of it quite that way, but I won't argue. I ought to go. And I would except for my affair—carrying on with that gooseneck lamp.

As soon as the word slips out he knows it was a poor choice; but

Puig, tenderly feeling the tip of his sunburnt nose, only looks mildly thoughtful.

What is it about this man, Muhlbach reflects, that bores me half to death? Why don't I care what he believes, or what he's done, or what finally becomes of him? When we were students I was interested in his ideas. I thought he was profound. I thought there were reservoirs in him, but there aren't any. He's commonplace. I suppose he always was. His forehead shows practically no expression, strange I never noticed. It's the forehead of a fascist or of a priest. His mind lacks resonance, I believe; even when he surprises me I realize the surprise is shallow. There's no deliberate evil in him, nor much magnificence. He's like other men. I guess that's why he bores me. He's bored with me, too, because he thinks I'm dull and cold, because I'm restrained, but that doesn't insult me in the least. How could it? I'm not concerned with what he thinks about me. I know there's more of me than there is of him. Remind myself that from a distance we're the same size—yes, but I know better, although I don't know how. Given enough to drink he'd announce that he doesn't amount to much, which is a confession I'd never make. Not now, drunk as I may be, or ever, or anywhere. Not even before Jehovah's throne. Let him abase himself if that pleases him, I respect myself too much. Three gold stripes, considerable prestige, yet his confidence is still that of a sophomore. How is it possible? He doesn't—what is it that he doesn't? A sort of growth must be what I have in mind, the way coral grows. But that doesn't explain him because we're not marine organisms, or plants with rings to count. You can't analogize a man. It must be some lack of human deepening that I can't describe. He hasn't deepened since I saw him last. Two years. He was in a good humor then and now he's annoyed at me for something that isn't my fault, otherwise it's as though these two years had never been. Which means it'll be the same when we meet again. Which means I haven't anything else to learn about him or from him. Which makes me wonder what I ever learned from being around him. Is he a great waste of time? And if he is, can I afford it? My life's half over. Come back as a white bull along the Ganges and I wouldn't mind so much, but I'm not expecting that. So what am I doing here with him? because he's nothing more than he appears to be. I doubt if he's ever gotten absolutely and hopelessly lost inside himself. Never peeled away the leaves looking for the innermost bulb. He doesn't know it's there, and that's why I don't think about him, only where he is in my imagination. I don't dislike him, not really. I suppose I like him. However, I'm not sure about that either, he's so fatally easy to forget.

How long have you been here? asks Puig, pretending to pick a bit of lint from his sleeve. And it's this—the calculated gesture—that betrays him. The question isn't casual. Puig is troubled; he opened the door and discovered another man.

How long? Muhlbach asks, and pretends to consider. Quite a while. We were beginning to think you'd never get here.

What'd you and my wife talk about?

Not "Huguette" but "my wife." What did you talk about with my wife? What were you and my wife doing before I got here?

To be decently honest, I'll say only that your wife did most of the talking.

Puig laughs.

Why do I sit here acting like a friend? Muhlbach wonders. I manipulate him and consider myself superior. I could have had his wife and that, too, makes me feel I'm better than he is but maybe I'm not as good. He's artless and coarse, and he's destructible, but his passions are honest. Mine are contaminated. Who's better? I don't know. I don't know. Maybe I worry it too much.

In the bathroom the shower is turned off.

Takes them forever, Puig remarks. Hey! Huguette! he calls.

A moment later the door opens a crack, a wisp of steam curls out, and Muhlbach can see her eye. Somebody wants me?

Snap it up, will you? Puig answers without turning around.

Are you hungry, cheri? I'll hurry. One minute. Okay? And then before disappearing the eye regards Muhlbach. The look is very brief but unequivocal. The eye of Cleopatra, or of Messalina, gazing across her husband's shoulder.

I should have done it, Muhlbach says to himself. That's what she wanted, so why didn't I? What difference would it make. I should have taken my cheap revenge. Puig would never know.

And then while the steam is clearing he realizes that he can see the interior of the bathroom; not much, because the door is almost shut, but it isn't completely shut.

Getting back to war, says Puig. This "peace" is just an introduction to what's coming up next. We're in the middle of another Hundred Years War, that's how I figure. All right, India. Sure, why the hell not?

Muhlbach can make no sense of what Puig is saying; it's as though the words conceal something more important, but what? Puig is not really talking about war, he's explaining something.

It's not going to blow over, you can lay a bet. Not for a long while. Maybe never. You sit in an office so you forget what most people actually are like under the surface. At each other's throat. That's human nature. You ought to remember that. Puig takes a swallow of his drink, belches, and wipes his lips on the back of his fist. People can be bloody unpleasant if they got a good reason.

The meaning becomes clear as soon as he finished; nearly everything Puig says is an allusion to his wife.

You've got to treat people with respect, he adds, but then changes the subject. What kind of food you want? Any preference?

Muhlbach lifts his glass slightly to indicate that he doesn't care.

Pizza's good enough for me, Puig mutters, fumbling around in the pockets of his uniform. Out comes a crumpled package of cigarettes, which he holds up with a questioning expression.

Muhlbach shakes his head.

Ten days is all I'm going to be here. I put in for shore duty last October but so far not a word. Ten short days. Then out we go. Ten bloody days.

You must like New York.

What do you mean?

You're here instead of at home.

How did you know about that?

About you buying a house in Trenton? She told me.

Puig settles back thoughtfully and feels the tip of his nose again. I've been at sea such a long while I wanted—oh, you know how it is. Lie in your bunk and think about it and think about it. So I wrote her to meet me here. We'll leave in the morning. I didn't want to lose any time. You know how it is.

I shouldn't have come. I assumed Huguette called me because you suggested it.

That's all right, Puig says awkwardly, and seems to say something else but shrugs and sips at his drink.

Maybe some other. . . .

Sit still, Puig replies irritably. You're here so you're here. If my wife ever gets dressed—I don't know what takes so long. You look like you lost a few pounds, he goes on without much interest.

Muhlbach nods.

You look younger. I usually put on weight aboard ship, he adds suddenly and then calls: Huguette! God damn it!

But, cheri, I am hurrying! she answers from the bathroom. Do be patient. One minute more, I promise.

Did I tell you that last year I was in the Orient? Some difference the way those people look at life. Means nothing to them. So courteous but the next thing you know they're torturing some poor bastard. You remember that time we went to New Orleans?

What's he doing? Muhlbach wonders. It's as though his brain has been short-circuited.

Puig smiles. We bought that old rattletrap car for twenty bucks to drive down. Seems like yesterday. You remember?

Yes. Of course. Muhlbach remembers. Rainy green bluffs along the Mississippi. The soft dialect of the people. Negroes everywhere. Crisp greasy fried shrimp and gray beans with red-eye gravy. Lying on the warm salty beach at Pontchartrain, a Gulf breeze blowing stiffly through the late afternoon. But then he hears Puig mention the street fight. That, too, had been part of the trip. A slow, savage beating more like a ritual than a fight. Muhlbach remembers the grotesque figure in a painted leather vest, with a black nail-studded belt and loose motorcycle boots. The fleshless wolf-like Slavic features, Asiatic eyes peeping out from beneath the dinky cap with a look of amusement while he kicked and beat the victim. A pair of gloves flapped from his back pocket when he swaggered away, the vest dangling from the muscular shoulders. Puig calls it a fight, but it was an assault. And the people standing around asking each other how it started, waiting to see if the thug would come stalking out of the night to attack his victim again—a man sprawled against the curb, resting near the base of the streetlight because he had held on to the streetlight with all his strength while being beaten, but at last slid to the sidewalk where he sat gazing up at the spectators until he was kicked in the back of the head and dropped over lifelessly. Muhlbach remembers the deep sexual pleasure in the hoodlum's face, and how slowly the victim was beaten. He remembers thinking that a man's body is like a heavy rubber ball without much air in it. The body scarcely moved when it was kicked.

Too bad we missed out on the beginning, says Puig, and Muhlbach finds Puig looking at him with mockery or contempt.

Now don't tell me you were going to stop it. Come on, mister, you must think I'm stupid. Nobody was going to—nobody in the whole crowd. That punk was dangerous. You knew it, I knew it, everybody knew it. So don't tell me you were about to step up and shake your finger in his face. You didn't make a move. You stood right next to me quiet as a lamb and watched a man get his brains kicked loose. Let's see—what street was that on? Dauphine, was it? Dumaine? It was close to the convent. We ate someplace near Jackson Square; afterward we walked around. Bought some pralines for dessert. Listened to a jazz outfit. Then what'd we do?

Puig continues reminiscing but Muhlbach no longer listens. What Puig has said is true, he had stood watching quietly while a man was being kicked in the head. He remembers standing on tiptoe to find out what was going on, wondering if there had been an accident, or if it was a play being performed under the streetlight. It had seemed almost like a play, as though at any minute the hoodlum would bow to the applause, then take off his cap and approach for a donation, and the motionless man who lay there bleeding from the mouth and ears would jump to his feet with a grin, wipe away the blood, and the two of them would move along the street to a different corner.

Puig is still talking. You couldn't let the thing alone. After it was done you had to go through it again and again. But while it was actually happening you didn't risk your neck, did you? No, you watched. Then an hour later you decide we ought to go to the cops to report what we witnessed. Sometimes you make me sick at my stomach.

The one act in my life that I'm still ashamed of, thinks Muhlbach with astonishment. How did he guess? After all these years how does he know I've never gotten over that feeling of shame? We did talk about it, yes, and I suppose I was the one who kept bringing it up, but of course we used to talk about all sorts of things. And he himself didn't try to stop the fight.

How many people in the world? Puig inquires. Worry about what happens to one of them and you got to start worrying about the others. I didn't lose any sleep over it. I never pretended I did. I didn't go around for the next two weeks throwing ashes on myself. I'm no hypocrite.

Everything Puig has said is the truth. And yet, thinks Muhlbach, why am I suspicious? He's trying to degrade me, that's clear enough, but I don't know why. He was as afraid as I was, maybe more, because he was the fine physical specimen, not I. He was the one who might have been a match for that thug, but he knew I wasn't. So! Is it possible? Does he feel as guilty as I do? Is he condemning himself?

But why did he bring it up now? What were we talking about—war, for some reason I've forgotten, then all at once he asked about New Orleans. How strange! Muhlbach looks again at Puig. War. Violence. Threats. The shapeless conversation while waiting for Huguette to dress. There it is! Of course! She can hear us talking.

Muhlbach glances toward the bathroom. The door has opened a few more inches and he sees Huguette brushing her hair. As she turns toward the cabinet he sees that she is naked.

What's she doing? asks Puig.

Brushing her hair.

Then there is nothing to do but wait, and Muhlbach waits. One more word may cause Puig to look around.

He knows the bathroom door is open, Muhlbach says to himself, and he knows I've been watching his wife. But that's all he knows. What will I do if he looks around? What could I say—nothing. Good God. And it's her fault, not mine.

Puig mutters. He scratches his jaw, swallows the rest of his drink, and seems about to stand up.

He's warned me. This ridiculous talk about fighting in the street—he was telling me how he feels. And he's convinced I've had his wife. He's almost certain. The only thing he needs is some proof. The way he's been peeking at me I should have guessed. If he makes a move to get up I've got to stop him. If he gets up he'll look around. If he sees her like that he'll know we were in bed together. What will I do if he starts to get up?

Then the solution appears, as obvious as a cartoon.

What's so funny? asks Puig.

Your suspicions.

Puig grins uncomfortably.

Now that you've asked, I don't mind telling you. I can practically see them. They're all over you like the measles. What if the bed had been wrinkled when you came in? Let's suppose your wife decided to lie down for a while before I got here but didn't straighten the bed when she got up. You were hardly in the door before you glanced at the bed. Isn't that right?

Puig continues grinning because he has no choice.

You suspected me before you bothered to say hello. And you've kept right on hunting for evidence. You decided I was a cuckoo and all you wanted was proof. Isn't that true? It is, isn't it?

Puig wipes his face, bites his lip.

Let's try another example. Let's suppose that while I happened to see Huguette brushing her hair she wasn't fully dressed. Suppose that had been the case, what would you have thought? No doubt you'd have manufactured something from that, too. Am I right?

Puig hesitates, but then accepts the stroke, and now unless he doesn't mind being ridiculous he can't possibly turn around. Muhlbach after studying him decides that the position is fixed. However, there's no particular reason to stop, so he continues.

What might happen, I asked myself, if he started misinterpreting? What might happen if—well, it hasn't been very pleasant to contemplate.

Puig is deeply embarrassed, unable to speak. For the first time he feels defensive. If I'm going to be hanged for a thief, Muhlbach goes on, I must admit I wish I'd stolen something.

Puig is writhing on the couch.

You practically challenged me to a duel, but I was so puzzled by the way you were acting. . . .

Oh come on, says Puig very miserably. Knock it off, will you?

If you want to drop the subject, all right.

This should be enough, Muhlbach thinks. This should satisfy me. Why do I feel like torturing him some more? But the fact is, I do. I finally got a taste of revenge and I like it. I want more, I guess because of what he did to me.

The scene in all of its glorious and ferocious schoolboy stupidity comes streaming back; wrestling with each other on the dormitory sun deck because half a dozen girls were watching, even though they pretended they weren't. Muhlbach remembers rolling closer and closer to the edge. I gave up, he remembers, to keep us from being killed. If I'd held on we'd have gone over and dropped sixty feet. And he was so pleased with himself. So proud that he'd won. We both knew he'd won. So did the audience. But what was the sense of it? Why did we do it? For what? For the admiration of a few girls who were busily snubbing us both. On account of that ridiculous humiliation I've hated him. And of course at the same time I've always liked him. Hated? That's not quite right, because hate is total. I never have hated him. What I feel is the nub of something stiff, like a cork or a corroded plug, that he forced down into me. I think only some kind of revenge could soften it. But I suppose I can go on living with it, I've lived this long in spite of what he did to me. And of course I've always liked him. I couldn't have spent four years in one room with him unless I liked him. With all those sorry masculine traits I like him. He's my friend. He always has been, although sometimes I'd like to split his skull. He always had to prove he was better than I was. He had to prove he was stronger, which he was, and smarter, which he wasn't, and better with the girls, which is something only they could answer. Well, that's how he was made, and it's how I was made, and otherwise I guess there's not much to choose between us.

Muhlbach, lifting his glass to finish the drink, because surely Huguette must be ready by now, finds himself looking into the bathroom again. She is standing in full view, leaning toward the mirror to add the last touch of lipstick. Her hair is beautifully brushed and arranged. She has put on her shoes and stockings and a red garter belt, but nothing else. She is watching him from the corner of her eye. She has been standing there waiting.

Muhlbach is too shocked to look away. This is no accidental tableau—if Puig should look. This is not the same as a door that's not quite shut. This is something out of the depths.

For an instant she gazes at him. Then as though he did not exist she turns her back, the worst and oldest insult.

Do you see? she seems to ask. This is what I think of you! And with that she pushes the door shut.

For the rest of her life, Muhlbach reflects, that's what she's going to think of me, because I denied us a round of cheap pleasure—a loveless struggle on a rented bed. Have I humiliated her so much?

A few minutes later Huguette reappears, exquisitely dressed and ready.

I am sorry to take so long but there are certain things a woman must do, she begins brightly. Now if you gentlemen will be good enough to get to your feet. . . .

They stand up, neither saying a word. Muhlbach is too amazed to speak and Puig obviously is bored by the idea of three for dinner.

Huguette takes each of them by an arm.

Alors, she asks, shall we go?

GUADALCANAL

IN THE OFFICERS' quarters of the naval hospital at Bremerton,
Washington, two men lay on adjoining beds. One was a Marine
captain who had been wounded in the fighting at Guadalcanal and
the other was a Navy pilot with catarrhal fever who had not yet left the
United States. The pilot had expected to start for his assignment in the
South Pacific on the following day, but now he was delayed by the fever
and was asking the marine what it was like on the front lines.

The captain, whose legs had been amputated, did not feel like talking but had answered a number of questions out of courtesy, and now
was resting with his eyes shut. He had said to the pilot that many of
the men under his command were very young and that many of them
were volunteers, and that for the most part they were excellent shots.
Some of them, the captain said, were the finest marksmen he had ever
seen, although he had put in almost twenty years as a marine and had
seen more good shooting than he could begin to remember. Many of
these boys had come from small towns or from farm country and had
grown up with a rifle in their hand, which was the reason they were so
deadly. They had been picking Jap snipers out of trees as though they
were squirrels. Often the Japs tied themselves to the trunk of a palm
or into the crotch where the coconuts grew, so that if they were hit
they would not fall, and when they were hit sometimes it seemed as
if there was an explosion among the palm fronds as the man thrashed
about. Other times an arm might be seen suddenly dangling alongside
the trunk while the man's weapon dropped forty feet to the ground.
Or nothing at all would happen, except that no more shots came from
the tree. The captain had narrated these things with no particular
interest, in a courteous and tired voice.

The pilot understood that he had been too inquisitive and he had decided not to ask any more questions. He lay with his arms folded on his chest and stared out the window at the pine trees on the hill. It had been raining since dawn but occasional columns of light thousands of feet in height burst diagonally through the clouds and illuminated the pines or some of the battleships anchored in Puget Sound. The pilot was watching this and thinking about Guadalcanal, which he might see very soon. He felt embarrassed because the captain had talked so much and he felt to blame for this. He was embarrassed, too, about the fact that he himself would recover while the captain was permanently maimed, but there was nothing he could say about that without making it worse.

Presently the captain went on in the same tired and polite voice.

Lieutenant, he said without opening his eyes, I can tell you everything you need to know about what the war is like on Guadalcanal, although I don't know about the other islands because I was only on Guadalcanal. Listen. In my company there was a boy from southern Indiana who was the best shot I believe I ever saw. I couldn't say how many Japs he killed, but he thought he knew because he would watch where they fell and keep track of them. My guess is that he accounted for at least twenty. There were times when he would get into arguments over a body we could see lying not very far away from us in the jungle. He was jealous about them. One night I observed him crawl beyond his post, which was the perimeter of our defense, and go some distance into the jungle. The night was not very dark and I observed him crawling from one body to another. I thought he was going through their wallets and pulling the rings off their fingers. The men often did that, although they were not supposed to. However I was puzzled by what this boy was doing because he made a strange motion over several of the Jap bodies. He appeared to be doing some sort of difficult work, and when he crawled back into the camp I went over to him and lay down next to him and asked what he had been doing. He told me he had been collecting gold teeth. He carried a tobacco pouch in his pocket, which he showed me. It was half-filled with gold and he told me how much gold was selling for by the ounce in the United States. He said that if he lived long enough and got onto enough islands he expected that he would be a rich man by the time the war ended. It was not uncommon to collect teeth and I had suspected he might be doing that also, but I told him I had been watching and was puzzled by the strange movements he had made over several of the bodies. He explained that he had been cutting off their heads and what I had observed was him cutting the spinal cord and the neck muscles with his knife. I asked why he had done this, if it was just for the sake of cruelty, although the men were dead, and he seemed very much surprised by this and looked at me carefully to see why I wanted to know. "They're mine, sir," he said to me. He thought that the bodies of the men he killed belonged to him. Then he said that he did not sever a head unless the man had died face down. I didn't understand what this meant. I thought perhaps it served some purpose that I knew nothing about, relating possibly to the way animals were butchered, but his explanation was so simple and so sensible that I felt foolish not to have thought of it. He reminded me that the jungle was full of snipers and that he did not want to expose himself more than necessary. In order to get at the mouths of the men who had died face down it would have been necessary to turn them over, and he did not want to risk this. A dead man is heavy and it takes a lot of work to turn him over if you yourself are lying flat, so he had severed these heads that, by themselves, could be turned over easily. You wished to know what the war is like on Guadalcanal, Lieutenant, although as I say, it may be different on other islands.

The captain had not opened his eyes while he was talking, and having said this much he cleared his throat, moved around slightly on his bed, and then lay still. The pilot decided that the captain wanted to sleep, so he too lay still on his painted iron bed and listened to the rain and gazed at the fleet anchored in the sound.

There's one other thing, the captain continued. I had not known how old the boy was, except that he was very young. I thought he might be eighteen or nineteen, or twenty at the most. It's hard to tell with some of them. They look older or younger than they are. I've seen a man of twenty-six who looked no more than eighteen. At any rate this boy soon afterward was discharged from the service because he had run away from home in order to enlist and managed to get all the way to Guadalcanal before his mother, who had been trying to locate him, discovered what had happened. He was fourteen when he was sworn in and apparently he celebrated his fifteenth birthday on the island with us, telling his buddies it was his nineteenth. But finally, as I say, it caught up with him and he was sent home. His mother, I was told, was very anxious for her son to finish high school. Perhaps he's there now.

I believe what I'm going to remember longest, the captain added in a mild voice, is the moment he stared at me while we were lying side by side. We were closer than you and I. He was young enough to be my own boy, which is a thought that occurred to me at the time, although it seems irrelevant now. Be that as it may, when I looked into his eyes I couldn't see a spark of humanity. I've often thought about this without deciding what it means or where it could lead us, but you'll be shipping out presently, as soon as your fever subsides, and will experience the war yourself. Maybe you'll come to some conclusion that has escaped me.

The captain said nothing more. The nurse came around a few minutes later, looked at him, and held one finger to her lips because he had gone to sleep.

Yellow Raft

From the direction of the Solomon Islands came a damaged Navy fighter, high in the air, but gliding steadily down upon the ocean. The broad paddle blades of the propeller revolved uselessly with a dull whirring noise, turned only by the wind. Far below, quite small but growing larger, raced the shadow of the descending fighter. Presently they were very close together, the aircraft and its shadow, but each time they seemed about to merge they broke apart—the long fuselage tilting backward, lifting the engine for one more instant, while the shadow, like some distraught creature, leaped hastily through the whitecaps. Finally the engine plunged into a wave. The fuselage stood almost erect—a strange blue buoy stitched with gunfire—but then, tilting forward and bubbling, it disappeared into the greasy ocean. Moments later, as if propelled by a spring, a small yellow raft hurtled to the surface where it tossed back and forth, the walls lapped with oil. Suddenly, as though pursuing it from below, a bloody hand reached out of the water. Then for a while the raft floated over the deep rolling waves and the man held on. At last he drew himself into the raft where he sprawled on the bottom, coughing and weeping, turning his head occasionally to look at the blood on his arm. A few minutes later he sat up, cross-legged, balancing himself against the motion of the sea, and squinted toward the southern horizon because it was in that direction he had been flying and from that direction help would come. After watching the horizon for a long time he pulled off his helmet and appeared to be considering it while he idly twisted the radio cord. Then he lay down and tried to make himself comfortable. But in a little while he was up. He examined his wound, nodded, and with a cheerful expression he began to open a series of pouches attached to the inner walls of his raft: he found dehydrated rations, a few small luxuries, first-aid equipment, and signal flares. When the sun went down he had just finished eating a tablet of candy. He smacked his lips, lit a cigarette, and defiantly blew several smoke rings; but the wind was beginning to rise and before long he quit pretending. He zipped up his green canvas coveralls to the neck, tightened the straps and drawstrings of his life jacket, and braced his feet against the tubular yellow walls. He felt sick at his stomach and his wound was bleeding again. Several hours passed quietly except for the indolent rhythmic slosh of water and the squeak of rubber as the raft bent over the crest of a wave. Stars emerged, surrounding the raft, and spume broke lightly, persistently, against the man huddled with his back to the wind. All at once a rocket whistled up, illuminating the watery scene. No sooner had its light begun to fade than another rocket exploded high above; then a third, and a fourth. But darkness prevailed: overhead wheeled the Southern Cross, Hydra, Libra, and Corvus. Before dawn the pilot was on his hands and knees, whispering and stubbornly wagging his head. Then the world around him seemed to expand and the fiery tentacles of the sun touched his face as he waited, drenched with spray, to challenge the next wave. The raft trembled, dipped, and with a sickening, twisting slide, sank into a trough where the ocean and the ragged scud nearly closed over it. A flashlight rolled to one side, hesitated, and came rolling back while a pool of water gathered first at the pilot's feet, then at his head, sometimes submerging the flashlight. The walls of the raft were slippery, and the pouches from which he had taken the cigarettes and the food and the rockets were now filled with water. The drawstrings of his life jacket slapped wildly back and forth. He had put on his helmet and a pair of thin leather gloves to protect himself from the stinging spray. Steep foaming waves swept abruptly against the raft and the horizon dissolved into lowering clouds. By noon he was drifting through a steady rain with his eyes closed. Each time the raft sank into a trough the nebulous light vanished; then with a splash and a squeak of taut rubber it spun up the next slope, met the onrushing crest, whirled down again into darkness. Early that afternoon a murky chocolate streak separated the sea from the sky. Then the waves imperceptibly slickened, becoming enameled and black with a deep viridian hue like volcanic glass, their solid green phosphorescent surfaces curved and scratched as though scoured by a prehistoric wind; and the pilot

waited, motionless, while each massive wave dove under the bounding yellow raft. When the storm ended it was night again. Slowly the
constellations reappeared.

At dawn, from the south, came a Catalina flying boat, a plump and
graceless creation known as the PBY—phlegmatic in the air, more at
home resting its deep snowy breast in the water. It approached, high
and slow, and almost flew beyond the raft. But then one tremendous
pale blue wing of the PBY inclined toward a yellow dot on the ocean
and in a dignified spiral the flying boat descended, keeping the raft
precisely within its orbit until, just above the water, it skimmed by the
raft. Except for the flashlight rolling back and forth and glittering in
the sunshine the yellow raft was empty. The PBY climbed several hundred feet, turned, and crossed over the raft. Then it climbed somewhat
higher and began circling. All morning the Catalina circled, holding
its breast high like a great blue heron in flight, the gun barrels, propellers, and plexiglass blisters reflecting the tropical sun. For a while at
the beginning of the search it flew tightly around the raft, low enough
to touch the water almost at once, but later it climbed to an altitude
from which the raft looked like a toy on a pond. There was nothing else
in sight. The only shadow on the sea was that of the Navy flying boat
moving in slow, monotonous circles around and around the deserted
raft. At one time the PBY angled upward nearly a mile, its twin engines
buzzing like flies in a vacant room, but after about fifteen minutes it
came spiraling down, without haste, the inner wing always pointing at
the raft. On the tranquil sunny ocean no debris was floating, nothing
to mark the place where the fighter sank—only the raft, smeared with
oil and flecked with salt foam. Early in the afternoon a blister near
the tail of the Catalina slid open and a cluster of beer cans dropped
in a leisurely arc toward the sea where they splashed like miniature
bombs and began filling with water. Beyond them a few sandwich
wrappers came fluttering down. Otherwise nothing disturbed the
surface of the ocean; nothing changed all afternoon except that a veil
gathered softly across the sky, filtering the light of the sun, darkening
the metallic gleam of the Coral Sea. At five o'clock the PBY banked
steeply toward the raft. Then it straightened up and for the first time
in several hours the insignia on its prow—a belligerent little duck with
a bomb and a pair of binoculars—rode vertically over the waves. The
prow of the Catalina dipped when it approached the raft and the pitch

of the engines began to rise. The flying boat descended with ponderous dignity, like a dowager stooping to retrieve a lost glove. With a
hoarse scream it passed just above the raft. A moment later inside the
blue-black hull, a machine gun rattled and the raft started bouncing
on the water. When the gunfire stopped the strange dance ended; the
yellow raft fell back torn into fragments of cork and deflated rubber
that stained the ocean with an iridescent dye as green as a rainbow.
Then the Catalina began to climb. Higher and higher, never again
changing course, it flew toward the infinite horizon.

The Cuban Missile Crisis

RUSSIAN FREIGHTERS were approaching Cuba, but Kennedy had said they would not get there: "All ships of any kind bound for Cuba from whatever nation or port will, if found to contain cargoes of offensive weapons, be turned back." The freighters had been en route for several days. Now they were approaching the point at which they would be stopped.

Koerner thought about the blockade and the Russian ships as he strolled along Broadway. In front of Ristorante Sergio he paused to consider the menu. *Prosciutto e fichi. Zuppa di pesce. Insalata Nizzarda. Fagiano. Costoletto di agnello piccante. Abbacchio al forno. Montebianco.* Everything sounded good, but it occurred to him that he might as well be reading the farmer's almanac. Two weeks earlier Vice President Johnson had stated that if the United States stopped a Russian ship it would be an act of war. Nevertheless, President Kennedy had ordered a blockade.

Just inside Sergio's window a checkered curtain hung from a brass rail. This was intended to give the diners a certain amount of privacy, but the rail was too low. Koerner stood on tiptoe and looked over it. Sergio's was not crowded; there would be no problem getting a table. He told himself that he should go inside and order something but his stomach felt like a cockroach. He had not eaten very much for two days because of Kennedy's decision to stop the Russian ships and the closer the Russians got to Cuba the more difficult it was to swallow. He imagined freighters plunging across the Atlantic and wondered what the men in Washington who had decided to stop them were doing at this moment. In San Francisco it was almost nine o'clock so it would be almost midnight in Washington. No doubt some of the policy makers were asleep. Others might be up late discussing the matter. Kennedy and his wife might be at a party. Maybe they were dancing. On the other hand, he was no fool; he might be going over the latest information with his advisers.

Koerner thought about the presidential election while he gazed at the diners in Sergio's. He had been worried about the election. Nixon was one of the worst—maybe the very worst of all the politicians—so it had been a great relief when Kennedy strode into the White House with that enormous grin and his beautiful wife. As long as he was in the White House it would be possible to hope. Of course he had started out clumsily, stupidly. Following Eisenhower's lead he was crawling into Vietnam, which was about as smart as invading Russia in December. Then there was the Bay of Pigs. You didn't have to be very bright to know the Cubans would object to American interference even if they didn't like Castro. Still, he wasn't Nixon. Even with two strikes against him, he wasn't Nixon. If Tricky Dick got into the White House there would be no hope; the ugliness and corruption could only get worse.

Exactly what were the Russians doing in Cuba? Kennedy said they were building missile sites. His Yankee voice reverberated: "The purpose of these bases can be none other than to provide a nuclear strike capability against the Western hemisphere." When these missile sites became operative they could launch nuclear warheads against Washington, Cape Canaveral, Mexico City, the Panama Canal, or anyplace else within a thousand miles—which meant the entire southeastern United States, Central America, and the Caribbean. McNamara was asked what would happen if a Russian freighter carrying offensive weapons chose to run the blockade and McNamara replied that the United States would use force. In other words, the United States would sink the Russian ship.

Koerner decided that he felt no animosity toward the Russian sailors who were delivering this equipment. They were doing a job—making a living, one might say. It was quite probable that most of them had no idea what was aboard. Trucks or trains delivered containers of various sizes and shapes to the pier; cranes hoisted the containers aboard; the ship transported this cargo across the Atlantic to another pier where it was unloaded. But what about the captain? Without doubt he knew what he was carrying and he understood the implications. Therefore was it possible to hate the captain of a Russian freighter? He, too, was obeying orders and quite possibly he felt that he was doing the right thing. Koerner wondered if the captains of these ships crossing the Atlantic had heard Kennedy's speech. This wasn't likely, but one way or another they probably had gotten the message and must be reflecting on the significance of their cargo.

Why didn't Kennedy go to the UN? There was plenty of time. The first ship wasn't expected to reach Cuba for another couple of days, so there was plenty of time to convoke an emergency session. That's what the UN was all about. It was supposed to handle international problems. Why didn't Kennedy go before the assembly with whatever evidence he had collected and say, look, here is what we've found and we're not going to have Soviet missiles on Cuba ninety miles from our shore and we want the UN to tell the Kremlin to recall those ships. Here's the evidence. Do something and do it quick because if you sit on your hands—if those ships don't turn around—the United States is going to blow them out of the water and nobody on earth knows what will happen next.

But he didn't go to the UN, Koerner thought. At least he hasn't done it yet and apparently he doesn't intend to. All he did was ask the Security Council to approve a measure requiring the Soviets to dismantle those things and get them out of Cuba. He said he'd been studying the evidence for a week. What was he waiting for? Why didn't he go to the UN immediately? Maybe they can't do anything or won't do anything, but at least he should have tried. What he's telling the entire world is that we have no confidence in the United Nations.

Koerner realized that he was glaring over the curtain at an old gentleman sprinkling cheese on a dish of pasta. He turned away from Sergio's with his fists clenched and walked toward Mike's Pool Hall. Mike's had a counter where you could eat and the hamburgers were famous. I've got to eat, he told himself. I had a quart of coffee and one orange for breakfast and coffee instead of lunch. My nerves feel like watch springs. Those people who govern us have lost their minds. They study their maps and charts and push buttons on their electronic toys and at the head of their table sits the Mad Hatter and I can't do a thing about it. I'm helpless. Kennedy may be right, but what if he's wrong? One flash of light—that's all I'll ever know.

He remembered the primitive hole in a neighbor's backyard. Every Saturday the neighbor was out there digging like a dog trying to find a bone. When the hole was deep enough he would pour cement. In another three months, the neighbor had said with cheerful satisfaction, it would be finished. If the alert sounded he and his wife and their daughter would scuttle into the shelter and pull the trapdoor shut. They could live underground for ten days. By that time Russia would be destroyed.

People were scared witless. They dug holes in the ground. They peeked in the broom closet and under the bed. The recited the Domino Theory. They pasted *Better Dead Than Red* stickers on their cars and told each other that Communism had to be stopped. If the Communists weren't stopped in Vietnam, for example, America would have to fight on the beaches of Hawaii or maybe on Sunset Boulevard.

Koerner walked into Mike's and sat at the end of the counter where he could see the pool tables. Half a dozen people strung along the counter were eating, others gossiped while they waited. He ordered a hamburger and a Mexican beer and settled back to watch the games.

After a few minutes he decided that the players were nothing special, no better than himself. He slumped on the counter stool with a bottle in one hand while he listened to the agreeable clicking sounds as the colored ivory balls rolled to and fro. Pool was a silly, comfortable gentleman's amusement like golf, a relic from the Age of Reason.

He was still waiting for the hamburger when one game ended and another began. These new players were good so he watched attentively. It was instructive and interesting to watch people who were good at something. He thought about the odd rituals of sprinters before a race. One might prance and snort and toss his head like a horse. Another would slap his thighs, quiver like a religious fanatic, touch his palms to the cinders, or dance a quickstep toward the finish. Finally all of them knelt at the starting blocks to wait for a pistol shot.

Koerner looked around. Everybody in Mike's was waiting, although nobody admitted it. They drank coffee and beer and ate spaghetti and sandwiches and played pool and nobody spoke of Russian freighters loaded with missiles wallowing toward the blockade. In Cuba by this time it would be midnight. On the Atlantic it would be morning.

Just then the hamburger arrived piled with tomato and lettuce and pickle and bacon and cheese and onion so that it looked as big as a football. Juice seeped through the thick French bread and the aroma would draw cats down from the rooftops, but Koerner knew that eating this majestic sandwich would be impossible. He thought about the first bomb. He remembered what Oppenheimer had said after the thing exploded above Hiroshima: "A few people laughed. A few people cried. Most people were silent." And this complex individual who directed America's greatest scientific accomplishment recalled a line from Hindu scripture:

Now I am become death, the destroyer of worlds.

Now I am become death. I am become death, the destroyer of worlds, and have grown weary from gathering them in.

Kennedy hadn't started this insane waltz, but that wasn't the point. Missiles were on the way, no matter who was responsible, and incomprehensible numbers of people would die if somebody in the Kremlin or in Washington miscalculated.

Why should I hate this man? Koerner wondered. I like him and I think he is our best hope. As long as he's in the White House we can hope for better government. We can hope that the terrible reign of dinosaurs may come to an end. Maybe that's naive. Maybe it won't. Maybe it will never end, but with this clever and amiable president we have a chance. So why do I want to attack him? I understand how a political assassin feels. I hate Kennedy worse than I've ever hated anybody. If a motorcade passed Mike's and I saw him in the back of a limousine—if right now I saw the president of the United States with his wife riding in triumph through the streets of San Francisco and there was a gun in my pocket, what would happen?

He remembered what Admiral Leahy had said after Hiroshima and Nagasaki, that the weapon had been of no material assistance in the war against Japan. The Japanese had lost and were attempting to surrender, but Truman wanted to send a message—not to the defeated Japanese but to the undefeated Russians. What Admiral Leahy said was that by annihilating two cities America adopted an ethical standard common to barbarians of the dark ages. What President Truman said was, This is what we will do to Moscow. This is what we will do to Leningrad.

A pool player bent across the table—his long skeletal fingers arched, the cue balanced like an arrow. He was as pale as Dracula and he wore a black motorcycle jacket. It seemed that he was about to shoot, but after a few seconds he straightened up. He appeared to be thinking.

Suddenly he whirled and flung his cue with terrific force against the brick wall. Koerner saw the cue explode and saw five or six pieces drift through the air. One piece bounced off the table. Nobody moved. Then the pool player asked in a wondering voice:

Why didn't he go to the UN?

The only noise in Mike's was the sizzle of frying meat. Koerner looked at the fragments of the shattered cue. Before long somebody would pick them up; but now they lay where they had fallen, as though they held some totemic power, and touching them might affect the delicate suspension of life.

ANCIENT MUSICK

H ERODOTUS vowed to record all matters of interest on
earth. Aye!
Wonders he admired. Two years he loitered in Egypt
gazing at mummies,
crocodiles, and people that kneaded dough with their feet
and wrote their language from right to left,
but I have seen as much. O yea! Twenty times more.
I have encountered men eating the flesh of their god in biscuits
and watched Poseidon gather up clouds with one hand,
so I think there must be no end to marvels.

I have chased knowledge across five continents.
I know why the agitated spirit vomits tumultuous speech,
why that anchorite suffered palsy at sight of a woman,
why Albategnius perceived a ship descending upon his deathbed.
I understand how our world revolves, as Galileo demonstrates
with his Fourth Dialogue, why decrepit old men have hollow brains
commanding them to see and hear what is not. Why our forefathers
heard Cerebrus bark. Why those that squint through red glass
think the universe red. Why that Greek yclept Pythagoras
deciphered messages on the moon. Why we believe what we want,
like Antipheron marveling at reflections of himself
wherever he looked. Truly, much of this world
I understand, but how men are corrupted
I would not presume to say.

Nightly we observe fresh motion overhead, planets lately detected
that come and go and hide and exhibit themselves anew, now close,
now afar, as if a musician should alter his tune on the sackbut

by pulling up or down. So do planets proceed upon their course
albeit we know not why. What hath Nature in her joynts?

By the radiant Pharos beacon did mariners leagues at sea
identify majestic Alexandria. Here lived such scholars as Euclid,
Callimachus, and Strato, as well as merchants eager for trade:
Persians, Moors, Jews, Macedonians. And here in Alexandria
while the sun rose to its zenith above a well at Syene
Eratosthenes calculated the circumference of the earth.
It is true that many request guidance from Heaven. Myself,
I look to those mysteries, riddles, fables, acrosticks,
splendors, and wondrous harmonies that consume us.

Thebes and Daulis prove inhospitable to sparrows,
but why is this? Does Theban soil excrete poison?
Does the moon over Egypt glow too brightly?
Why does Africa breed venomous beasts
whereas none exist in Ireland?
What accounts for such discrepancy?
Why do Scythian pigs stumble to their knees, groan,
and die? If Nature is proportionate and constant,
how should matter be at odds? Verily
we sing and dance bewildered.

What might explain those hideous torrents
when out of cloudless sky we are assaulted by frogs,
stones, rats, snails, fishes, corn, filaments of wool,
and snakes? Could these be illusions or effusions
from embittered souls? As Barcellus argues,
objects could be attracted toward a Middle Region
by the comeliness of heavenly beams, later descending
in frantick showers. Many point to celestial virtue, magnetick
influence, or to the possibility of disengaging elements,
which some regard as feasible yet others think preposterous.
So much doth ebb and flow with our conceit.

Hath not the Red Sea most vehement, irregular,
and divers contractions? Behold the Atlantick! Behold
the Pacifick! See how they stretch and sink upon their season.

Accordingly, no man should complain of tumor, gall, or flatulence,
or because the eaves of his neighbor's house throw long shadows.
We have been granted a while to strut, to boast of transient
accomplishment, yet what use have we for such theatricks
with nightfall imminent? Who limns himself against Providence?
Who would arrest the declining sun?

Theodoret has said that our Lord diversely distributes gifts,
riches to one, art to the next. Thus, wealthy men encourage
and employ laborers, this being all for the common good.
Like sumptuous brocade neatly woven of luxurious thread
such as gold and turquoise, others from disparate sources,
all serve to embellish the entirety, even as we compose musick
out of various keys and discords to fabricate a totality
from the infinite matrix of terrestrial design. Similarly
do we build a commonwealth among equal trades and callings.
Otherwise, if all were prosperous, who should till the land?

Geographers fix the Cape of Good Hope and Italy
equidistant from the equator, yet Blackamoors populate the Cape
while citizens of Italy are white. Beset with conundrums
we lie awake at night gnawing our thumbs.

In a sepulchre at Bologna have we deciphered the epitaph
of Aelia Laelia Crispis who succumbed neither to poison,
stiletto, nor famine. Neither male, female, nor androgyne,
neither harlot, virgin, nor hag. Neither wife nor mistress
to Lucius Agatho, Priscius. Neither in Heaven nor on earth
nor in the water does this creature rest, but everywhere.
She knows and knows not why she should be buried.

In Genoa they speak of a Prince that deceived his Princess,
tumbling through each adventure toward the next.
Vulcan whistling after Venus. Menelaus
feasting upon Helen. Viper tongue,
heart of a dove, caul,
horse pintle,
stone from an eagle nest,
herb of cyclamen. Grief. Shame. Regret.

Hath some radiance passed away? Do we keep within us
the decadent face of God?

They say of Herakles that he fought to subdue monsters
and purge the earth. So did he battle egregious vices,
duplicity, imposture, subterfuge, dissimulation, all such
monsters of the mind. Therefore we ask why His Holiness Leo
deceived Baraballius of Gaeta that he excelled Petrarch
in verse, was destined soon to be chosen Laureate,
and must invite companions to his installment.
Jovius wonders how this venerable old man of sixty
might let himself be persuaded. But inquire among us
who would not be likewise humored.

Socrates advised his friends to beware of poets
since they are irritable and words cut worse than a sword,
nor do they speak except they bite and would sacrifice a brother
to make a jest. Do they not preen their withered souls
on laughter? Do they not lick their feathers
with misfortune? Sarcasmus moulders in their mouths.
As for me, I think poetry and musick most forcible medicine
to erect the mind and heart. I recall how Pythagoras,
hearing the melodic chime of hammers from a blacksmith shop,
paused to meditate on the nature of acousticks.

Near Cornwall live whales that rise eagerly to dance
and otherwise disport themselves at the blast of a trumpet.
Similarly does Calcagninus write of bees that hesitate
to listen when they hear tingling in the air.
Arion caused little fishes to follow him.
Elephants, crafty serpents, horses, swine, and wolves
feel much affected. Nor is the stolid oak exempt
as we know from Orpheus singing to the lyre,
which tempted haughty trees to draw up their roots
with longing. Indeed, we hear of buoyant islands
much given to dance upon hearing a merry tune.
Myself, I am overcome with unhappiness
and sit myself down to weep at delicate harmonies.

Listen! Listen! We are told of a Fish that deliberates,
that enjoys clasping with his teeth the prey he expects to devour,
who is called Escarius, albeit his true name is Wickedness
since if he espies a lesser fish he swims in pursuit,
seizes it, and reflects upon the taste. O yea!
Like his victim, does Escarius perceive too late
that he was meant to nestle in the maw of another.

Look you! Is not the Salamander fearful and grotesque?
Is he not a reptile without remorse? Does he creep into a cistern
he poisons the water. Should he clamber into a tree
he taints the fruit with venom. By nature is he frigid,
slithering through fire without difficulty. Indeed he quenches fire.
Malignant, ghastly, and prophetic is the Salamander. Unwittingly
does he advise Mankind to be watchful.

The Crow. Is not this bird omniscient?
Round about the chamber of sickly men does the crow
hover and croak because he smells a corpse. Plutarch saith
how crows did flock and scream against Tully when he expired,
snatching the pillow from beneath his head. Hence,
like Mardonius that brought tragedy to Persia,
the ragged bones of Tully nourish scavenging dogs.

Regard the Eagle that with sharp talons
plucks chicks from the nest one after another
to learn which is courageous and which contemptible
by exposing them to the sun. Does a chick glare upward,
he is worthy. Those that blink from the sun
she hurls to earth with disgust.
Yet is the universe all of a piece.

The Wolf. Is he not dangerous and cunning?
Into the sheepfold he creeps against the wind
so as not to be detected and like some household dog
pretends to sleep. Should he make a noise

he will bite his paw for punishment.
Rank is his breath. Terrible are his teeth.
His eyes glow more fiercely than torches at midnight.
His belly he likes to stuff with succulent lamb.
Yea! He is ravenous! Lupus is he named
and those he pounces upon must die.
Yet I have met men three times more deadly
and skillful.

See the unlettered peasant guide his plow.
Behold the muddly alchymist unable to distinguish
ambition from talent that would have his name engraved
on a rippling stream for washing lapis lazuli fifty times.
Watch the tenacious huntsman snare a rabbit
while multitudes escape his net.
Do our best efforts lack perfection?

Now look you upward!
Cosmas, surnamed Indicopleustes,
signifying one who traveled through India,
hath elucidated for our benefit in twelve volumes
a theological portrait of the world: *Topographia Christiana*,
demonstrating how earth must be a parallelogram with Jerusalem
at its heart. If not relevant to all, where might the Holy City
be found? And to the north doth Cosmas postulate a lofty summit
about which the moon and sun revolve to illuminate our lives
both night and day. Thus, earth need not be spherical. Otherwise
those dwelling at the Antipodes must conduct their business
upside-down. Holy Scripture and human logic therefore attest
that empires and oceans shall conjoin horizontally.
And when the last trumpet resounds from Heaven
heretics seduced from truth by science
must stand humbly before God
with empty hands.

Water hurries downhill
because it longs to unite with Ocean.
Similarly doth earth seek to unite with itself,

but cannot. Why is this? Should the Lord prove less artful
than Satan? We know the Evil One manipulates our lives
through irregular shapes and feeds upon calamity,
disguising himself as a lion rampant,
a fish asleep in the current,
a goat nibbling at tender shoots.
Lactantius warns us that he exults
each time we stumble. He directs us
to the yawning sink of Perdition.
Numerous stratagems doth he invoke,
machinery to assemble against our souls,
this agent of deceit who would take us hostage.

Michael Parapinatius, Emperor of Greece,
finds devils to have bodies like those of humans.
Thus, if they have been injured they experience pain
and minister to themselves if their limbs are broken.
Facius Cardan relates how his father conjured up seven
wearing Greek apparel, some forty years of age, some pallid,
others ruddy, and put to them questions which they answered,
and told him they fly briskly about their affairs as people do,
excepting they live eight hundred years and govern us.
And no more do we perceive the nature of devils
than does a mouse perceive that of a man.

We learn of a housewife in Milano devoted to lechery
who is thought to cavort with devils at midnight.
Others thus afflicted are known to writhe and tremble,
raving across languages they do not speak,
discoursing on physick, astronomy, or pagan lands.
Galen writes of one mad as a weaver hearing such musick
waft from vapours as made his skull reverberate.
Who can identify the ten thousand mouths of madness?
Montaltus contends that insanity feeds upon bodily humours.
Arculanus would hold the Prince of Darkness responsible.
Who can be certain? Paracelsus would trace the roots of lunacy
to degenerate and squalid fear.

Florilegus relates how a distinguished gentleman of Rome,
having got himself married, went out to supper with his bride.
Afterward, loitering by the tennis court, he for amusement
slipped his wedding ring on a marble statue of Venus,
but when he would have it back she would not give it up.
Vile curses being no help, he thought to retrieve it next day,
Therefore, off to home with his weeping bride
and thus to bed whereupon Venus insinuated herself,
claiming she was his wife, so he could not perform his duty.
Pox, Phrensy, Abscess, Convulsion, Palsy, Gout, Caligo,
all such grievous aches many declare less onerous
than vehement perturbation of the mind.

Boissardus tells how a German diplomat in Sweden
set out for Livonia to converse with spirits.
Now, in Livonia one told him where his wife was,
what clothes she wore, and showed him a goodly ring
he placed on her finger the day they were married.
When he got home he discovered that all of it was true.
Are we not surrounded by vast and fluctuant influences
whose presence we divine but fail to apprehend?
Do not fireflies dance the meaning of their lives?

Philostratus speaks of a likely youth traveling from Cenchreae
to Corinth when a spirit took him by the hand, saying
she was Phoenician, and led him to her home
promising to sing sweetly for him,
saying if he would linger awhile
he would have such wine as no man ever drank.
And she was gracious and fair to behold,
and he tarried awhile and vowed to marry her.
But to the wedding came Apollonius who found her out
as a serpent, a Lamia. And all about her
was like the gold of Tantalus,
mere illusion.

We hear that Roger Bacon devised some curious instrument
to cast a simulacrum of himself walking on air. Perhaps.

I admit to little understanding. Mountebanks,
gammoners, exorcists, cheap-jacks, and such-like
speak inside their throats as if they were leagues distant
and counterfeit the voices of birds until I am riddled with wonder,
but contemplation of these things I leave to stronger wits.
Like a blinded gladiator striking back and forth,
no matter how I turn I lose the way.

Anaximander asserts that Man emerged from the spawn of fishes.
Ah! Do flies give birth to elephants? Disciples of Plato
claim that within His limitless mind Theos contemplates
a model of the Universe. Myself, I am subject to doubt
within doubt and would not build unneeded obelisks,
pretentious pyramids, or labyrinths.

Centuries ago in order to divert himself
Albertus Magnus constructed the image of a man
which would answer questions and work as a domestic
but grew uncommonly turgid with pride. Thomas Aquinas,
disturbed at his studies by such loquacity,
snatched up a hammer to destroy the abomination.
Even so, this automaton called Brazenhead
hath untidily reassembled itself
and goes by many names.

Albertus in his tract concerning old age
boasts how he would restore every man to youth
until he live three and four hundred years,
emulating the juggler Passetes with a magic obol
that returned to his pocket each time he spent it.
Some would devote these centuries to love. Others complain
how women have tossed them on a blanket often enough
and think one life sufficient.

Hieronymus argues that every creature must have its love.
How comes the lode-stone to draw iron, if not for love?
How comes the earth to covet showers? Now, the vine
holds little sympathy for the bay nor his fragrance

and endeavors to kill him, yet both vine and elm
manifest deep sympathy toward one another.

For love of Aurelia Orestilla
the rebel Catiline murdered his only son.
For love of a scrivener's daughter in Thessalonica
Constantine Despota dispossessed his wife and children.
Alexander set Persepolis afire to please a concubine.
Xenocrates, knowing how ivy doth suffocate the oak,
withheld himself from Lais of Corinth.
Caligula, importuned by the Senate
to fortify the crumbling walls of Rome,
offered 6,000 sesterces
while lavishing 100,000 on his mistress.
Are we not subject to frantick acts and scenes?

Aristophanes writes that at the beginning of the world
men boasted four arms and feet, but suffered from vanity.
Now, lacking humility and the grace of women,
they struggle to be united.

Seneca would have us marry while we are able, lie in mutual
and lusty embrace. Still, many converse with Sappho
on the noise of water through apple orchards
when sleep falls like rain through shimmering leaves.

Anon, I open the ivory box of dreams.

Divers authors profess knowledge of realms beyond the Sea.
Theopompus mentions cities on some distant continent
where people live twice as long as Europeans
and express contempt for gold! What next?
That Carthaginian navigator Hanno recounts a voyage
westward through the Pillars of Herakles.
Indeed! Furthermore shall Tethis
the Sea Goddess disclose new worlds. Mercy!

Cosmas of Alexandria doth blindly argue
that men below the horizon anticipate another dawn.
Lord help us! Meantime we hear Gregory, Horace,
Aristotle, and similar slip-slop Solomons
muddle the wits of credulous citizens. But I would ask
with Xenophanes: How old were you when the Persians came?
And where do the wild white horses graze?

Honorius of Autun scribbles in his *Chronicle*
how the fairest, most bountiful island on earth
awaits discovery somewhere in the Atlantick.
Pedro de Ayala tells how Bristol merchants
fit out three and four caravels to investigate.
A most experienced shipmaster, by name John Lloyd,
sails west to look for the island yclept Brasylle
which mariners equate with Paradise, returning
after nine long weeks empty as a keg.
Many claim to have set foot on this island
but were not able to find it again.
Providence offers to each of us
a glimpse of Paradise, if little else.

In Ethiopia where bronze is hugely esteemed
prisoners are bound with golden shackles
and the body of a man when he dies
is colored white with gypsum,
enshrined in a crystal tower
overlooking the village of his birth.
And every woman is lovelier than Rhodopia.
And there is a fountain redolent of hyacinth
bequeathing long life to those who drink from it.
So much and more do travelers allege.
What marvels we perpetuate in imagination.

Herodotus claims to have spoken with Egyptians, Libyans, and
    Greeks
regarding the origin of the Nile. Not one presumed to know
but for a scribe in Thais tabulating the wealth of Egypt

who declared that near Thebes rise two symmetrical mountains,
Crophi and Mophi. Between them flows water from the fountainhead
of the Nile. Pharaoh Psammetichus sought to measure the depth
by lowering a rope many thousands of fathoms in length,
encountering nothing substantial. Therefore, say Egyptians,
the mainspring of the Nile must be fathomless. I think otherwise.
In my opinion the rope of Pharaoh Psammetichus entangled itself
among mountainous whirlpools generated by subterranean roots.
I am persuaded that immutable laws determine natural phenomena
and those oddities we report are little but errors of observation.

From Egypt's first regent to the Priest-King Hephaestus
three hundred and forty-one generations have been numbered
during which period no deity assumed the guise of Man.
So much according to Egyptian priests. Four times
the sun reversed its course, twice declining
in the east, rising in the west. Perhaps.
Perhaps not. Who directs the orbs of Heaven?

What of cartographers that depict Ocean
embracing earth like a river? What of Phoenicians
despatched by Pharaoh Necho to circumnavigate a continent?
Where but in Africa does one encounter such phantasy?
Mewling infants unable to dive into profundity, travelers
flickering back and forth gnawed by vultures of doubt,
bleary, toothless, breath stinking, lumpy bone-bags
clattering at every joynt, one foot stuck on Charon's scow,
we acknowledge a life wrapped with uncertainty.

Should it be that earth is a Moon, as Burton saith,
then are we giddy, vertiginous, and lunatick
amid our sublunary maze. As to myself,
night upon night with Homer beneath my pillow
I slip across the universe like Alexander
seeking distant worlds.

Vagabonds sift the beaches of Mare Rubrum
searching for jewels cast up by the sea.

Suppose I go there, what awaits me?
If I travel as far as Cyrenaica
will I pass over the rainbow bridge?

Neither awake nor asleep I ask what impels the Lord
to create unstable matter. Zeno of Elea,
for biting off his tongue to spit at Nearchus,
was pounded to death in a mortar.

Lucilio Vanini, for composing a book on natural secrets,
was strangled, burnt at the stake,
ashes scattered.

Xerxes, having flogged the Hellespont three hundred times,
scored the oblivious waves with incandescent iron.
Amestris, his wife, sacrificed fourteen Persian boys.
Ah, but what miller counts every bubble passing by?

Sisanes the jurist was flayed alive for accepting a bribe,
strips of his body stretched across the judicial bench
where he had been accustomed to sit while presiding at court.
From the summit of Olympus might we observe the tumult
and meseraick veins of this wavering world?

Behold the philosopher, Ancius Manlius Severinus Boethius,
requested by Theodoric the Ostrogoth to build a water-clock
for King Gundobad of Burgundy. Appointed Consul, anno domini
     510.
Subsequently, Magister Officiorum. Behold him accused of treason,
condemned without trial, executed at Ravenna, anno domini 525.
Is it not the worst of ill fortune, he wrote while awaiting death,
to have once been happy?

Bishop Roger of Salisbury, distraught from torture,
could not decide if he wanted to live or die.
So do we struggle between fear of life
and dread of annihilation, buckets in a well
riding up or down.

Lycidas, being accused of disloyalty, was stoned to death
in the council chamber. Athenian women gathered at his home
encouraging one another to stone his wife and children.
Some voice within us whispers against this.
We ask if humanity is but a shadow,
a leaf, a transient thing.

Thucydides writes how noxious plague befouled the peninsula
where each acted as he list with utmost licentiousness,
caring naught for legality nor the fury of God
because all were swept aside, bad or good,
worshipping or not, keeping whores
or not, since each must perish
beneath cataracts of grief. Futile magistrals.
Cathartick. Medicament. Epithyme. Clove. Orpiment.
Does plague stink worse than corruption in high office?

Do monarchs govern through divine anointment
or some furious disease of the mind?
Does intolerable arrogance precede catastrophe?

Clay tablets disclose how Cambyses succeeded his father
as King of Elam, how Cambyses invaded Egypt, how each conquest
invited another until a witless, vainglorious sovereign
chose to enter the cave of blind gods.

We are told how Onesilus, a Cypriot, besieged Amathus,
how the Cypriot army was destroyed, the head of Onesilus
lopped off, exhibited at the gate where a colony of bees
replaced the foreign brain with honeycomb.

Consider Darius who marched against Scythia
despite good counsel. Scythian archers retreated.
Darius followed. Again these archers fled.
Darius, stuffed with contempt, hurried to engage them
until the King of Scythia sent as messengers a frog, a mouse,
a bird, and five arrows, meanwhile bidding him be damned:
Hear ye, Persian! Jump into a pond like a frog!

Burrow in the earth like a mouse! Hear me! Fly away
like a bird lest Scythian arrows darken the sun!
Who should illustrate imperial misjudgment if not Darius
pursuing phantoms through emptiness toward emptiness?

Is it true that the deeper men go down to defeat
the more stubbornly they cling to dogma?
How often we declare a beginning
yet do not guess the end.

Reflect upon those Paylii after a thievish desert breeze
sucked the water from their storage vats.
Mad with rage, justified by loss,
they rode against the desert
where an east wind buried them in sand.

Human affairs hold their track. Ancient and terrible
pieties linger.

Now have I read myself near to sicknesse
with Mathematick, Classick, Medicine, Divinity,
Astrology, Geography, and much else I forget,
ofttime leavened by profanity of bargemen
at the dock. Therefore, I pray you,
tell me how I could be other than I am,
stepchild of a stupendous dream.

Acrid fumes seep through fissures in the earth,
Bubbling clouds foretell tomorrow.
Locusts gather.

I have more to relate, but it is almost dawn
and the river wind blows cold.

THE PALACE OF
THE MOORISH KINGS

O FTEN WE wondered why he chose to live as he did, floating
here and there like a leaf on a pond. We had talked about
this without ever deciding that we understood, although
each of us had an opinion. All we could agree upon was that he never
would marry. In some way he was cursed, we thought. One of those
uncommon men who follow dim trails around the world hunting a
fulfillment they couldn't find at home. Early in a man's life this may
not be unnatural, but years go by and finally he ought to find a wife
and raise children so that by the time his life ends he will have assured
the continuation of life. To us that seemed the proper pattern because
it was traditional, and we were holding to it as best we could. Only
J.D. had not.

From the capitals and provinces of Europe he had wandered to
places we had scarcely heard of—Ahmedabad, Penang, the Sulu archi-
pelago. From the Timor coast he had watched the moon rise above the
Arafura Sea. He had slept like a beggar beside the red fort in Old Delhi
and had seen the Ajanta frescoes. Smoke from funeral pyres along the
Ganges at Varanasi had drifted over him, and he'd been doused with
brilliant powders during the festival of Bahag Bihn.

Three hundred miles south of Calcutta, he had told us, is a thirteenth-
century Hindu temple known as the Black Pagoda of Konorak, which
is decorated with thousands of sculptured sandstone figures—lions,
bulls, elephants, deities, musicians, dancing girls, and frankly explicit
lovers. Its vegetable-shaped peak, the *śikhara*, collapsed a long time
ago, but the *mandapa* is still there, rising in three stages. It represents
the chariot of the sun. This fantastic vehicle is drawn by a team of

elaborately carved horses, and century after century it rolls toward the Bay of Bengal. Nothing equals it, he said. Nothing. The temple complex at Khajuraho is marvelous, but Konorak—and he gestured as he did whenever he could not articulate his feelings.

What he was after, none of us knew. Seasons turned like the pages of a familiar album while he traveled the byways of the world. He seemed to think his life was uncircumscribed, as though years were not passing, as though he might continue indefinitely doing whatever he pleased. Perhaps he thought he would outlive not only us but our children, and theirs beyond them.

We ourselves had no such illusions. We could see the clean sweep of youth sagging. Not that we had considered ourselves old, or even badly middle-aged, just that there was some evidence in the mirror. And there was other evidence. Zobrowski's son, for example, was in Asia fighting a war that had begun secretly, deceptively, like a disease, had gotten inside of us, and was devouring us before we understood its course. We who had fought in the Second World War had gone along confidently supposing that if war broke out again we would be recalled for duty, but now the government ignored us. It was somewhat embarrassing, as if we were at fault. Young Dave Zobrowski did the fighting while all we did was drive to the office. A boy hardly old enough for long pants had been drafted.

The war offered a deep and bitter paradox. We had succeeded. Beyond all possible question we had succeeded: we had defeated the enemy, yet we had failed. Davy, too, attacked the riddle, unaware at his age that an insoluble problem existed, just as it had existed for us and as it existed for our fathers after the war they called the Great War. Maybe young Dave was more conscious of this than we had been, because we were more knowing than our fathers; still, not much had been changed by our evident sophistication. One conflict ended. Another began. Awareness was irrelevant.

So, against this, we were helpless. We could only hope that our bewilderment and dismay were misplaced. The acid we tasted while listening to newscasts and hearing the casualty figures—"body count" the Pentagon secretaries chose to call it—we could only hope that these falsified and shameful statistics would soon be forgotten. During the Second World War we would have thought it degenerate to gloat over corpses. Now this had become official practice. Apparently it

was meant to reassure and persuade us that the government's cause
was just.

The slow spectacle of ourselves aging, a dubious war, the decay
of our presumably stable nation—these matters were much on our
minds when J.D. wrote that he had decided to stop traveling. He was
planning to come home. Furthermore, he intended to get married.

We were, of course, astonished. At an age when his friends might
become grandfathers he had concluded that perhaps he should stop
amusing himself like a college boy in the summertime.

Our wives were not surprised. They considered marriage inevitable and they were relieved that J.D. had at last come to his senses.
They were merely irritated that he had waited so long. They regarded
his solitary wandering as some kind of pretext for taking advantage of
women all over the world. If we were in charge, they seemed to say,
he'd have been suitably married years ago. The news affected them
quite differently than it affected Zobrowski and Al Bunce and the
others who used to play football and marbles with J.D. in those tranquil days when it was safe to walk the streets, and the air in the city
was almost as sweet as it was on a farm.

Then we didn't think of our city the way we do now. Sometimes
in winter or when the earth was soft after a rain we would find deer
tracks across a vacant lot, and occasionally we caught a glimpse of what
we thought must be a strange dog vanishing into the shrubbery—only
to realize that it was a fox. Now we go about our business in a metropolis. The sizable animals have disappeared, nobody knows quite where;
but we don't see them, not even their prints. Gray squirrels once in
a while, some years a good many, but little else. Robins, jays, bluebirds, cardinals, thrashers—we used to sprinkle bread crumbs on the
snowy back porch just to watch a parliament of birds arrive. Today
our luncheon guests are the ubiquitous sparrows who can put up with
anything.

Smoke fouls the sky and we find ourselves constantly interrupted
by the telephone. Billboards, wires, garbage. We have difficulty accepting these everyday truths. How can we admit that the agreeable past,
which we thought was permanent and inviolable, has slipped away
like a Mississippi steamboat? We like to think that one morning we
will see again those uncultivated fields thick with red clover, streams
shaded by cottonwood and willow, and butterflies flickering through

the sunlight as clearly as illustrations in the heroic books we read when we were eight.

We used to discuss what we would do when we grew up. We made splendid plans. First, of course, we would be rich. Next, we would marry beautiful exciting women with names like Rita, Hedy, or Paulette. We would race speedboats and monoplanes, become as famous as Sir Malcolm Campbell and Colonel Roscoe Turner, or perhaps become wild animal trainers like Clyde Beatty, or hunters like Frank Buck, or great athletes like Glenn Cunningham and Don Budge. There were jungles to be explored, mountain peaks that had never been scaled, cities buried in the sand.

One after another these grandiose ideas acquired the patina of dreams. We could perceive as we grew older that we had not been realistic, so it was natural for Bunce to stop talking about an all-gold motorcycle. Art Stevenson would laugh when reminded of his vow to climb Mount Everest. But there were less ambitious adventures that still seemed reasonable. It's not so hard, for instance, to visit the ruins of Babylon; apparently you can go by jet to Baghdad and hire a taxi.

All of us intended to travel—we agreed on that—just as soon as matters could be arranged. As soon as we finished school. As soon as we could afford a long vacation. As soon as the payments were made on the house and the car. As soon as the children were old enough to be left alone. Next year, or the year after, everything would be in order.

Only J.D. had managed to leave. Surabaja. Brunei. Kuala Lumpur. The islands of Micronesia. He had sent us postcards and occasionally a letter describing where he had been or where he thought he might go next, so in a sense we knew what the world was like.

Once he had returned for a visit. Just once. He stayed not quite three days. We felt obscurely insulted, without being able to explain our resentment. He was not obligated to us. We had played together, gone through school together and exchanged the usual juvenile confidences, but no pacts were signed. We couldn't tell him to come home at Christmas, or insist that he stop fooling around and get a job. Nevertheless, we wished he would; bitterness crept into our talk because we knew he meant more to us than we meant to him. We suspected he seldom thought about us. He could guess where we would be at almost any hour; he could have drawn the outline of our lives day after day and year after year. Why should he think about us? Who thinks about a familiar pair of shoes?

Nor could we explain why we so often discussed him. Perhaps we were annoyed by his indifference toward our values. The work we did was as meaningless to him as the fact that our children were growing up. To us nothing was more significant than our jobs and our families, but to J.D. these vital proceedings had less substance than bread crumbs in the snow. When he wrote, usually to Zobrowski, he never asked what we were doing. He considered us to have a past—a childhood involved with his own—but a transitory nebulous present and a predictable future.

During his visit we questioned him as if we might not ever talk to him again. We asked about Africa—if he had seen Mount Kilimanjaro. He said yes, he had been there, but you seldom see much of Kilimanjaro for the clouds.

Millicent asked if he had shot anything. He said no, he was not a hunter. But he had met an Englishman who did some sort of office work in Bristol and every year came down to hunt, and they had sat up all night drinking gin and talking while the clouds opened and closed and opened again to reveal different aspects of Kilimanjaro in the moonlight, and it sounded as though the lions were only a few yards away. This was as close as he had gotten to hunting the big game of Africa he told her with mock seriousness. Unless you counted the flies, which were savage brutes.

Nairobi, he said, was a delightful town, surprisingly clean, and the weather was decent. We had assumed that it was filthy and humid.

The Masai live not far from Nairobi, he said, and you can visit their compounds if you care to. They eat cheese and drink the blood of cattle and have no use for twentieth-century marvels, except for ceramic beads with which they make rather attractive bracelets and necklaces. Their huts are plastered with animal dung, yet you can tell from watching a Masai warrior that once they were the lords of this territory just as you see in Spanish faces the memory of an age when Spaniards ruled Europe. But it's embarrassing to visit the Masai, he said, because they start to dance whenever a tourist shows up.

I should guess they look forward to the tips, Zobrowski remarked.

They get paid, J.D. said, but you don't tip a Masai. And nobody needs to tell you.

Barbara asked how he liked Ethiopia. He said he'd been there but hadn't stayed long because of the cholera and the mud. He mentioned this Ethiopian mud twice. We thought it strange that his principal memory of such an exotic country should be something as prosaic as mud.

Nor did we understand why he chose to cross and recross a world of dung-smeared huts, lepers, starvation, and cholera. No doubt he had seen rare and wonderful sights, he must have met a good many unusual people, and he had tasted fruits we weren't apt to taste. Granted the entertainment value, what else is there? His pursuit of ephemeral moments through peeling back streets struck us as aimless. He is Don Quixote, Zobrowski observed later, without a lance, an opponent, or an ideal.

Perhaps J.D. knew what he wanted, perhaps not. We wondered if the reason for his travels could be negative—ridiculing the purpose and substance of our lives. In any event, we had assumed that he would continue trudging from continent to continent as deluded as Quixote until death overtook him in a squalid cul-de-sac. We were wrong.

He was planning to settle down. Evidently he had decided to emu-late us. When we recognized this we felt a bit more tolerant. After all, what sweeter compliment is there? Then, too, it should be interesting to learn what the Black Forest was like. Dubrovnik. Kabul. Goa. The South Seas. At our leisure we would be able to pick the richest pockets of his experience.

Leroy Hewitt was curious about Moslem Africa and meant to ask if there were minarets and cool gardens, and if it was indeed true that the great square at Marrakesh is filled with storytellers, dancers, acrobats, and sorcerers just as it was hundreds of years ago. Once J.D. had traveled from Marrakesh to the walled city of Taroudent, rimmed by dark gold battlements, and he had gone over the Atlas Mountains to Tiznit and to Goulimine to the lost Islamic world of women wear-ing long blue veils and of bearded warriors armed with jeweled daggers.

From there we had no idea where he went. Eventually, from Cairo, had come a torn postcard—a cheap colored photo of a Nile steamer. The penciled message told us that he had spent a week aboard this boat and the afternoon was hot and he was drinking lemonade. How far up the Nile he had traveled we didn't know, or whether he had come down from Uganda.

Next he went to some Greek island, from there to Crete, and later, as closely as we could reconstruct his path, to Cyprus. He wrote that the grapes on Cyprus were enormous and sweet and hard, like small apples, and he had bought an emerald that turned out to be fraudulent, and was recuperating from a blood infection that he'd picked up on the Turkish coast. Months passed before we heard any more. He wrote next from Damascus. The following summer he was in Iraq, thinking he might move along to Shiraz, wondering if he could join a camel train across the plateau. He wanted to visit Karachi. What little we knew of these places we had learned from melodramatic movies and the *National Geographic*.

But what brought J.D. unexpectedly into focus was the Indo-China war. We saw him the way you suddenly see crystals in a flask of treated water. Dave Zobrowski was killed.

When we heard that Davy was dead, that his life had been committed to the future of our nation, we perceived for the first time how J.D. had never quite met the obligations of citizenship. During the Second World War he had been deferred because his father was paralyzed by a stroke and his mother had always been in poor health, so he stayed home and worked in the basement of Wolferman's grocery. Nobody blamed him. Not one of us who went into the service blamed him, nor did any of us want to trade places with him. But that was a long time ago and one tends to forget reasons while remembering facts. The fact that now came to mind most readily concerning J.D. and the war was just that he had been deferred. We resented it. We resented it no more than mildly when we recalled the circumstances; nevertheless we had been drafted and he hadn't. We also knew that we had accomplished very little, if anything, while we were in uniform. We were bored and sometimes terrified, we shot at phantoms and desperately appealed to God. That was about the extent of our contribution toward a better world. It wasn't much, but still there was the knowledge that we had walked across the sacrificial block.

After the war we began voting, obeying signs, watering the grass in summer, sowing ashes and rock salt in winter, listening to the six o'clock news, and complaining about monthly bills. J.D. had not done

EVAN S. CONNELL

this either. As soon as his sister graduated from secretarial school and got a job he packed two suitcases and left. He had a right to his own life; nobody denied that. Nobody expected him to give up everything for his parents' comfort. But he had left with such finality.

Problems sprang up around us like weeds, not just family difficulties but national and international dilemmas that seemed to need our attention, while J.D. loitered on one nutmeg-scented island after another. Did it matter to him, for instance, that America was changing with the malevolent speed of a slap in the face? Did it make any difference to him that American politicians now ride around smiling and waving from bullet-proof limousines? We wondered if he had an opinion about drugs, ghettos, riots, extremists, and the rest of it. We suspected that these threatening things that were so immediate to us meant less to him than the flavor of a Toulouse strawberry. And now young Dave was among the thousands who had been killed in an effort to spread democracy—one more fact that meant nothing to J.D. He was out to lunch forever, as Bunce remarked.

While we waited for him to return we argued uncertainly over whether or not it was a man's privilege to live as he pleased. Wasn't J.D. obligated to share with us the responsibility of being human? We knew our responsibilities, which were clear and correct, and hadn't disclaimed them. Maybe our accomplishments were small, but we took pride in them. We might have no effect on these staggering days, no more than we had affected the course of the war, but at least we participated.

We waited through days charged with electric events that simultaneously shocked and inured us, shocking us until we could feel very few shocks, until even such prodigious achievements as flights to the moon appeared commonplace. At the same time our lives continued turning as slowly and methodically as a waterwheel: taxes, business appointments, bills, promotions, now and then a domestic squabble. This was why we so often found ourselves talking about J.D.—the only one whose days dropped from a less tedious calendar. He had gone to sleep beside the Taj Mahal while we occupied ourselves with school bonds, mortgages, elections, auto repairs, stock dividends, cocktail parties, graduations and vacations and backyard barbecues.

Because we had recognized adolescent fantasies for what they are, and had put them away in the attic like childhood toys, we felt he

should have done the same. What was he expecting? Did he hope
somehow to seize the rim of life and force it to a stop? Implausibly,
romantically, he had persisted—on his shoulders a rucksack stuffed
with dreams.

He drifted along the Mediterranean littoral like a current, pausing
a month or so in Yugoslavia or Greece, frequently spending Easter
on the Costa del Sol; and it was after one of these sojourns in Spain
that he came back to see us. His plans then concerned the Orient—
abandoned temples in a Cambodian rainforest, Singapore, Macao,
Burma, Sikkim, Bhutan. He talked enthusiastically, youthfully, as
though you could wander about these places as easily as you locate
them on a map.

He had met somebody just back from the foothills of the Himalayas
who told him that at Gangtok you see colors more luminous than
any you could imagine—more brilliant, more hallucinatory than the
wings of tropical butterflies. The idea fascinated him. We asked what
sense it made, quite apart from the danger and the trouble, to go such
a long distance for a moment of surprise. He wasn't sure. He agreed
that perhaps it didn't make sense.

He'd heard about prayer flags posted on bamboo sticks, the water-
ways of Kashmir, painted houseboats, mango trees on the road to
Dharamasala. He thought he'd like to see these things. And there was
a building carved from a cliff near Aurangabad. And there was a forti-
fied city called Jaisalmer in the Rajasthan desert.

Then he was gone. Like a moth that flattens itself against a window
and mysteriously vanishes, he was gone.

A friend of Art Stevenson's, a petroleum engineer who was sent to
the Orient on business, told Art that he happened to see J.D. sitting
under a tree on the outskirts of Djakarta. He did not appear to be doing
anything, the engineer said; and as he, the engineer, was pressed for
time he didn't stop to say hello. But there could be no doubt, he told
Art, that it was indeed J.D. dressed in faded khaki and sandals, doing
absolutely nothing there in the baking noonday heat of Indonesia. He
is mad, Zobrowski commented when we heard the story.

This, of course, was an overstatement. Yet by the usual standards
his itinerant and shapeless life was, at the very least, eccentric; and
the word "madness" does become appropriate if one sits long enough
beneath a tree.

However, some lunacy afflicts our own temperate and conservative neighborhood. We meet it on the front page every morning—a
catalogue of outrageous crimes and totally preposterous incidents
as incomprehensible as they are unremitting. What can be done? We
look at each other and shrug and wag our heads as though to say well,
suppose we just wait and maybe things will get back to normal. At
the same time we know this isn't likely. So it could be argued that
Zobrowski's judgment was a trifle narrow.

Anyway, regardless of who was mad, we waited impatiently for J.D.
When he arrived we would do what we could to help him get settled,
not without a trace of malicious satisfaction. But more important, we
looked forward to examining him. We need to know what uncommon
kernel had made him different. This, ultimately, was why we had not
been able to forget him.

Our wives looked forward to his return for another reason: if he
was planning to get married they wanted to have a voice in the matter.
They thought it would be foolish to leave the choice of a wife entirely
up to him. They were quite in league about this. They had a few suitable divorcées picked out, and there were several younger women
who might be acceptable.

We knew J.D. had spent one summer traveling around Ireland
with a red-haired movie actress, and we had heard indirectly about an
affair with a Greek girl who sang in nightclubs along the Riviera. How
many others there had been was a subject for speculation. It seemed
to us that he amused himself with women, as though the relationship
between a man and a woman need be no more permanent than sea
foam. Leroy Hewitt suggested, perhaps to irritate the ladies, that
their intricate plans might be a waste of time because J.D. probably
would show up with a Turkish belly dancer. But the ladies, like Queen
Victoria, were not amused.

We tried to remember which girls interested him when we were
in school. All of us agreed that he had been inconstant. It was one girl,
then another. And as we thought back to those days it occurred to us
that he had always been looking for somebody unusual—some girl
with a reputation for brilliance, individuality, or beauty. The most
beautiful girl in school was Helen Louise Sawyer. J.D. would take
her on long drives through the country or to see travel films, instead
of to a dance where she herself could be seen. This may have been

the reason they broke up. Or it might have been because she was conceited and therefore rather tiresome—a fact that took J.D. some time to admit.

For a while he dated the daughter of a Congregational minister who, according to the story, had been arrested for prostitution. Almost certainly there was no truth in it, but this rumor isolated her and made her a target. J.D. was the only one with enough nerve to date her publicly, and the only one who never boasted about what they had done.

His other girls, too, were somehow distinctive. Gwyneth, who got a dangerous reputation for burning her dates with a lighted cigarette at intimate moments. A cross-eyed girl named Grace who later became a successful fashion designer in New York. Mitzi McGill, whose father patented a vending machine that supposedly earned him a million dollars. The Lundquist twins, Norma and Laura. To nobody's surprise J.D. went out with both of them.

Rarities excited him. The enchanted glade. The sleeping princess. Avalon. We, too, had hoped for and in daydreams anticipated such things, but time taught us better. He was the only one who never gave up. As a result he was a middle-aged man without a trade, without money or security of any sort, learning in the August of life that he shouldn't have despised what might be called average happiness— 3 percent down the years, so to speak. It wasn't exhilarating, not even adventurous, but it was sufficient.

Now, at last, J.D. was ready to compromise.

I've expected this, Zobrowski said. He's our age. He's beginning to get tired.

He's lonely, said Millicent. He wants a home.

Are we echoing each other? Zobrowski asked.

On Thanksgiving Day he telephoned from Barcelona. He knew we would all be at Zobrowski's; we gathered there every Thanksgiving, just as it was customary to drop by the Hewitts' for eggnog on Christmas Eve, and to spend New Year's Day at the Stevensons'.

It was midnight in Barcelona when he called. Having gorged ourselves to the point of dyspepsia we were watching football on television, perfectly aware that we were defaulting on a classic autumn afternoon. Somebody in the next block was burning leaves, the air was crisp, and through the picture window we could see a maple loaded like a treasure galleon with red gold. But we had prepared for the feast by drinking too much and by accompanying this with too many tidbits before sitting down to the principal business—split-pea soup, a green salad with plenty of Roquefort, dry heavy salty slices of sugar-cured Jackson County ham as well as turkey with sage and chestnut and onion dressing, mushroom and giblet gravy, wild rice, sweet potatoes, creamed asparagus, corn on the cob, hot biscuits with fresh country butter and honey that would hardly flow from the spoon. For dessert there were dense flat triangles of black mince pie topped with rum sauce. Nobody had strength enough to step outside.

As somnolent as glutted snakes we sprawled in Zobrowski's front room smoking cigars, sipping brandy, and nibbling peppermints and mixed nuts while the women cleared the table. Embers snapped in the fireplace as group after group of helmeted young Trojans rushed across the miniature gridiron. It was toward such completed days that we had worked. For the moment we'd forgotten J.D.

His call startled us, though we were not surprised that he was in Spain again. He had gone back there repeatedly, as though what he was seeking he'd almost found in Spain. Possibly he knew the coast between Ayamonte and Port-Bou better than we knew the shore of Lake Lotawana. He had been to Gijón and Santander and famous cities like Seville. He'd followed baroque holy processions and wandered through orange groves in Murcia. During his visit he spoke fervently of this compelling, strict, anachronistic land—of the apple wine *manzanilla*, fringed silk shawls, bloody saints, serrated mountains, waterless valleys, burnt stony plateaus, thistles as tall as trees lining the road to Jaén.

We remembered his description of goat bells tinkling among rocky Andalusian hills and we could all but feel the sea breeze rise from Gibraltar. One afternoon he ate lunch in a secluded courtyard beside a fountain—bread, a ball of cheese, and some sausage the color of an old boot. He insisted he'd never eaten better.

He imitated the hoarse voices of singing gypsies—a strident unforgotten East beneath their anguished music—and told us about a cataract of lavender blossoms pouring across the ruined palace of the Moorish kings of Málaga. As young as another Byron he had brought back these foreign things.

There's a town called Ronda that is built along a precipice, and he

told us that when he looked over the edge he could feel his face growing damp. He was puzzled because the sky was blue. Then he realized
that spray was blowing up the cliff from the river. It was so quiet, he
said, that all he heard was wind through the barranca and he was gazing
down at two soaring hawks.

He thought Granada might be Spain's most attractive city. He had
told us it was the last Arab bastion on the peninsula and it fell because
of rivalry between the Abencerrages and Zegris families—information anybody could pick up in a library. But for him this was more
than a musty fact. He said that if you look through a certain grate
beneath the floor of the cathedral you can actually see the crude iron
coffins containing the bodies of Ferdinand and Isabella; or if you go
up a certain street near the Alhambra you pass a shop where an old
man with one eye sits at a bench day after day meticulously fitting
together decorative little boxes of inlaid wood. And he liked to loiter
in the Plaza España, particularly while the sun was going down, when
swallows scour the twilight for insects.

He had ridden the night train to San Sebastián along with several
members of the Guardia Civil in Napoleonic leather hats who put their
machine guns on an empty seat and played cards, with the dignity and
sobriety peculiar to Spaniards, beneath the faltering light of a single
yellow bulb. Outside a station in the mountains where the train paused
to build up compression there was a gas lamp burning with vertical
assurance, as though a new age had not begun. Wine bottles rolled in
unison across the warped floor of the frayed Edwardian coach when
the train creaked around a curve late at night, and the soldiers ignored
a young Spaniard who began to speak of liberty. Liberty would come
to Spain, the young man believed—even though Franco's secret police
were as common as rats in a sewer.

From everything J.D. said about Spain we thought it must be like
one of those small, dark green olives, solid as leather, with a lasting
taste.

He returned to Barcelona more than to any other city, although
it was industrial and enormous. He liked the Gothic barrio, the old
quarter. He enjoyed eating outside a restaurant called La Magdalena
which was located in an alley just off the Ramblas. Whenever a taxi
drove through the alley the diners had to stand up and push their
chairs against the wall so it could squeeze past. Whores patrolled the

barrio, two by two, carrying glossy handbags. Children who should have been at home asleep went from café to café peddling cigarettes. Lean old men wearing flat-brimmed black hats and women in polka dot dresses snapped their fingers and clapped and danced furiously with glittering eyes on cobblestones that were worn smooth when the Armada sailed toward England.

Flowers, apple wine, moonlight on distant plazas, supper in some ancient alley, Arabs, implications, relics—that was how he had lived while we went to work.

Now he was calling to us from a boarding house in the cheap section of Barcelona. He was alone, presumably, in the middle of the night while we were as surfeited, prosperous, and unrepentant as could be. It was painful to compare his situation with ours.

So, Zobrowski said to him on the telephone, you're there again.

J.D. said yes, he was in the same boarding house—*pensión*, he called it—just off Via Layetana. He usually stayed at this place when he was in Barcelona because it had a wonderful view. You could understand Picasso's cubism, he said with a laugh, if you looked across these rooftops.

I'm afraid my schedule won't permit it, Zobrowski remarked.

What a pity, said J.D.

Zobrowski took a fresh grip on the telephone. It would appear, he said, that Spain continues to stimulate your imagination.

Actually, no, J.D. answered. That's why I'm coming back.

Then he explained. He wasn't altogether clear, but it had to do with progress. With jet planes and credit cards and the proliferation of luxury hotels and high-rise apartments you could hardly tell whether you were in Barcelona or Chicago. Only the street signs were different. It wasn't just Barcelona, it was everyplace. Even the villages had begun to change. They were putting television sets in bars where you used to hear flamenco. You could buy *Newsweek* almost as soon as it was published. The girls had started wearing blue jeans. There was a Playboy club in Torremolinos.

Years ago he had mentioned a marble statue of a woman in one of the Barcelona plazas and he had said to us, with an excess of romantic enthusiasm, that she would always be there waiting for him.

Zobrowski asked about this statue. J.D. replied that she was growing a bit sooty because of the diesel trucks and cabs and motorbikes.

He said he had recently been up north. The mountain beyond Torrelavega was completely obscured by factory smoke and there was some sort of yellowish chemical or plastic scum emptying into the river with a few half-dead fish floating through it.

The first time he was in Spain he had walked from Santillana del Mar to Altamira to have a look at the prehistoric cave paintings. There wasn't a tourist in sight. He had passed farmers with long-handled scythes, larks were singing, the sky was like turquoise, and he waded through fields of flowers that reached to his knees. Now, he said, he was afraid to go back. He might get run over by a John Deere tractor, or find a motel across the road from the caves.

That bullfighting poster you had, Zobrowski said, the one with Manolete's name on it. Reproductions of that poster are for sale at a number of department stores.

You're flogging me, J.D. said after a pause.

I suppose I am, Zobrowski said.

However, I do get the point, J.D. said. Another decade and the world's going to be as homogenized as a bottle of milk.

Millicent is here, Zobrowski said. She would like a word with you.

J.D.! Millie exclaimed. How marvelous to hear you're coming home! You remember Kate Van Dusen, of course. Ray Van Dusen's sister?—tall and slim with absolutely gorgeous eyes.

J.D. admitted that he did.

She married Barnett Thomas of Thomas Bakery Products, but things just didn't work out and they've separated.

There was no response. Millie seemed about to offer a transatlantic summary of the marriage. Separated was a euphemism, to say the least. Kate and Barnett were in the midst of a reckless fight over property and the custody of their children.

She's asked about you, Millie went on. She heard you might be coming back.

I'm engaged, J.D. said.

We didn't realize that, said Millie without revealing the horror that flooded the assembled women. We simply understood that you were considering marriage. Who is she?

Margaret Hobbs, he said.

Margaret Hobbs? Millie sounded uncertain. Is she British?

You know her, J.D. answered. She's been teaching kindergarten in Philadelphia.

Oh! Oh, my God! Millie said.

We had gone to grammar school with Margaret Hobbs. She was a pale dumpy child with a screeching voice. Otherwise she was totally undistinguished. Her parents had moved to Philadelphia while we were in the sixth grade and none of us had heard of her since. Her name probably hadn't been mentioned for twenty-five years.

We met by accident last summer, J.D. said. Margaret and some other schoolteachers were on a tour and we've been corresponding since then. I guess I've always had a special feeling for her and it turns out she's always felt that way about me. She told me she used to wonder what I was doing and if we'd ever meet again. It's as though in a mysterious way we'd been communicating all these years.

How interesting, Millie said.

It really is, isn't it! J.D. said. Anyhow, I'm anxious for all of you to make her acquaintance again. She's amazingly well informed and she remembers everybody.

I think it's just wonderful, Millie said. We're so pleased. I've always wished I could have known Margaret better. Now here's Leroy.

Is that you, young fellow? Leroy asked.

Hello, said J.D. You don't sound much different.

Leroy chuckled and asked if he'd been keeping himself busy. J.D. said he supposed so.

Great talking to you, Leroy said. We'll have a million yarns to swap when you get home. Hang on, here's Aileen.

We look forward to hearing of your adventures, Aileen said. When do you arrive?

J.D. didn't know exactly. He was going to catch a freighter from Lisbon.

Aileen mentioned that last month's *Geographic* had an article on the white peacocks.

After a moment J.D. replied that the connection must be bad because it sounded as if she was talking about peacocks.

Have you been to Estoril? Aileen almost shouted.

Estoril? Yes, he'd been to Estoril. The casino was jammed with tourists. Germans and Americans, mostly. He liked southern Portugal better—the Algarve. Faro, down by the cape.

Faro, Aileen repeated, memorizing the name. Then she asked if he would stop in Philadelphia before coming home.

J.D. was vague. The freighter's first two ports of call were Venezuela and Curaçao. Next it went to Panama. He thought he might hop a bus from Panama, or maybe there would be a boat of some sort heading for British Honduras or Yucatán or maybe New Orleans.

Aileen began to look bewildered. She was sure that he and Margaret would be able to coordinate their plans and it had been a pleasure chatting. She gave the phone to Art Stevenson.

Art said a lot of water had flowed under the bridge and J.D. might not recognize him because he had put on a pound or two. J.D. answered that he himself had been losing some hair. Art proposed that they try to work out a deal.

Neither of them knew what to say next. Art gave the phone to Barbara.

Barbara asked if he and Margaret would be interested in joining the country club. If so, she and Al would be delighted to sponsor them.

Not at first, J.D. said. Maybe later. Let me talk to Dave again.

He was thinking of buying a car in Europe because he had heard he could save money that way, and he wanted Zobrowski's advice. He had never owned a car.

Zobrowski suggested that he wait until he got back. Bunce's brother-in-law was a Chevrolet dealer and should be able to arrange a price not far above wholesale. Zobrowski also pointed out that servicing foreign cars in the United States can be a problem. Then, too, you're better off buying from somebody you know.

J.D. inquired about jobs.

We had never learned how he supported himself abroad. As far as we could determine he lived from day to day. There have always been individuals who manage to do this, who discover how to operate the levers that enable them to survive while really doing nothing. It's a peculiar talent and it exasperates people who live conventionally.

A job could be found for him, that wasn't the issue. What disturbed us was that he had no bona fide skills. Zobrowski was a respected surgeon. Bunce was vice president of the Community National Bank and a member of the Board of Education. Art Stevenson was director and part owner of an advertising agency. Leroy Hewitt was a successful contractor, and so on. One or another of J.D.'s friends could find him a place, but there would be no way to place him on equal terms. He could speak French, Italian, Spanish, German, and Portuguese well enough to make himself understood, besides a few necessary phrases of Arabic and Swedish and Hindi and several others, but language schools want instructors who are fluent. He knew about inexpensive restaurants and hotels throughout Europe, and the best way to get from Izmir to Aleppo. No doubt he knew about changing money in Port Said. Now he would be forced to work as a stock clerk or a Western Union messenger, or perhaps as some sort of trainee competing with another generation. The idea made us uncomfortable.

Margaret would soon find a job. Excluding the fact that Bunce was on the Board of Education, she was evidently an experienced teacher with the proper credentials. She could do private tutoring until there was a full-time position. But J.D. in his coat of many colors couldn't do anything professionally.

I have a suggestion, Zobrowski said to him on the telephone. This will sound insulting, but you've got to face facts. Your capacities, such as they are, don't happen to be widely appreciated.

I'm insulted, J.D. said.

Zobrowski cleared his throat before continuing: Fortunately, our postmaster is related by marriage to one of the cardiologists on the staff of Park Lane Hospital. I have never met this man—the postmaster, that is—but, if you like, I will speak to the cardiologist and explain your situation. I cannot, naturally, guarantee a thing. However, it's my feeling that this fellow might be able to take you on at the post office. It wouldn't be much, mind you.

Well, said J.D. from a great distance, please have a talk with that cardiologist. I'm just about broke.

I'm sorry, Zobrowski said, although not surprised. You enjoyed yourself for a long time while the rest of us went to an office day after day, whether we liked it or not. I won't belabor this point, but I'm sure you recall the fable of the grasshopper and the ant.

J.D. had never cared for lectures, and in the face of this we thought he might hang up. But we all heard him say yes, he remembered the fable.

If I sound harsh, forgive me, Zobrowski said. It's simply that you have lived as the rest of us dreamt of living, which is not easy for us to accept.

J.D. didn't answer.

Now, as we wait to greet him, we feel curiously disappointed. The end of his journey suggests that we were right, therefore he must have been wrong, and it follows that we should feel gratified. The responsibilities we assumed were valid, the problems with which we occupy ourselves are not insignificant and the values we nourish will flower one day—if not tomorrow. His return implies this judgment. So the regret we feel, but try to hide, seems doubly strange. Perhaps without realizing it we trusted him to keep our youth.

LOST IN UTTAR PRADESH

I ONLY SAW Uncle Gates drunk on one occasion. I had gone back to Kansas City for my parents' fiftieth wedding anniversary and Uncle Gates had driven up from Springfield. My parents didn't want him to drive because he was eighty years old and sometimes forgot where he was, but that didn't stop him. I know what's what, he said. My parents didn't think so. Ever since Aunt Ruth's death three years earlier he had become more obstinate and quarrelsome. He was an emeritus professor of history and literature at Springfield College and when I was a child he terrified me. I would squint at the ceiling or inspect my shoes or notice something on the other side of the universe if he aimed that little pear-shaped head at me.

My parents reserved the Shawnee Country Club ballroom and invited enough people for a convention. My flight from San Francisco was delayed, so I arrived late. I thought at first I had walked into a World War II reunion—gray hair, canes, wheelchairs, hearing aids. Near the bandstand was a table heaped with hors d'oeuvres and I saw three bartenders wearing maroon jackets with the gold SCC crest. I had almost reached the bar when Uncle Gates clutched my arm.

William! he exclaimed.

He was listing a few degrees like somebody on a sailboat and I could smell alcohol. He had shriveled and wrinkled. He was an elf, a munchkin, no longer a monster, nothing to be afraid of. I asked what he had been up to since his retirement. Not that I cared, but at the moment I couldn't think of anything else.

I knew it, he said. I knew you would ask. All right, sir, I have commenced work on a book of recollections. Memoirs, if you will.

He stood directly in front of me, too close. His glasses were so thick that he looked like a mutant bug in a horror film. He peeled them off, held them to the light, cleaned them with his handkerchief, hooked them to his beak, and stared at me. I thought his eyebrows were still growing, though the crabby expression hadn't changed for as long as I could remember.

Yes, William, that is what I have been up to. It should be quite a project. I am unable to estimate how long it will take. Can you guess the title?

The title? I asked.

Since you are unable to guess I must tell you. I intend to call it *A la recherche du temps perdu*. He chuckled. I have sprung that on various acquaintances. Thus far only one — a colleague in the foreign language department — has managed to get it right.

I looked over the top of his head at the bar. It occurred to me that after a couple of quick ones I might locate my parents somewhere in the crowd, say I forgot to feed the dog or something and had to catch the next flight to San Francisco.

Uncle Gates waved at the punchbowl. May I suggest a beverage? Whatever they put in that concoction, it does the trick. You betcha, Bob!

I stood in line for a martini while he helped himself to the punch.

That's the ticket, he said after smacking his lips. Year before last when I saw you in San Francisco we left a few matters unresolved. We should have a long chat.

It had been almost five years. I said maybe I ought to look for my parents, but I don't think he heard me. He belched and glared at the crowd. A daisy hung from his lapel so I asked where he got it. In the kitchen, he said, but didn't explain why he was in the kitchen. One of the dishwashers gave him the flower, a pretty young girl from Cuba. He asked if I had been to Cuba. No. He advised me not to miss it.

Be sure to see Morro Castle. The execution chamber will turn your hair white.

I was in no mood to hear about executions, so I asked if he had sampled the buffet.

Speak up, he said.

The buffet. Are you hungry?

No, he said. Let me tell you what they did.

In the dungeon was a huge wooden chair, solid as a throne. The heretic, traitor, scoundrel, thief, blasphemer, brigand, atheist — whatever his transgression—would be strapped into it. A primitive iron helmet immobilized his head.

Well, sir, on either side of that iron contraption was a long screw. Now, William, listen to this. The executioner would manipulate those screws to bore holes in the fellow's skull.

A few steps from the chair were cells that reminded him of holding pens at the Kansas City stockyard. Prisoners next in line would be able to watch and listen to the shrieks. Uncle Gates thought a good many of them probably wet their britches.

I had bumped into a woman and turned around to apologize. She was about my mother's age, with spools of gray hair, too much lipstick, and watery blue eyes.

Aren't you Willie? she asked.

Yes, I said, though nobody had called me that since I'd left Kansas City.

Gladys Spreckels. You wouldn't remember me, of course. How nice to see you again. Isn't the floral display exquisite?

Her talcum powder was stifling. I tried to hold my breath. My mother used that sort of powder and I held my breath whenever she hugged me.

How are your parents, Willie? Newfield and I have searched high and low, but they seem to have vanished.

I don't know where they are, I said. I've been looking around.

Newfield and I are delighted to hear of your success. How marvelous that you are doing so well.

I didn't know what she was talking about. I hadn't been doing anything particularly well. Then I remembered. At these country club affairs you were expected to hand out bouquets. Jensen Puckett is doing quite well at First Fidelity. Myra Sue Partridge is doing awfully well in Chicago.

Gladys went on talking. Lucy Smoot's engagement. The Board of Education, taxes, crime, City Hall, the new golf course—nothing mattered as long as you kept talking. Aren't those enormous Mexican trucks a disgrace? We let them into the United States and they just ruin our highways, but Washington looks the other way. Isn't it shameful? Newfield thinks we ought to shut the door this very minute. I certainly agree. Newfield and I have been married forty-eight years. Can you believe that?

Uncle Gates tugged my sleeve. I want to finish telling you about Morro Castle, he said. After the fellow gave up the ghost they would drag him to a ramp, give him a shove, and he would go rolling down the cobblestones like a log until he fetched up kerplunk against an iron grate at the edge of the water. Now, by means of a pulley they could lift the grate and my guess is that every shark in the neighborhood hung around waiting for lunch.

I had been looking at the hors d'oeuvres so I wished he would stop talking about sharks and corpses. I asked if he enjoyed his visit to San Francisco.

I did. Your friend Hazel is a charmer.

Rachel, I said.

Yes, yes. The similarity confused me. That young woman reminded me of someone I used to know. She quizzed me about Europe. I regret I wasn't better informed.

You gave her an earful, I said. You were all she talked about for the next six months. Visigoth crowns or whatever they were, dancing with the prettiest girl in France at some festival, the tombstone of a magician. You went on and on.

Visigoth crowns? Ah! She remembered that?

Listen, I said. A couple of weeks after your visit Rachel and I had lunch together and she didn't know me from Abner Gooch. You lectured us on Euripides and Montaigne and Alexander von Humboldt and I forget what else, but she remembered. My God, she sat there with her hands clasped over the braised duck and looked right through me while she talked about you.

Uncle Gates frowned. He didn't recall the tombstone of a magician. I said it was bolted to the wall of a museum in Paris.

Musée de Cluny. Nicolas Flamel. He was an alchemist, William.

You told us he changed lead into silver.

He did. He transmuted eight ounces of lead on January 17, 1382. His wife Pernelle witnessed the transmutation.

Well anyway, I said, she fell in love with you. I couldn't believe it. My God, you were two generations older.

Your education is incomplete, he said.

'Much education doth make one mad,' I said.

Uncle Gates sucked his teeth while considering this. You botched it, he said after a while. You misappropriated that from the New

Testament. 'Much learning doth make thee mad.' Hazel is a dancer, is she not?

She was, I said. She finally gave up. Critics always described her as promising. She got sick of it and married an electrician from Ukiah.

Can't hear a thing in this nuthouse, he said. Damn carnival of animals. Hazel married an electrician?

Rachel, I said. An electrician from Ukiah.

Ukiah. Ukiah, he said. Ukiah. Such a lovely name.

It's north of San Francisco, I said. I think they harvest trees or something.

It reminds me of Malaysia, he said. I cherish the memory of one long salty afternoon on a Malaysian beach. William, you should manage a peek at the world. You are a stick-in-the-mud.

I worked five days a week and earned just enough to pay the bills, so I didn't expect to be loitering in Malaysia or anywhere else. It occurred to me that I didn't know much about him. He used to visit us once or twice a year when I was a child and he had traveled quite a lot, otherwise my uncle was a stranger. My father told me he had made a bundle playing the market and I hoped he would teach me how to get rich on soybean futures or whatever it was.

You don't look well, he said. Have you a touch of indigestion?

I told him I felt all right but my parents must be wondering where I was. He poked me in the stomach with a finger that looked like a rusty nail and suggested another trip to the punchbowl, which he called the mead basin. He got to the bowl without falling down, but he wobbled.

Drink deep or taste not, he said, and lifted the ladle.

I expected a rickety little jig. The daisy slipped out of his lapel and fell on the floor but he didn't notice.

Let me tell you about the Nizam of Hyderabad, he said. Croesus incarnate. Once upon a time the wealthiest potentate on earth.

I had never heard of the Nizam, but at least we got away from the sharks. He had spent a few months traveling through India when he was young so I asked if he went to Hyderabad.

I did. Indeed I did, sir. The Nizam's treasure was on display.

Well, that sounded like a trip to the land of Oz, although I wasn't surprised. The only thing that surprised me was how Uncle Gates and my father could have been hatched in the same nest. My father wouldn't go three blocks to look at the Nizam's treasure. He wouldn't gamble on soybeans, pig bellies, football games, or anything else.

A Dutchman at the hotel in Hyderabad told Uncle Gates the Nizam's palace wasn't far away, so he started walking. He walked the better part of an hour.

I was beginning to think that fellow sent me on a wild-goose chase, he said.

Finally he saw it. What the Dutchman had neglected to mention was a bridge crowded with lepers. Many of them were blind and as he got closer they turned their faces toward him. He thought they had been told of a tourist approaching. He said their eyes were cloudy white.

They reached out to me, William. They dragged themselves toward me. They held up disfigured hands. Some of them held up stumps instead of arms. They clutched my trousers and my sleeves, trying to bring me down. And do you know what popped into my head? Dante's Hell. Keep walking, Gates, I told myself, because if you stop for a second they'll devour you. Gobble you up!

Hunched like an owl at the Shawnee Country Club, he recalled a day fifty years earlier when he tried to keep from going insane while lepers moaned and struggled around his knees.

When I asked about the treasure he waved it aside. The palace was a warehouse. Commonplace artwork exhibited alongside emeralds. The Nizam had no more taste than a magpie or a packrat. The richest man on earth didn't know junk from jewels.

Uncle Gates had wandered around India before he met Aunt Ruth. All right, I said, there you were—a young man in a mysterious foreign country surrounded by exotic women. You must have gone romping through the daffodils. He barked like a terrier and said he wasn't cut out for that sort of nonsense, but he appeared to be thinking.

Well, now, the woman at the airport, he said with a tight little smile, but it didn't amount to much.

His plane landed at Calcutta in midafternoon. It was so hot that he paused before going out in the sun. An attractive young woman wearing the Alitalia uniform asked if she could be of any help. Did he need anything? A hotel reservation? Yes, that was exactly what he needed.

Well, sir, this young lady found me a room at the New Eastern. She got me a taxi and gave instructions to the driver. I hadn't expected such service. And the room turned out to be rather posh. My introduction to Calcutta was altogether favorable, excepting that infernal heat.

As soon as he got to the room he collapsed on the bed, fell asleep, and didn't wake up until the telephone rang. A woman's voice asked if she could be of help. Did he need anything? No, he said, everything was fine. He thought she was a hotel clerk making a routine call to be sure the guests were satisfied. He thanked her for calling and she began to laugh.

Do you know, William, what that woman said to me just before hanging up? 'Sweet dreams, American!' He paused. I wondered if he saw her once again, as young and appealing as she had been at the Calcutta airport decades earlier. Year in, year out, I was seldom troubled by hunger of the flesh, he went on. More a blessing than a curse, perhaps.

He thought the New Eastern quite comfortable, a fading grande dame somewhat tarnished and frayed. He liked the musty Victorian dining room with unobtrusive music and discreet Indian waiters fancied up in white linen coats and turbans. Embossed silverware, perfumed napkins, flowers on the table, all sorts of curries. His first meal was a shock. When I looked at the dessert menu I was thunderstruck, he said. There, plain as the nose on your face: American Hot Fudge Sundae. I'd not tasted one of those things since high school. My Lord, when I was a boy I could put away two of those monstrosities at Watkins' drugstore. Uncle Gates shook his head in disbelief.

He didn't recall what he had for the main course, most likely a curry dish. He couldn't think of anything except dessert. The dining room was full by the time he rearranged the napkin on his lap and, feeling rather proud to be American, told the waiter he would have a hot fudge sundae.

It took longer than expected but a hot fudge sundae must be prepared with attention to detail. A fat dollop of vanilla ice cream, fudge oozing warmly down the slope. Pecans, cashews, walnuts, almonds, Brazil nuts, anything you like scattered on top, puffy whipped cream, a bright red cherry crowning the summit. Without a cherry it wouldn't be authentic. J. S. Watkins made the best hot fudge sundae in Kansas City. Perhaps the New Eastern could equal it, or possibly do better. The New Eastern dessert chef might have a secret recipe.

Uncle Gates said the very thought of it caused him to remember his boyhood. Kansas City became an idyllic place. He recalled tennis games with his friends Evered and Dink and Scotty on the cracked asphalt court across the street from Border Star grade school where he learned to read. He thought about Miss Hagedorf who taught singing, the class divided into bluebirds and robins. Miss Elmo with oily black hair who taught geography and blistered his hands with a ruler because he was shooting spitballs at Winifred Gupta.

At last the hot fudge sundae arrived, a mound of gray slush on a gold-rimmed New Eastern dessert plate. Uncle Gates told the waiter there had been a mistake. The waiter looked attentively at the slush. Uncle Gates said he had ordered a hot fudge sundae.

The waiter cocked his head for another look.

Hot fudge sundae, Uncle Gates said. This is not it. You've brought me the wrong dish.

The waiter moved a little to one side for a better look. Ah, he said. Yes, sir. There it is, sir.

No, Uncle Gates said. American Hot Fudge Sundae. I have no idea what this is, but this is not what I ordered.

The waiter pursed his lips and seemed to be thinking. Hot fudge, sir?

Yes, Uncle Gates said.

There it is, sir.

Take it back, Uncle Gates said. Tell the chef I ordered the American Hot Fudge Sundae. Hot fudge! Do you understand? Don't forget the hot fudge! The waiter picked up the plate and hurried away.

I believe his feelings were hurt, Uncle Gates said.

Ten minutes later the waiter returned. On the plate was an enormous pile of slush.

William, Uncle Gates said to me, do you remember from biology class the smell of formaldehyde? That gelatinous soup might not have been treated with formaldehyde, but to this day I have doubts. When I touched it with a spoon I suspected it was alive. Uncle Gates looked thoughtful.

I asked if he ate it.

I am a cautious man, he said. I was of no mind to experiment. I thought I might try once again. Now look here, I said, where is the

hot fudge? And as he didn't seem to understand, I asked for a menu.
Right there, I told the fellow. Look. Do you see? That's what I want.
Bring me that dessert.

Why do you think they had it on the menu? I asked. Obviously they
didn't know what it was.

Many a time I have puzzled over that, he said. India can drive a
Westerner cuckoo.

He remarked that his voice might have risen while he and the waiter
discussed the problem because people at other tables looked around.
Uncle Gates spoke with an abrasive Midwestern accent and I had no
trouble imagining how he sounded in Calcutta. I could almost see a
party of Englishmen or Frenchmen turn around to stare at the uncouth
American quarreling with a waiter about hot fudge.

I asked if he had escaped the usual fate of tourists. India, I had heard,
was notorious. Everybody got sick. Not Uncle Gates. He never got
seasick and nothing he ate made him sick. He declared that the cuisine
of India was marvelous. He could scarcely wait to unfold his napkin.
Only once during his travels had he suffered from that unspeakable
malady, after a meal at the American Club in Paris. A dish of ratatouille
laid him low.

A week or so after the hot fudge he was window-shopping on a busy
commercial street when everything stopped. Each shop had a metal
shutter in front and almost simultaneously they came rattling down.

Quick as a wink, he said, snapping his fingers, I had that street to
myself.

He began to hear what might have been an avalanche or a distant
waterfall and here came a mob of infuriated citizens pouring into
the street, chased by cops. The cops held wire screens resembling
medieval European shields, except that they could look through the
screens as they advanced.

And those fellows carry bamboo sticks rather than guns, he said.
Oh, I should guess the sticks might be four feet long. Get whacked
with one of those and your bones feel it till Christmas.

He reasoned that nobody cared about him, the mob wasn't after
him and the cops were chasing the mob, so he flattened himself against
a shutter. I played possum, he said.

Rocks soared overhead, bounced from police shields, ricocheted
from metal shutters, tumbled, hopped, skittered across the street.

Once, he said, he had to jump. Never in his life did he pay such close attention to rocks. It seemed to me that he wasn't as cautious as he thought. He hadn't been very cautious when he elbowed his way through a crowd of lepers and he just about got his skull cracked in a riot.

At last the bamboo sticks prevailed. He supposed he might have been trapped for a good fifteen minutes. I asked what caused the trouble. He found out that the soccer stadium wasn't far away and there had been an important match, but too many tickets were sold. I said that in my opinion he used up one of his nine lives because he might have been torn apart. Not likely, he said. Those people rioted because they were cheated. Maybe he was right. In any case I would have retreated to the New Eastern for a couple of heavy-duty drinks. Not Uncle Gates. He planned to visit the museum. He wanted to learn more about Hindu sculpture.

Nobody holds a candle to those birds, he said.

Elephant-headed Ganesha. Vishnu with nine avatars and eleven heads or some such. Shiva. Parvati. Dravidian characteristics. Nandi the sacred bull. Vamana the dwarf. On and on. Krishna married 16,000 women, which was worth thinking about. A monkey expired from a surfeit of happiness after meeting Gautama Buddha. The Buddha expired after eating some rotten pork that he was too courteous to refuse. Uncle Gates might as well have been teaching class in Springfield. I listened once in a while, sipped a martini, and thanked Vishnu that I never had to sit through a semester of his lectures. I remembered how he used to bore my parents by discussing Sophocles or the drainage system at Mohenjo Daro or some Assyrian general they had never heard of.

Vishnu took three giant steps by which he measured out the universe. So do the Upanishads recognize man's burgeoning moral conscience by asking: 'Whence are we born? Where do we live? Whither do we go?'

I thought for the tenth time I ought to find my parents and explain how sorry I was to leave but I had to get back to San Francisco.

Now listen to this, William. Krishna died after being struck by an arrow on the one vulnerable spot of his body—the heel. Doesn't that sound familiar? You bet! Achilles. Then, too, his kingdom sank into the sea. Atlantis! What do you make of it?

I didn't make anything of it.

He had gone to a number of ancient shrines and found many of them severely damaged. Thieves appeared at night or if they knew the site was unguarded. Heads, arms, legs—oh, he said, they chisel off a complete figure if they can manage it. I've seen fragments and torsos in galleries from New York to Geneva. Deplorable, of course, but don't forget the Elgin marbles. Traffic around the Parthenon would have eaten those figures halfway to nothing if they'd not been kidnapped. What's the answer?

He stopped, glared at nothing, took one step backward, and stiffened. I thought he was having a heart attack. Then he sneezed. A shining bead emerged from the tip of his nose. He looked like the evil magician in a fairy tale.

It was late afternoon when he decided he had seen enough Hindu sculpture. Behind the museum was a park almost overgrown with semitropical shrubbery. He slumped on a bench, exhausted by the heat. Flatter than a wet pancake, he said.

A middle-aged woman with tangled yellowish hair and half a dozen scabs on her face came shuffling along the path, Caucasian to judge by her features. At the bench she hesitated, looking him up and down. She wore battered shoes with the laces untied and a greasy pink dress. He suspected she was living on alcohol and drugs and might not have bathed for a month. She asked if he was waiting for anybody. The accent was Australian. No, he said. You buy me a beer? No. You want me to come to your hotel? No. You come to my room? No.

We had nothing else to discuss, Uncle Gates said. The woman appeared to be considering the situation. I expected her to go away, but after a few moments she sat down next to me. Excepting that rank odor, I felt quite at ease and I believe she felt comfortable.

He remembered birds darting through the twilight, a sudden tiny squeak from a thicket that probably meant the end of a tiny life.

Along the path came a barefoot Indian boy with luminous brown eyes, perhaps eight years old, who stopped at the bench to inspect them. He wore a loincloth, nothing else. And having no immediate business he sat down cross-legged in the dust at their feet. Nobody spoke.

We sat there like three monkeys in the jungle watching it grow dark, Uncle Gates said.

He remembered thinking he could spend the rest of his life in Calcutta. For several hundred dollars a year some Indian family would give him food and a pallet. He could visit the museum whenever he wished. And this woman whose desperate face registered such hard experience, she might be worth knowing. There would be any number of things he might do in Calcutta. Why return to a lunatic asylum?

Well, I said, how did the tea party break up? You and that Australian good-time girl and Sabu.

Stop mumbling, he said.

You and the hooker and the Indian boy. Did you buy a round at the local pub?

He didn't recall who was the first to leave. It didn't matter. Nothing mattered. India had begun to absorb him just as India had absorbed innumerable millions over the centuries. He said he could understand why British colonials met at the club night after night, decade after decade, promised one another that they would return to England, and drank themselves silly.

NOT LONG after declining the hooker's invitation he looked at his immunization booklet and discovered that the smallpox vaccination had expired. Wise travelers don't gamble. Malaria, jaundice, cholera, smallpox, yellow fever, typhoid—many surprises welcome a fool to the Orient. What to do? The public health service should be able to take care of it.

In the doctor's office he produced his booklet while a couple of dogs scratched and coughed. The doctor leafed through it, pulled open a drawer, and fumbled around. Bottles, needles, scalpels, cotton swabs, pencils, syringes, and whatnot rolled back and forth. Uncle Gates said he didn't care for the looks of that.

Two nights later he turned on the bedside lamp to inspect his vaccination: a sinister red line extended three inches up the inside of his forearm. He sat on the edge of the bed and watched. After a while he was convinced. All right, you're in a pickle, he told himself. He got dressed and walked down to the lobby, which was deserted except for the night clerk and another Indian. Uncle Gates rolled up his sleeve.

The night clerk hissed and clucked. Very bad. Not good.

Uncle Gates said he needed a doctor.

The night clerk talked it over with his friend. They spoke Hindi. At least that's what I assumed, Uncle Gates said. I couldn't make heads or tails of it.

The night clerk studied his watch. Umm. Very late.

That other fellow had a look at my arm and they talked some more. There was a lot of clucking.

The night clerk's friend beckoned. Uncle Gates followed him down a mouldy corridor, through the kitchen, out the back door, and into a wooden shed. There was a motorbike. At first the night clerk's friend couldn't get it started. Then they tore through Calcutta while Uncle Gates clung to him like a long-lost brother. They bounced across broken pavement, sped around a Victorian monument, and roared into an alley. The night clerk's friend braked to a stop and shouted at what appeared to be a warehouse. Somebody answered but no lights came on. The night clerk's friend got off his bike and pounded on a door. No response. Uncle Gates suspected that the doctor or whatever he was had rolled over and gone back to sleep.

Hospital, Uncle Gates said. Hospital! Hospital!

The night clerk's friend shrugged. They roared out of the alley.

At the hospital a grossly fat woman in a peacock-blue sari led him into an office. He sat down to wait for the doctor. She was the doctor. He said he felt a degree of apprehension. He rolled up his sleeve. The red line had climbed to his elbow. She glanced at it, walked out, and returned with a bottle of tablets. One tablet every four hours.

After another thrilling motorbike ride he swallowed a tablet and sat on the edge of his bed for half an hour watching the thermometer on his arm. It seemed to him that he had done the best he could and there was no sense worrying. Either he would be all right in the morning or he would wake up delirious or he wouldn't wake up, so he went to sleep.

Sunrise woke him. The arm didn't look any worse. He swallowed a tablet. At ten o'clock another tablet, another at two in the afternoon, another at six, and he thought perhaps the villainous red line had begun to retreat. The next day he felt certain.

I told him I would have panicked. He asked what good that would do.

Outside the New Eastern he got into a serious argument with a ricksha boy. He explained that the word ricksha derives from the Japanese word for man-power-carriage, being a two-wheeled vehicle pulled by one or two men. Therefore those vehicles were not rickshas, strictly speaking, because they were pedal-driven tricycles. However, that wasn't the point. Ricksha boys hurried forward screeching like bats whenever he stepped outside. He didn't want anybody pedaling him around Calcutta so he told them to go away. Off with you! Scat! Be gone!

After several days they recognized him and gave up, all except a wiry little nuisance the color of cinnamon who looked tough as a one-dollar steak.

In very short order, William, that fellow and I became enemies. A dozen times I told him to let me alone. Did he listen? Not on your life.

One afternoon Uncle Gates decided to go for a walk. There had been a violent rainstorm and the air smelled uncommonly fresh. Another storm might develop because the sky remained cloudy, so he took his umbrella. Before stepping outside he peeked through a glass panel beside the entrance. And there like a saturated monkey on a tricycle sat the hated ricksha boy.

You should have asked the concierge or somebody to drive him away, I said.

It was a matter of pride, said Uncle Gates.

He gripped the umbrella, marched out, and walked rapidly away from the New Eastern while his enemy pedaled alongside screaming insults in two languages. Off to the right lay a bumpy field, difficult terrain for a ricksha.

I cannot explain what came over me, he said. I remember thinking that if I didn't escape that brown devil I would lose my mind. Well, sir, I'd not taken three steps off the pavement when I knew I'd gotten myself in a fix. The field was a swamp. That bugger was shrieking at me and when I looked over my shoulder I saw him leaping around in the street like a grasshopper. Going back was out of the question.

He marched ahead and experienced what he called a secular epiphany, which he described as though it had happened to some-body else. He could see a wretched traveler floundering through muck like Bunyan's pilgrim lurching from the Slough of Despond to the Valley of Humiliation. It was nobody but himself struggling across a muddy field, waving his umbrella, shaking his fist, raving at the earth and the sky.

I am unable to explain that, he said. Even today, William, I cannot explain my performance.

He wanted to visit the famous black pagoda of Konorak three hundred miles south of Calcutta on the Bay of Bengal. This meant overnight on the train. He decided to indulge himself by traveling second-class because third-class meant sleeping on a board or sitting up all night if the boards were occupied. He shared a compartment with a pleasant young university student from Bangalore who enjoyed talking and who kept the overhead light burning.

I felt a bit groggy next day, he said.

As he walked toward Konorak he saw an old woman lying in the dust, moaning and flailing her arms. He said she was lying quietly in the dust when he returned.

Not many kilometers north of Konorak the Bhubaneswar complex of temples sprouted from the plain like giant ears of corn. He was on a bus waiting for the trip to begin when he noticed something flopping and scuttling up the road, possibly an injured dog or a baboon. Whatever the creature was, it appeared to be in a hurry. When it got close, he understood that it was human—a naked boy twisted like a pretzel, shaggy with black hair, the rump above the head. When that thing scuttled past the bus, he said, it looked up at me. The humanity was plain as a broken bone.

In Bombay he saw a woman die of starvation on the sidewalk while a cop wearing a white pith helmet and clean white gloves stood on a box at the intersection directing traffic. He said the cop knew she was there but wouldn't investigate. Nothing would be accomplished by sending the woman to a hospital. After being treated and released, she would die of starvation.

Rounding a corner he met a procession led by an elephant, monstrous, stately, painted, bejeweled. He called it a sight to behold. Yes, William, I have met the elephant with a ruby on its forehead.

From Bombay east to Ellora because he wanted to see the eighth-century Kailasa temple—a fantastic subterranean tour de force quarried from living rock. Jain, Buddhist, Hindu, all three worked on it. He thought Jain sculpture less provocative than Jain theology, which teaches that matter of any sort, animate or inanimate, is immortal. The orthodox Jain wears a mask to avoid breathing on other creatures, he carries a broom to sweep aside whatever might be in his path, he refuses to eat at night because he might accidentally swallow a bug. Uncle Gates said quite a few were moneylenders, which seemed to amuse him.

North to Ajanta for a look at early Buddhist frescoes. The bus let him off at a desolate stretch beyond Aurangabad, a mile or so from the nearest cave. He had to make a decision: carry his luggage up a dusty slope in exhausting heat or leave it beside the road. He noticed twenty or thirty men squatting on the hillside who appeared to be watching with considerable interest, which he thought justified because he was the only foreign object in sight. The Ajanta murals and sculptures were almost two thousand years old and tourists had been visiting for a long time, so he expected an information booth, possibly a guide.

Little did I know, William. That bus dropped me on another planet.

He didn't have much luggage, one suitcase and a ragged cotton laundry bag for leftovers. Still, it would be a long disagreeable hike from the road to the caves. He declared that it was hot enough to fry a lizard. For several minutes he stood in the road trying to decide. Maybe Vishnu would protect the luggage. Vishnu is supposed to help whenever man bungles it. All right, pull yourself together, he told himself.

He smiled and beckoned to his audience on the hillside. Nothing happened. He took the wallet out of his pocket and waved it. This brought one of the spectators downhill. Uncle Gates pointed to the suitcase, the laundry bag, the cliff, held up five fingers, and showed a banknote. He didn't know if the man understood, but there was nothing else to do and nothing would be gained by standing around, so he opened his umbrella and started walking.

I asked what would happen if the suitcase and laundry bag vanished. He answered a little sharply that he had his wallet and umbrella.

Ajanta was lost for a thousand years, William. Some British soldiers out tiger hunting met a wild Indian youth who led them into a ravine and up to the cliff where they saw a gigantic statue of Buddha. Here, too, those principal orders—Buddhist, Jain, Hindu—painted and carved their beliefs. The place had no electricity when I was there.

A boy squatted at the entrance to the first cave holding up a polished sheet of tin so he could take a look by reflected sunlight. He called the illumination imperfect but sufficient. He guessed he spent two or three hours exploring. When he got back to the road his possessions were exactly where he'd left them. He paid his employee and didn't open the suitcase, which would have been an insult.

From Ajanta north to Agra, home of the Taj Mahal. When he was a child in Kansas City, he saw a photo of the Taj in the rotogravure section of the *Star*. He pasted it inside one of his schoolbooks and began saving nickels and dimes from his allowance.

The train to Agra stopped late at night. A sign in English said Uttar Pradesh—not a city but a state—and he decided to stroll around instead of loitering in the depot. Once outside he smelled urine.

I have toured Mexico and various Central American countries and I have touched the fringe of Africa, he said, but nothing rivals India, especially if you happen to be near a wall.

He said that the farther he walked from the depot the darker it got. Blacker than Hades. Couldn't see his hand in front of his face. After a while he became disoriented and thought perhaps he should start back. The idea of getting hopelessly lost troubled him somewhat. A few minutes later he passed a courtyard where a small fire was burning. He glanced at it and continued walking. Then he stopped, wondering if he might have seen a ghost. He decided that before proceeding he ought to find out if he was losing his mind so he went back for another look. Next to the fire sat a man with a blanket drawn over his head like a monk from the Middle Ages, beside him a heap of skeletons. I don't mind telling you I felt relieved, Uncle Gates said. I was afraid I had invented that bird.

He found his way to the depot a few minutes before the train pulled out. He said nothing else about the skeletons or the mysterious guardian warming himself beside a fire. Just as a hot fudge sundae belonged to America, that belonged to India.

When I asked if the Taj lived up to its reputation Uncle Gates snapped at me.

For goodness sake, William! The thing is a masterpiece.

He called it dynamically feminine, a subtle fusion of Hindu and Muslim styles. White marble inlaid with lapis lazuli, bloodstone, jasper, and he didn't recall what else. Muslim chevrons. Flowing Arabic script aesthetically more gratifying than our efficient but graceless Western alphabet. Shah Jahan built it during the seventeenth century to honor his favorite wife, Mumtaz Mahal.

Now let me think, he said.Yes, the woman died in 1631.That would be correct.They were married nineteen years. Mumtaz Mahal died while giving birth to their fourteenth child. Fourteen! His wrinkled face lit up with a vinegar smile. Would you say that Mumtaz Mahal lived horizontally?

It was probably the sort of joke he used in his lectures.

Shah Jahan intended to build a similar mausoleum for himself, of black marble, across the Jumna River—the mausoleums to be connected by a silver bridge—but Shiva the destroyer intervened. Shah Jahan died.

And so, William, he rests beside Mumtaz in a crypt beneath the marvelously intricate floor of theTaj.That crypt, I believe, is now open to the public, though I don't think infidels were admitted when I was there. Sheets of gold embellished with Lord knows how many jewels lined the ceiling and walls. Canopies of pearls hung above both caskets. And you might suspect what happened when Muslim power declined. Vandals sacked the place.Vanitas vanitatum, et omnia vanitas.

What he remembered most clearly about the week he spent in Agra was a nightclub show. On the top floor of his hotel was a theater and every night the management presented a song-and-dance spectacle for tourists. From his seat he could look out a window.There, drenched with moonlight, stood theTaj. Under optimum conditions, he said, it conveys the impression of music or a dream. It reminded him of Coleridge high as a bluebird on opium who imagined that he beheld Kubla Khan's vaporous palace where bloomed many an incense-bearing tree.

Uncle Gates lifted his glass. Ah! Beware that man who feeds himself with honeydew and drinks the milk of Paradise!

During the show he nearly succumbed to grief. He described Shah Jahan gliding after Mumtaz Mahal like a snake, bounding frantically back and forth across the stage every time she escaped.

William, I choked up, he said. He thought everybody else felt the same. He could hear sobs and sniffles.

Stage décor didn't amount to much, a sequence of gauze curtains, filmy nothings. Mumtaz wore a harem outfit, but he suspected it might not be an authentic seventeenth-century costume.Around each ankle was a string of bells and she wore tiny brass finger cymbals.Whenever Shah Jahan reached for her she would touch the cymbals and slide away—easing behind one diaphanous curtain, then the next, retreating languorously from our world as the cymbals chimed more and more distantly.

Uncle Gates sighed, put his glass on the bar, and blew his nose.

Oh, he said while stuffing the handkerchief into his pocket, that was a heartbreaker. 'Because of one with hair dark as violets I am broken with longing.'

I didn't have the slightest idea who he was quoting. Fifty years teaching literature and history and grading student papers. All for what? He could probably lecture until Halloween on Roman emperors and Egyptian pharaohs and the novels of Henry James and whatever else had accumulated in his head after decades of reading. Who cared? Students would joke about his lectures and prehistoric bow ties and the cuffs that were too long or too short, but soon enough they would graduate and get on with the business of life while he decomposed in the dustbin of college memories. I wondered if the trustees or whoever was in charge of such things had honored him with a gold watch and a testimonial banquet when he retired. The college might publish his memoirs in a handsome leather-bound limited edition. Nobody would read them.

He frowned and took another sip of punch. He had bumped into something, a purplish bloodstain was spreading beneath the skin of his hand.

From Agra to Delhi where he chose a good hotel because in those days just about any Westerner could afford it. The hotel posted a boy on each floor to watch for thieves. The boy sat in a chair at the end of the corridor. Another boy sat there all night. Uncle Gates wanted to visit Khajuraho so he bought a plane ticket on a flight that left Delhi early in the morning and returned before sundown. He told the corridor guard he would be gone all day.

Lord knows I have made my share of mistakes, he said, but that was a dandy.

When he returned from Khajuraho he noticed that his suitcase had been moved—not much, only a few inches, but he noticed. Right away he knew what to expect. The traveler's checks were gone. They would enter the black market. The rate for unsigned checks was fifty cents to the dollar.

The boy stole them, he said, his voice taut. When I told that little bugger somebody had been in my room he hopped to his feet shouting: 'We find bad mans!' He ran up and down the corridor scowling at everything. Never in my life have I seen worse acting.

I asked if he reported it to the management.

Speak up, William. Speak up.

Did you report the theft?

Of course. Not that it would do any good.

An hour later the house detective arrived, fat as a hippo, with soulful brown eyes and a mustache like a dirty whisk broom. This fellow parked his carcass in my room without asking permission and set about interrogating me. I pointed out that the desk clerk asked if I wanted to change money on the black market and if he was looking for crooks he might begin with the hotel staff.

I told Uncle Gates I didn't think it was a good idea to antagonize cops. He may not have heard me.

He said the detective carried a huge key ring and probably could unlock everything—every room and lavatory and storage closet and linen supply and laundry room in the hotel. He jingled and fondled and stroked those keys, William. He was worse than a Turk with a string of beads. Besides, he farted. There was just one chair in the room so I had to sit on the bed.

The detective questioned Uncle Gates for quite a while. At last he grunted, sighed, and waddled out of the room, leaving his mammoth key ring on the nightstand.

He sounds like the world's dumbest gumshoe, I said. He probably thought you were black marketing, he forgot his keys, and he farted.

He did, said Uncle Gates. I suppose it could happen anywhere.

I asked if somebody reimbursed him for the checks.

American Express, but I had a feeling they were suspicious. Now, William, I'm afraid I've lost the thread. Where are we?

Khajuraho, I said. We were going to Khajuraho or we just got back. I'm not sure which.

Yes, yes. Now I recall. It wasn't much of a flight—oh, four hundred kilometers—and from Panna airport some forty-five minutes on the bus. They've a circuit house if you wish to stay overnight, though I didn't like the look of it. The place is altogether different from Konorak. Hardly the spot for a picnic. Shrines and temples scattered across a baking hot field. Right away I wished I had brought my umbrella. And do you know, William, Khajuraho used to be something of a metropolis with brick and wood buildings all around. Hard to believe.

He expected a crowd of tourists but saw no more than a dozen, most of them snapping pictures. I asked about thieves and vandals. A good many figures had been mutilated, although he doubted it was vandalism. Rupees. Rupees. Rupees. No matter how much those buggers pocket, he said, they wouldn't believe what a choice Shakti will fetch on Madison Avenue. He thought a moment and remarked that in the Calcutta museum he probably admired a number of body parts stolen from Khajuraho. Fragments accessible to the public in galleries all over the world seemed to him more tactile, sensuous, and alive than anything he saw while squinting at deserted temples in a barren field south of Delhi.

At Khajuraho, as at Konorak, every surface was decorated, hardly a centimeter left untouched. Vishnu and his surrogates nearly omnipresent. Kings and queens and elephant fights. Shiva with his consort Parvati. Hybrid monsters. Flowers. Surya the Sun God sporting high boots, driving a seven-horse chariot. Women, oh yes, Uncle Gates said with a chuckle, women and more women. A thousand and one nights. He especially liked a sinuous dancing woman whose great breasts had been darkened and polished by millions of caresses. He guessed she might be ten centuries old. The carving reminded him of Mumtaz Mahal dancing for Shah Jahan. Western goddesses—Venus of this or that—he considered pleasing, yet in the shade of voluptuous Hindu creatures these famous women appeared somewhat repressed.

He loved the ancient and unfamiliar. Broken columns, paintings, books, coins, medieval sculpture, manuscripts, artifacts, pyramids, mausoleums, anything crusty with age. I thought he must be looking for something, maybe the end of the rainbow. He had made a fool of himself over an ice cream sundae, dodged rocks in a soccer riot, marched across any number of godforsaken fields carrying his umbrella like a crazed Englishman in the noonday sun, got himself poisoned by the Calcutta public health service, battled lepers and a farting detective and a maddened ricksha boy, and parked his baggage on the road somewhere beyond Aurangabad. It seemed to me that his laundry bag was stuffed with horror stories and pratfalls.

After exploring Delhi and the suburbs he climbed into a rusty cargo plane for a shuddering trip across a mountainous ridge to Katmandu where he came upon three Nepalese down from the Himalayas. Fur boots, fur helmets with earflaps. Mongols who might have ridden with Timur Leng.

Rustics enjoying the sights and bright lights of Katmandu, he said. When we passed on the street I told myself I wasn't apt to meet the likes of that again so I turned around. And wouldn't you know it, William, those birds turned around for another look at me.

He traveled to Benares because he wanted to see the Ganges, which he called the filthiest river on our planet. Hindus wade into it and bathe, he said, though he didn't know how they survive. One dip in that water would knock a Caucasian silly.

He had watched funeral ceremonies, corpses of men wrapped in white, women in colored garments. The stench of burning flesh nauseated him. He noticed a slender bone, probably the arm bone of a woman, drop off a pyre and roll downhill toward the Ganges. A man who was tending the fire brought it back and tossed it into the flames like a stick of wood.

To this day, he said, I do not know why I continue to see that scorched bone rolling toward the Ganges.

I asked about souvenirs. In a fly-specked Delhi shop stuffed with manufactured debris he uncovered a stack of seventeenth-century Mughal drawings. Rajahs. Peacocks. Cobras. Monkeys. Lions. Wrestlers. Ogres. Ladies bathing in a river. Musicians. Lovers. Cranes. Acrobats. Sword swallowers. He bought two dozen. One rupee each. Dabs of color on several drawings suggested that a teacher was instructing a student. When he returned to Springfield he had the drawings framed and hung them on the walls of his library.

Did he plan any more trips?

Yes, he wanted to visit Persepolis. For a very long time he had wanted to do that. He had found Persepolis on the map but it would be a tiresome journey. From Teheran south to Isfahan, farther south to Shiraz, northeast to the ruins by some sort of conveyance. He was young, twenty-five or so, and could walk all day without blinking, but he worried about the expense and decided against it. He had been cross with himself ever since.

Like Alexander to ride in triumph through Persepolis—ah, William, such lines rank with Marlowe's mightiest. The Upstart Crow himself might be envious. Well, perhaps next summer. I'm giving it some thought.

I heard from my father several months after the anniversary. Uncle Gates apparently fell asleep in his library and never woke up. I thought if he had known how everything would end he would have considered it appropriate. I remembered him saying, 'I have met the elephant with a ruby on its forehead.'

ACKNOWLEDGMENTS

The author wishes to thank the editors of the various magazines and journals who have encouraged his work by publishing early versions of many of these stories.